THE
INSPECTOR
OF
STRANGE
AND
UNEXPLAINED
DEATHS

'Rich with historical detail and macabre atmosphere… a story full of intrigue and secret societies'

Culturefly

'Fans of Sherlock Holmes-esque mysteries will be enraptured with this historical crime thriller set in pre-Revolutionary France'

France Magazine

'A heretic monk, a fortune teller, a secret society and petticoats, this is a historical mystery with style'

Le Point

'A compelling thriller set in pre-revolutionary France with engaging characters that you are never entirely sure if you can trust – a CUB must read!'

CUB Magazine

'Behind the numerous plot twists you can sense the turning points of history, when alchemy becomes science, when philosophers start to oppose the church, when liberty and free-will are valued for the first time'

Alibi

'The author makes use of a singular alchemy to blend the scheming and plotting of past days with contemporary concerns'

NVO

'A series to follow'

Memoire des arts

OLIVIER BARDE-CABUÇON is a French author and the creator of *The Inspector for Strange and Unexplained Deaths*, who has featured in seven bestselling historical mysteries so far. *The Inspector of Strange and Unexplained Deaths* (previously published as *Casanova and the Faceless Woman*) won the Prix Sang d'Encre for crime fiction in 2012 and is the first of the series to be translated into English.

LOUISE ROGERS LALAURIE's translations from French include books by Antoine Laurain and Jean Rolin, as well as Gabrielle Wittkop's *Murder Most Serene*, which was shortlisted for the 2016 Best Translated Book Award. She has also translated Frédéric Dard's *The King of Fools* for Pushkin Vertigo.

THE
INSPECTOR
OF
STRANGE
AND
UNEXPLAINED
DEATHS

OLIVIER BARDE-CABUÇON
TRANSLATED FROM THE FRENCH BY LOUISE ROGERS LALAURIE

PUSHKIN VERTIGO

Pushkin Press
71–75 Shelton Street
London WC2H 9JQ

The Inspector of Strange and Unexplained Deaths was first published
as *Casanova et la femme sans visage* by Actes Sud in 2012

Previously published as *Casanova and the Faceless Woman* in 2019

This paperback edition published 2020

1 3 5 7 9 8 6 4 2

ISBN 13: 978-1-78227-623-4

Designed and typeset by Tetragon, London
Printed and bound by CPI Group (UK) Ltd, Croydon, CRO 4YY

www.pushkinpress.com

For Christine, Thibault,
and all my family

I go where I please, I listen to the people I meet,
I answer to those I like; I gamble, and I lose.

CRÉBILLON FILS

I

*Nothing in all Creation exerts such power over
me as the face of a beautiful woman.*

CASANOVA

Night swarmed through the streets of Paris, casting its black
veil over the carriage standing motionless in the middle of the
deserted thoroughfare. Buttoned tightly in his dark coat, the
driver kept a close rein on the horses as they jostled nervously.
A slender, cloaked silhouette climbed down from the coach.
The hood, pulled low, concealed the features of a young girl.
Shadows stole over the surrounding walls, extending hooked
fingers in her direction. A horse tossed its mane. The driver
stared straight ahead, imperturbable.

'It's late. Take care, child: good people cleave to daylight,
but the wicked come out at night!'

The voice came from inside the carriage. Tired, but with
a rich timbre that was pleasing to the ear. As if in response
to some invisible signal, the vehicle shuddered into life with
a clatter of wood and iron. The unknown girl trembled. She
stood alone, her white fingers clenched as if preparing to strike
out with her fist. The darkness made everything unfamiliar.
Fantastical forms suggested themselves to her searching eyes.
Unwittingly, throughout her childhood, her mother's bedtime
stories had peopled her nights with werewolves, thieves and
ghosts. For an instant, she thought she heard footsteps, and
froze to listen. But there was nothing. Only silence.

At that moment, the clouds shredded and pale moonlight
flooded the street, revealing the entrance to a small courtyard,
and the red glow of a bread oven on its far side. The young

girl started forward, happy and relieved. A tinkling, crystal laugh rose unbidden in her throat, and she strode quickly in the direction of the wavering light.

A sudden movement pierced the night. A shadow loomed and spread over the walls, in the girl's pursuit. Presently, a scream tore through the dark.

A mild spring night in the year 1759. The light from the oil lamps and candles, flickering in their lanterns, had drawn a crowd of onlookers, like fascinated moths. The precinct chief swallowed hard and averted his gaze from the bloody spectacle before him.

'Dead,' he stated. 'I have no idea why or how it was done, but the skin has been completely torn from her face. No one could recognize her in that state.'

'As though it had been eaten away by a wolf!' declared one of his men.

A muffled cry greeted his words, and a low rumour spread through the assembled company.

'Wolves! The wolves have entered Paris!'

The precinct chief shot a dark look at his officer.

'I'll thank you to keep your thoughts to yourself, in future!'

The man shrank back, colliding as he did so with a solemn, impassive figure—a recent arrival, who had been watching in silence.

'Ah!' There was a note of irritation in the precinct chief's greeting. 'The Inspector of Strange and Unexplained Deaths… Who in hell's name sent for you, Volnay? And how did you get here so quickly? Do you never sleep?'

Volnay stepped forward. He was a tall young man with a pleasant enough face, offset by his dark gaze and stiff bearing. The moonlight modelled his features in stark relief. He wore no wig and his long, unpowdered, raven-black hair floated behind him on the gentle breeze. From the corner of his eye, a scar curled around his temple, prompting its share of speculation. He was plainly dressed in a black jerkin, with a bright, white, frill-necked shirt and cravat. Despite the late hour, he was impeccably turned out. He made no reply to the precinct chief, but knelt and examined the body from head to toe before turning to his colleague.

'I want the body brought for examination—not to Châtelet. Not the city morgue. You know the place.'

The precinct chief shivered and tried to protest.

'You've only just got here. Let us begin our inquiries before we decide if this is a case for the scientific police!'

Volnay gave him not so much as a glance.

'By order of the king,' he said firmly, 'I am authorized, as you know, to investigate every strange or unexplained death in Paris. As you can see, we are in the presence of a victim who has had the skin torn carefully from her face, so as to render her unrecognizable.'

He took a bell lantern from the grasp of an officer of the Royal Watch and cast the dim light of its tallow candle over the body.

'As you may also see, there is not a trace of blood on the woman's clothing. From which it seems clear she was killed first, then had her garments removed, was disfigured after that, then dressed again, and finally placed here. And sure enough, even though your officers have trampled everything and very probably spoilt any available clues, I have observed no spot or trail of blood in the vicinity.'

The precinct chief shook his head and breathed a long sigh.

'Clues! You're obsessed, Volnay…'

'If I can trouble you to establish a police cordon and keep everyone at bay,' Volnay continued smoothly, 'I would prefer us to attend the scene of the crime in privacy.'

He waited while the order was issued and carried out, then took the victim's hands in his and examined them carefully.

'The hands are well cared for, and show no signs of manual labour,' he said quietly, as if thinking aloud. 'This is a person of some standing.'

'Or a whore from one of the finer parts of town.'

Volnay gave no reaction, but scrutinized the dead woman's body, pausing briefly at her breast, and stopping at her neck. Delicately, his long, slender fingers lifted a small chain and medallion engraved with an image of the Virgin. On the reverse, he read a Latin inscription, and translated it with ease.

Lord, deliver us from Evil.

Volnay turned to his colleague with a thin smile.

'A somewhat unusual whore, if so!'

Half stooping, he began a methodical examination of the ground. But so many feet had trodden the area around the body that it was impossible to make anything out. He searched in his pocket, took out a stick of charcoal and a piece of paper, and began to draw the dead woman and her surroundings. The precinct chief grinned in amusement.

'So, it's true what they say: you're quite the artist. You've missed your vocation!'

Volnay answered with a cold stare. At times, his blue eyes appeared veined with ice.

'Every detail is important in its own, particular way. I commit them all to memory, but not only that—I note everything down on paper, too. A murderer may leave traces of his presence at the scene of a crime, just as a snail leaves its trail of slime. Observation is the bedrock of our work. Take an example—have you counted the number of people in their nightclothes at the front of the crowd?'

The precinct chief had not.

'Six,' said Volnay smoothly, sketching all the while. 'Unless others have arrived in the last minute. Am I right?'

'Dear Lord, so you are!'

'I should like your men to question them. They are here in their nightclothes because they live nearby and were alerted by the noise. They may have seen something, or noticed someone.'

Their exchange was broken by the creak of cartwheels on the cobblestones. At the sight of the new arrival, the precinct chief's stomach churned, and he swallowed hard. Volnay raised one eyebrow.

'Ah, here he is! I had him sent for. Only the Devil himself is quicker, as you can see!'

The cart was driven by a dark, spectral figure shrouded in a monk's habit, the cowl pulled down to conceal his face. Many of the onlookers crossed themselves. Noiselessly, fearfully, the crowd shrank back as the vehicle passed.

'Ah yes—and who discovered the body?' asked the inspector sharply.

'That gentleman there.'

Volnay looked in the direction of the tall individual who had been pointed out. His jaw dropped in recognition. Serene and self-assured, the fellow stepped forward. He had a pleasing, sallow face. He was elegantly dressed in a velvet coat of deep yellow with a woven pattern of small flowers and cartouches, and buttons covered with silver thread. His jabot and frilled cuffs were of costly bobbin lace. His entire person radiated natural good humour and an irresistible, lively charm.

'The Chevalier de Seingalt, sir!' His tone was bright and amiable.

'I know who you are, Monsieur Casanova,' said Volnay, quietly.

Who had not heard of Giacomo Casanova the Venetian, by turns banker, swindler, diplomat, army officer, swordsman, spy, magician, and of course, ever and always the arch-seducer? Casanova was a walking legend, whose reputation preceded him wherever he went.

Volnay's expression left no doubt as to his profound disapproval of the immoral behaviour of such as Casanova, a man who bedded barely pubescent girls, and sometimes even mother and daughter together.

'The Chevalier de Seingalt, at your service!' persisted the other, ever-eager to be addressed by his title. 'Decorated with the Order of the Spur by His Holiness the Pope himself!'

'Indeed. Who among us is not?' retorted Volnay, with a scowl.

He knew perfectly well that the title—pronounced *Saint-Galle* in the French manner—was a fabrication. The chevalier himself responded with insolent charm to anyone who laughed at his affectation, urging them to make up their own title if they were jealous! Volnay observed him quietly. He had no liking for Casanova and his kind, but the man was a creature of the great of this world, or tried his best to seem so, at least. He had arrived in Paris three years earlier, and his energy, vivacity and intellect had secured him an entrée to the highest circles. He frequented the loftier ranks of the nobility—the Maréchal de Richelieu, or the Duchesse de Chartres—and the country's intellectual elite. He was a man to be handled with care.

'How did you discover the victim?' Volnay asked, curtly.

'It happened that I was accompanying a delightful young lady back to her place of residence. As you know, nothing in all Creation exerts such power over me as the face of a beautiful woman! Well, we were going on our way when, quite simply, we ran into the body lying here. I bent down to lift her hood and... my companion screamed, very loudly.'

'Did you notice anyone nearby, when you discovered the dead woman, or just before?'

'Absolutely no one, Inspector.'

Without a word, Volnay turned on his heels and knelt once more beside the body, forcing himself to scrutinize the bloodied mask of the face, in an effort to understand how the murderer had proceeded. A wolf? Certainly not, but very likely something far worse.

The scene was bathed in silvery moonlight. Volnay cursed suddenly, under his breath. Transfixed by the dead woman's face, he had omitted to search her body. Now, mechanically, his hands discovered and pulled a letter from the victim's pocket, almost before he knew what he had done. Volnay felt Casanova's eyes on him. He glanced at the seal and experienced a wave of dread.

'Well look at that, Inspector! A letter in the dead woman's pocket!'

'You're quite mistaken, Chevalier,' said Volnay, allowing Casanova his usurped title for once. 'This letter just fell out of my sleeve.'

'But I assure you—'

Volnay shot him a cold stare.

'It's mine, I tell you!'

Casanova fell silent, but he continued to watch the inspector with keen interest.

Among the onlookers, a black-clad figure stood watching Volnay's every move, long and lean as a hanged man against a winter sky. His face and the skin of his bald scalp shone disconcertingly white, like milk or a faded flower on a tall stalk. His grey eyes seemed washed of all colour. They held not a shred of humanity. He turned at the approach of the cart. The monk sat waiting placidly for the corpse to be lifted aboard.

The pale man frowned, as if struggling to remember where he might have come across the hooded figure—the source of such fear and astonishment—before. A hideous grin lit the pale man's face, but stopped short of his eyes. His mouth spat a silent curse. Hastily, furtively, he made the sign of the cross. He noted Casanova's presence with interest, and gave a short gasp of surprise when Volnay slipped the letter discreetly into his pocket. His features hardened. After a moment's hesitation, he pushed through the crowd and hurried away, as if the Devil himself were at his heels.

It was late when Volnay made his way home. The night was beset with shadows. He gripped the hilt of his sword as he walked, alert to the silhouettes of furtive figures who crossed his path, and others who kept out of sight, behind pillars or under the dark overhangs of the houses. Each morning, the street sweepers of Paris gathered up the bodies of incautious nightwalkers.

A cobbled passage led from Rue de la Porte-de-l'Arbalète to Rue Saint-Jacques. Stone wheel guards jutted from the walls, protecting them against passing carriages. Partway along, the passage opened onto a series of tiny courtyards, the first of brick and stone, with a stone well in the middle; a second, smaller court, and a third, even tinier, the last almost entirely filled with a tall acacia tree. Here Volnay lived, happy with his own company, and that of his tree, glimpsed from every window on both floors of his little house. The acacia was a symbol of life in this unfrequented place, a link between the earth with all its woes, and the indifferent eye of heaven.

Volnay stepped inside and bolted the heavy door behind him. The ground floor served as his parlour, study and dining room. But the house's *raison d'être*, its defining, unifying force, was its books. The books filled Volnay's living room, glowing in the candlelight. Their remarkable sheen lit the walls, nooks and corners with scattered specks of ochre and gold. There were books bound in leather or parchment, and books with studded or embossed covers. Their presence and prominence hinted at the scope of their owner's inner life, and its limits. Two mismatched armchairs and a wooden table set with fine candlesticks stood their ground with a determined air. Faded tapestries—family heirlooms, perhaps—contributed an unexpectedly soft touch.

'And how are you, my fine friend?'

The question was addressed to a splendid magpie, eyeing Volnay through the bars of her cage. She had a long tail, and black plumage with a purplish sheen on her back, head and chest. Her underbelly and the undersides of her wings were pure white, and her tail showed flashes of oily green.

'What, no answer? Are you sulking?'

The bird kept her silence. Volnay shrugged lightly and crossed the room to one set of bookshelves. He chose a volume bound in red vellum, caressed its cover lovingly and settled himself into his favourite armchair beside the chimney, piled with extinct logs. After a moment's hesitation, he placed the book on a side table and fished in his pocket for the young victim's letter. He had taken it—unusually for him, and right under the nose of the Chevalier de Seingalt—for one very simple reason. He stared gloomily at the seal, and sighed heavily. The wax was imprinted with the seal of His Majesty the king.

Why me?

Dark thoughts flooded Volnay's mind. The monarch's depravity knew no bounds. It was rumoured that he purchased or stole young girls from their families and took them to live in the palace attics, as fodder for his debauched appetites. In Versailles, Volnay knew of two quarters—the Parc-aux-Cerfs and Saint-Louis—where one or more secret houses were used as trysting places for the king and his young conquests. When royal bastards were born of these illicit liaisons, they were removed from their unfortunate mothers forthwith and placed in the care of wet nurses.

What if the young woman had come from the king's bed?

Louis XV's favourite, Madame de Pompadour, had installed the young girls in the Parc-aux-Cerfs, the better to satisfy the king's unstinting desires. No longer the object of royal lust herself, and fearing to lose her position at Court, she had devised a way to pander to His Majesty's pleasure with a hand-picked array of willing girls from the lower orders, all thoroughly unversed in the intrigues of Court life. In this way, La Pompadour nipped potential rivals in the bud, by ensuring none of the king's mistresses rose too high in the royal favour. Ultimately, she dispensed with the girls by marrying them off to members of the royal household.

Volnay often wondered how Louis XV reconciled his vices and his very great fear of God. But the king considered himself a ruler by divine right. Hell was for other people. And he was at pains to ensure that the unfortunate children recited their prayers after he had taken his pleasure, so it was said, to avoid eternal damnation!

Deep in thought, Volnay turned the letter over and over in his fingers, but he did not break the seal. The king's secret harem of young mistresses was common knowledge, but Paris was rife with even wilder rumours: the king was said to have contracted leprosy as a result of his debauchery. Bathing in the blood of innocent children was the only thing that kept him alive.

What if the young woman had come from the king's bed? Volnay asked himself, again. What should I do then?

His logical, deductive mind had run ahead, to the inevitable conclusion: doubtless, one day, he would be forced to return the letter to its rightful owner. He was even more careful not to break the seal now, despite his burning curiosity. He swore under his breath.

'To think that that arch-rogue Casanova saw the whole thing!' he declared out loud in exasperation. 'Casanova!'

'Casa! Casa!'

Volnay jumped half out his skin, then turned to look at the great birdcage and its splendid occupant.

He smiled.

'Yes, that cretin Casanova!'

'Cretin Casa! Cretin Casa!' repeated the magpie obediently.

Volnay laughed aloud.

Casanova had played a superb hand, drinking little but frequently refilling his opponent's glass, losing at first to raise the stakes, then delivering his fatal blow with immediate, sobering effect.

'I played on my word, Chevalier…'

The Venetian straightened himself in his armchair, a slight smile playing at his lips.

'A gambling man keeps his money about his person, Joinville,' he said quietly.

His opponent rolled his shoulders uncomfortably and ordered more drink. He peered anxiously into Casanova's face, from which all trace of affability had now disappeared. The pair sat in a smoke-filled den where a player's rank in society counted for less than the cash he could lay on the table. A place for cavagnole and manille, faro, biribi and piquet. Ladies pressed their generous bosoms against the shoulders of the luckier players. The Chevalier de Seingalt's eye alighted on a girl in pink silk stockings, then turned coldly back to his debtor. He never mixed money with pleasure, unless the money belonged to someone else.

'You had a run of luck tonight, Giacomo,' said Joinville, gruffly.

The Venetian gave a quick smile and sat back in his arm-chair, eyes half-closed as if remembering things past.

'There have been times in my life,' he confided lazily, 'when I gambled daily and, losing against my word, found that the prospect of having to pay up the next day caused me greater and greater anguish. I would fall sick at the very thought, and then I would get over it. As soon as I regained my health and powers, I would forget all my past ills and return to my usual pursuits.'

'So you played on your word, too!'

Casanova opened his eyes wide.

'Could that be because my word was valued more highly than yours?' he retorted, wickedly.

A peculiar, bitter smell wafted from the candles on the table, stinging the nostrils. With forced gaiety, Joinville snatched his tankard from the serving girl's hands and tried, clumsily, to pinch her backside. She trotted off, giggling. Joinville shrugged, and boomed out a song that had been a great source of merriment the length and breadth of France under the previous reign, when the Italian-born Mazarin was first minister, governing the country with Anne of Austria, his supposed mistress, the erstwhile infanta, and mother of the child king Louis XIV:

> 'Mazarin's balls don't bounce in vain,
> They bump and bump and rattle the Crown.
> That wily old Sicilian hound
> Gets up your arse, princess of Spain!'

Casanova wasn't singing. He sipped his Cyprus wine and kept his opponent firmly in his sights.

'I'll take your credit,' he said suddenly, 'if you can tell me a good story. I know you're privy to all the secrets at Court.'

'Well now! Where to start?'

'With whatever is of greatest interest.'

Joinville took a deep breath. He was a wine merchant, serving the finest households in Paris. His honourable dedication to sampling all of his merchandise had given him a fine paunch; and his dutiful drinking bouts with each eminent client made him an inexhaustible fount of gossip, ingested more or less accurately, depending on his state of drunkenness at the time.

'Do you know how La Pompadour first seduced the king? She attended a costume ball dressed as Diana the Huntress, with threads of silver plaited in her hair, and her breasts very much on display, carrying a quiver of arrows and a bow on her back. The king had her there and then.'

Joinville heaved himself to his feet and declaimed:

> 'What care I, who seem so bold?
> What if my husband be cuckold?
> What care I for anything,
> When I'm the mistress of the king?!'

Casanova stifled a yawn. Joinville watched in alarm as he got to his feet.

'Wait! Wait! There's fresher meat than that! The Devout Party—the religionists—detest La Pompadour, as you well know. They'll do anything to destroy her...'

'Nothing new there,' remarked Casanova, adjusting his waistcoat and looking around for the girl in the pink silk stockings.

'Wait, I tell you! They say the Devout Party have found a way, and soon La Pompadour will be a mere memory.'

'A plot?' Casanova was interested now.

'So it seems. But I know nothing more for the moment. Father Ofag, a Jesuit, is the leader.'

'Is that all?'

'His devoted accomplice goes by the name of Wallace. A soldier. Visionary type. Skin as white as milk, and eyes to make your hair stand up straight on your head. He's very dangerous.'

Joinville underscored his message by dragging his thumb across the skin of his throat. Casanova looked at him thoughtfully for a moment, cold and calculating.

'I'm not sure I believe you,' he said at length. 'But get me some first-hand information and I'll cancel our debt. I may even throw in a few coins, but only if it's truly worth my while.'

He glanced at a woman in a low-cut corset standing at a table nearby, then reluctantly turned his attention back to Joinville.

'Do you know a police officer by the name of Volnay?'

Joinville laughed heartily.

'Of course! Volnay saved the king's life a couple of years back, when Damiens tried to assassinate him. The king knighted him, made him a chevalier.'

'Indeed!'

'He is known as an upright man of great integrity. The king asked if he might grant Volnay a favour for having saved his life, and Volnay answered that he should like to be put in charge of investigating every strange and unexplained death in Paris. The king laughed at the idea, but he was in Volnay's debt. And so, for the past two years, Volnay has been just that: His Majesty's Inspector of Strange and Unexplained Deaths, with no particular mandate other than to investigate especially nasty or complicated cases of murder in the capital. It was he who solved the Pécoil affair. You've heard about that?'

The Venetian shook his head. Joinville lit a cigar and leant forward with a slight, condescending smile.

'Pécoil had accumulated vast riches from the *gabelle*, the salt tax. He kept it all under his house, in a vault sealed by three doors of solid iron. Like any self-respecting skinflint, he would go down each evening and revel in the sight of his gold. One evening, he failed to come back up. His wife and son were concerned, of course, but it was two days before they sent for the police and forced the three doors. They found Pécoil with his throat cut, lying on the floor beside his treasure, from which not a single crown was missing. His arms were outstretched, reaching into his blackened, burnt-out lantern, the flesh partly consumed by fire.'

Joinville blew a thick cloud of smoke.

'Volnay solved the case in less than a week. They say he's highly competent.'

Casanova raised one eyebrow.

'I hope he is,' he said coldly. 'For his own sake.'

II

*What is beauty? We cannot say, and
yet we know it in our hearts.*

CASANOVA

In the darkness, the wood cracked and the furniture creaked.
Were they truly inanimate, and devoid of a soul? The sounds,
and the memory of the faceless woman, woke Volnay with
a start in the depths of the night, just as a pair of blood-
drenched lips placed themselves upon his own. He fell back
into a deep sleep, but the woman with her bloodied mask
returned again, holding out a letter which he stubbornly
refused to take. He tore himself from his nightmare when
she threw off her clothes and sat astride him, like a she-devil
come to ride him as he slept.

*Whoever sleeps on his back is sometimes suffocated by spirits of
the air, who torment him with attacks and tyrannies of every sort,
and deplete the quality of his blood with such sudden effect that
the man lies in a state of exhaustion and cannot recover himself.*

His learned collaborator, the monk, would doubtless have
explained it thus. But he would be busily occupied now, with
a meticulous examination of the body of the faceless woman.

Volnay thought of the letter he had removed from the body.
He fought the temptation to read it. He rose from his bed and
lit a candle. The silence of the night fed his thoughts, and he
tried to get his ideas in order. He examined the sketches he
had made at the scene of the crime, elaborating theory after
theory, but still he could not sleep. And so, early that morning,
it was with a haggard face that he answered the beating of a
fist on his front door.

Opening it, Volnay had expected anything but the apparition that met his eyes: a young woman, her waist most admirably clasped in a brocade gown in three different shades of blue, trimmed with silver lace. The cut and fabric flattered her well-rounded breasts, pushed up tight in her stays. She was enveloped in a delicious fragrance of roses, by turns sweet, peppery and fruity, with base notes of amber and musk. She looked not yet twenty; her features were pure and clear, yet already an application of crimson gloss and a touch of silver glaze emphasized the dark brilliance of her almond-shaped eyes. Her hair was blacker than the blackest night, held in place by a multitude of pins, so that it seemed speckled with stars. There was a luminous quality to the skin of her throat, and her waist was slender but healthy and firm. Volnay lowered his eyes, and discovered a delicate foot, light as air, that quickened his pulse.

'Madame…'

'*Mademoiselle* Chiara D'Ancilla, Chevalier,' she said in a charming, cajoling voice.

Volnay blinked briefly. He was rarely addressed by his title, and never used it himself. Who was this beautiful young Italian woman, and what did she want? He employed a woman to keep house, and see to his provisions and laundry, but no other female presence ever brightened his simple dwelling. It was a place dedicated to rest, reading and reflection.

'May I come in?'

He realized that he had been standing there in the doorway without the least show of manners. Hastily, he stepped aside to let her pass, noting how the tiny pleats in the back of her dress showed off the sheen of its silk and the softness of the satin. Once inside, the young woman stood motionless, gazing at the gold-tooled bindings that lit the room with their refulgent glow. She admired their elegant, abstract patterns, their azure motifs, the foliage and palm fronds entwined in their decorative frames.

'Oh, I see you're a lover of books!' she breathed appreciatively. 'So am I—they hold all human knowledge!'

She turned to him and added, in a charming voice:

'All human hopes and desires, too.'

She ran her delicate hand along the spines, and Volnay trembled, in spite of himself, as if she had caressed some part of his body. She took out a book bound in a pretty pattern of five fleurons around a central lozenge, framed by four triangular corner pieces.

'*Treatise on the Condition of the Human Body after Hanging,*' she read in horror-struck tones. 'Dear God, why ever do you read such things?'

Gently, Volnay removed the book from her grasp.

'It is thanks to this book that I understood how to determine whether a person has been strangled or hanged. The marks upon the neck are different in each case, and the angle of the break at the nape is also…'

He broke off, seeing her shudder.

'Forgive me such unpleasant details. It was merely by way of explaining to you that my trade obliges me to take an interest in how people meet their deaths. It is possible to discover a great deal by examining the scene of a crime, and the victim's body. The corpse alone holds a wealth of clues, as do the clothes, and everything must be examined with the utmost care. My collaborator, a monk and a learned man of science, devotes himself to the task. The deciphering of footprints, or how blows have been delivered and received, is truly an art.'

He paused, and sighed.

'Yet it interests no more than two people in the entire kingdom!'

The young woman stared thoughtfully at Volnay, who was scarcely much older than she was herself. Her gaze lingered on the fine scar running from one eye to his temple. And on the half-moons of shadow beneath his lower lids. So this was what an Inspector of Strange and Unexplained Deaths looked like? Suddenly, Chiara D'Ancilla froze, and shivered, as if a new thought had just struck her.

'Have you ever burnt books, Inspector?'

Her passionate feelings on the subject were quick to find expression in her beautiful, dark eyes.

'Indeed not, Mademoiselle, never!' said Volnay, hurriedly, because it was the truth and because he had no desire to incur this woman's displeasure.

He might have added that he had even saved books on occasion, stealing back volumes that had been confiscated by the censors, without a second thought. His answer brought a smile back to the young woman's face. She spoke animatedly.

'I knew it—one cannot be both a reader and a destroyer of books! Ah, you've read all our philosophers: Rousseau, Voltaire, Diderot and Baron d'Holbach! How very bold of the king's personal policeman. What does Monsieur de Sartine, our city's chief of police, have to say about that?'

'He hardly ever comes here,' said Volnay, unsmilingly.

She took a few steps around the room, and again he admired her graceful but unaffected carriage. Morning light bathed the walls with a honeyed glow. A delicate shaft of sunshine caught her figure, so that she stood in a radiant halo of gold. She had stopped to admire a red morocco binding stamped with a mesh of fine dots. Just at that moment, the bird shifted in its cage. She had not noticed it until now.

'Oh! A magpie!'

'Mag-pie! Mag-pie!' The bird echoed the familiar exclamation.

The young woman clapped her hands in delight.

'What is this miracle of nature?'

Volnay joined her beside the cage, pleased to have found a pretext to step inside her fragrant cloud.

'There is nothing miraculous in it, Mademoiselle. Magpies are even more accomplished than parrots when it comes to reproducing human speech. Few people know this, but a little teaching is all they require.'

They stood in silence for a moment, contemplating the bird's magnificent plumage as it perched motionless now, its beak pointed in their direction. Slowly, almost regretfully, the young woman turned to Volnay.

'Monsieur, the reason for my coming here will doubtless surprise you,' she said in tones of the utmost seriousness. 'And so first I must tell you who I am. I am Italian, as my name suggests. My father is a widower: the Marquis D'Ancilla. He has significant interests in your country, and we live here all year, apart from the summer, which we spend in Tuscany. Like you, I read a great deal, but while you devour philosophy, I am drawn to the natural sciences, astronomy, mathematics—'

'Indeed, you are a scientist at heart.'

She frowned very slightly with one eyebrow, displeased at having been interrupted.

'A scientist in practice too. I like to test theories through practical experiments, and—'

'Doubtless you have a laboratory?' he ventured, knowing full well that every person of means with an enquiring mind had their own private workroom.

This time she took a step closer, eyes flashing.

'You must find me feeble-minded indeed to keep finishing my sentences for me. Or is it because I'm a woman?'

Volnay excused himself hurriedly. The young aristocrat was placated, and continued:

'I should like to visit the place where the police take all the corpses!'

The stupefaction on Volnay's face must have been comical indeed, because Chiara burst out laughing. But the Inspector of Strange and Unexplained Deaths took no offence at her gentle mockery.

'You see, sir, I am interested in the natural sciences. I have devoted much time to the study of the human anatomy, and I am… very inquisitive.'

Volnay sighed. He thought of the hideous place she was asking to visit, where the corpses were salted, then stacked like loaves in an oven.

'It is no spectacle for a person of your quality.'

'Inspector…'

She moved closer and placed her hand lightly on his arm.

'Mademoiselle, believe me, it can be done, but you would regret the sight of it your whole life.'

Volnay thought she seemed vexed, but he was wrong. She continued briskly:

'Well then. Enough of that.'

Then she seemed to hesitate for a moment.

'They say you'll be leading the investigation into the murder of a woman whose face was torn off.'

'News travels fast in Paris!'

Chiara smiled sweetly, with her hands clasped behind her back, like a good little girl.

'Paris is such a small city.'

She paused for the briefest of moments, before asking innocently:

'Have you been able to identify her?'

'Mademoiselle, all the skin on her face has been removed. Who could recognize her in such a state?'

She turned pale. Volnay was alarmed and led her to a chair.

'We shouldn't speak of such things! Shall I fetch you a glass of port?'

'A glass of water, please.' She took a deep, slow breath. 'And you say you haven't been able to identify her? Did she have anything about her person? A name embroidered into an item of clothing? Any papers?'

She noticed Volnay's cold stare.

'Some jewellery, perhaps?' she ventured.

She gave a forced laugh and added:

'Some women can be recognized by their jewellery alone!'

Volnay was perplexed. He shook his head.

'A glass of water,' murmured Chiara. 'Please…'

'Straightaway,' said Volnay.

He was surprised, on his return, to find her standing at his desk, examining his papers.

'Mademoiselle?'

She turned to him, and her expression was open and candid.

'I was admiring your lacquered work cabinet. It must have cost a small fortune.'

'It came to me from my father,' he answered, coldly. 'I'm pleased to see you are feeling better.'

Relinquishing any attempt at manners, he held the glass out for her to take, but did not move. She walked slowly to where he stood, her eyes fixed firmly on his, but pouting sulkily like a naughty little girl who has been caught in the act. She took the glass, and their fingers brushed. Volnay felt a tremor of excitement throughout his body.

'It is very fresh, thank you.' She returned the glass, after taking the tiniest of sips.

Volnay was troubled indeed. He took the glass, resisting the urge to drink from it in turn, in the delicate trace of her lips. She hesitated for a moment, then walked across to admire the magpie once again, and played with it through the bars of the cage. The bird beat its wings and set about smoothing its feathers.

'Is she any more of a prisoner than we poor humans, labouring under the yoke of our own rules, conventions and prejudices?' she pondered.

The question took Volnay by surprise. He watched her closely.

'You must find me very strange,' she went on in some embarrassment, 'but you see, my lady-in-waiting left to care for her sick mother, and has sent no word since. When I heard the news of the killing, I wondered if…'

Volnay relaxed. Here at last was the reason for her persistent questioning.

'The post can be inefficient, Mademoiselle. But I can assure you that—'

There came a knock at the door. Irritated, Volnay excused himself and went to open it. He was a man who seldom entertained, and kept the company of no one but his magpie and his monk, yet he was receiving more visitors than ever before this morning. His surprise was all the greater when he saw the man standing outside his door:

'Casanova!'

'Chevalier?'

Chiara D'Ancilla's delicate presence in the room he had just left prevented him from inviting the Chevalier de Seingalt to come inside. His visitor was clearly offended, but said nothing.

'I come with greetings.'

'What can I do for you?' asked Volnay, standing his ground in the doorway.

'Well, you might invite me in off the street for a start,' said the Venetian coldly.

Reluctantly, Volnay stood aside.

'I have a guest; I must ask you to be brief.'

He heard the rustle of Chiara's gown and was alarmed to see a sparkle in Casanova's well-trained eye. She had appeared behind him, and Volnay saw straightaway that Casanova was sizing her up as a potential conquest. For her part, the young woman seemed quite struck by the tall, handsome man—who stood a good head above Volnay—with his robust figure, healthy complexion and smiling eyes. Cold fury gripped the inspector, but he retained his composure.

'Mademoiselle…'

Casanova had sunk into a deep bow.

'Allow me to introduce myself, since our friend Volnay will not. The Chevalier de Seingalt, at your service.'

And he bowed once more, but without taking his eyes off Chiara this time.

'Forgive me, I'm quite forgetting myself,' said Volnay drily. 'Chevalier de Seingalt, allow me to introduce Chiara D'Ancilla.'

'Your family is widely known,' declared Casanova, bending again to kiss the tips of the young woman's fingers. 'These are the moments I treasure most in life: chance encounters, unforeseen, unexpected, and all the more delightful for that!'

Volnay rolled his eyes to the ceiling, but Chiara considered the Venetian carefully.

'Are you not the one they also call Casanova?'

She pronounced the name with a certain anxiety, and a glimmer of excitement, too. The Chevalier de Seingalt was unsurprised. His reputation preceded him, and he attracted the attention of women wherever he went.

'What did you want to tell me?' asked Volnay brusquely.

The Venetian mimed a gesture of comic despair.

'To be perfectly honest, I have quite forgotten. It must have been something connected with last night's business, but the sight of this charming young lady has quite driven it from my mind.'

Casanova often fell in love at a glance. His smouldering gaze left Chiara quite disconcerted. Her fingers toyed nervously with a flower of gold that she wore about her neck. Volnay noticed, and felt a rush of anger at the Venetian. He thought of a stratagem to rid himself of this unwelcome visitor. He invited his guests to sit in his two armchairs, and seated himself on a stool. Pleasantries were exchanged about the late coming of spring.

'You are a lover of science, Mademoiselle,' said Volnay, suddenly. 'Madame d'Urfé's laboratory will certainly fascinate you. They say it is crammed full of stills and jars of every kind, with a furnace that is kept burning even through the height of summer. Madame d'Urfé has been working there night and day for years, in hopes of discovering the elixir of life. The Chevalier de Seingalt here is sure to know all about it.'

Casanova raised one very aristocratic eyebrow, feigning incomprehension. Chiara D'Ancilla turned to address him.

'Whatever does our friend mean?'

'I haven't the faintest idea. Though I have indeed met Madame d'Urfé, of course...'

Volnay gave a thin smile.

'And extorted money from her on the pretext of initiating her into the mysteries of the Kabbalah!'

The Venetian jumped to his feet.

'You cannot say that, sir! I have never received so much as a penny from the lady, I give you my word of honour!'

'Gemstones, to be precise,' insisted the policeman.

'Oh, that...'

Casanova affected a gracious wave of the hand.

'I used them to show her the constellations...'

Chiara was unable to suppress a loud giggle. Volnay turned to her, furiously.

'Does it amuse you to think of swindling a fifty-three-year-old lady? Do you believe the Chevalier de Seingalt, here present, behaved in a manner befitting his freshly bestowed title when he told the poor, credulous woman that she would become pregnant, die in childbirth and be reborn sixty-four days later?'

Chiara pressed her hands to her chest, struggling unsuccessfully to contain her laughter.

'Did you really tell the lady that, Chevalier?'

The Venetian gave an exasperated sigh.

'How the devil did you hear about that, Volnay?'

The inspector sat impassively, in silence. Casanova turned to Chiara D'Ancilla and saw straightaway that she found the story greatly amusing.

'You shouldn't mock the Marquise d'Urfé,' he said indulgently. 'She was the mistress of the regent, and he is passionate about alchemy. They say he was conducting his experiments with the express aim of meeting the Devil himself! The marquise is researching the balsamic properties of plants, to create an elixir of life. It's an obsession with her. A harmless enough obsession if it weren't for her private genie.'

Chiara's hilarity increased. Volnay was transfixed by her charming lips, chilled by a secret horror that he might see them offered to another.

'Yes indeed,' Casanova continued enthusiastically, 'she has a genie who talks to her at night! He's thoroughly well intentioned, and advised her to elicit my help in securing the passage of her soul into a male child born of the philosophical coupling of a mortal man with a divine female being. She was even prepared to poison herself to that very end! I dissuaded her…'

He broke off with a modest smile, as if expecting to be congratulated.

'If I had been thoroughly honest,' he continued, with aplomb, 'and assured her that her ideas were absurd, she would never have believed me. And so I thought best to go along with her, for her own safety. But I formed no plan whatsoever to rob her of her riches, though I could have done it most easily, believe me, if I had been in any way ill-intentioned.'

'And how did you "go along" with her?' asked Chiara, wickedly.

Casanova fixed her with a penetrating stare.

'I developed a theory, according to which we would achieve union with the elementary spirits by engaging in hypostasis. The Marquise d'Urfé was eager to carry out the experiment, in order to bear a miraculous child, in which form she would be reborn. This would help her overcome her absurd fear of death!'

Volnay gave an exasperated groan.

'Her children have filed a complaint: there's more trouble ahead for you, dear Chevalier.'

Chiara D'Ancilla turned to the Venetian, to scold him.

'You have made me laugh, but I cannot approve your actions: robbing a poor woman who has taken leave of her senses!'

Casanova's face lit up with a mocking smile.

'Robbing her? The lady is vastly rich, and a miser. Securing a few gifts for myself won't ruin her. Those who have money distribute it to those who do not—it's a very good system. It's my belief the rich should be subject to taxation, and the proceeds distributed to the poorest in the land, rather than the opposite, as we do today.'

Chiara smiled affectionately.

'Well, hark at you.'

'Her money should go to her children,' grumbled Volnay, 'not to you!'

The Venetian's smile froze on his lips.

'It will go to her offspring minus a few baubles, rest assured. And her stupid, stubborn children will be a little less rich and fat as a result, Monsieur, the great defender of the rich and powerful of this world! I have no employment, hold no office, as you know. My freedom is unconstrained. All I have are women to love, and the purses of others to spend. Allow me that privilege, at least.'

'A dubious privilege indeed,' growled Volnay.

Casanova shot him an icy look.

'What am I to do? I'm a man of considerable merit, but I live in a century where such things go unrewarded.'

'Casanova, the great, misunderstood genius.' Volnay's response was heavy with irony.

'Chevalier de Seingalt, if you please.'

'Your name is not Seingalt, it's Casanova!' objected Volnay. 'The latter is true, the former is false.'

The Venetian responded with a gesture that suggested the conversation was beginning to bore him.

'Both names are as true as I'm sitting here talking to you now. The alphabet belongs to everyone, as far as I am aware.'

'You have no more status than a stage valet,' said Volnay scornfully.

'Watch your words,' said Casanova, losing none of his sangfroid. 'Many's the stage valet who ends up beating his master with a stick!'

He rose and took his leave of Chiara, elegantly addressing a few words to her in Italian, to which she responded most charmingly. Then he gave a stiff nod to the Inspector of Strange and Unexplained Deaths and left.

'Chevalier de Seingalt! Wait, please!'

Chiara turned to Volnay with a playful look.

'Forgive me, Monsieur, for leaving so quickly, but I've just remembered that I am expected elsewhere. Please consider my request. You are a police inspector—you will know how to find me.'

Out on the street, Volnay watched darkly as Casanova gallantly helped the young woman into her carriage, then joined her. The driver cracked his whip and the vehicle shuddered. Volnay shook his head, trying to rid himself of his black thoughts. It was said that Casanova had raped a young woman in her carriage and that she hadn't even reported the crime. But then, what woman would dare report such a thing in this day and age?

The chevalier's pronouncements about money lacked conviction. Casanova was often short of funds, but as the protégé of the abbé de Bernis, the former French ambassador to Venice, with whom he had shared a mistress in Venice, Volnay knew that he had secured an introduction to the Duc de Choiseul. After which, praised by Bernis as an expert in matters of finance (especially the finances of others), he had persuaded the financier Joseph Pâris-Duverney of the infallibility of a plan he had devised, for a lottery. D'Alembert, the mathematician, had been persuaded, too. Casanova had obtained six offices and a comfortable salary of four thousand francs per year to set up the lottery, the aim of which was to finance the new military college, without raising taxes! Since when Casanova had been living in luxury, in a magnificently furnished villa, with a stable of horses, carriages, grooms and a retinue of servants.

Volnay walked slowly back to his house. Again, his thoughts turned to the carriage bearing away the young woman who had awakened a heart imprisoned in ice for so long. Then he thought of the Venetian and sighed.

'Ah! Casanova…'

He swore out loud. The magpie broke its silence, cackled and called out:

'Casa! Casa Cretin!'

Casanova studied Chiara's face as she turned to him. She radiated an unexpected light, just as some paintings of the quattrocento subtly show Mary to be more woman than Virgin. And with that, memories rose to the surface of his mind, in a disorderly rush he had not experienced for many years. First, the face of a mother who never granted him so much as a single loving look. Yet he would have paid dearly, in his childhood, to see his own reflection even for a second in the sparkle of her eyes. Next, the face of Henriette, his dearly beloved, and the message she had left him, carved on the windowpane with the point of a small diamond she wore in a ring: 'Henriette shall be forgotten, too.' Twelve years had passed, and he had forgotten nothing. He half closed his eyes, allowing his feelings to subside and his carapace to shut tight once more. He was alone with his memories. There was nothing to be gained as a lover of women.

'Why were you in such a hurry to leave Volnay?' he asked.

'Because he was in too much of a hurry to chase away one of my countrymen, and doubtless for the wrong reason.'

'Really?' he asked, innocently. 'And what reason is that?'

She stared him straight in the eye, discovering all the Venetian's legendary vitality as she did so, concentrated in his gaze.

'A reason I'm sure you can guess.'

Casanova allowed an amused smile to flutter at his lips. This young woman was vivacious indeed, and very sharp.

'And what about you, Chevalier?' she went on. 'What brought you to visit the inspector? Have some young girl's parents filed a complaint?'

Casanova looked slightly annoyed. The fact was, he had been thinking all night about the faceless woman, and the letter that Volnay had removed from her body. His mind, ever alert to the possibility of securing some advantage in life, told him that this was fertile territory, worth exploring. The inspector must have taken the letter for good reason. From what he knew of Volnay, he was a man of integrity. Was he trying to protect someone? The affair was worth a closer look. Often enough, knowing all there was to know had helped him keep body and soul together: one reason why he had called on the Inspector of Strange and Unexplained Deaths. But this young woman had distracted him from his purpose.

'A simple courtesy call,' he replied, and said no more.

Chiara laughed.

'A courtesy call to an officer of the police—a rebel like you!'

'Me, a rebel?' Casanova was astonished.

'You've been in prison; you escaped. You don't care a jot for the law, you have dared to revolt against authority!'

Her eyes were so bright with excitement that the Venetian was loath to disappoint. But some reputations were best not lugged across Europe in a man's baggage.

'I am no threat to society, Mademoiselle.'

'And yet you challenge it, by not living according to society's conventions!'

Casanova watched her attentively. He was seldom seen as a man at war with his own time. He had no bone to pick with anyone, though he enjoyed duping the gullible, and making a mockery of the law. And yet no one on earth was freer than he: he loved women madly, but when pushed he would always choose his freedom.

'It is true that I often pass from Their Royal Highnesses' courts to their prisons,' he admitted, elegantly.

She chuckled, and again he enjoyed her refreshing laughter, a reminder of Venice and more carefree days. *What is beauty?* he wondered, observing her with rapt devotion. *We cannot say, and yet we know it in our hearts.*

'Why did you take the name Seingalt, which seems to annoy our friend Volnay so?' she asked him suddenly.

'Oh, that's very simple,' he said, with a twinkle in his eye. '*Seing* means "signature" and *alt* is short for *altesse*: Highness.'

She looked at him, and her expression was grave once more. The Venetian's insolent disregard for society as a whole was enormously pleasing.

'How did you become what you are, Chevalier de Seingalt?'

'I grew up surrounded by women, from infancy,' he replied, in a tone of sincerity that surprised even him. 'That certainly influenced me in some way, for I have always loved the opposite sex, and have made sure to be loved as much as I was able.'

She leant forward, intrigued. Immediately, he was enveloped in her wonderful scent. He breathed it discreetly, alert to its elegance and sensuality.

'Tell me about that, Chevalier.'

The Chevalier de Seingalt affected an air of discomfort.

'As a child, I lost my father at a very young age, and my mother Zanetta was too busy acting and taking lovers to raise me herself. My memory developed only after the age of eight years and four months. I remember nothing before that.'

Not even if his mother had ever taken him in her ams. He paused for a moment. When seducing a woman, he was not in the habit of talking about his childhood. A quality of light in the girl's dark eyes encouraged him to go on.

'My mother took me for an imbecile, and never cared for me herself. I was placed in the care of my grandmother, who despaired because I seemed insensate, with my mouth hanging half-open. The doctors were at a loss, endlessly conjecturing as to what ailed me. My imbecility was due to frequent nosebleeds. Picture me standing in my bedroom at the age of eight, my grandmother supporting my head while I gaze, transfixed, at the blood trickling across the floor.'

He paused with a sigh and saw the interest his words had sparked in Chiara's eyes. She sat waiting attentively for him to continue.

'My grandmother, who loved me, had me taken in secret by gondola to the island of Murano, near Venice. She delivered me to an old witch, surrounded by black cats, who shut me—still all covered in blood—in a chest. I could hear her laughing, crying, shouting, singing and beating on the box, hard, with her fists. When she took me out, I was bleeding less profusely. She caressed me, undressed me and laid me down on a bed. Then she burnt medicinal herbs, and collected the smoke in a sheet, and wrapped me in it like a mummy. Then she gave me sweets with a pleasant taste, and rubbed the nape of my neck and my temples with a sweet-smelling ointment.'

Chiara hung on his every word. Her lips were parted slightly, revealing the small, pink tip of her pointed tongue.

'Then, the old hag cast a spell on me, telling me that a very beautiful, quite extraordinary young woman would come to me in the night, who would cure my ills. And so when I returned home, I tried hard not to fall asleep when evening came, despite a certain apprehension. *Somnia terrores magicos, nocturnos lemures portentaque Thessala rides…*'

'Can you laugh, unafraid, at dreams, spirits of the night and Thessalian monsters!' Chiara knew the poetry of Horace, and supplied the translation.

Casanova nodded, smiled and continued:

'My patience was rewarded by the dazzling apparition of a woman made of flesh and light. Her dress was of the finest fabric, and on her head she wore a crown dotted with precious stones that sparkled in the night. She bent over me as if to kiss me, and drew out my sickness, through my mouth. That was my first experience with a woman, and my life began that very night.'

'Tell me more!'

The young woman's eyes shone. Casanova continued eagerly. He knew that women delighted in men who talked to them and made them laugh.

'To think that the witch made me swear never to tell anyone what had happened, for fear of being bled dry. Dear God!'

He turned pale and pressed a hand to his heart. Chiara started violently in her seat, then broke into nervous laughter when she saw Casanova's wicked smile.

'When I had completed my studies,' he went on hurriedly, so as not to embarrass her, 'I took the cloth as a priest for a time, before leaving Rome and the clerical life to become a soldier! I soon gave that up, too, and became a lawyer, but relinquished that for lack of any appetite to see it through. Since then, I have been a financier, a professional gambler, a businessman—'

'A spy—and a swindler, too, some say.'

'People are always ready to speak ill of their fellow man,' said Casanova smoothly.

'And now, are you without a trade, or an income?'

The Venetian gave a charming, careless wave of the hand.

'What can I say? I am a feather-brained friend of pleasure, and the enemy of planning ahead! I delight in everything and blind myself to nothing.'

'And is that why you exploit the credulity of old women?'

Casanova shot her a piercing look.

'The idea came to me when I returned penniless from Corfu. In Venice, I was a forgotten man. The only work I found was playing the violin at the Teatro San Samuele, but I knew Fortune had not forsaken me. She exerts her powers for all mortals who truly desire her, especially in their youth.'

He turned to her.

'I am no longer very young, you know.'

'It hadn't escaped me,' she said, drily. 'But you'll get no pity from me. Go on with your story.'

Pleased to have caught her once again in the net of his narrative, he went on:

'I had sunk to the bottom when Fortune knocked at my door. One April night, a man collapsed in the street. I hurried to help him and by my treatment, or by chance, I saved his life. The man was a senator, wealthy and well known. He took me into his home after that, and treated me like a son.'

'And then?' asked Chiara, in spite of herself. She was trying in vain to conceal her eagerness.

'With age, the man developed a passion for the occult sciences—a passion he shared with two of his friends. I had read enough to be able to discourse knowledgeably on the possibility of communication with the hidden spirits, water sprites, nymphs and salamanders. I had read the *Clavicula Salomonis*. I invented a game using numbered pyramids that enabled me to decipher the desired answer to any question that was asked. I was asked what its secret was. Cleverly, I replied that I had it from an old hermit in the mountains, who swore I would die if I divulged it. I was well liked, and so no more questions were asked.'

He went on brightly:

'What man has never resorted to the basest of means when in need? But rest assured, I exploit only the credulity of those with the means to pay, unlike the sovereign heads of Europe, who live solely by pressuring the poorest of all!'

And as he laughed, he covered the young woman's hand with his own. She smiled, and withdrew it gently, though she had savoured the caress.

'You see,' she said solemnly, 'I was right. You care nothing for the established order, and convention. You obey nothing but your own desires. And you show boundless ingenuity when it comes to luring women to your bed.'

'Then you must also know that they are rarely disappointed, and often discover new sensations.'

The Venetian's tone was more urgent now.

'Chiara—permit me to call you by your first name. Women's bodies are inexhaustible founts of sensual pleasure, if only they knew it, which all too often they do not.'

He had whispered the last words in Italian, in her ear. She trembled, in spite of herself.

'Chiara…'

He seized her hand and lifted it to his lips.

'Chiara, man is born to give pleasure, and woman to receive. Will you be my light, and my host?'

Casanova froze. The young woman's body shook violently, and again a second time. It was then he realized she was in the grip of an uncontrollable fit of the giggles.

'What do you take me for, Chevalier, a mere child?' she asked, laughing. 'Do you think I don't know who you truly are? I know how you use and abuse your charms to seduce. One more little act of treachery is nothing to you, if you can get what you want! You're playing your sincerity card with me because you think that's what I'll like. Well you're right, but I know your game, nonetheless.'

Casanova said nothing. He had been caught off guard, but he did not show it.

'You have an abject opinion of me, based on a handful of gossip,' he declared ardently.

'And your reputation rides much too far ahead of you!'

She paused. When she spoke again, her tone was tinged with regret.

'I do not belong in your world. Yours is turned in upon itself, whereas mine is devoted to others. I am interested solely in the progress of science and the intellect, for the greater good of humanity. Your world and mine are destined never to meet.'

She turned suddenly, to look out of the carriage window. When she turned to look at him once more, there was a hint of sadness in her eyes.

'But I am charmed to have met you nevertheless, Chevalier.'

The carriage had pulled up in front of a magnificent mansion, its facade decorated with busts of figures from Antiquity. The flat roof was crowned with a balustrade supporting vases and trophies. A servant in purple and gold livery hurried to open the coach door and pull down the steps.

'I must leave you now,' said Chiara graciously. 'My driver will take you home.'

She stepped down with a rustle of silk and climbed the steps to the house without looking back. Alone in the coach, Casanova repeated her parting words: 'But I am charmed to have met you nevertheless, Chevalier!'

'That woman,' he whispered to himself, under his breath, 'I must have her!'

III

*I have loved women madly, but I have
always preferred my freedom.*

CASANOVA

The street swept him along and spat him out, deafened by
the cries of the merchants and street traders, each compet-
ing to holler the loudest and sell their fish, milk, cheese or
fruit. Volnay strode along the Rue du Loup-Perché, his mood
darker than usual. Thus far, in life, he had distanced himself
from passionate liaisons which he knew to be hopeless. But
Chiara D'Ancilla's spirited ways and looks had awakened new
interest in him, before that smug fool Casanova had arrived
and ruined everything. The sight of so rare a pearl leaving his
house in the company of that scoundrel and ladies' man had
left him seething with rage.

His first thought was to quell his fury by draining a glass or
two, though he was not in the habit of drinking. He marched
angrily along, jaw clenched tight, until the cool spring air
brought him to his senses. Little by little, he recovered his
calm, though the blood still buzzed in his ears. What did that
charmer Casanova and the frivolous Italian aristocrat matter
to him? Why form an attachment to someone about whom
he knew nothing? In the gilded, decadent, doomed world
of Chiara and Casanova, women were for the taking, or gave
themselves freely, on a whim.

Life for gaudy nobles such as them had no meaning beyond
present enjoyment and the satisfaction of their desires from
one moment to the next. Love was an illusion, a pretty illusion indeed, but feelings were transient things, and however

solid-seeming, the day always came when they crumbled to nothing, leaving an inescapable void. Love was always unreliable.

Volnay hesitated a moment. He was on Rue du Paradis now, near the palace of the Prince de Soubise. A fountain stood nearby, and around it a crowd of water-carriers and housekeepers busied themselves fetching their supply. He felt suddenly empty, drained of energy, incapable of advance or retreat. Volnay turned and paced slowly back to his house, pushing through the crowded streets, past the picklocks, whores and beggars who clutched at his sleeve with one hand while they felt for his purse with the other. Here was a trader selling purgative pills, there another selling greasy fried sweetmeats and spices, and, further along, a third selling her own body. The spectacle left him feeling suddenly, overwhelmingly weary.

At home, an extraordinary sight met his eyes. His orderly dwelling had been reduced to chaos. Books and notes from his desk lay scattered over the floor. The armchairs had been overturned. A candelabrum lay on the floor, beside a broken glass. He hurried into the room and swore vehemently. Suddenly, as if to warn him, the magpie cackled. Alerted by the bird's call, he felt a presence at his back and moved to defend himself, just in time.

All hell broke loose.

A fist glanced off his temple. Half knocked-out, he sank to the floor on one knee. A kick hit him hard in the stomach. He gripped his assailant's ankle and chopped the calf with the side of his hand. He suffered another kick for his pains. Hot blood filled his mouth. He was struggling to his feet when a thin knife blade was laid against his throat.

'Stop twisting about, Chevalier! Now, tell me the whereabouts of the letter you took from the faceless woman.'

Volnay was at his attacker's mercy, gasping for breath, when a hoarse, nasal voice rang out behind him.

'Quick! Quick!'

It was the magpie. Caught off guard, the intruder loosened his grip and glanced over his shoulder. Instinctively, Volnay turned and brought his knee up hard and fast between his attacker's thighs. The man howled in pain. Without a second's thought, Volnay head-butted him, and almost knocked himself out in the process. He threw haphazard punches after that. His foot found a soft belly and kicked it sharply, over and over. Then he heard a ringing of steel. Through a blood-red fog, he saw the dagger clattering across the floorboards and threw himself after it. A moment later he was on his feet, staring in disbelief at the tall, thin man with milk-white skin, brandishing at arm's length the thing he held dearest in all the world: the magpie in her cage. He lunged forward on instinct, trying to grab the bird. His attacker made a dash for the door. Volnay tried to follow and tripped over the cage. When he reached the street, the man had disappeared. Volnay tore back inside and scrabbled feverishly to turn the key in the door. The terrified magpie flapped and fluttered in her cage.

'Quiet, quiet!' Volnay soothed her as he caught his breath. 'Good bird!'

Gently, he took hold of the cage and placed it on his side table, talking to the bird all the while, to reassure her. His mouth was still dripping blood as he knelt and began to dislodge a flagstone hidden under a carpet. His hands were shaking violently, so that it took several attempts before he succeeded. A narrow space was revealed, containing a roll of gold coins, a packet of herbs which, when infused in water, could fell an ox, a few carefully sealed documents and the letter from the king. Volnay removed the last of these items, carefully replaced the flagstone, then sank into his favourite chair. He sat for a moment or two, with the letter in his hand. The relative, specious quiet of his existence was at an end.

He was determined now. He broke the seal, and read with growing astonishment:

Louis XV, king of France,
to Monsieur le Comte de Saint-Germain,

Monsieur le Comte,
   Madame la Marquise de Pompadour has spoken highly to me of your skill in the natural sciences, in particular the science of herbs. You are hereby instructed, with my grateful thanks, to accord the bearer of this letter the treatment this wicked creature has earned. You may verify the identity of the bearer of this letter by asking her for the affectionate name by which I called her, viz. My Little Kitten.
   My very best to you, dear Monsieur le Comte.

Volnay rose heavily and poured a glass of Bordeaux wine, which he drank down all at once, with no enjoyment. With the letter in one hand, he paused in front of the magpie's cage, stroking its plumage.

'Thanks are in order, for saving my life,' he said quietly. There was true affection in his voice.

He opened the cage door to place the bird on his shoulder, then, feeling suddenly burdened as if by a great weight, he walked slowly back to his chair. He read the letter through once more, then sat with his head in his hands.

Volnay muttered to himself: myriad scraps of information about the Comte de Saint-Germain. The fellow had arrived in Paris the previous year and had petitioned the brother of the Marquise de Pompadour, the Marquis de Marigny, director of the king's buildings, asking for the use of one of the royal houses, in which to install a laboratory so that he might continue the research he had been carrying out over the past twenty years and more. He had promised the king a rich and rare discovery, hitherto unparalleled. And the marquis, far from dismissing the comte out of hand, had offered him the palace of Chambord! The comte had been so busy installing his laboratory that he had quite disappeared from society for a time, and attracted no attention until he was presented to the king at Court.

Everyone surmised what had happened next. Each evening, the monarch visited the apartments of Madame de Pompadour at Versailles, using a hidden staircase. There, the marquise organized small, intimate dinner gatherings, designed to afford the king a chance to relax and converse in agreeable company. The Comte de Saint-Germain was a striking figure: understandably, La Pompadour's brother had brought him along for the entertainment of a monarch afflicted by ennui. Louis XV had taken a liking to the comte and invited him on a number of occasions. He had become part of the king's close circle, and the Marquise de Pompadour counted him her friend.

Volnay knew that during one such dinner in Paris, the comte had told a series of anecdotes about the court of François I, with great accuracy and wit. Questioned on any subject or period of history, he showed surprising knowledge—or powers of invention—and his plausible tales often shed new light on things hitherto shrouded in the greatest mystery.

When the party had moved to the drawing room, the elderly Madame de Gergy, who had been listening with passionate interest, approached the comte. She told him she had met him in Venice, during her time as the wife of the ambassador to the Most Serene Republic, fifty years before, and that he looked much younger now! She even remembered that at the time he called himself the Marquis de Baletti. Smiling all the while, the comte had assured her that her mind was as fresh now as it had been fifty years ago.

The anecdotes, and their exchange, overheard by the other guests, were reported all over Paris and Versailles, and incited much curiosity. A rumour spread that the comte, to all appearances a man in his forties, was in fact several hundred years old.

Suspicions were confirmed when, at subsequent dinners, the comte told how he had met King David, attended the wedding party at Cana at which Jesus had turned water into wine, hunted with Charlemagne and gone drinking with Luther. He sat at the piano and played the march that had accompanied the entry of Alexander the Great into Babylon. The high point of the entertainment came when he spoke of his friend Jesus Christ, the finest man who ever lived, though possessed of so wild an imagination, and so reckless and impulsive, that the comte had predicted he would come to a bad end. After that, he told how he had intervened in person with the wife of Pontius Pilate, a woman he knew well, to beg for Christ's life to be spared. Asked if he had found it difficult to live for several thousand years, he would reply that 'the first thousand are always the worst!'

But while the comte had indeed been present at the dinner with the Comtesse de Gergy, everything that took place subsequently had been a trick. The king's minister, Choiseul, who loathed the comte for having a liaison with his wife, had paid a man by the name of Gauve, an actor known for his clever impersonations, to make the rounds of the Paris salons and the streets of the Marais, passing himself off as the Comte de Saint-Germain. This, then, was the source of the tall tales, but contrary to their intended purpose, the comte suffered no ridicule, but instead found himself at the centre of a web of mystery that fascinated the popular imagination.

The comte was greatly amused by this and delighted in perpetuating the myth. Volnay supposed that in reality the man possessed a flair for narrating historical episodes in astonishing detail, and had mastered the art of portraying famous figures from the past. When he spoke of them, he seemed to have known them personally, and was happy to let his listeners believe that he had truly lived in those distant times, rather than telling them so outright.

Volnay pondered all this while stroking the magpie's long, layered tail fathers with his finger, admiring their metallic sheen. That the king should write a letter to the Comte de Saint-Germain was unsurprising in itself. Louis XV considered the comte a friend and suffered no one to mock him. It was even rumoured that the king, who had an obsession with genealogy, had spoken of the comte as a person of very high birth. But now the king's own inspector had found this royal letter, with its surprising contents, on the corpse of a faceless woman, and secretly removed it.

'What can all this mean?' Volnay asked the magpie.

The first man was tall, his face and head entirely devoid of hair of any kind. His skin was white as milk, and his gaunt silhouette resembled a stalk struggling to support a faded flower. He stood as if to attention, stiff and straight, and his fixed gaze was disconcerting. The second man, smaller and older, resembled a fat cat purring in front of the fire. The room they occupied was sparsely furnished with a large oak table and two uncomfortable-looking, straight-backed chairs. In front of the smaller, seated man, a psalter lay open somewhere towards the middle, richly illuminated and annotated in its margins. A shaft of sunlight shone through the only window, casting its golden rays upon a crucifix bearing the twisted form of the dying Christ, like a butterfly pinned to a board. A thin veil of dust particles floated on the air, like the harbinger of some supernatural apparition.

'Are you quite sure it's the girl who stepped down from the carriage you were following?' asked the older man.

'The same dress, Father Ofag, the same ribbons and shoes.'

He lowered his eyes and continued, with a hint of shame: 'Black silk stockings with fine, pale pink stripes…'

Father Ofag saw the other man's discomfort, and hid his smile behind his hand.

'Tell me again about this mysterious letter,' he commanded.

'I saw it, Father,' repeated the other, 'with my own eyes. The inspector removed a sealed letter from one of her pockets. I was not close enough to identify the seal, but I saw the amazement on his face.'

'And what did he do with the letter, my dear Wallace?'

'He concealed it, Father, doubtless in order to secure himself some advantage by it.'

Father Ofag shook his head. His heavily lidded eyes gleamed with cunning.

'Have you never heard talk of the Chevalier de Volnay? Well, I have. He is not a corrupt man.'

He paused.

'Alas, he is not one of us, but happily, neither is he a creature of the king's favourite, that second-rate whore who has turned the Court into a brothel—La Pompadour!'

He spat out the name like a bitter clot of blood, causing the other to take a step back in alarm. Father Ofag observed his companion's grey eyes, so pale they seemed to have been washed of all colour. Had the light of heaven ever truly shone there? Wallace blinked briefly at the mention of the favourite's name.

'Do you think this letter has anything to do with La Pompadour?' asked Father Ofag, silkily.

'She sent one of her creatures, the girl Chiara D'Ancilla, to Volnay's house the next morning to recover the letter.'

'That's bad! Very bad! An old Milanese family, the D'Ancillas, very rich, very noble—sixteen quarterings. Their ancestors accompanied the crusades to the very foot of the walls of Jerusalem. They hold the ancient right to ride into church on horseback—one they seldom find occasion to exercise, I might say.'

Father Ofag thought for a few moments.

'Have you nothing else to tell me?' he asked, staring into space.

'I do, indeed! The policeman works with that heretic, the fornicating monk, a sinner spat out of hell by the Devil himself for the misery of us all!'

Ofag nodded.

'I know the man you speak of. He's the Devil incarnate, he must be dealt with without delay. In fact, I thought you had already taken care of him…'

'Fear not—he is my next priority.'

For the first time since the beginning of their interview, Father Ofag seemed, almost imperceptibly, to relax.

'Inestimable Wallace! Inestimable.'

Wallace straightened up, part anxious, part triumphant.

'I, er… I went to search Volnay's house for the letter, but I didn't find it, and he surprised me there. We fought…'

He gestured to his battered lip.

'But no one was killed, my dear Wallace?' asked Father Ofag, quietly.

'Not yet, not yet…'

Rue de la Corderie was a narrow street with a sharp turn that opened onto a small, dark square enclosed by tall houses. Volnay walked straight up to the oldest of these. Either side of the door, the stone figures of a crane and a cockerel, symbolizing patience and vigilance, surveyed one another.

The monk opened the door. He had pulled his hood down over his face. He stood aside to let Volnay pass, and locked the door behind him as a precaution before uncovering his head to reveal a finely featured face with a high forehead, a narrow, almost aquiline nose and a firm chin covered by a short, greying beard. His eyes were bright and penetrating. His lively features bore the traces of the many passions he had learnt to discipline and conquer over time, with considerable effort and at great personal cost. His voice was deep and warm, but tense, as he greeted his collaborator.

'Here you are at last! Before I forget, take this sachet—you who are such a poor sleeper. It contains pills to send you to sleep. I made them myself from cynogloss root, henbane seed, myrrh and saffron. You'll have marvellous dreams, believe me! I saw myself surrounded by the most wonderful, sensual harem any man could hope for. Quite the most wanton experience of my life!'

They stood in a narrow hallway, dimly lit by a small window. Still talking volubly, the monk led the way down a long, dark passage to a double iron door. He turned a key and Volnay, who knew this place well, followed him into a stone-walled room housing an extraordinary laboratory full of crucibles, alembics, retorts and, above all, furnaces, some cold and others snoring faintly with the muffled roar of fire. The monk danced about like an excited child, moving agilely around the cluttered room, with seemingly boundless energy.

'It's hot as hell in here,' said Volnay.

'I've become used to it. I don't even sweat any more under my habit,' said the monk. 'I shall be hardened and ready to confront the afterlife, though of course I don't believe anyone or anything lies waiting on the other side!'

'Have you succeeded?' asked Volnay, anxious to avoid a theological argument.

'Of course, but with the greatest of difficulty.'

The monk drew him closer to the body. An amused smile fluttered at his lips. His gaze was attentive, and unshakeably confident, but frequently softened to gentle laughter, as if granting the imperfect world around him the indulgence it deserved.

'The mask is ready,' he said, 'but the circumstances of her death remain a mystery. Her body shows no sign of any blows, only slight bruising to the knees and elbows, when she collapsed to the ground. I can assure you, nonetheless, that she died this night, and suffered appallingly: she writhed and twisted like a soul in damnation. It appears she suffered heart failure.'

Volnay winced in horror.

'She was skinned alive?'

'Probably. Though there should be traces of cuts, as she tried to defend herself. And there are none. Who could have done such a thing? My inquisitive, weasel mind took me to my records of murder from the past few years. I consulted them all, and found two cases of flaying, but of the whole body. The first murderer was executed. There was some doubt as to his guilt, but, fortunately for his judges, he confessed after having his hands and feet immersed in boiling oil. The other died under questioning, when both of his legs were broken. People have no stamina these days!'

Impervious to his colleague's humour, Volnay paced the length and breadth of the room, taking long, thoughtful strides.

'With regard to the act itself,' the monk went on, 'I examined the body as soon as it was loaded onto my cart. I know from experience that the rigor mortis—the stiffening of the muscles—can reveal the time of death. It begins with the eyelids and jaw, in the first six hours, before spreading to the whole body in the following six hours. I can certify, therefore, that the young woman died very shortly before her body was discovered.'

The monk bent forward and, with great delicacy, took hold of one of the dead woman's hands. He turned it over with extreme care, as if it were made of porcelain.

'The palms of her hands have been partly stripped away. You and I have been working together for over two years now, and in all that time I have never seen so strange a corpse. I simply do not understand…'

'Neither do I!' growled Volnay. 'The whole business looks like witchcraft.'

'Ha! Indeed, witchcraft is a convenient explanation for many things.'

The monk watched Volnay for a moment. He raised one inquisitive eyebrow.

'What if you were to tell me the whole truth?'

Volnay gave short, plaintive sigh.

'Last night, I found a letter on the corpse, bearing the royal seal.'

The monk swore at length, and Volnay shuddered to hear it. Saints-turned-whores were involved, and a sodomite pope.

'And what does the letter say?' asked the monk, finally.

'Last night, I thought it prudent not to open it,' said Volnay. 'I thought I might have to justify myself one day, to someone of importance.'

The monk nodded, with a thin smile.

'But your curiosity got the better of you?'

'Particularly after a hired killer broke into my house this morning and attacked me, in order to get it back.'

The monk started in surprise.

'Are you hurt?' he asked, anxiously.

'Wounded pride, nothing more!' sighed Volnay.

He told his story. At the description of the attacker, the monk's face darkened.

'Wallace, without a shadow of a doubt. A fanatical soldier-monk, wholly dedicated to the so-called Devout Party—the Company of the Holy Sacrament. His moral fibre wouldn't stretch to cover a gnat's wing! He is highly dangerous and stops at nothing. I have no idea how he knew you were in possession of the letter from the king, but its contents will doubtless shed some light on the nature of the danger we face…'

'The letter is our only clue, at any rate,' said Volnay. 'I'm left with an unidentifiable corpse, and no witnesses. How can I possibly carry out an investigation?'

'What does the letter say?' his companion was impatient to know.

Volnay sat himself in an appallingly uncomfortable straight-backed chair and told his collaborator what he had read.

'Unbelievable,' said the monk, quietly. 'The king might be asking the Comte de Saint-Germain to slay the poor girl, punish her, or—jokingly—to grant her a favour. You are someway nearer to discovering her identity, at least: simply find out if anyone has heard talk of an adorable Little Kitten.'

'And who do you suggest I ask, the king or the Comte de Saint-Germain?'

Both fell silent.

'Or La Pompadour,' sighed the monk thoughtfully, at length. 'She and the king share so much. And the Comte de Saint-Germain is one of her intimate circle.'

Volnay said nothing, and the monk changed the subject.

'The dead woman is young, no more than sixteen or seventeen. The fact that she was no longer a virgin will come as no surprise. She had been intimate with a man shortly before her death. I found traces of semen.'

'Was she raped?'

'Not immediately prior to the murder, if that's what you're asking. No, I estimate the intimacy to have taken place an hour or two beforehand. Ah, and judging by her hands and nails, she must have taken great care of her person.'

'And her appearance in general?'

The monk said nothing. Volnay was accustomed to his long silences, interspersed by flashes of ironic wit. But he was worried now.

'What else did you find?'

The monk gave a long and heart-felt groan.

'This was not one murder, but two. The young woman was with child.'

Volnay froze. His mind raced. What if the victim had been carrying the king's child?

'This might give the king's letter a new and quite different meaning,' said the monk, as if reading his companion's thoughts. 'Viz. the young woman is with child: be sure to put an end to it.'

'The Church preaches coitus interruptus, and the use of vaginal sponges,' said Volnay, icily. 'But the termination of an unborn life is a crime which even the king would hesitate to order.'

The monk buried his hands in the sleeves of his habit and raised his eyes to the ceiling, talking as if to himself.

'The king turns to evil while the cold of the tomb seeps through the Court. We may expect anything and everything of him now.'

He rose and crossed to the dead woman's body, over which he had laid a black cloth.

'As a rule,' he said reflectively, 'the king likes them younger than this. Is this one of his former mistresses? They say he tires of their bodies in the space of a few weeks. Or abandons them as soon as they are with child. It's a thing he abhors.'

He gestured furiously, and his eyes glittered.

'They say that at fifty, the king's private pleasures are more and more perverse. You may have heard the same?'

'Yes, and worse.'

The monk gave a caustic laugh.

'Strange indeed, when you consider that our monarch was deflowered at the age of fourteen, in the palace of Chantilly, by an experienced marquise, on the orders of the regent, who feared he was exhibiting unnatural tendencies.'

Volnay glanced at him in surprise.

'It's unlike you to spread such gossip.'

His companion frowned eloquently.

'You must know, my young pupil, that I never venture to assert anything unless I am absolutely certain of my sources. My remark was also intended to remind you of the nature of the man you serve—a person for whom, at base, you feel no respect whatever.'

'I serve the king, that's how it is.'

Another ironic laugh from the monk.

'We'll see about that! Your king is an incompetent fool, politically and economically—and militarily. We have just lost Canada and the Indies. And we are about to lose another campaign. Our finances are pathetically inadequate. The State's creditors remain unpaid. The people are unaware of it, but our debts are heavy indeed. France is bankrupt!'

He stared into space.

'And what of the freedom of religion? The Protestants suffer appalling repression: the royal troops hunt them down, the men are arrested and sent to the galleys, their women are shaved, clubbed and imprisoned in the Tour de Constance in Aigues-Mortes, with their children. There are boys and girls there, six years old, who have known nothing all their lives but one room and the bars of a cage.'

Volnay knew what was coming next, and steeled himself, as so many times before.

'If you had not saved the king…'

And closing his eyes, Volnay remembered the evening in January 1757 when a man named Robert-François Damiens had joined the crowds entering the palace of Versailles in hopes of an audience with the king. At six o'clock, Louis XV had walked to his carriage, for the ride back to the Trianon, when Damiens broke through the line of guards, in a downpour of rain. With his scarlet breeches, he had doubtless been mistaken for a Court valet. The crowd was so dense that no one noticed him but Volnay. Damiens attacked the king in plain sight, but no one saw anything. The monarch was stabbed with an eight-centimetre blade, easily deflected by his thick winter clothing and leaving only a shallow wound between his ribs. Thinking he had been struck by a drunkard, Louis XV even observed to his neighbour, the Duc d'Ayen: 'Someone has punched me with his fist!' Then he pressed his hand to his side, and withdrew it covered in blood. Meanwhile, Volnay had flung himself forward and prevented Damiens from stabbing the king a second time. In the ensuing struggle, Damiens had slashed Volnay's face.

The king, as morally bankrupt as he was stupid and deluded, had cried out:

'Who would kill me? I've done no harm to anyone!'

The blade had left a cut just a centimetre deep between the royal ribs. After receiving the last rites, and confessing his sins, which took some considerable time, the king had made a full recovery. He became a laughing stock in certain quarters, and bills were posted all over Paris proclaiming: 'By order of the Royal Mint: a badly struck louis must be struck a second time!'

Damiens was a person of no importance, a one-time soldier

turned dealer in white clay, for the removal of stains. By way of explanation for his actions, he said merely: 'The king is ruling his country badly, which is why I sought to kill him, for the public good.'

The king wanted Damiens thrown in a dungeon, but the Paris parliament found him guilty of attempted regicide, and he suffered an appalling end. Spectacular punishment was a pillar of the king's justice, and Damiens's demise was carefully staged to leave a lasting impression. He was led to the scaffold on Place de Grève, where his chest and limbs were slashed and molten lead, burning oil and pitch poured into the gaping wounds. His right hand, which had held the knife, was completely charred with burning sulphur. Damiens screamed and howled. Dozens in the crowd fainted or vomited in disgust. Some even swore at the executioner.

After these initial tortures, the condemned man's limbs were tied to four horses, and he was torn apart. Several attempts were necessary, and even with his limbs torn off, Damiens was still alive. Sombre and pensive amid the vast crowd that had packed Place de Grève, Volnay watched the execution in silence, noting sadly how many aristocratic ladies applauded the spectacle from the balconies of townhouses rented for the occasion, at one hundred livres apiece. Not one of them looked away, he noted, while Damiens, in possession of barely half his body, continued to howl and scream like a soul in perdition.

In recognition of his bravery, Volnay had been knighted by the king. Since then, His Majesty's Inspector of Strange and Unexplained Deaths had held a special place in the king's police force. Legend had replaced fact, and the scar on his face led everyone to believe that he had thrown himself between Damiens and the king, and received the knife wound in the latter's stead.

Nothing of this mattered to Volnay, in the end. All that tormented him now was the nagging question: should he have allowed the king to be killed?

Volnay was on his way to pay a call. Eager not to arrive at mealtime, rather than to satisfy a hunger he did not feel, he stopped at an inn with a tumbledown roof and a curious-sounding name: the Singing Rabbit. The floor was strewn with dirty straw, but bundles of juniper twigs burnt in the hearth, casting an agreeable glow around the room. A cauldron placed on a tripod released a sour, meaty smell mixed with cloves, cinnamon and the green-grape acidity of verjuice. In a corner of the room, a group of diners ate chicken livers wrapped in bay leaves, dipped in a brown sauce floating with croutons. Volnay ordered a baked hare terrine and a piece of cheese, with a glass of bitter wine that scorched his throat.

After eating, he rode his horse through the narrow, filth-strewn streets, thronged with the eternally noisy, restless Paris crowd. The populace was incapable of keeping quietly indoors. Paris lived, hollered and died in the street. Artisans kept their doors and windows open all day long, and passers-by could see the masters and their apprentices at work. Gradually, the din of the crowd subsided. The streets were broader; stone replaced wattle and daub. Volnay rode past carriages and crowds of well-dressed gentlefolk.

He stopped outside the superb, marble-clad mansion that was home to the family of the Marquis D'Ancilla. A liveried servant asked him to wait in a small salon. Volnay paced to and fro impatiently. The ceiling was painted with garlands of flowers highlighted in silver against a white ground dotted with gold. The luxurious decor announced the residence of a fine aristocrat: a Murano chandelier, silk carpets, varnished woodwork and panelling, mirrors reflecting into infinity the image of a young man of twenty-five, with a pleasant if austere bearing, solemn and utterly determined.

'Chevalier de Volnay, what a surprise!' exclaimed Chiara on entering the room. 'I left you only a few hours ago. Are there any developments in your investigation, so soon?'

Volnay paled imperceptibly under the dazzling gaze of her magnificent, dark eyes. She had changed her clothes and was no longer bejewelled, but wore a simple gown of blue satin that showed her slender waist and marble-white bosom to marvellous effect. Lowering his eyes, he saw with surprise that her tiny feet were in slippers. He allowed a few, precious moments to elapse in silence, under the young woman's amused gaze. Recovering himself, he heard Chiara explain that she had been working on an experiment in her laboratory. She even offered to take him to see it. Politely, Volnay declined.

'But what is it you do in your laboratory?' he asked none-theless, seeing her disappointment.

The young woman's dark eyes glittered with unexpected fire.

'I observe nature, I calculate the distance from the Earth to the sky... I am most interested in volcanic rocks at present.'

'Indeed?' asked Volnay, politely.

She laughed lightly.

'Yes, indeed. You are aware that the Earth owes nothing of its creation to God? It was a mass of burning, molten rock and then, as the heat diminished, the first mountains rose up. Imagine the mists floating gracefully all around the globe, enveloping it in a mantle of gauze. They settled, at length, and covered the whole planet in one, great ocean. The first inhabitants of our world emerged in those waters. Vast caverns lay at the bottom of the sea. They collapsed over time, swallowing down part of the oceans with them, and causing a new world to rise.'

'Wherever did you read all that?' asked Volnay, astounded.

'In Monsieur de Buffon's *Natural History*. He says that, after that, the sea retreated slightly, everywhere, and that mountains thrust upwards under the effect of fire.'

She broke off.

'I have a piece of lava rock in the laboratory—would you like to see it?'

She was in such ecstasies of excitement that it seemed she saw the volcanoes forming, and burning lava pouring down their flanks, right before her eyes. Volnay watched Chiara's delicate hands fluttering in space as they recreated the forms of lost worlds.

'Life developed slowly and gradually,' she added. 'It struggled every day for its right to exist; it changed form; it adapted to its environment.'

'And so you do not believe in God?' demanded Volnay, abruptly.

Coming from an officer of the police, the question was anything but innocent, in the present climate. Chiara faced him calmly, challenging him with her firm gaze. He saw how beautiful this young woman was, and that she was afraid of nothing.

'I do not believe in God, Monsieur, I believe in Nature.'

She scrutinized his face, trying to fathom his reaction.

'And you, Monsieur, do you believe in God?'

'Less and less, Mademoiselle.'

'Why is that?'

Volnay blinked rapidly. A blazing bonfire shone in the eyes of a small boy who stood weeping. The image gnawed at his soul. The small boy was him.

'I no longer believe in God, Mademoiselle, because it is said of him that he made man in his own image. And so he must be a thoroughly detestable individual.'

There was a startled silence. Two creatures who knew nothing of one another were expressing beliefs that would take them to the scaffold or worse. The punishments for blasphemy were barbarous indeed: the human imagination knew no bounds when it came to the infliction of suffering. The image of the Chevalier de La Barre lingered in every mind's eye: a young man of nineteen, condemned to have his fists and tongue cut off, then beheaded and burnt for having sung a lewd, disrespectful song on the subject of religion, and for refusing to remove his hat for the passing of a church procession. 'I did not believe a gentleman could be put to death for so little,' were his last words.

Chiara came closer. For a brief moment, Volnay's ears were filled with the loud rustle of her gown.

'I have faith in progress,' she said quietly. 'What do you have faith in?'

He stared at her in silence. A chasm yawned between them, though he longed to cross to her side.

'I have faith in truth,' he said at last. 'There should be no such thing as lies.'

Chiara shrugged her shoulders gracefully.

'Is that all?'

'I believe in equality among men.'

She stood rooted to the spot in astonishment. *What a strange police officer this is!* she thought.

'I would not go so far, Monsieur,' she said, after moistening her lip nervously with her tongue. 'But I have faith in humanity because it is capable of the very best.'

'Indeed it will be, when men are capable of putting the common good ahead of their personal interests. For now, I will quote Monsieur de Voltaire: "One day, all will be well, that is our hope! All is well today, that is our delusion."'

'You're forgetting,' she said brightly, 'that the quotation

ends like this: "But good or bad as things are, we must strive for better!"'

She gazed at him with her beautiful, shadowy eyes, framed by silky lashes. Silence fell once more, but it was a thoughtful silence now, tinged with respect on both sides.

'Mademoiselle,' said Volnay finally, and with a hint of regret, 'I came quickly to find you because I have the dead woman's mask, now. I will show it to a number of people, of course, but yesterday you were concerned for the safety of your lady-in-waiting, and I thought I should bring it here to reassure you. Are you ready to see it?'

Her eyes were wide with surprise.

'How is that possible? There was no skin on her face!'

'Someone has worked to reconstruct it. With quite expressive results, I find.'

And from the satchel he carried with him, he withdrew a fine gold mask that glowed with a seemingly supernatural light. Chiara cried out.

'That's Mademoiselle Hervé, one of the king's wig-makers!'

The young woman seemed quite overcome. Volnay took note.

'Are you quite certain?'

Chiara seemed to be thinking fast, as Volnay noted with some surprise.

'Well,' she stammered, 'I believe so, but I can't be quite sure. I met her only once or twice, I suppose…'

Volnay watched her with interest. To remember the face of a person of low estate, a servant, whom one has met *only once or twice* was extraordinary. And why the cry of recognition, followed by the hasty retreat? His curiosity was whetted.

'Where did you meet her?'

The young woman flushed deeply.

'Well, I don't remember…'

'Mademoiselle, do you know something about the victim, or about her death?'

Chiara looked him straight in the eye, unblinking, and answered:

'I know nothing.'

She spoke without hesitation, and yet it seemed to Volnay she was lying. His methodical mind analysed the facts he had carefully stored away: a young Italian aristocrat comes to see him the morning after an appalling murder, pretending first to request a visit to the city morgue, and then to ask about the disappearance of her lady-in-waiting. The same woman is able to identify the victim from her death mask, but incapable of providing any further information about her.

Volnay bitterly regretted his initial impulse to trust Chiara, and the feelings he had been prey to when he first saw her. She was the same as all the rest: lying, selfish, indifferent to others. Like all women, and all men. This world was dead to him, it was a world without hope.

Again, he felt the icy carapace close around his heart. Again, he banished any human sentiment that might have obstructed him or held him back. The only thing of importance was the mission he had accepted, the mission that gave his life meaning. He realized he was fixing Chiara with a cold, hard stare, and saw her discomfort. Hastily, he recomposed his habitual mask. The look, some said, that gave the impression of gazing into a bottomless, perfectly still lake.

'Who suggested you come to see me yesterday?' he asked at length, in studiedly neutral tones.

She paused before answering.

'My father.'

'Ah…'

Another lie, from the tone of her voice. To maintain her composure, Chiara had seated herself with a loud rustling of silk. Her annoyance at this thinly veiled interrogation showed clearly in her face. Meanwhile, Volnay's thoughts travelled from the salon to a certain letter, with a certain royal signature.

'Have you ever heard of the Comte de Saint-Germain?' he asked suddenly.

She was caught completely off guard.

'Of course!' she exclaimed. 'He's the darling of all the salons. They say he's the man who has seen everything and knows everything. He can remember his past lives and will happily tell you what went on at the wedding in Cana, and all the intrigues at the court of Babylon, as if he had been there himself. They say he has lived for one thousand, eight hundred and fourteen years already, thanks to an elixir of life given to him by the queen of Judea!'

'And do you believe him?'

The young woman gave a mocking laugh.

'Monsieur, I am not like those other, silly girls! I reason by science alone, and science says that such things are impossible.'

'I'll grant you that.'

Volnay bit his lower lip thoughtfully.

'Why do you ask me about the Comte de Saint-Germain?' asked Chiara evenly. 'Does he have anything to do with your investigation?'

'Not at all, Mademoiselle. I will go now and show the mask to a person in the king's household, to confirm your identification. For the good of the inquiry, I ask you to keep what we have said here today absolutely secret. Do you give me your word?'

Chiara straightened her shoulders haughtily, but quickly recovered her habitual charm, and her smile.

'On one condition, Monsieur. Come and visit me again soon, or I'll blab it at every society dinner!'

*

The monk bit off a chunk of his salt pork pie and chewed it thoughtfully while staring at the corpse. He was perplexed. *Strange! Strange!* he thought, as he contemplated the bloodied flesh, which was turning putrid now. This was all too perfect. The face couldn't have been cut away like that with a knife. It demanded the precision of a surgeon, or a furrier to achieve such a result. And why had the palms of her hands been partially skinned, together with the tips of her fingers? *Truly, I do not understand!*

He pondered the problem, muttering under his breath as usual, because he disliked keeping his thoughts to himself, and because his years in prison had accustomed him to these solitary conversations. The candles were burning down around him, casting only a feeble light. The deep cellar was riddled with damp. A sudden rush of air flattened the flames, and extinguished some.

'Back again?' he said, without turning around. 'This faceless young lady has certainly captured your attention. What of the visit to the young Italian aristocrat?'

He received no reply.

The monk lifted his eyes without moving his head, and stared at the shadow making its way around the wall. His hand slid silently to the knife he had just used.

'Yes,' he added calmly, 'a strange business indeed—'

He span around, narrowly avoiding the fatal strike. A gleaming dagger pointed at his throat, clasped by a hand gloved in black leather. The monk elbowed the man sharply in the ribs before throwing himself clear and retreating. The other man stepped calmly to one side. He wore a thick leather jerkin of the kind used by robbers as protection in sword fights. His face, half-hidden under a felt mask, was riddled with pockmarks. Calmly, he unfastened his leather cape, keeping his eyes firmly on the monk, and folded it swiftly over his arm before holding it in front of him like a shield, while he tried to run his victim through the heart. The monk struck sidelong at the sword with his knife, thwarting the blade. He slashed his assailant's face, then struck down at the man's stomach with brutal force.

The monk had not always lived the life of the mind. His wild youth had taken him to a fair number of battlefields. Later, his nocturnal activities had brought him into confrontation with old soldiers forging new careers as cheap killers for hire. This man was certainly one of their kind. He was quick, and said nothing. Their blades clashed again. His aggressor charged once more, ferociously, his face glistening with sweat. Again, the monk parried his thrusts, methodically and with a mastery that betrayed his experience of hand-to-hand combat, hindered only by the voluminous folds of his habit. He moved back behind the table, upon which—impassive amid the commotion—lay the body of the faceless woman.

The monk parried a hail of blows as he retreated, and suffered a cut to the hand. With remarkable lucidity, he ignored it and concentrated on redoubling his defence. Between two clinks of their blades, at last, his hand found the candelabrum he had been groping for. He seized it and brought it down violently on his opponent's gaunt face. The other man howled and dropped his guard. Coldly, the monk sank his knife into his right eye, deep enough to touch the brain.

With his visit to Chiara at an end, Volnay made his way to the Pont Neuf early in the afternoon. Down on the quaysides, laundry workers of all ages rubbed their hands raw on the city's washing. The Pont Neuf was crowded with carriages, people on foot, street performers and bear-tamers. Astride his horse, the Inspector of Strange and Unexplained Deaths threaded his way adroitly through the tide of humanity. The silhouette of the Châtelet rose before him. In medieval times, the ancient castle had defended Paris against the Norman invaders. When the city walls were extended by Philippe Auguste, the building had become the headquarters of the military police, and the seat of Paris's criminal justice court. It had been the scene of innumerable acts of violence, and outright massacres. Its walls were steeped in the blood of its victims. Prison cells and rooms set aside for torture compounded its sinister reputation: in the notorious Fosse dungeon, prisoners were left standing in water, day and night, barely able to straighten up. Few survived more than two weeks in such hell.

Antoine Raymond de Sartine kept his office in this grim place. The son of a financier ennobled by the king of France and appointed sheriff of Catalogne, Sartine had purchased the post of police chief for the city of Paris in 1752. He had proved a competent administrator, with a keen political sensibility. Through the broad scope of his office, he had improved not only food supplies to the city through the construction of a new grain market, but also public safety through the installation of street lanterns. It was rumoured that he was eyeing the post of chief of police for the whole of France, one of the most important positions in the land. He was judged a fair-minded and honest man compared to his peers, but an instrument of the king, too, and unflinching in his devotion to duty. He had shut down the city's clandestine gambling dens, but established authorized gaming houses in their place, overseen and taxed by his own agents.

At the news of the identity of the faceless woman, he sank into a tremendous state of nervous anxiety.

'The king's wig-maker? The young woman was the king's wig-maker! Do you realize what this means?'

Volnay understood only too well. He had no liking for this monarch, who was indifferent to the everyday lot of his people and loved only hunting and women. Before the Marquise de Pompadour had 'furnished' the king's house, or houses, in the Parc-aux-Cerfs, Louis XV had enjoyed the services of a small harem of three: shop girls or artist's models who were recruited officially as wig-makers, and housed in the attics of his palace: Mesdemoiselles Fouquet and Hénaut, and the victim, Mademoiselle Hervé. They were a lively trio, noted for their gaiety, and for making more noise overhead than a colony of rats. Now one of these *petits rats* had been silenced.

'I don't want the king mixed up in this, at close quarters or from afar,' ordered Sartine. 'You don't need me to remind you of the usefulness of all this to the king's enemies. Calumny is rife against him as it is.'

'Let them talk,' said the Inspector of Strange and Unexplained Deaths, in a careless tone that was very unlike him.

Sartine raised an ill-tempered eyebrow.

'I attach a great deal of important to public gossip. A docile populace is a subject populace. When the people talk, the established order is threatened!'

Volnay's face darkened.

'There is worse to come, I fear. People are taking an interest in the case.'

The chief of police eyed him coldly.

'What "people" are they, if you please, Chevalier?'

Volnay shrugged slightly.

'How should I know? Everyone spies on everyone else in Paris and Versailles.'

And perhaps the 'people' are you? he added to himself.

Sartine opened a tobacco pouch, sniffed a pinch or two then brushed the remaining strands from his jabot with a long, slender white hand. He had a high forehead, a receding hairline and a pointed nose. With age, his complexion had acquired the colour of old ivory. He adjusted his wig, as he did a hundred times a day, with the regularity of a metronome. The headpiece was one of a whole collection he kept closely guarded in a steel closet. His only foible and, all things being equal, a relatively harmless one at that.

'The perpetrator of this outrageous murder must be found,' declared the chief of police, drily. 'But I hesitate to leave you in charge of the inquiry. The precinct chief could handle it just as well as you.'

Volnay felt his heart beat faster. Paris was divided into forty-eight precincts or *quartiers*, each with its own police chief under royal authority, but who among them had the scientific expertise that was needed to solve this mystery? He reminded Sartine of the fact.

'It's a strange death, I grant you that,' muttered the chief, 'but it's uncomfortably close to the king himself. Well, do what you can! Act swiftly, but be discreet. If speech or silence must be bought, you have limitless credit. Throughout this whole business, you will have in your sights nothing but the service of our king and the country under his care.'

He opened a drawer in his desk and took out a purse full of écus, tossing it noisily onto the desk.

'Keep me informed regularly of progress, as soon as you have anything new to report. Are there no leads?'

'Not as yet,' replied Volnay with superlative calm.

Sartine shot his colleague a suspicious glance, then walked quickly up to him and stared him in the eye.

'Are you hiding something, Volnay?'

Volnay made no reply. His impassive expression matched Sartine's own. Not a muscle in his face twitched. Sartine scrutinized the inspector's expressionless blue-grey eyes in vain. His stiff bearing, distance and reserve were as impregnable as any armour. If it were not for that madman, the monk, Sartine would have had no idea how to keep such a man down.

'Tell me everything, Volnay!' he growled.

But Volnay said nothing. He knew that Sartine had spent three years searching on the king's behalf for a young girl who had caught his attention while out riding in his carriage. When he found the girl, her father had tried to protect her virtue, and the king had threatened him with imprisonment in the Bastille. The girl had been taken to the king's house on Avenue de Saint-Cloud. Volnay had no more respect for Sartine than the man deserved. The inspector's blank composure exasperated the chief of police still further.

'Truth be told, Volnay, I've never fully understood why you entered the police in the first place! The profession has no appeal for you—you are interested solely in the workings of the criminal intellect. People are raped, robbed and have their guts spilt on every street corner in Paris, day and night, yet you are content to solve two or three fine mysteries a year and nothing more! Is that what this city needs, in your opinion? Watch yourself, Volnay—you're far from untouchable! Like everyone else in this kingdom besides the monarch himself. Remember, your own father was almost burnt at the stake!'

The flames. Again! Suddenly, Volnay was a child of ten, watching as his father was strapped naked to a post. The executioner arranged a pile of wood and bundles of sticks at his feet. If the wood had been green, his father would have died swiftly, from smoke inhalation, but it was dry, and he would burn to death, in agony. While the executioner smeared oil on the condemned man's torso and armpits, to exacerbate the burns, the child pleaded with his father to abjure his heresy and be spared. Weeping, his father had replied that Volnay was all he loved in the world, but that he could not deny the truth. The executioner set about attaching small packets of gunpowder to his father's genitals and ears, designed to explode with the advancing flames, and the little boy had fainted.

Sartine's iron gaze remained fixed on Volnay, whose complexion had paled to transparency. Satisfied that he had asserted his rank by summoning the frightful memory, the chief of police dismissed the inspector with a scornful flick of the hand.

It took all Volnay's authority and powers of persuasion to reach the two wig-makers in Versailles. One was absent on the day of his visit, and he was forced to confine his questions to the other. Her name was Chloé, a lithe creature with a slender, nymph-like waist. Her wicked countenance and small, upturned nose were a delight to behold. The Inspector of Strange and Unexplained Deaths found himself alone with her in her bedchamber under the eaves. It was suffocatingly hot. A sickening smell of excrement filled the air, though it seemed not to bother her at all. With nothing else in the room, he had ordered her to sit on the straw mattress on the floor, and as if by force of habit, she had made to stretch out at full length. Volnay's outraged glare had stopped her short.

'Have you seen Mademoiselle Hervé recently?' he asked, careful not to arouse suspicion.

'No, Monsieur, I haven't seen her these past two days.'

'She lives here with you?'

'Yes.'

She pointed to another mattress in a corner of the room. Volnay searched it, quickly. Nothing. He sat down next to the young woman and felt the warmth of her body close to his.

'Has she any other lodgings, elsewhere?'

He thought of her corpse, discovered on a quiet street with no place of entertainment nearby. Chloe frowned delicately.

'I heard her say she had a room at her disposal, in Paris. She would meet men friends there, sometimes. I don't know where exactly. She told me once that at night, her room was lit up by the glow from a bread oven in the court-yard.'

Volnay listened intently, trying to spot any chinks in her story, any waver in the tone of her voice. Immediately, he connected her description with the place where the body had been found.

'Do you know any of these… friends whom she meets?'

The young girl shook her head, and with it the two, pretty kiss-curls that hung down over her forehead. Her chest betrayed her quick, staccato breathing. She knew she was losing control of the conversation, and attempted to redress the balance of power by pressing against Volnay's side. She was anything but shy, and clearly knew men's weaknesses. Volnay swallowed, uncomfortably.

'No fiancé?'

'No, Monsieur.'

'Any family?'

She seemed ill at ease.

'A grandfather. A strange man…'

'What does he do?'

Again, she hesitated.

'He works for the jewellers on Ruelle de l'Or, but…'

'Yes?' asked Volnay, encouragingly.

She gave him an enticing look and leant closer still, as if she were about to fall forward. She leant her weight against his shoulder and continued in a conspiratorial whisper:

'They say he's been trying to make gold, too.'

Volnay received the information without flinching. They were living in the century of enlightenment, yet never before had so many gone chasing after such idle nonsense.

'And where does he live?' he asked casually.

She told him. He shifted away from her. Her strong, carnal smell was masked by a heavy, woody fragrance over a heart note of jasmine. Volnay recovered his own space, and his self-control. His mind was lucid once more—a cold, perfectly balanced machine that had found the answers to so many unexplained crimes.

'Was Mademoiselle Hervé pretty?'

The girl's face lit up with a sardonic smile.

'She knew how to please a man, Monsieur, as we all do.'

And she accompanied her remark with a sustained and knowing stare. But it took more than a flash of eyes to deflect the inspector.

'Does she have clients here in Versailles?'

She nodded cautiously.

'And elsewhere?'

Another nod.

'And where would that be?'

He had slipped a silver écu into the palm of her right hand. She closed her fingers around it, but instinctively she placed her left hand over Volnay's. He played along, entwining his fingers in hers. He felt his pulse quicken.

'In Paris?'

'In the Châtelet,' she whispered.

'And who would that be?'

He was stroking her hand now. She was enjoying it and made no attempt to stop him. He insisted, and she whispered in his ear:

'I don't know his name, but she told me he often changes his wig and keeps a whole closet full of them.'

Her fingers played with his. She seemed anxious. Volnay felt acutely uncomfortable, too. He knew the shadowy figure's name all right: Sartine, chief of police. A man who had received the news of his young lover's death with scarcely more emotion than a wall of stone.

He felt suddenly giddy. Sartine's every move was calculated. Doubtless he had made Mademoiselle Hervé his mistress, to spy on the king or secure a reliable informant from the royal bed itself. Or perhaps Mademoiselle Hervé had been his spy, and nothing more. Heart pounding, he extricated his hand from Chloé's grasp and removed the gold mask from his satchel.

'Is this Mademoiselle Hervé's face?'

The girl gave a low cry, before stifling it immediately with both hands.

'Is this her?' He pressed the young woman, knowing he should take advantage of her state of shock.

'Yes. But what's all this about?'

He leant over her and breathed her smell once more. It filled his senses, and excited him. Experience had taught him that witnesses spoke the truth only in the first few seconds following a shock or surprise, and seldom when they had time to think.

'Mademoiselle, I know that Mademoiselle Hervé was with child. Can you say by whom?'

The girl opened her mouth as if to gasp for air. Volnay leant closer still, never once taking his eyes off hers. When he spoke, his voice was a barely audible murmur:

'Was she carrying the king's child?'

The wig-maker had turned deathly pale. She glanced at the door. Volnay leapt to his feet and ran to open it. The man crouching on the other side straightened up quickly and observed him with breathtaking indifference and aplomb.

'Who the hell are you?' growled Volnay.

The other man scrutinized him in dignified silence.

'I am Le Bel, first valet of His Majesty's bedchamber,' he said at length. 'I came to enquire as to the reason for your thoroughly inappropriate presence here.'

Volnay glared at the king's private pimp with all the scorn he could muster. The other man paled.

'Monsieur, you are in Versailles!' he declared, as if that alone were sufficient explanation.

Volnay glanced at the wig-maker and noted her stricken expression. There was nothing more to be gleaned now, and it would be pointless to try: the girl's terrified reaction had told him everything he needed to know. He was practically certain the victim's child was of royal blood. He left the room, pushing roughly past Le Bel, who received this parting affront with hate-filled silence.

Dusk was falling as Volnay fetched his horse and turned towards Paris, advancing at a walk through the crowds and vehicles thronging the road. Along the way, he thought again of the young woman, and the smell of her body. Gradually, his feelings of disarray subsided, and he felt sick at heart: they had murdered a young wig-maker, who was carrying the king's child.

IV

*On the eve of my birth, my mother felt
a great craving for shrimps*

CASANOVA

Casanova had taken advantage of his good fortune and bought himself a country house near Paris. He fancied he would call it La Petite Pologne—Little Poland. He kept chickens, feeding them on rice, and cultivated a kitchen garden as a source of fine, fresh vegetables. He had opened a workshop, too, employing twenty women, all of whom—naturally—had come to his bed, individually, and two by two, in various combinations. His little helpers all adored him, and he was mindful of their lot and their condition, paying them a higher salary than they would find anywhere else in Europe. Inexorably, he was running his business into the ground, though this did not concern him excessively. Money should be redistributed. Casanova upheld the free movement of people, goods and capital in equal measure.

For Casanova, fine cuisine was a source of enjoyment almost as vital as the pleasures of the flesh. He savoured the aroma of his dishes, their colours and flavours, be they rich or light. He loved all foods, bitter or sweet. He could not bear to take to his bed without eating first, and regaled his conquests with oysters, game, sturgeon and truffles.

Boasting proudly that his table was as divine as his love-making, he had invited Madame Ferraud, the wife of a public prosecutor, to dinner at his home. Every woman had her weak spot, and Casanova delighted in instinctively identifying the foible that would ensure he had his way. Madame

Ferraud was a delicious, full-bodied woman of barely twenty-five, whose sensual nature revelled in the pleasures of the flesh, not least when it was perfectly cooked and served.

Naturally, the lady's visit began with a guided tour of the kitchens. The aroma of vegetables fresh from the garden, cooking gently in warm butter, assailed them at the very top of the stairs leading down to the lower floors. At the bottom, they were engulfed in the stifling heat. Logs were fed regularly into the bread oven and the roasting pit. Beneath the low, vaulted ceiling they admired the great stone *potager* oven, with fifteen separate compartments and plates, and the endless ballet of cooks adding truffle essence to the fish stock or whisking the lobster butter.

'Can you believe, dear lady, that lately, at a princely table, I was served a dish of peacock's brains and parrot tongues?' said Casanova. 'It was *quite* extraordinary.'

'Goodness me!'

'Well, that's what our host told us,' he added, delighting her now with his scurrilous gossip. 'It might very well have been cat's brains and old wives' tongues for all I know!'

Crooking his arm gallantly for the lady to take, he escorted her to the dining room, hung with tapestries in delicate pastel shades. The table was decorated with flowers, and the crystal glasses gleamed in the light from the wall sconces. Shrimps were served.

'On the eve of my birth,' remarked Casanova, 'my mother felt a great craving for shrimps. Imagine this: I was born on Easter Sunday, the day of the Resurrection, with my mother's complexion still tinged pink by the shrimps she had eaten the day before!'

They laughed together, then savoured a generously salted dish of eels' livers and rockfish. Casanova was careful to accompany the succession of dishes with equally piquant observations, to titillate his prey. His gaiety, perfect manners and tremendous good humour worked marvels, as they always did.

'What are we to have next?' asked his guest, in total innocence.

'Carp stuffed with butter, egg yolk and crushed almonds, the whole seasoned with fragrant herbs,' replied Casanova. 'But we'll take a moment's repose in the small salon first, where we shall be served apple sorbet, and a liqueur of the same fruit.'

The Chevalier de Seingalt was anxious for his guest not to become drowsy. Hence he had ordered refreshing sorbets and liqueurs to be served in an intimate setting, after which they were to be left alone. Madame Ferraud thought this a fine idea. He led her to a panelled room painted in eau de Nil, in the middle of which stood an expansive, voluptuous ottoman couch decorated with gold fringe-work and laden with red silk cushions. The shutters were closed, and the slats drawn down. The room was suffused with soft light. In each corner, on the rosewood floor, an exquisite scent of violets and jasmine rose from a ceramic jar. Whenever Casanova was in funds, he spent lavishly, as if the money burnt his fingers.

'What a great shame it is, Chevalier,' said Madame Ferraud, 'that people speak only of your prowess in certain endeavours, and not in others.'

'But those "certain endeavours" are not to be scorned, Madame. Every woman expects a man to show vigour in the rites of Venus. And God has granted me such extraordinary vigour that I am capable of satisfying any and all who desire it...'

'Chevalier, what language! Truly, I regret having accepted your invitation.'

She affected a pained expression, while the Venetian enveloped her in the velvet gaze of his soft, dark eyes.

'Your regrets are unjustified, Madame. I aspire to delight you with nothing but the story of my life, and the latest gossip from every royal court in Europe. And in return, perhaps you will favour me with the news at Court here in Paris? That public prosecutor husband of yours must know a thing or two about all the worst crimes!'

'I'll tell you anything you like, but first, tell me about your most dramatic adventure—your escape from the cells under the leaden roof of the doge's palace in Venice.'

'The Piombi? You'll be surprised to know, Madame, that I was in far greater danger in Rome than in Venice. I witnessed the most appalling debauchery in the Holy City. I was forced to keep my hand firmly on my sword, the entire evening, for fear of being sodomized!'

She laughed.

'But will you tell me how you escaped from the Piombi?'

The Chevalier de Seingalt gave a slight bow.

'I shall indeed, Madame, but in return, you will indulge my curiosity as to the criminal underworld of Paris!'

'It's a promise! My husband tells me *everything*.'

Satisfied, Casanova launched into his account:

'One day, in Venice, I was warned of a plot against me by a league of wicked and—above all—jealous gentlemen. I was told I must flee. I laughed it off, and found myself imprisoned in the Piombi the very next morning. The place from which no one had ever escaped.'

Casanova's companion gave a small chuckle.

'So typical of you, Chevalier—you never listen to anyone, or anything!'

The Venetian acquiesced with an ironic smile, and went on:

'From the moment I found myself in prison, I began ceaselessly to plot my escape. I stole a key when I was escorted into the open air for a walk, and I used it to scrape a hole in the floor of my cell, leading down into the apartments of my guards, which I knew were directly underneath. I had almost finished when, thinking to please me, they moved me to a new cell with a higher ceiling and a view of the lagoon!'

The lady chuckled again. Casanova had bound his audience with rings of steel, as always. He continued:

'I began scraping with the key again, but this time at the ceiling, to reach the cell of a monk that lay above mine. From there, I could make my escape with him over the rooftops. One night, after a month of sustained effort, I reached his cell. The monk had succeeded in scraping a hole in his own ceiling. I led my reluctant companion out onto the roof. From there, I spied an attic window, which I reached by means of a rope fashioned from sheets and towels. I forced the window, then pulled my companion down after me. I almost broke my neck ten times over but, bloodied and battered, I reached the palace archives. There, I picked a lock to gain access to the Cancelleria, but the great doors leading to the doge's staircase were locked and impregnable.'

'And so, Chevalier, what then?' cried Madame Ferraud.

'I had brought all my clothes with me in a bag. I dressed, and thus attired, I leant out of the window and called down into the palace courtyard, to one of the sentries. I told him he was an idle good-for-nothing, and ordered him to fetch the warden, who was swiftly brought. I told him that my friend the monk and myself had been locked in by mistake, and that we had fallen asleep. He seemed reluctant at first, but I gave him a thorough scolding, and he hurried to open the doors!'

He snapped his fingers.

'And there you have it! Now you…'

The lady leant towards him with a greedy smile.

'What do you want to know, you rascal?'

'Your husband is involved in a curious case: a faceless woman... Do we know yet who she is?' he asked.

'We do,' she said, triumphantly. 'Imagine this—the Inspector of Strange and Unexplained Deaths has established her identity by means of a delicate gold death mask, made by a sinister monk!'

'A monk?'

'His colleague.'

Casanova remembered the eerie figure of the monk, tall and straight as Mozart's Commendatore himself, on the driver's seat of his cart.

'Ah yes, I saw him! A strange figure indeed. What is his role in all this?'

Madame Ferraud broke into a knowing smile.

'Officially, he examines the bodies of the victims of the crimes investigated by the Inspector of Strange and Unexplained Deaths.'

'To what end? When a fellow's dead, he's dead!'

'No, no, you don't understand. He is looking for the cause of death.'

The Chevalier de Seingalt looked troubled.

'But anyone can see whether a fellow's been strangled, or had his throat slit.'

The prosecutor's wife shook her head vigorously.

'Don't be so sure. This is the scientific police! My husband has told me that bones break differently depending on the nature of the blow, and that the shape of a wound can reveal whether it was made using a single or a double-edged blade.'

'And where does that get us?' asked the Venetian, unconvinced.

'You mentioned strangulation. Well, thanks to his colleague, the inspector once showed that a person did not die by his own hand, from hanging, but was murdered. The murderers—two brothers—sat astride their victim and blocked his nose and mouth until death ensued.'

'A serviceable monk, indeed,' Casanova was forced to agree.

'Serviceable, but a heretic!'

Casanova's guest lowered her voice, and whispered conspiratorially:

'They say he roams the cemeteries at night and exhumes newly buried corpses to take back to his mortuary. He opens up the bodies to study their anatomy! They say he eats the brains, to expand his own knowledge.'

'Dear God! And what of our faceless victim? Who did you say she was?'

'Highly confidential information, my friend. My husband has sworn me to secrecy. He should never have told me, but what's the point of knowing all the best secrets if you can't share them with a living soul?'

She burst out laughing.

'But you can tell me,' Casanova insisted. 'My lips are as mute as that carp's, which we are about to eat.'

'Not a word to a soul: she's one of the king's little whores, a wig-maker!'

Volnay pushed the door with a sudden feeling of dread. The monk stood waiting in silence. His expression was dark, and his habit was stained with blood.

'Not mine I assure, you,' he said, seeing his colleague's anxious expression. 'Alas, I left the doors to the laboratory ajar, and someone forced his way in, hoping to cut my throat. I killed him.'

He showed Volnay an adjacent cellar, to which he had dragged the body. The room contained a few bottles of wine, sealed with wax. Hams and bunches of flowers hung from the ceiling to dry. On the floor, the corpse lay in a pool of its own blood.

'I washed the laboratory floor—you could eat your dinner off it now, if you so desired! We must dispose of the body straightaway—we'll take it to the Seine, like everyone else! No corpse, no questions asked. Now is not the time to be attracting Sartine's attention.'

Volnay squatted beside the corpse and turned it over, to reveal the gaunt, weather-beaten face, covered with scars and dotted with smallpox.

'The face of a true villain,' said the monk, scornfully. 'I found a large sum of money in his pockets, his wages for my life, and the sum total of its worth, in the eyes of whoever paid him. I'll keep his money and drink to his very good health!'

'Drink to the angels if you've no one better to toast,' muttered Volnay, dropping one knee to the floor.

Briefly, he examined the wound.

'A single, fatal strike,' he said appreciatively. 'You've not lost your touch!'

There was a note of pride and respect in his voice.

'No sense in wounding an assailant like him first,' said the monk.

Volnay nodded gravely. He was utterly at a loss. What had he got himself mixed up in this time? Who possessed enough information, and the certainty of his own impunity, to attack an inspector of the king's police, and his partner? The attack was all the more worrying given that few people knew where the monk lived and worked. Plainly, an attempt had been made on the monk's life. Volnay stared at the dead man, and reflected that he himself might have had his throat cut, by Wallace, if he had handed over the royal letter.

He slipped his fingers inside the man's buffalo-leather jerkin, half opening it, and registered in silence the small rosary around his neck. He exchanged a knowing look with the monk. His partner was noticeably unmoved, and gazed at the body with the calm serenity of a man returning from vespers.

'A good Christian and a murderer…' he observed, simply.

A deathly silence ensued.

'I questioned one of the king's wig-makers,' said Volnay, at length, tearing his gaze from the corpse's chest with some difficulty. 'I secured little in the way of hard information, but I did ascertain that Mademoiselle Hervé was with child, by our dearly beloved monarch!'

The monk's face darkened.

'And worse than that,' Volnay continued, 'Le Bel, the first valet of the king's bedchamber, spied on us during our interview.'

The monk sighed.

'Everyone spies on everyone else at Versailles. People have nothing better to do with their day. It's even said that the king finds the queen's company so tedious, he kills the flies on the windowpanes to pass the time.'

The monk locked the cellar door carefully behind them, then led Volnay back to the laboratory. The furnace glowed red in the half-light. Rows of pipettes were filled with liquid, coloured spinach green, walnut brown or purple as a bishop's robe.

'The truth goes beyond what you say,' he observed acidly. 'There's a Court spy behind every door, and every minister has several of his own.'

The monk smiled into his short beard.

'Ministers always want to know whatever ill is being spoken of them!'

'They even pay off the police informers, to get information about themselves,' said Volnay. The thought revolted him. 'There is no such thing as idle talk, now. Every unfortunate joke or slip of the tongue is reported to the chief of police. Friends at dinner together guard against saying too much, because so many men of quality are professional spies. Not to mention the household servants, who are all in the pockets of some aristocrat and enemy of their master. Royal family secrets are never kept for long.'

He sat astride a high-backed chair and refused the glass of water pushed towards him by the monk.

'You shouldn't drink that stuff,' he told his colleague.

'I infuse my water with lemon balm, iris root and a small glass of eau de vie,' said the monk. 'Delicious to drink and thoroughly hygienic!'

But Volnay's mind was far away; he reconsidered, analysed and compared each fact, each piece of information.

'You should know, too,' he said, 'that Mademoiselle Hervé was Sartine's mistress.'

To his astonishment, the monk burst into delighted laughter.

'This whole affair is so entertaining! First the Devout Party, as they like to call themselves, and now our own chief of police is mixed up in it all! But I doubt the girl was his mistress. Sartine doesn't mix business with pleasure. She was his informer, most likely... The police's interest in prostitutes is dictated solely by their clients. Well—I hope Sartine isn't after the letter, along with the religionists!'

'I know what you're going to say,' Volnay cut in. 'You and I are the only people who know about the existence of the letter, and we've spoken of it to no one. The only explanation for these attacks on us is that someone saw me remove the letter from the body. Casanova saw me do it, quite plainly, and he's a man who knows how to negotiate for information of that sort.'

The monk looked sceptical.

'I can't see Casanova selling that to the Devout Party when as far as they're concerned he's the Devil incarnate! His dealings with the Church are confined to orgies with pretty young nuns.'

He could see Volnay was becoming impatient.

'If Casanova saw you remove the letter,' he went on quickly, 'others are sure to have seen it, too. The precinct chief, for example. Those people are always in someone else's pay.'

Volnay got to his feet and paced slowly around the room, as if to make space for his thoughts.

'If not Casanova, then I wonder how the person who saw me managed to arrive so quickly at the scene of the crime, unless—'

'Unless he was already there, is that it?' The monk was accustomed to following his partner's logic.

Volnay stopped pacing and stood deep in thought.

'Yes, either because he was the murderer—though I doubt that, because the murderer would have thought to recover the letter before cutting away his victim's face—or because the young woman was being followed. In either case, whoever ordered the attack on me is very likely one of the Devout Party, because my attacker was that man Wallace. As for the second attack, it was doubtless ordered by the same people, in an angrier mood now…'

Silence fell, broken only by the buzzing of a fly at the neck of an empty bottle.

'So many questions, so many possible answers!' exclaimed the monk. 'The king, the Devout Party, Sartine—suspects aplenty! I suggest you keep a very cool head. Take care and do as St Thomas Aquinas said: "Be not indiscreet, but watch your words, and like a prudent son, do not cast pearls before swine." For my part, I shall leave this place for a time, and return to one of my old hideouts.'

He laughed merrily.

'Why, it's almost like the good old days, when my heretical books were burnt! But you cannot retreat like me into the shadows. And so, be on your guard with everyone.'

He paused. His tone was harder, and darker, when he spoke again:

'Because now, there are just three things you can trust in this world: me, your talkative magpie and the tip of your sword!'

Night fell over the city, with its cortège of shadows, phantoms and thieves. Honest citizens sought a peaceful night's sleep in their beds of straw, feathers or wool. Here and there, windows glowed with dim yellow light. But the inns and gambling dens were ablaze with tall wax or tallow candles. Loud bursts of laughter rang out in the darkness. Volnay walked fearlessly, a pistol in his belt and his sword at his side. He was constantly on the alert, and his eyes followed every suspect shadow. He picked his way carefully along the dark, filth-strewn streets. His nostrils quivered in disgust. He glanced more than usual at the prostitutes, who did their best to attract him, like supernatural sirens taunting a lost mariner. He paused for a moment, then went on his way. He walked down a narrow lane that turned a sharp corner before skirting the gardens of a fine mansion and petering out on the banks of the Seine.

'Watch out below!' yelled someone overhead, before emptying a bucket of slops from a window.

Volnay leapt to one side to avoid being splattered, then made his way to the Rue des Lanternes, populated by cloth brokers, wig-makers and corset-makers. There he saw her. A girl, cleanly and decently dressed, but whose dark eyes were full of fire. She gave a small sign, then pushed at the door of an inn, the Leaky Barrel. Before disappearing inside, she shot him a penetrating stare: a mix of conflicting emotions, and an invitation to follow her. Intrigued, he stepped through the door.

He found himself in the main room of the inn, long and low-ceilinged, its floor strewn with fresh straw. Near the entrance, an old man sat with his head nodding on his chest. He seemed to have tossed his goblet aside. Volnay surveyed the room but saw no female presence. Tallow candles lit the tabletops, each one the centre of a still life or tavern scene, as if freshly painted on canvas. A small group ate chunks of bread dipped in pea soup. At another table, diners were devouring small cuts of pork fillet pricked with sage and washed down with thick, syrupy wine. Then Volnay spotted the men sitting in the darkest corner of the room. Three of them, all dressed in black, and watching him with particular attention. One, with a swarthy complexion and a square jaw, possessed a natural authority. He rose, as if to drink Volnay's health. The inspector paled. The man gestured discreetly, and Volnay moved forward, as if in a trance.

'Welcome, brother,' said the man with the swarthy complexion.

And he made the sign of the Brotherhood.

'What do you want from me?' stammered Volnay under his breath. 'It's been so long—'

'And the time has come for you to join us once more. We need you.'

'In what way?'

'You're in charge of an investigation that is of interest to us. A letter meant for us has come into your possession by mistake. You must hand it over.'

Volnay reeled slightly, but stood his ground.

'It's not addressed to you,' he said.

'Have you opened it?'

'No, but—'

'Do you know who wrote it?'

'Yes, absolutely—'

He stopped short. This cross-examination was pointless.

'If you know who wrote the letter,' he said scornfully, 'tell me yourself.'

The man leant closer.

'Someone of great importance!'

'Then you will know why I am unable to give you the letter,' said Volnay, lowering his eyes. 'I am the king's servant.'

One of the other men—fat, with piercing grey eyes and a black beard—leant across. He seemed sprightly indeed for a man of his constitution. His German-accented voice was curiously soft.

'You serve the king! Come on, Volnay, you know us. Your life is as spotless as your reputation. The worst anyone can pin on you is a penchant for our modern philosophers, and saving the king's life!'

Volnay stared down at the floor. The men in black had been watching him in silence. Now, all eyes turned to the fat man. Volnay scrutinized him. His neck beard hid a voluminous double chin, and the moustache brought a certain depth and majesty to his upper lip. His eyes burnt with passionate fire. The inspector understood. Here was the true leader of this little party.

'I followed the orders of the Brotherhood of the Serpent at the time, nothing more. Damiens was one of us, but he lost his nerve and wanted to kill the king, far too soon. That was what the Grand Master told me. He had to be stopped.'

'And you stopped him,' said the other man, drily.

'I had sworn an oath.'

'And that oath still holds!'

Regretfully, Volnay shook his head.

'I left the Brotherhood after Damiens's death. I am no longer one of you.'

'The oath of the Brotherhood binds all who swear it, for ever. It is broken only by death!' said the square-jawed man icily.

Volnay ignored him. 'What is your objective?' he asked.

'The same, as ever, and what was once yours,' sighed the fat man. 'An end to the monarchy. We have here an extraordinary opportunity to discredit it for ever. Across France, people are in revolt against the war and its mindless slaughter, against speculation in the price of grain, against taxes. There are mutterings of rebellion. People spit at La Pompadour's carriage, and wish the king dead. But that's not what we want. Another will only take his place. This king is good enough for our purpose: he stains the royal fleur-de-lys. Your investigation has the potential to ruin what remains of his reputation, for good. He will be viewed with horror throughout Europe!'

'What does the Grand Master say about all this?' asked Volnay, at length.

There was an embarrassed silence.

'He is unaware of your plans!' he exclaimed in amazement.

'The Grand Master is very advanced in years. He is living far from Paris now.'

Volnay's mind raced. The errors of his youth, his entire past had caught up with him. This was no accident of fate. The young woman in the street, the letter. A world of shadows was teeming all around him: Sartine's spies, the Devout Party, the Brotherhood of the Serpent. They all knew something he did not.

'What is your decision, my brother?' asked the leader.

'I have not changed my mind,' said Volnay, though his voice quavered.

'You swore an oath before,' one of the three men in black reminded him.

'To the Brotherhood, to the Grand Master, not to you. And I am no longer one of your number.'

The fat man sighed.

'Oh, but you are. No one leaves the Brotherhood of the Serpent quite so easily, as you will very soon discover. When the Brotherhood needs you, it calls you back. If you change your mind, come to this tavern. There will always be someone waiting to talk. But act quickly, brother: the Devout Party is at your heels; you need our protection. You cannot act alone. Terrible forces have risen, and they are on the march. You will be crushed if you stand in their way!'

He shot a dark glance at Volnay and added:

'You are a bird that throws itself into the void, unsure whether it will fly.'

V

The only God I worship is liberty!

CASANOVA

When morning came, Casanova saw to it that he was immaculately powdered, before setting out for the Marquis D'Ancilla's mansion. Clad in a grey tailcoat lined with blue, and a waistcoat and breeches of purple silk, he presented himself at the gates. To his annoyance, he found his heart beat a little faster than was usual. A liveried footman walked ahead of him up a marble staircase. Chiara received him in the prettily decorated music room, lined with panelling. Through the window, he glimpsed a garden of touch-me-nots, enclosed by gilded railings.

Chiara wore a green dress, beneath which Casanova glimpsed a skirt of satin edged with lace, and a whole, rustling world of undergarments he had hopes of exploring. She wore a choker at her throat. Her black hair was gathered into a chignon, fixed by a single gold pin, gleaming in its midst. The Venetian's heart melted at the sight.

They seated themselves in blue-painted armchairs decorated with a fine silver fillet, and chatted of everything and nothing until Chiara declared, rather abruptly:

'I do not like this world in which we live, ruled by the accident of birth: riches for a small number, and misery for so many.'

'Did you know my parents were poor?' said Casanova, humbly.

Chiara made no reply. From childhood, her days had been filled with pure delight: playing with her dog in the mornings,

97

then practising the harpsichord and singing. Before luncheon, she studied plants with her tutor. In the afternoons, after a short siesta, she would conduct experiments in the little laboratory that her natural sciences tutor had equipped with the latest instruments. After that, she would read until dinner, then gaze at the stars through her telescope before bed.

Casanova saw that Chiara was fiddling nervously with the silk of her dress.

'You must have suffered greatly,' she said.

'Not at all! I'm a pauper untouched by adversity, and I have always found my own solution to every difficulty.'

Chiara lowered her eyes. Her head was filled with dreams of equality for all mankind, yet she had been born to a silk-lined cradle, and her path had been strewn with rose petals ever since. For that, she felt guilt, even a vague sense of shame.

'You are of one mind with our great philosophers,' said Casanova, who sensed the young aristocrat's discomfort. 'I saw that in you straightaway. I have met many of them: Rousseau, Favart, Fontenelle, Voisenon, Crébillon…'

'And you agree with their philosophy?' asked Chiara, incredulously.

'I agree with Diderot. According to him, and I quote, man is "a material creature, nothing more, and can have no aim but the pleasure of the senses. We have no rights, no obligations, and act solely in our own self-interest."'

'If that is indeed our nature, then we must fight against it. A world in which inequality is the rule can only go from bad to worse.'

Casanova shrugged his shoulders. He was a fatalist.

'That is the way of the world. Some get richer and richer, others get poorer and poorer. It's up to us to stay rich if we are already, or to become rich if we are not. No one helped me become what I am—why should I help others?'

'Yet many have shown you great generosity: women in their beds, and men with their purses!'

The Venetian gave a modest smile.

'Indeed, and I have received richly endowed offers of marriage, too, but there it is: the only God I worship is liberty!'

I stand as a lesson, he thought to himself. A lesson to all those in positions of power, who gaze down on me with the arrogance that comes from centuries of security, plying me with gifts so that I might decipher their horoscope or give them the secret of cultivating gold under a full moon! Duping them gives me greater pleasure than if I were to beat them with a stick.

Silence fell. The Chevalier de Seingalt looked up. In front of him, the room stood reflected in a mirror, and with it the nape of a most delectable neck. Chiara was nibbling pensively at her lower lip and staring at her right foot. Casanova was torn by conflicting emotions. His memories beckoned, but he refused to listen. He had no desire to know who it was that Chiara so resembled. Not yet.

'Tell me about your childhood,' she said suddenly. 'I like it when you tell me about that.'

Casanova hesitated. His childhood was the only time in his life when he had felt vulnerable. Then he thought of Bettina and began a curious confession.

'At the age of nine, I was sent to board with an extraordinarily mean, avaricious woman,' he said, very softly. 'I slept in the attic with three other boys, and was bitten all over by bedbugs, and terrified by the rats that jumped onto my bed and nipped me. Food was so scarce that I stole in order to feed myself. My master, Abbott Gozzi, had a sister who was three years older than me: Bettina. She took pity on me, because I felt so lonely, far from my home, and my mother. Bettina wore long shifts, and her hair hung loose down her back, rippling like snakes. I was a small boy. She was like a mother to me. She called me "my dear child". Each morning, she came to comb my hair and help me with my toilet. She had gentle, expert hands. Too expert. One morning, seeing my thighs were grubby, she scrubbed hard in her desire to get me clean, provoking a state of voluptuous excitement in me that ceased only when it had attained its highest peak. And then my very soul seemed to burst and melt in the hollow of her hand.'

He lowered his eyes and added darkly:

'No mother would have done such a thing, do you agree?'

Raising his chin, Casanova saw with astonishment that the young girl's eyes were filled with tears.

'What is it?' he asked gently.

'It's nothing. The black kohl on my lashes makes my eyes water,' she said.

A heavy silence fell between them. Overcome with embarrassment, neither could find a way to break it.

'Have you seen that curious police officer, the Chevalier de Volnay, since our visit?' asked Casanova, suddenly.

The question was unexpected, and Chiara seemed troubled by it.

'I have indeed. What concern is that of yours?'

The Venetian smiled charmingly.

'I merely wanted to know if a rival stood in my way.'

Chiara was briefly surprised, then burst out laughing. Gallantly, Casanova laughed too.

'Your rival! Since when do the great seducers of this world inform their victims that they have been chosen?'

Casanova gazed into her eyes, and there was no trace of gaiety in his expression now.

'When they wish to give them some small chance, Chiara. I hope I have afforded you the possibility of escape.'

The young woman was speechless. A strange shade of red flooded her cheeks.

'What an actor you are!' she said hurriedly.

Casanova nodded. He had spoken the truth, and now he was accused of play-acting! He was growing older and softening in the process. It was no good, no good at all.

'You didn't answer me, regarding Volnay,' he said cautiously.

'Indeed not. The Chevalier de Volnay is a serious, conscientious man.'

'Who thinks of nothing but his work?'

'Yes, but I cannot say a word about that—he has made me promise.'

Casanova savoured the moment. When a person declared they had been sworn to keep a secret, they were generally about to confess it.

'Well,' he said innocently, 'I am glad to hear it. He has sworn me to secrecy too, over the death of the king's wig-maker.'

Chiara looked taken aback.

'He spoke of that to you too?'

'He needed my help. I am a material witness in the affair, and I have a great many contacts in Paris, which can help ease things along. I wonder whether he has told you the rest, however…'

It was worth trying, he thought, though he held little hope of success. His astonishment was all the greater when Chiara asked, fresh and innocent as a daisy:

'About the Comte de Saint-Germain?'

Casanova could have bowed to kiss both her hands, there and then!

The Comte de Saint-Germain bowed low before the Marquise de Pompadour. He wore a braided, fur-trimmed coat and a lace jabot spilt from the unbuttoned top of his waistcoat. His thoroughly aristocratic face wore an expression of rare sensitivity and intelligence. His olive complexion made his host's appear whiter than ever, indeed drained of all colour. Around them, the entire room was decorated in harmonious shades of blue: vivid blue motifs on the Persian carpet, a muted blue for the woodwork, the delicate blue of a Flemish-inspired painting, turquoise blue for the upholstery—and the florets decorating his hostess's gown—a dusty blue-grey for the cover of a piece of piano music, and the ribbons attaching a portfolio of drawings. And lastly, the pale blue of her eyes.

'See here,' said the comte, eager to entertain his host, 'I have brought you this very fine box. I had it fitted with an amusing mechanism!'

She took from him a black tortoiseshell box, its lid decorated with an agate.

'Watch,' said the comte, carefully taking hold of the object once more.

He held the box over the fire. When the marquise took it back, she was astonished to see that the agate had become a pretty miniature of a shepherdess holding a basketful of flowers. She held the box over the fire once again and saw to her amazement that the shepherdess disappeared, to be replaced by the agate.

'Truly, you are a magician!' she exclaimed with childlike excitement.

Then she bit her lip, as if she had let slip some inappropriate comment, and sighed.

'Thank you, my friend, for trying to help me forget my troubles.'

She glanced around with a conspiratorial air, then signalled to the comte to come closer and listen to what she had to say. Even within the walls of her private mansion, she was not safe from inquisitive ears.

'I need your advice—I am terrified at the thought of that letter falling into the wrong hands. How have we come to this?'

The comte gazed sympathetically at the Marquise de Pompadour. He knew she was exhausted and had no idea where to turn. She was profoundly ill at ease.

'We have come to this, Madame, because we live in a country in which a shadowy committee intercepts all correspondence, acting on behalf of the king. They even have expert cryptographers, for coded messages. You were the letter's safest means of conveyance.'

'Then it is all my fault—'

'No, Madame, trust in God and the Chevalier de Volnay.'

The marquise gave a small gesture of irritation. Nervously, she rearranged her gown with her left hand, in a loud rustling of silk.

'The Inspector of Strange and Unexplained Deaths? He is so young...'

'Perhaps, but he is possessed of two qualities in short supply in our royal administration: integrity and efficiency. I beg you to do everything in your power to ensure that he remains in charge of the investigation.'

'And so I shall. But he has no weight against Sartine or the Devout Party. They will sweep him aside like a wisp of straw. As for the rest, my dear Chiara tells me that he has made little progress and knows even less than we do.'

The Comte de Saint-Germain maintained his neutral expression, but the marquise caught the bright gleam that lit his eye like a tiny lantern in the night.

'A vision,' whispered the marquise. 'You have had a vision! Am I right?'

The comte shook his head slowly.

'*Sum quia sentio*: "I feel, therefore I am." Trust me, Madame, I have never hidden anything from you, and never will. Talk to the king and see to it that Volnay reports to no one but him for this investigation—certainly not to that cursed devil Sartine, who serves nothing but his own interest.'

'I will do what I can,' she promised him. 'But I cannot be sure the king will listen to me.'

A dry cough rose in the marquise's throat. When it had subsided, she asked anxiously:

'How much time do I have?'

'What do you mean, Madame?'

Her cough worsened, as if determined to assert itself.

'You know very well, as my medical adviser!'

The comte remained impassive, but pity shone in his eyes.

'Now is not the time, Madame, to talk of such things. And while your mission is far from over, forces are mobilizing, of a brutality you cannot possibly imagine.'

The marquise paled.

'What now, the Devout Party? We know they will stop at nothing. Monsieur de Sartine? He is merciless.'

The comte leant towards her. Two dark, attentive eyes scrutinized La Pompadour's face.

'Worse! Have you heard talk of the Brotherhood? The Brotherhood of the Serpent, to be more precise…'

People yelled in the street at the tops of their voices for no reason. The din was so great that it was known to induce panic in visitors to Paris. At the corner of Rue Vieille-Place-aux-Veaux the crowd parted suddenly, torn asunder by a carriage at full gallop, driven by a crazed coachman. The cracks of his whip masked the curses and cries of terror from those on foot. It was noon. The Inspector of Strange and Unexplained Deaths and the monk were returning to the scene of the crime to subject the surroundings to close scrutiny, as was their habit. Directly overhead, the midday sun cast a thin scar of bright gold along the right-hand side of the street.

'Now then,' said Volnay, his eyes screwed up against the light, 'Mademoiselle Hervé's young companion told me that, from her apartment, her friend could see the fires from the baker's oven at night. We shall enter the courtyard and examine it.'

They passed under the archway and concluded that two of the buildings overlooking it afforded a direct view. The place was like an anthill, full of nooks and corners, traversed by narrow passageways, endlessly busy with the comings and goings of the inhabitants, their visitors and their clients. Shops faced the street, workshops lined the courtyards. The cries of the sellers mingled with the cheerful singing of the artisans. A ragged child of about ten, its face blackened and filthy, held out a hand as they passed.

'Take this, boy,' said Volnay, slipping him a six-livre coin. 'But watch out, the police have orders to arrest anyone found begging and take them to the Châtelet, whatever their age!'

The child's eyes widened at the sight of the coin in the hollow of his hand. Then he raced away as fast as his legs would carry him, as if the two men might snatch his treasure back at any moment. The monk smiled benevolently.

'You have a generous heart, just like me! It pleases me to see it.'

Volnay shrugged lightly. They knocked at a door of one of the buildings overlooking the courtyard. The door was opened by a tall, surly woman perched on long, thin legs. She peered at them suspiciously. Her features looked rough-hewn, as if her creator had lacked the time needed to finish the job properly. The two visitors' civilized demeanour, Volnay's fine bearing and the monk's spotless habit seemed to reassure her. Volnay explained the reason for their visit.

'Mam'selle Hervé, yes,' she mumbled. 'She is my lodger. I'll take you to her room.'

They followed close behind her, up the first staircase, beside the courtyard entrance.

'My husband's dead,' explained the landlady on the rickety stairs. 'He came over all dizzy and weak one day. I called a doctor. He was bled four times from the arms and feet, but to the doctor's surprise that left him weaker still. The fifth bleeding was what killed him.'

'I have always maintained that bloodletting is too much practised nowadays,' said the monk.

'In my misfortune,' the woman went on, breathing heavily, 'I was thankful at least that he left no debts and that he had bought one floor of this building, where I now live. I rent it all out, thank God, and I don't ask too many questions. What has Mam'selle Hervé done?'

Volnay said nothing, He preferred to ask the questions.

'I know that she received men at this address. Could you describe the last visitor she saw?'

The stairs were steep. The landlady paused for breath.

'Dear Lord! Do you think I keep a lookout for all the comings and goings of her wretched trade? This is no house of debauchery, but I can't prevent a lady lodger from receiving visitors… Anything for a quiet life.'

'Did she receive many visitors?'

'No denying the appeal of a pretty girl in a saucy dress…' said the woman, continuing her climb up the stairs.

'Well?' Volnay was impatient now.

'Not many, truth be told. Because I heard it said she lived at Versailles and only came here on occasion, for… pocket money. God's mercy upon her!'

'In the eyes of the Lord, the greatest virtue is love,' intoned the monk.

And he added, wickedly:

'For the rest, better say your prayers between two bouts of sinning!'

'Come now…' Volnay frowned at his colleague. They had climbed to the third floor as they talked. The landlady's chest heaved noisily as she selected a key on her bunch.

'Oh!' she exclaimed suddenly. 'The lock has been forced.'

'Leave it,' ordered Volnay. 'Kindly wait for us downstairs.'

She shrugged and disappeared down the staircase, muttering unintelligibly. Volnay drew his pistol from his belt and moved inside the room. He turned on the spot, taking in the scene, his features set hard as flint.

'Who has been here before us?'

They paced around the single room with its lime-washed walls. The mattress had been ripped open, and cupboards, bookcases—even the stove—had been overturned. Everything had been systematically ransacked and searched.

'Go no further!' ordered Volnay.

He dropped down on one knee.

'The young lady does not come here regularly—the floor is dusty,' he said. 'I see the print of a fine pair of boots here. And there… it seems the sharp tip of a rapier has been dragged over the floor. Another swordsman, it seems.'

He lowered his pistol.

'A wooden bedframe, a feather mattress, a woollen blanket, curtains at the windows,' he observed. 'Here is a person with money, hence benefactors.'

The monk pointed out the iniquity of a figure of Christ, twisting on the cross above a bed reserved for pleasure.

'She must have turned it to the wall before love-making, as so many Christian women do.'

They moved to the bedside table, where the contents of a collection of small boxes had been tipped out.

'Powders and pigments. A woman who strove to please.'

Volnay walked across to the window and folded his arms.

'There is a great lack of privacy in these buildings. Everyone knows everyone else's business, and it is advisable to keep your voice down, so as not to be overheard. We shall go and talk a little with the neighbours.'

They walked along the wooden gallery overlooking the courtyard and knocked at a door. On the promise of an écu, it opened. They found themselves face to face with a young woman, clutching a baby to her bony ribs. The infant was suckling at her breast. She introduced herself as a fruit-seller. Fortunately, she explained, her husband worked fifteen hours a day as a master joiner. But even with that money, they could afford only one meal each day because the rent was very high.

Volnay took her meaning and slipped her another écu while he pressed her with questions about Mademoiselle Hervé.

'I only spoke to her once, to ask her to make less noise when decent folk were trying to sleep,' she said pointedly, 'and that filthy whore dared to call me a "stuck-up bitch". After that, we'd hear her at night, telling the men, "Gently now, you're hurting me, and you'll wake up the cow next door!"'

'Did you notice any man in particular?'

'Never saw them, only heard them!'

'What can you tell me about Mademoiselle Hervé?'

The fruit-seller thought for a moment.

'They say she used the money from her men to buy herself powders and ointments. You know, lotions, for a youthful appearance.'

'Had any men come to her apartment lately? By day or night? Have you come across any strangers on the stairs, or in the passageway, in the last two days?'

'Well,' she said, hesitating, 'yesterday there was a man out on the gallery, tall, bald and beardless, with very white skin. He had nasty eyes. Quite frightened me.'

Volnay and the monk shared a look and took their leave.

'Our friend Wallace has been putting himself to a great deal of trouble,' said the monk.

Volnay nodded, and asked to go back to the victim's apartment. He positioned himself at the window, and gazed thoughtfully down at the bread oven in the yard below.

The early afternoon sun shone brightly in a clear sky. Crowds were out walking in the streets of the capital. Among the passers-by, the courtiers had spotted two fourteen-year-old girls with adorably pretty faces and figures. They were a little anxious but allowed themselves to be talked into climbing aboard the carriage to accompany the party to Versailles. Certain of payment for their services later, the courtiers showed the girls around the gardens. They admired the fountains. A thousand birds chattered in the trees shading the fine, sandy paths. A thousand water jets spurted at intervals from the mouths of mermaids and Tritons. A thousand flowers bloomed in the ornamental beds.

The young girls uttered small cries of delight at the sight of Neptune, recognizable by his beard and his menacing trident, riding in his chariot pulled by six seahorses. To his left, Proteus, shepherd of the monsters of the deep, rode on a unicorn's back. To the right swam a herd of sea dragons, ridden by cherubs. The myriad jets, shooting out like watery lances, made a sound like a great waterfall as they poured into the huge stone-rimmed basin. The gentlemen courtiers exchanged glances and decided to conclude with a visit to the Grotto of Love.

Three high arches were decorated with golden seashells. Inside, the two ingénues sighed ecstatically. The ceiling of the grotto represented the sun; the walls were covered with seashells and colourful mother-of-pearl. At the back of the cave, the god Neptune held an upturned wineskin, from which water poured into a crystal lake at his feet. More water poured from great seashells carved in mottled marble. In places, the jets fed sheets of water that rose in steps, like a fairy-tale staircase leading nowhere. Tritons and Nereids, their bodies coated in mother-of-pearl, fed four fountains shaped like chandeliers, whose jets crossed to form the silhouette of a flame. Mirrors set into the biggest seashells offered infinite reflections of the graceful birds painted in relief on the walls. Hidden organ pipes played rustic melodies that, coupled with the rippling water, mimicked the sound of birdsong, as if in the depths of a wood.

The two friends wept with emotion at the sight of such marvels. The gentlemen courtiers took advantage of their near-swooning state to support them gently with an arm passed nonchalantly around their slender, girlish hips. At which moment Le Bel—first valet of the king's bedchamber and His Majesty's personal pimp—appeared from out of nowhere like a pantomime devil.

'We' had picked out these young ladies, he reminded the gentlemen, and 'we' had desired to offer them some light refreshment...

Knowing full well who 'we' were, the two courtiers regretfully abandoned their prey to the king, who greeted them in one of his nearby villas, before a mountain of cold meats, pastries and bonbons. The girls' names were Marion and Mariette, they declared. After much charming banter, and aided by alcohol, 'we' asked the girls to undress. The king followed suit and sneezed as he did so.

'Oh, Rachel!' giggled the older of the two. 'He's getting cold feet!'

'What did you say your names were?' asked the king, who was worried now.

'Begging your pardon, Majesty, but we've been playing a game. Our true names are Rachel and Sarah: Rachel David and Sarah Lévy…'

The king, who was a devout Christian, stared at them, quite taken aback, and began yelling out loud.

'Jewesses! They are Jewesses!'

He rushed from the room in his undergarments, his voice ringing out still, all around the house:

'Jewesses!'

Fortunately, other young girls were on hand to satisfy his desires and chase away his anxious fears. The king soon forgot the disappointment of his ill-fated tryst in the Parc-aux-Cerfs, with a visit to another house: number 20, Rue Saint-Louis, purchased by a proxy.

'Find me some young women of the world!' he ordered. 'Tonight, I feel in need of a little *savoir faire!*'

In the dim, late-afternoon light just before sunset, Volnay entered the Ruelle de l'Or, a narrow lane lined by houses so low that a man might touch the eaves of some of them just by stretching out his hand. Life in this neighbourhood went on at its own mysterious pace. The area was home to a dubious population of dealers in potions and lotions, spiritualists, exorcists, astrologers, witches and necromancers. The cellars of the houses lay deep, and rumour had it that the lane and the cemetery nearby were the object of strange comings and goings on certain nights, when the moon was full. It was said, too, that some of the local magi would scratch the earth beneath the feet of hanged men, to collect the putrid mosses that formed there, and harvest a magical plant: the mandrake.

Faceless shadows, clients careful to keep their identity secret, would slip into one or other of the houses from time to time, and emerge later, their faces covered. What strange ceremonies had they engaged in? No secrets escaped these peeling walls. The spirits conjured there remained firmly under lock and key. In the shadowy street, the smell of mould and incense filled the air. There were no sudden noises; no merchants clamoured for the attention of passers-by. The silence was broken only by occasional, quickly stifled mutterings. Everyone knew precisely where they were going, and no one dawdled along the way.

Volnay made his way hesitantly along, struggling to find his bearings. Behind the smoky windowpanes, pale faces cast curious glances. A man whose features were concealed beneath a hood muttered to him in passing:

'Amulets and wax figures for enchantments—follow me if you're interested!'

Volnay ignored him. Further along, a woman with a masked face took him by the hand. Volnay started in surprise, for he had neither seen nor heard her approach.

'Fear grips your heart—will you come and couple with Death?'

There was a hint of a beautiful face beneath her mask, but she was dressed in rags. Volnay pushed her away, saying simply:

'I have no fear of death. I am afraid of nothing.'

But he was lying. His heart was beating fast. He hurried along, and soon found the house mentioned by Chloé, the king's troublingly sensual wig-maker. Some of the windowpanes were broken, and bundles of rags had been stuffed into the holes. The door was so low that Volnay was forced to bend double to step into the smoke-filled lair, its walls coated with soot. The fire in the chimneypiece cast a blazing light over the convoluted forms of the alembics and crucibles. A shelf to the left of the door bore an array of phials and bottles containing strange, stagnant liquids.

A bent figure turned slowly to greet the visitor: a very old man, clad in a long, dark robe, his forehead deeply furrowed. He held a pair of pincers in one hand. His face was red, and his temples glistened with sweat.

'Well, Monseigneur, what brings you here? Do you wish to know your fate? The key to life, and death? Or perhaps it's a simple case of stiff joints? I am your servant! I have the remedies!'

His voice was low and wheezy, unpleasant to the ear. He shuffled across to a huge table covered with clay vases, alembics and stones carved with symbols of the Kabbalah. He took hold of a dull-coloured globe, wiping the dust from it with his sleeve.

'There are truths aplenty to be revealed in this orb, and a veil to be lifted on the future, in exchange for a modest sum indeed...'

'Indeed! My concerns are more monetary...'

'Ah!'

The other man's face darkened.

'My services are not free of charge.'

'You mistake my meaning: I have too much but, on a private whim, I should like still more, and very quickly.'

The old man's eyes shone with greed.

'Oh, that's good! A wise resolution. Only one solution for that: the coition of King Sulphur and Queen Mercury! The Great Work.'

'Coition?'

'Monseigneur, sulphur is the male element, associated with fire and the sun. Mercury is the feminine element, symbolized by water and the moon. They must be married with the addition of salt, the breath of life that animates all things.'

He shuffled over to the glowing furnace. He noticed Volnay watching his hunched gait and shrugged with a resigned air.

'My vertebrae are rusted with age, Monseigneur, but a year from now I shall walk straight as the letter *I*! I am nearing my goal, the ultimate secret: the secret of eternal youth!'

His fingers brushed the furnace in a curiously sensual caress.

'But to get back to the business in hand,' he said in hon-eyed tones. 'I cannot lie, Monseigneur. If I had discovered the secret of turning base metal into gold, I would not be living here. I am impeded in my research only by a lack of means— 'tis all that stands between me and that moment when, after torturing my metals in the alembics, and under the crucible, I see them reveal themselves to me, as silver or gold!'

His hand swept the room, and he pointed a finger at the rickety, dusty shelves.

'Look there! Mandrake roots, toad venom, the sting of the queen bee, dragons' teeth! I speak of the primordial dragon, ancestor of us all! And that tooth there is a sea unicorn's canine!'

He hobbled over to a shelf, and gazed in ecstasy at a ter-racotta pot.

'Do you know what's in there? The plant like no other: the moon spittle that contains the universal spirit! It grows only in Paradise, and by night in a mere handful of places on this earth. Who can claim to possess such marvels? All I need now is money to fund my research, because still I need colophony powder, iron filings, red sulphur, borax, red arsenic and a list of other materials too long and tedious to recite for you here.'

He held out his gnarled, bony hands to Volnay.

'Eaten alive by the fire and the acid! I have worked night and day for more than twenty years to wrest the secrets of Nature from her bosom.'

His expression was cold and calculating now.

'A small injection of funds is all I need to take up my research once again, and I promise you that in a year from now, or two, I will succeed in transforming the basest lead into gold.'

Volnay stood for a moment, saying nothing. His smile had frozen, and he observed the man with some severity now. He moved swiftly over to the furnace.

'You think I don't know your tricks? You think I don't know how you tamper with your dishes, the double bottom of clay concealing a stash of gold powder? Your *aqua fortis* peppered with gold pellets! Even if your experiments were real, they would be a blasphemy in the sight of God and a challenge to the authority of the king!'

'Monseigneur!'

'*Inspector.*'

Volnay's icy tones lowered the temperature of the room by a good ten degrees.

'I am investigating the death of your granddaughter, Mademoiselle Hervé.'

'My little girl? Dead? Woe is me!'

The old man sank heavily onto a chair and began sobbing unconvincingly. Unmoved, Volnay pressed him with questions. At length, he was satisfied and left, but not without casting a curious glance at the furnace glowing in the corner of the room.

Outside, he chased the polluted air from his lungs. He scanned his surroundings and froze at the sight of a familiar figure, quite out of place in the Ruelle de l'Or. The capacious habit and hood did nothing to disguise the familiar gait of the monk. Volnay hurried after him, and soon caught up with his colleague. Idiotically, he thought to startle him by placing a hand on his shoulder. But the monk's long years incognito, in hiding, on the run, had sharpened his senses to a state of perpetual alert. He turned with astonishing speed, and blocked Volnay's wrist.

'You?' he exclaimed.

He released Volnay immediately and sighed.

'*In flagrante delicto!*'

'What brings you here?' asked Volnay.

A faint look of unease spread over the monk's face.

'Oh, some purchases for my experiments. You can find anything here.'

Volnay whistled between his teeth.

'You haven't given up, either. You're all the same, chasing after mirages!'

'Scientific curiosity!'

'It will be your downfall. You shouldn't come around here, you who were accused of heresy.'

'*De haeresi vehementer suspectos.* Strongly suspected…' said the monk, pointedly.

He broke into a broad smile.

'That said, not all the goals I pursue are without name. Here is where I buy my supplies of myrrh, for foul breath, and to clean the teeth and repair the gums. You crush an ounce of myrrh and mix it with two spoonfuls of the finest white honey and a little green sage. You apply this to the teeth before retiring and…'

His voice trailed away, seeing his colleague's obvious lack of interest.

'If I'm boring you, perhaps you'd like to tell me why you're here, on Witches' Alley? When you left me earlier, you said you were going to question Mademoiselle Hervé's grandfather.'

'And that is exactly what I came to do,' replied Volnay. 'If I had known where you were going, I would have suggested you accompany me, but you're as secretive as ever when it comes to your experiments. The grandfather in question is a charlatan who looks out for gulls he can pluck naked on the pretext of securing funds for his research into the transmutation of lead into gold.'

'Ha! His kind are cunning indeed,' said the monk feelingly. 'They put mercury and copper vitriol in a copper crucible, mixed with a little water. The salts in the copper dissolve, and it melts and combines with the mercury to form an amalgam that looks for all the world like gold. Similar results are achieved by treating leather shavings with *cadurie*, a sort of greenish soot which they use to coat the sides of their furnaces.'

'Yes, yes,' Volnay interrupted, smiling. 'I have no doubt you are quite the universal scientist! No one knows more than you about anything.'

The monk looked vexed. He shrugged his shoulders.

'I don't say there is no one wiser or more learned than me, merely that I have never had to the honour of being introduced to them.'

He dug his fingers into his short beard.

'And what did you conclude from your interview?'

They walked a few paces along the lane, both glancing up on a reflex, at the same moment, to catch sight of a stone niche in the wall of a house, and the incongruous presence of a group of saintly statuettes.

'Mademoiselle Hervé was only interested in what she could get out of her grandfather,' said Volnay evenly, casting his eye all around him. 'She dreamt of magical powders, potions to seduce and bind men to her, and an ointment of eternal youth, to preserve her beauty down the years. For his part, he managed to extort a few coins from her from time to time, by selling her creams for her complexion.'

The monk looked up at the reddening sky.

'Our victim was a girl of inconstant morality, and her attraction to things magical was genuine. Interesting—our desires and our centres of interest exert considerable influence on our behaviour.'

He broke off to point to a tumbledown cottage with a roof of worn thatch.

'Here are talismans for every eventuality: eternal passion, or requited love. They even sell one that prevents your wife from making a cuckold of you!'

'I have precious little use for that…' said Volnay, tonelessly.

The monk shot him an anxious look, then walked on, changing the subject.

'Here is a dealer in ointments, who distils a very fine *eau d'ange*, for embalming.'

Volnay burst out laughing in spite of himself.

'Well, I see you are familiar with everyone's speciality along this street!'

'Indeed.' The monk lowered his voice. 'And I can take you to eat a meal with the dead of your choice, in one of these buildings, where they practise incantations using bones, oil, flour, honey and, of course, human blood.'

He turned into a tiny blind alley as he spoke. Volnay followed him, unthinking, then drew close behind him and caught him by the wrist.

'Where are we going?'

The monk turned, with a mysterious smile.

'My scientific mind is not wholly closed, as you know, to certain processes unexplained by nature. Follow me!'

They entered a house whose front door opened directly onto a staircase that descended in two spirals to a vaulted cellar, curiously clean and well aired. Cushions were scattered over the floor in front of an unlit fireplace. Incense was burning, clouding the air with fragrant smoke. Candles cast a wavering light. A woman with silver hair, dressed all in white, turned to greet them. Her face was pale and serene, and long lashes framed her sea-green eyes.

'It's been a long time, gentle monk,' she said simply.

The monk bowed gallantly and kissed her hand.

'Too long, mistress of my thoughts,' he said, straightening up.

'I waited for you for a long time, once,' she said, reproachfully.

'I remember. But I was forced to flee abroad. To a country where I was unhappy indeed, for they clapped me in prison. You should know that you peopled my cell with sorrowful memories and piquant dreams.'

She placed a finger to her lips with an amused look.

'I'll hear no more, I am no longer of an age for such words.'

The monk shook his head in protest.

'To say so is an insult to your charms.'

He seemed to have quite forgotten the Inspector of Strange and Unexplained Deaths at his side, but quickly recovered himself and turned to introduce him.

'My friend Volnay.'

He added, for the inspector's benefit:

'Our hostess is skilled in a most venerable art, which she learnt in Germany, beneath a walnut tree in Aachen, the ancient capital of Charlemagne. The art of divination.'

Volnay stifled an exasperated sigh.

'Wait!' said his friend. 'This honourable lady has done me proud service in the past. There are things in heaven and earth that even science remains powerless to explain. Which is no reason to reject them out of hand!'

He bowed before their hostess.

'Madame, would you do us the signal honour of lifting the veil on a portion of our destiny?'

'I can refuse you nothing,' she replied indulgently.

She filled a crystal cup brimful of limpid water and covered it with a white cloth, before lighting two candles to either side. She signalled to Volnay to sit facing the cup, and placed herself behind him, placing both of her hands on his forehead. Her touch was light, almost cold. His tension eased and his mind cleared. He seemed for a moment to be falling asleep. Clouds rolled and passed before his eyes, then vanished to make way for a spectre of light. Suddenly, the sky darkened, and it was night. He saw the figure of a woman stumble among the shadows, and turn around. The pale flash of a dagger shone in the moonlight, illuminating her terrified face. He cried out, and woke.

His hand was covered in blood. He stared at it, aghast, before realizing that he had overturned the magical cup, and that the monk was holding him firmly by the shoulders.

'It's only water! By Beelzebub, whatever did you see?'

Volnay recovered himself. Haltingly, he described the images.

'There will be a second murder,' the monk concluded, coldly.

It was midnight on Rue Saint-Louis, in the Parc-aux-Cerfs, and people were still dancing in the garden to the sound of violins. The trees were hung with multicoloured lanterns. Some of the little Sultanas sought the cool air beside the stone-rimmed pond. A girl emerged from inside the private mansion. She addressed one of her comrades, who was making her way up the steps, with a complaint about the king.

'The old rogue did me good and proper! My cunt's still sore!'

'You would do well to remember, Marcoline, that your cunt is blessed indeed to have known such an honour,' retorted her friend.

120

'A royal honour!' the other agreed, chuckling.

She walked down the long promenade lined with privet hedges, to the gates. The lanterns in the trees scattered flecks of light over the grounds, but the street was black as night. Marcoline hesitated, almost imperceptibly. All at once, her spirits failed her. The air was filled with foreboding. Had she heard something, or seen a tremor of movement in the darkness? She walked on, and her shadow on the wall seemed to grow beyond all reason. She shivered. She thought she heard footsteps pounding the cobblestones behind her. She stopped to listen. Nothing.

'Is someone there?' she asked.

There was no answer but silence. Her imagination was playing vile tricks. She continued on her way. Soft lights shone through the shutters of some of the houses. In one, a party was at its height. She heard laughter and singing. The noise and gaiety were reassuring.

But she had not been dreaming. A second shadow loomed against the wall, a shadow even bigger than her own, though it did not engulf it, yet.

'Who is it?' she asked in a frightened voice.

There was no reply, but the shadow seemed to shrink into itself. The girl hurried on. The shadow loomed once again. It seemed to want to seize her, to swallow her up. She glanced desperately at the lighted windows. When a light shines it is hard to believe that evil is near. Now, the two shadows seemed to blend into one. She began to run. She heard the pounding of feet behind her. Just at that moment, a carriage turned into the street. She was saved. She ran out in front of it.

'Help! Please help me!'

The coachman cracked his whip, and the young woman was forced back against the wall to avoid being crushed. The vehicle passed without stopping, with a hellish racket. The carriage lamps cast a brief pale glow on the cobbles, before the shadows returned. The poor girl turned, shaking all over. There was no one behind her now. Her breathing eased, and she gave a long sigh of relief. The stranger had been frightened off. She waited for her pounding heart to subside. Then she turned to continue on her way. Something blocked her path. A firm, strong torso. As if in a trance, she saw fingers reaching towards her, and when she recognized their owner's face, she gave a small cry of surprise.

'You!'

The last sound ever to emerge from her throat.

VI

A woman has only one way to be beautiful,
but a hundred thousand to be pretty.

CASANOVA

A whirl of lace, jabots, powdered wigs and colourful satins danced in the iridescent light of the chandeliers, and the flickering glow of the candelabra. Precious stones glittered at the women's white throats. Not for the first time, Volnay pondered the motive behind his invitation to dine with this rich and noble company. Doubtless the mystery of the faceless woman had attracted the attention of some, but many were rightly suspicious of officers of the police, fearing they may be spies of the king.

He was annoyed to find Casanova had been invited, too. The Chevalier de Seingalt greeted him warmly and, seizing him by the elbow in a sudden show of familiarity, drew him aside.

'Chevalier de Volnay...'

The inspector started in surprise.

'Ah yes!' said Casanova brightly. 'I learnt of your title, and a great many other things, too. Don't look so enraged...'

Volnay understood:

'It was you who secured my invitation this evening!'

Casanova gave a dismissive wave of the hand.

'I thought it an occasion to patch things up between us.'

Three words fought to escape from the inspector's tightly pursed lips: *imposter, swindler, schemer!*

'You have troubled yourself for nothing,' he said drily. 'I do not feel coldly towards you. Neither am I your friend.'

Casanova looked hurt.

'What a shame. I have an appointment tomorrow with the Comte de Sainte-Germain. I had thought you might like to come along.'

'Why the devil would I come with you?'

'Because you are as curious as I to know how an individual who proclaims himself immortal can appear out of nowhere. No one knows where he was born, whence he comes, nor how he acquired the riches which are so obviously his.'

Volnay was about to give a colourful reply when Chiara entered the room. Once again, the sight of her left him quite breathless. She wore a dress of light, glossy silk with a satin ground and a large damask pattern of stylized, scrolling leaves. Her double-flounced pagoda sleeves were pushed up to reveal layers of fine embroidered lace. She had stuck a beauty spot at the corner of her lips, and that simple change had revolutionized her appearance. Volnay found himself considering her in a completely new light. She came towards them, her eyes shining. Casanova kissed her hand most gallantly. Volnay did the same, though rather more stiffly.

'Mademoiselle,' said the Chevalier de Seingalt, 'a woman has only one way to be beautiful, but you have found a hundred thousand ways to be pretty!'

Chiara accepted the compliment with an indulgent air.

'I was just explaining to the Chevalier de Volnay how we came to be invited by the Comte de Saint-Germain,' he went on.

'You've explained nothing whatever,' growled Volnay, who had positioned himself instinctively between Chiara and the Venetian.

Casanova laughed brightly.

'Well, it happens that I met him at a dinner given by Madame d'Urfé.'

Chiara gave an amused smile and added, for Volnay's benefit:

'You know, the lady who is to be reborn on the seventy-fourth day.'

'I am not easily impressed,' Casanova went on, as if he had heard nothing, 'but I confess that I found the comte quite astonishing. He drinks no wine, ale or spirits, and refuses anything of animal origin. He eats chiefly grains and seeds, pecking at them like a bird.'

'And what does he do while everyone else is eating?' asked Volnay.

'He talks! All the time! And I am forced to admit his conversation is fascinating. He knows everything about everything. You can question him on almost any subject and be certain of an answer. In particular, he has an extraordinary flair for detail, and casts the great events of history in a thoroughly new light.'

'As if he had been there himself…'

'Yes, that is indeed his gift!' declared Casanova, and there was a hint of envy in his voice.

They were interrupted by the call for the company to be seated at dinner. The silver sparkled amid the fine porcelain and crystal glasses. The table overflowed with flowers. Volnay tried awkwardly to manoeuvre himself into a seat beside Chiara, but failed hopelessly and was relegated to the far end of the table. He felt uncomfortable in this bejewelled, gleaming microcosm, obsessed as it was by appearances, rumour and scandal. He overheard one diner commenting idiotically to another: 'The people lack for bread? Let us feed them the crusts of the *pâté en croute*…'

Volnay was listening without enthusiasm to his neighbour's comments on her iced dessert, when a burst of laughter drew his attention. Casanova excelled in the subtle art of salon conversation, by turns erudite and playful, and especially in the company of women. Just at that moment, he was enjoying great success with one of his anecdotes:

'And so, the Prince de Lambèse, with characteristic devotion to duty, ran to the burning thatched cottage and emerged carrying an elderly, paralysed woman in his arms. Her clothes had caught alight, and he raced to the pond and threw her in, to extinguish the flames, whereupon she drowned!'

The unexpected conclusion was greeted with gales of laughter around the table, as the first dish was brought in: veal sweetbreads with a shrimp coulis, truffled roe, pricked and stuffed pike, red partridge wings with puréed mushrooms, and white snipe on toasted bread spread with baked stuffing meat. The Chevalier de Seingalt knew how to captivate an audience by awakening its curiosity, but Volnay was no conversationalist, and his neighbours quickly lost interest. He looked from Casanova to Chiara, gazing at the young woman for longer than was seemly. He saw the Venetian staring at him long enough to secure his attention, before leaning towards Chiara, certain that he could be heard at the other end of the table.

'The talk is all of the Comte de Saint-Germain just now; it seems he's an accomplished artist.'

Another guest agreed.

'And an excellent musician! He sings and plays the violin wonderfully well, and he composes music, too. When the comte improvises on his violin, an expert ear may pick out the four parts of a full quartet!'

There were exclamations all round, and Madame de Genlis leant towards them, her eyes bright.

'The Comte de Saint-Germain paints in oils, too, and is extraordinarily skilled in the secrets of colour. You should see the colours he contrives for the floral decorations in his paintings. Emerald greens, sapphire blues, ruby reds… Truly, they have the sparkle, sheen and brilliance of precious stones. Van Loo, La Tour and some of the other painters told my father they had never seen such dazzling colours!'

The second course appeared, and occupied the company for a time, until Monsieur de Cobenzl, minister plenipotentiary of the Empress Maria Theresa, delicately replaced his fork and commented, in a somewhat reedy voice:

'For my part, I find him quite the strangest man I have ever encountered. He is possessed of great wealth but lives very simply. He is remarkably honest and demonstrates admirable kindness and decency to his fellow man. He has profound knowledge of all the arts. He is a poet, a musician, a physician, a chemist, a mechanic, a painter… In short, I have never seen such general knowledge and culture in any other man. His knowledge appears quite boundless.'

Volnay was fascinated, like everyone else. Casanova's presence was forgotten. The diplomat paused for a moment, and Volnay looked up to see the Venetian fixing him with a knowing stare. He shifted his gaze back to the minister plenipotentiary. Monsieur de Cobenzl had paused merely to dab at his mouth with a napkin, for fear that talking at table might have left some small trace. He continued in the same vein:

'Before my very eyes, the Comte de Saint-Germain performed a remarkable experiment, though for him it was a quite ordinary piece of work, so he told me. He stained pieces of wood in vivid colours, without indigo or cochineal, and went on to make a most perfect ultramarine blue, just as if he had extracted it from lapis lazuli. Finally, he took an everyday oil—walnut or linseed—as used in painting, and took away its smell and taste, making it the finest edible oil anyone could imagine.'

More exclamations were uttered around the table, including from those guests who had not fully understood all the terms employed. Casanova taunted Volnay in silence, and his look seemed to say:

See if you can resist accompanying me to the comte's tomorrow, after all that!

The Baron de Gleichen was moved to contribute a story of his own:

'I have had occasion to see his collection of precious stones, and I can assure you, it is quite unique!'

The ladies uttered piping, quail-like cries.

'Indeed, Mesdames! He has them in extraordinary number, and above all coloured diamonds of remarkable size and perfection. The king himself has nothing like it!'

'But how has he obtained stones of such quality, and where do these riches come from?' asked someone, voicing the question on everyone's lips.

Silence fell. Everyone around the table was thinking the same thing, thought Volnay. Had the Comte de Saint-Germain discovered the secrets of alchemy?

'I may have the elements of an answer,' ventured the baron. 'Our king learnt that the comte knew the secret of making the flaws in diamonds vanish, and he entrusted him with a stone that possessed a sizeable flaw. The diamond was estimated at six thousand livres, but ten thousand without the flaw. The king asked Saint-Germain, "Would you help me to gain four thousand livres?" The comte accepted, and returned one month later with the flawless diamond. The stone was weighed, and its weight was unchanged!'

Everyone marvelled at the news. Delighted with his success, the baron continued:

'They say at Court that he can enlarge pearls and give them the very finest lustre.'

'Does he also practise alchemy?' asked Volnay, abruptly.

Another silence fell around the table. Chiara gave him a knowing smile that warmed his heart.

'I have no idea,' replied the baron at length, somewhat disconcerted.

The tension eased slightly. All eyes turned expectantly to Volnay. The inspector pretended not to notice.

'Chevalier,' Chiara's clear, impassioned tones were heard around the table, 'do you believe the philosopher's stone may indeed exist?'

The subject touched on the immortality of mankind on earth, territory fraught with the utmost danger. Chiara's youth prevented her from realizing the full implications of her question. To answer 'yes' was blasphemy, and liable to punishment of the very worst kind. Adroitly, Volnay chose to answer the question with another of his own.

'People are seeking nowadays to turn base metals into gold, and to communicate with the spirits, water goblins and salamanders. Is it not strange that in this century of reason, the finest minds should be so fascinated by magic and alchemy?'

Some dinner guests lowered their eyes in discomfort, others smiled at the clever response. People turned their gaze on Chiara, hoping to spy her reaction, but the young woman wisely chose not to pursue this sensitive topic in public. Eager to maintain the flow of conversation, the mistress of the house leant towards Volnay, taking advantage of the attention he had secured.

'Chevalier, is it true that a woman was killed in Paris, and her face entirely cut away?'

Having posed her question, she swept the company with a look of triumph and satisfaction at the presence of the man in charge of the extraordinary investigation, seated at her table.

'Yes, Madame,' said Volnay. 'But I can say nothing further.'

He noted with pleasure that Chiara was unable to take her eyes off him now. His feelings were such that he quite failed to hear his hostess's next question, and was forced to stammer a convoluted, non-committal reply. Chiara smiled at his distracted state, knowing she was its cause.

'But what monster is capable of such a heinous crime? A madman?' his hostess persisted, raising one eyebrow.

Volnay recovered himself, just as great baskets laden with pyramids of fruit were brought to the table. Platters of candied fruits were brought, too, and quantities of pastries.

'Madame, experience has taught me that even a madman follows a logic all his own, and that for every effect, there is a cause.'

The company reflected on his words, and pondered what they might actually mean. The meal was over. Sorbets were served, with coffee from the colonies, and liqueurs. The company moved to the large salon for the games of cards and chance so beloved of the nobility, who had money to lose. Casanova seized the inspector's arm and led him aside, watched by Chiara.

'Chevalier, what a shame your conversation is so plain! The whole table was waiting for a few words from you about this strange business of the faceless woman, whose body I discovered. A wonderful opportunity to shine, if you were so inclined.'

'It is not my vocation to be a performing monkey for society at large!'

Casanova sighed.

'And that is why you will never shine at dinner! My invitation from the Comte de Saint-Germain is for tomorrow, late morning. Our mutual friend will be joining me. Are you sure you won't accompany us?'

Coldly, Volnay extricated his arm from Casanova's grasp. He could not bear to be in physical contact with this man.

'Please understand that I have no need of you, should I choose to visit the Comte de Saint-Germain.'

'Of course,' said Casanova, with a venomous smile. 'As part of an official investigation... Am I therefore to understand that the comte is part of your inquiries?'

Volnay thought fast. He did not want to give that impression. Viewed in that light, the offer was tempting: he would gain access to the comte in all innocence, without causing alarm. He would also be able to keep an eye on this sham seducer and his wagging tongue. Besides which, the Venetian was holding his beautiful young compatriot too close for Volnay's liking, and she seemed far from impervious to his charms.

Just at that moment, a commotion was heard in the hallway. A voice boomed. There was the sound of running feet, and a liveried valet entered the room, rather too hurriedly. All eyes turned to him, in curiosity. The man paced quickly across to Volnay and whispered something in his ear. The inspector invited him to lead the way and the two hurried from the room. Volnay did not notice the Chevalier de Seingalt following close behind.

The Inspector of Strange and Unexplained Deaths hurried down the main staircase, shadowed closely by Casanova. Chiara hurried after them, too. One of Volnay's men stood waiting in the great hallway, awkward and out of place beneath the crystal chandeliers.

'What's happened?' asked the inspector sharply.

The man's face was white and drawn.

'Another young woman has been found dead, and her face cut away!'

A small group of men in black surrounded the corpse. The precinct chief stared, dull-eyed, at Volnay as he approached.

'Never thought I'd have occasion to work with the Inspector of Strange and Unexplained Deaths. My colleague in Paris told me about the affair. This victim was killed in the same atrocious manner. No witnesses.'

His mouth stretched into a scornful grin.

'Seems your investigation just got a little more complicated, Inspector!'

Volnay made no reply. He knelt beside the dead woman. She was appallingly disfigured. Shreds of flesh hung from around her face.

'Shoddy work,' said the precinct chief solemnly. 'The murderer must have been in a great hurry.'

'Hurried, or disturbed,' said Volnay, quietly.

His fingers rested for a moment on the young woman's neck, marked by two elongated, purplish bruises.

'There were no marks of this sort this first time,' he noted.

He lifted one eyelid.

'The pupil is dilated, the lips are blue. The contusions on the neck and throat suggest to me that the victim was strangled bare-handed before being cut up. So much the better for her…'

Volnay placed both hands around the young woman's neck, enclosing it delicately, as if to strangle her a second time.

'God in heaven!' The precinct chief swore loudly. 'Have you gone stark, staring mad? You're fit for burning, man!'

Volnay turned slowly. His eyes blazed cold as ice.

'I am trying to form an idea of the size of the murderer's hands.'

In the heavy silence that ensued, he took hold of the corpse's wrist. As with the first victim, hers was the hand of a young woman who took good care of herself. A pretty ring glittered on one of her fingers, and she wore a band of gold. Volnay removed them carefully and placed them in a small pouch, where he kept his clues. Her clothes seemed well cut, though rather plain. They were bloodstained, and in disarray, as if the young woman had fought fiercely to escape her attacker. This time, he made a systematic search of the body, but found nothing. He examined the surrounding area with his lantern, and discovered what looked like a small, round grain, smooth as boxwood, stuck between two cobblestones. He removed it under the ironic gaze of the precinct chief and placed it carefully in his pouch of clues.

'Did you know,' he said quietly, 'that almost a thousand years ago, a magistrate of the ancient Tang dynasty, one Ti Jen-Chieh, studied crime scenes by examining every piece of material evidence?'

Without waiting for a reply, he took one of the victim's small, delicate hands in his. These were not the hands of a woman who worked by day and caressed her lover by night. They were too white, too delicate. Nor were they the hands of a society lady: the victim was not sufficiently well dressed. A woman who plied her trade by night, then? Seductive, immodest hands, Volnay decided. Hands that were unafraid to insinuate themselves beneath shirts and breeches. Delicately, he turned them palm upwards. The skin was white, soft and intact, unlike the first victim.

He's proceeded differently, thought Volnay. *Perhaps a different murderer altogether?*

The dull clatter of cartwheels rang out over the cobbles. Heads turned to look.

'Dear God!' sighed the precinct chief.

The cart drew to a halt. A rumour ran through the crowd that had assembled now. Pulling on the reins, a ghostly figure sat deeply swathed in a monk's habit, the hood pulled down over his face. He stared straight ahead, and his intense, fixed gaze was troubling indeed.

A number of onlookers made the sign of the cross. As people always did.

The dead woman lay stretched out on her bed of stone, in the foul depths of Paris's police headquarters. Other recently arrived corpses lay around her, by no means all in perfect condition, though they had kept their faces, at least. After the attack on the monk, Volnay had judged it preferable to bring the body to the basement gaol at the Châtelet, which served as the city morgue. The vast, gloomy cellar was the repository for any corpse found on the streets of Paris or fished out of the Seine, once they had been liberally salted, like fish on a market stall. The air was filled with the smell of decomposing flesh, at once sweet and fetid. The inspector insisted on special conditions for the work of his mysterious colleague: no salt, a private corner, with some daylight—for light entered the basement gaol only through a series of narrow slits, and it was famously dark.

'A word,' said Volnay. 'Could we possibly avoid the dramatic entrances with your cart, each time a corpse is discovered?'

The monk's face lit up with a half-smile, and his eyes glittered wickedly.

'But that's the best part! All eyes are on me!'

'And you play your part to the hilt! Is the mask finished?'

The monk skipped delightedly on the spot. He was never livelier, or more good-humoured, than when faced with a surfeit of things to do. It was his nature—or perhaps the effect of the herbs he collected at the forest edge and chewed for long periods, when he sought to stave off the effects of fatigue.

'It is,' he said. 'But it's far more rudimentary than the first.'

'Why is that?'

'The skin of the face was torn away very roughly this time. Not at all like the first victim. In so doing, the murderer has

134

splattered the victim's upper garments with blood. Perhaps he worked in a hurry…' he added.

Volnay nodded.

'He must have worked directly out in the street, while she was fully clothed, whereas before he stripped the body, probably inside the courtyard, then re-dressed and dragged it out onto the street once he had finished.'

The monk frowned and indicated the young woman's neck.

'As you saw straightaway, she was strangled. The bruises at her throat are doubtless due to the pressure from the murderer's thumbs: the central marks are circular and quite symmetrical. His nails have pierced the skin, too.'

He opened the dead woman's jaw, with extraordinary gentleness.

'The victim seems to have reacted by biting her tongue, alas. The murderer pressed very hard, because the curved tongue bone has been broken, and the cartilage in the trachea is crushed. I found no trace of wounding or strangulation on the first victim. The facial skin had been very neatly removed, like skinning a rabbit, truly it seemed like the work of a surgeon. Now, for the second murder, we have strangulation, followed by this act of butchery, and unskilled butchery at that, for I have no wish to slander a profession of such vital importance!'

With infinite delicacy of touch, the monk lifted one of the victim's hands and turned the fingers over for the inspector to examine.

'The girl put up a fight. There is blood under three of her fingernails, and scraps of flesh. If we could only identify to whom they belong. At least we know the murderer bears a livid scar on one arm, with three bloody scratches. And lastly, the palms of the hands are perfectly intact, whereas on the first victim, they seemed to have been burnt away.'

The monk pursed his thin lips in an expression of doubt.

'Thinking about it, the only thing common to the two murders is the torn-off face and the fact that—ah yes, I omitted to mention—the young women had both made love to a man an hour or two before their deaths. What do you think?'

'Either this is another murderous lunatic, copying the earlier crime, or the same murderer who, for reasons unknown, has proceeded differently this time. And in Versailles, a town crammed with agents and officers of the king! Not a place where people are murdered on the street, as a rule!'

Both fell silent. The inspector pressed his face briefly to the metal grille separating the decomposing bodies from the public. When he looked up once more, his eyes were cold as ice.

'There's something I didn't tell you yesterday,' he said quickly. 'The Brotherhood have found me. They threatened me with death if I didn't serve their interests.'

The monk's expression closed tight as an oyster at low tide.

'And what might those be?'

'To discredit the king and La Pompadour. In their eyes, the king is Bluebeard himself, and the marquise his procuress-in-chief!'

'Wait…'

Volnay had turned to go, but the monk caught his sleeve.

'You and I, we know the Brotherhood's true name: the Brotherhood of the Serpent. They pride themselves on their rational, pragmatic cast of mind, yet their leaders engage in bizarre ceremonies that perpetuate the cult of the gods of Egypt and Babylon! Isis, Osiris, Baal, Moloch, Semiramis… They are dangerous madmen! And you were mad to join them when you did. You know that once initiated, a brother can never leave. But you would not listen to me. You wanted to kill kings and topple their royal houses back then! Ah, the folly of youth!'

Volnay slipped from the monk's grasp.

'That's precisely why I have distanced myself from them ever since,' he said curtly.

'Keep it that way,' said the monk, who had turned white as a sheet. 'The Brotherhood of the Serpent seeks to emulate ancient Sumer, and Babylon. A fine example! The Sumerian and Babylonian civilizations invented slavery, conscripted standing armies and based their expansion on a state of perpetual war and the subjugation of other peoples. They destroyed their lands with the greed of their farming, and turned green fields into deserts. I have a feeling this second murder brings us closer to the king—all the more reason to flee the Brotherhood!'

He lowered his voice and bent closer to Volnay.

'A royal letter associated with the first body, and a royal setting for the second—Versailles, in the quarter they call the Parc-aux-Cerfs, just minutes from Rue Saint-Louis, the site of a house set aside for the king's amorous pleasures! The first victim may have coupled with the Comte de Saint-Germain before her death, the second with the king himself.'

The monk broke off and cursed softly.

'By the bowels of Christ, what have we got ourselves into?'

Volnay looked thoughtful.

'And was she with child, like the other victim?'

'If she was, I would have told you.'

The monk threw off his hood and drew Volnay's attention to the young woman's clothing.

'An habituée of the Parc-aux-Cerfs. That seems the most likely hypothesis, to me.'

He struck a theatrical pose and raised a finger, like a scholar delivering a lecture.

'I shall confine my remarks to a certain "habit", but there is much in that alone. Habit, habitual—from the Latin *habitudo*:

condition, plight, customary behaviour. But curiously, also, clothing, raiment, attire…'

He paused for effect. Volnay stared at his eccentric colleague in silence. One might know a man, or a monk, by his 'habits', and, in the present case, both seemed highly questionable.

'A person's habit describes their habits, for we may see how it is *worn*,' said the monk, emphatically. 'A well-worn garment acquires a certain patina. Over time, it cleaves to the wearer's form. It *conforms* to the thing we are. And so this garment reveals the gestures performed repeatedly by its wearer, such as the lifting of her dress.'

He caressed the fabric lovingly, and showed Volnay a patch more worn than the rest.

'You see,' said the monk thoughtfully. 'The hands are frequently placed here, in the same position. The repeated gesture *wears* the garment and testifies to the wearer's habits, which in turn reveal her true person. Our habits are what differentiate us one from another, they are what give a person's clothing, their habit, its movement, its life. I can read it like a book, and from my observations, I deduce that we have here a young woman of pleasure, with an irregular, not always substantial income, who frequently lifts her skirts.'

'A vulgar prostitute,' concluded Volnay. 'A young woman of the world.'

The monk's pale eyes rested in his.

'A prostitute is a woman of the world because she is the property of every man on earth, but where is the vulgarity in prostitution? Which is better, to starve to death or to sell one's body? Are our bodies such objects of shame that we must wear them out in drudgery and labour, and never enjoy them for our pleasure? As to selling one's body, we are all of us confronted with tragic choices in this life.'

He spoke with genuine emotion. The inspector lowered his head in silence. The monk prepared to leave.

'Where are you going?' asked Volnay, anxiously.

His colleague turned, and his eyes burnt with rage and despair.

'I am going to throw off this habit, for more civilized attire, because I intend to go and drink till I forget who I am. I'll thank you not to come along.'

At the inn, a handful of students from the Sorbonne were tucking into a fine, runny omelette with chives, washed down with a hearty, cheap, slightly bitter wine. Near the chimney, a group of severe-looking merchants devoured roasted woodcocks trickling with grease. In a corner, a man sat slowly drinking, watching the rest of the company out of the corner of his eye. He was clearly past fifty years of age, yet he appeared sharp and alert. His bright eyes were filled with humanity. He nodded his head and smiled to himself when the students broke into song:

> 'We must away to Paradise
> There we'll take an angel each
> Their heavenly cunts do smell of peach...'

Doubtless he knew the song, but his bearing was more aristocratic than scholarly. His short, greying beard gave pleasing definition to a patrician, Roman face. He had been a handsome man in his time, and the years had not dimmed his charm.

'And here's the rest!'

The innkeeper set down a golden, well-roasted chicken and another pitcher of wine in front of the man.

'Like Prezzolini, that great chef before all Eternity,' commented his client, wickedly, 'I am a loyal devotee of the spit roast and the purifying flame: no sauces with my roasts and fries! *Delirium dieteticum*. The secret of my good health and vigour, both physical and intellectual!'

The innkeeper stared at the man as if he were quite mad, then shrugged his shoulders and returned to his kitchen. A draught of cold air ran through the room, causing the candle flames to gutter. Night itself seemed to rush inside. Slowly, the monk—for it was he—raised his head. The door closed quietly behind a small man with an inquisitorial look, meticulously coiffed and powdered, dressed in a dark, wine-coloured coat and gilet decorated with buttons stitched with golden thread. He walked straight over to the table occupied by the man and his golden roasted chicken. The monk watched impassively as he approached, though his eyes darkened.

'Good evening, monk,' said the new arrival, seating himself without waiting to be asked. 'Shaking off your old habit tonight, I see.'

The monk gave a wan smile.

'Sartine! What ill wind blows you hither?'

'Ah, my friend,' sighed the other, 'you are seldom out of my sights. An object of perennial interest!'

'I am not your friend, and I'm surprised to see you're following me yourself today. Usually you send your filthy flies to buzz around me instead…'

'Is that what you think? In truth, I'm here quite by chance,' said the chief of police.

His jocular tone was unmatched by any gleam of gaiety in his eyes. His entire person radiated a subtle but implacable determination. The monk pushed his glass away. With such a redoubtable adversary, a man had better stay in full possession of his faculties.

'Your flies are everywhere,' he said, not bothering to hide his scowl of disgust. 'Why waste their time on me? They'd do better to spy on the great and powerful of this world—those you fear like a cur trembling before his master!'

Sartine gave vent to a grunt of anger but contained himself.

'A fearful master muzzles his own dog,' he said.

'Ha! You and your kind at Court, you prefer tongues that lick to fangs that bite.'

Sartine shrugged and lifted a hand to his wig, patting a curl into place, then swept an invisible mote of dust from the sleeve of his coat. The monk watched him, with no hint of indulgence. He knew Sartine spied on the nobility, even under their own roofs. The chief of police knew their most shameful secrets and brightened the king's days with his stories.

'Well, I fear I must a call a truce in our pleasantries,' said Sartine firmly. 'We have a second murder, and Volnay has sent me a most succinct note. He didn't even see fit to bring it to me himself. Does he truly believe he can keep me out of this?'

'Of course not,' said the monk cautiously.

His dark eyes were watchful, attentive to the slightest shift in the chief's expression.

'So, tell me more about your investigation,' growled Sartine.

'Why would I tell you any more than Volnay?'

The chief's face hardened.

'Need I remind you that you have known the horrors of prison, and risked far worse?'

The monk sighed.

'When I was young, I was an island, free to think and act exactly as I pleased, but there is no room for such people in a monarchic system…'

'You may find yourself back in prison if you're not careful! Think, quickly man!'

The monk leant back in his chair and blinked delicately. There was a fixed quality to Sartine's stare that quite made a man's hair stand on end.

'You're asking me to betray Volnay,' he said.

'For the common good,' replied Sartine, amiably.

VII

The Comte de Saint-Germain did not live in the palace of Chambord, where he had installed his pigment workshop, but in Paris, at no. 101, Rue Richelieu, in the mansion of the widow of the Chevalier Lambert. There, late in the morning, two lackeys in tobacco-coloured livery with gold braid, and collars and cuffs of blue lace, ceremoniously opened the doors to the three visitors.

The comte received them in the music room, decorated with statues of the nine Muses. Around the walls, mirrored pilasters reflected the splendid, richly varnished woodwork, alternating with others bearing garlands of golden leaves against a ground of lapis lazuli speckled with silver. With his habitual eye for detail, Volnay observed a *Treatise on Engraved Stones*, devoted to the art of intaglio and gem-cutting, on a side table. A print taken from the book lay unrolled beside it.

The inspector turned his attention to the Comte de Saint-Germain. Of average height, with a swarthy complexion and a high forehead topped by an expertly curled wig, the comte was elegantly dressed in a coat of Parma silk brocade with generous, turned-back cuffs, an elaborate waistcoat of many different fabrics, and a jabot and shirt-cuffs of Brussels lace. He seemed youthful and alert, though he must have been almost fifty years old. His skin was fresh and bright, and his features regular, with a hooked nose, well-defined lips and a dimple on his chin.

He had an undeniably aristocratic air, but there was otherwise no ostentation in his manner. He wore a lively, spirited expression, and his dark eyes fixed his visitors attentively. His manners were exquisite, and his bearing was one of noble, disinterested politesse. Volnay noticed the rings on his fingers, set with magnificent diamonds, and the fine rubies adorning his sleeves.

Chiara wore a damask gown embroidered with gold nasturtium flowers, and three-tiered pagoda sleeves. Her lips were coloured with Spanish vermilion, that most delicious and desirable of shades.

She is magnificent, thought Volnay, with a touch of bitterness. Clearly, the comte thought the same, for he hurried to greet her.

'Mademoiselle, I am honoured to receive you.'

He executed a perfect bow and kissed her hand. Chiara's cheeks flushed with pleasure. Next, the comte greeted the Chevalier de Seingalt and the Chevalier de Volnay with the courtesy he reserved for all of his guests.

'May I offer you a glass of Jerez wine? This is the oloroso, or "fragrant". It is aged for ten years in oak casks.'

Volnay tasted it and discovered an exquisite flavour of fresh almonds, ginger and prunes. Light conversation ensued, on topics of the day, until Casanova skilfully directed their talk to the subject of precious stones. The comte sensed his implicit request. It came as no surprise to him. All his visitors asked the same thing. He led the trio to a small side room. There, on a piece of black velvet, he emptied the contents of soft bag he had taken from a chest.

A torrent of colour seemed to pour out onto the table. The stones glittered and sparkled in the soft half-light. Volnay knew little about fine gems, but he recognized an opal of monstrous size, and a white sapphire the size of an egg.

'How beautiful,' whispered Chiara ecstatically.

Casanova, for his part, seemed to be weighing up the stones and estimating their value.

'A fortune, before our eyes!'

The comte gave an almost imperceptible shrug of the shoulders and declared lightly:

'Our riches are merely the measure of our needs.'

The Venetian gave a short sigh.

'Your Lordship has never known want.'

The comte turned to look at him sharply.

'I was not born to silks, Chevalier! At the age of seven, I lived a vagrant life in the forests with my governor. There was a price on my head, and my mother had fled.'

The revelation met with astonished silence. The comte held up a diamond.

'The Queen of Stones,' he said. 'Hard, limpid, brilliant.'

He let it sparkle for a moment in a shaft of sunlight, then ran his hand carelessly over the stones, spreading them across the velvet cloth.

Volnay understood now why the comte was able to lead the life he did. All the riches he needed for a contented existence, for centuries to come, were kept close to hand in a single bag. And suppose for a moment, as was rumoured, that he had the secret of making precious stones such as these, too…

'Forgive me for asking,' he said, 'but you must know what people are saying—that you have the art of removing flaws from diamonds.'

'And you are equally curious to know if I can make them, are you not?' supplied the comte, with heavy irony.

For a moment, the trio watched his lips, ready to hang on his every word. A delicate breeze blew in through the half-open window, tinkling the crystal droplets on the chandelier overhead.

'Well, of course I don't know how to make diamonds!' exclaimed the comte. 'That is a gift granted to Nature alone. Do not be tempted to believe every rumour they spread about me. The facts have always been supplanted by a wealth of supposition, in my regard. But I am merely a man of science and reason.'

'An exceptionally gifted man of science, so they say,' breathed Chiara, in curiously gushing tones. 'For example, you are rumoured—'

She broke off suddenly, conscious of her clumsy intervention. Her cheeks turned a ravishing shade of red. The comte finished her phrase:

'...to possess the philosopher's stone,' he said evenly. 'And to have pierced the mysteries of matter, and eternal life—why ever not, while we're on the subject? Every man dreams of eternal life! That's why they all talk about me.'

A hornet struck the window with a dull thud that startled them all, though not the comte.

'Strange indeed,' he observed delicately. 'Our philosophers preach the strictest logic and reason, and yet, in this era of universal incredulity, we prefer to question nothing, and to believe anything at all!'

'What of the dinner with Madame the Comtesse de Gergy, who seemed to recognize you as a man she had known in her youth?' ventured Volnay, as much out of his own curiosity as to come to Chiara's rescue: the young woman clearly felt she was being targeted. Her cheeks were still flushed scarlet.

The Comte de Saint-Germain gave a slight smile.

'Madame the Comtesse de Gergy confused me with another man she had known. All I did was ask whether the man in question, a Marquis de Baletti, had enjoyed an upstanding reputation. She said that he had, and I laughingly told her that, in that case, I would happily adopt him as my grandfather. That's the whole story! And so the rumours run…'

He stared Volnay in the eye.

'As an officer of the police, you will know that my enemies have hired an actor to impersonate me and discredit my reputation, throughout Paris. It doesn't do to be an intimate of the king and the Marquise de Pompadour; it incites mortal enemies.'

Volnay blinked nervously. So the Comte de Saint-Germain knew his profession, though he had been presented only under his—in this instance highly convenient—title of chevalier. An uncomfortable silence fell between them. The comte smiled impassively, while Casanova cast the inspector a knowing smirk.

'In truth, Monsieur le Comte,' said Volnay, recovering his sangfroid, 'I take little interest in Paris gossip. I prefer to concentrate on my work—a rather particular speciality.'

The comte's smile brightened.

'And you think I don't know that you are the king's Inspector of Strange and Unexplained Deaths?'

Seeing his guest's growing expression of surprise, he added quickly:

'I don't have the gift of divination, but people talk about you a great deal—and your mysterious colleague in his hooded habit, who reads corpses like books. Between you, you have solved a number of complicated cases. At least, that's what they say. There was the affair of the young nobleman who claimed to have been pursued by a vampiress who had granted him her favours, or the priest who was found in his confessional with his throat cut.'

Volnay seized the moment.

'I am currently investigating the murder of two young women, both of whose faces were cut away.'

'Indeed?'

The comte's expression was impassive, filtering nothing but polite curiosity.

'Doubtless you have heard talk of that?' Volnay persisted.

'None whatsoever.'

Another silence, which no one felt emboldened to break. At length, the comte addressed Volnay with a question, more out of politeness, it seemed, than any real interest.

'And do you have any suspects?'

The inspector held his gaze firmly.

'I cannot say, Monseigneur.'

'Of course, I understand…'

Volnay fished for a way to open up the conversation. In desperation, he asked:

'You are a man of reason—perhaps, with your enlightened mind, you are able to proffer me some advice?'

The compliment was heavy-handed, and the comte ignored it. He shook his head lightly.

'None that I can think of…'

Then his eyes lit up, and he added:

'I must, however, recommend the greatest caution. Such murders, in Paris, are likely to cause a considerable stir. I imagine they have already provoked much talk and dismay in many circles. You have very little time before others will start to encroach on your territory. Be careful, discreet, and trust to your intuition, more than the facts.'

'Whatever do you mean?'

The comte stared at him gravely.

'Often, we form an opinion, and then we bend the facts until they correspond…'

At that moment, a door opened abruptly, and a young man entered the room, making his apologies. He had a frank, pleasant face below a high forehead, framed by a long, curled grey wig. He wore a purple velvet coat over a yellow doublet.

Shreds of tobacco dotted his lace jabot: clearly, he had just taken a pinch of snuff.

'Forgive my intrusion, Monsieur le Comte, but you asked me to inform you when your carriage was ready, for your appointment.'

His message delivered, he bowed to the visitors with some ceremony.

'Allow me to introduce my assistant!' exclaimed the comte. 'Monsieur Mestral, I give you the Marquise Chiara D'Ancilla, the Chevalier de Seingalt and the Chevalier de Volnay.'

The assistant bowed a second time. He was about thirty years old, and his manners were every bit as polished as those of his master.

'I am most honoured to meet you. The comte is an extraordinary man. You will have heard many wonderful things about him already, but the truth is more remarkable still. Did you know that he mixes elixirs for the common good? There is nothing in this world which he cannot improve upon and make use of.'

For the first time, the Comte de Saint-Germain showed a glimmer of embarrassment. He rebuked his assistant gently, and asked him to wait outside. The comte excused himself to his guests: he would have to curtail their visit. They took their leave with great civility. On their way out, the comte signalled to Volnay and whispered quickly in his ear:

'Do not forget that however complex the situation, its causes are often very simple.'

Volnay pondered the phrase as he made his way down the staircase. Turning, he saw that the comte's eyes were fixed upon him still.

Outside in the courtyard, the inspector stopped the servant who had accompanied them and slipped an écu into the man's hand.

'Rumour has it your master is two thousand years old…'

'I cannot say,' said the other, coldly, as he handed back the money. 'I have only been in his service these past three hundred years!'

Chiara giggled, and Casanova burst out laughing. Volnay clenched his teeth and climbed into the carriage after them. They had just driven out into the street when he saw the comte's doorman hurrying along with a letter in his hand. He asked the driver to stop, and climbed down just as the man was passing.

'One question, friend!' he said. 'We have just come from Monsieur le Comte's. You are the servant who admits anyone who comes to his door, am I right?'

'Myself, or another by the name of Jean Folioure,' said the man, clearly uncomfortable at being addressed in the street.

Volnay pressed a louis into his hand.

'Has the comte received a visit lately from a young woman named Mademoiselle Hervé?'

'I don't know, Monseigneur,' replied the man, pocketing the coin. 'But when the Marquise de Pompadour paid the comte a visit yesterday evening, she was accompanied by a young woman. The lady waited in a side room while her mistress visited my master. Then she left with her in her carriage, one hour later.'

'Did she have anything in her hand?'

'I don't remember, Monseigneur.'

Volnay dug in his pocket.

'This, my friend, is for you to forget these questions were ever asked.'

The servant bowed solemnly.

'So be it, Monseigneur.'

Volnay turned to see Chiara and Casanova poking their heads out of the carriage windows, listening attentively.

Casanova laughed quickly, as he caught the inspector's eye.

'Truly, there is entertainment in everything!'

They walked in the Tuileries gardens, and the sun beat down on their shoulders. Streams of water flowed from the stone-rimmed ponds; antique statues were glimpsed in the copses, watchful guardians of their secret pleasures. Chiara seemed to delight in the play of the fountains, and the formal gardens with their charming borders of flowers. Along an avenue of fine sand, they came to a ring of box hedges and the statue of a lightly clad nymph, reclining on one side atop her plinth, lazily trailing one of her arms.

Casanova gazed attentively at the statue. His eye followed its seductive forms, then shifted nonchalantly to Chiara, who looked away sharply. Volnay's own thoughts at the sight of the nymph had taken a quite different direction.

'Do you really believe the Comte de Saint-Germain has broken the boundaries of human existence?'

The inspector's question was addressed to no one in particular, as if he were enunciating the parts of an equation. Chiara spoke up straightaway, nonetheless, but adding further questions of her own.

'None can escape death, the destiny of us all. Nature will not allow it, but what if scientific research could alter Nature? Has the comte discovered an elixir of life in his laboratories?'

Volnay stared at her in surprise.

'You seem beset by the question: you asked it at dinner last night. Never have there been so many fake healers and false prophets as now, in our age of reason. And you are like all the rest, in spite of your science and culture. You are fascinated by the regeneration of the body, and the soul!'

'I am not talking about magic, but about science, indeed!' said Chiara, in clipped tones. 'In particular, I am thinking about chemistry, in which the comte seems well versed.'

She turned to Casanova.

'What do you think?'

The Venetian gave a small laugh.

'I have seen plenty of conjuring tricks and outrageous impostures in my life.'

'Seen and practised,' grinned Volnay.

'But this is different,' Casanova continued, ignoring him. 'The comte speaks better than anyone. His tone is decisive, and pleasing, because he is erudite and at ease in every language. He cuts an agreeable figure and is skilled at befriending every woman he meets. He flatters them, too. He gives them creams for their complexion, and he alludes not to the possibility of restoring their youth, because that is impossible, as he tells them, but rather to the preservation of their present appearance by means of a special water, which costs a great deal, but which he most kindly presents to them as a gift. He possesses a kind of universal medicine; he can make Nature do his bidding—in short, he is most surprising, and never fails to astonish. He is, then, the cleverest and most seductive of impostors!'

They turned back the way they had come, along the shady avenues. And it seemed their thoughts had effected an about turn, too.

'They say the Comte de Saint-Germain is very close to the king, and La Pompadour,' said Volnay. 'Perhaps they know his secrets?'

'I'd be surprised,' said Casanova, wickedly. 'Two things are required to seduce the great and powerful of this world: first, you must agree with them, and second, you must retain a reasonable air of mystery. There is nothing a great man or woman likes better than to be flattered by a person who is themselves out of the ordinary.'

Volnay glanced at him sharply, but at a warning look from Chiara, he bit back the retort that was burning his lips. He addressed the young Italian:

'We speak of the Marquise de Pompadour, but they say her star is in the descendant and that her sworn enemies, the Devout Party, exercise a growing influence over the king.'

Chiara straightened her shoulders briskly.

'The Devout Party have no influence except with the dauphin. The Marquise de Pompadour retains all the king's favour and friendship. And the enlightened minds and free-thinkers of this country all fall into rank behind her, while the Devout Party rallies those who, lacking any special merit, press their court upon persons of power for the lowest of motives. They ruminate and plot against intelligence and reason.'

Casanova shot Volnay an appreciative glance that seemed to say: *Cunning, my friend! You have led her to confess which side she is on. Now try the same with me…*

But Volnay was taking no such risk. He had no need. He knew full well that Casanova took no side but his own. For his part, the Venetian had a great many questions for the inspector, but no guarantee of an answer.

They emerged from the circle of box trees to see the city bathed in scarlet sunlight. They paused for a moment to admire the effect, then made their way down a flight of steps towards a shimmering water basin. Chiara tripped, and both men reached out to stop her falling. Each held out his arm. Smiling, she took both, and they walked on between flower beds overflowing with blooms. Soon, it was Chiara who dictated the pace and direction of their stroll. And soon after that, the direction of their conversation.

'We all know,' she said, addressing the inspector, 'that you are determined to solve the murder of the young wig-maker…'

Casanova was unable to suppress a frown of disapproval. Volnay dropped the young woman's arm roughly and planted himself in front of her, outraged.

'What in heaven possesses you to talk about that in front of this man? I insisted you keep it secret.'

'But,' she stammered, 'you told him about it yourself.'

The inspector turned abruptly to Casanova.

'Explain yourself!'

Casanova gave a resigned shrug.

'Paris is such a small city, everything gets around very quickly. And so I learnt the identity of the victim whose body I had discovered.'

Volnay's logical mind worked fast.

'And so,' he said, 'you confirmed the information by making this young lady believe you had heard it from me.'

Casanova pursed his lips. He ventured a glance at Chiara, and saw the storm clouds gathering in her eyes.

'I was wrong, I confess,' he said, contritely.

'You have no excuse!' said Chiara.

The Chevalier de Seingalt glanced at Volnay out of the corner of his eye. The inspector appeared overjoyed at the young Italian's words.

If he thinks he's keeping her for himself, thought Casanova, *then he has surprises aplenty in store!*

'Mademoiselle, I beg your forgiveness.'

'Out of the question!' ordered Volnay.

Chiara's face flushed with rage. No one decided on her behalf.

'We three must be united,' she decreed. 'It is necessary, I feel it. This is how it must be.'

She spoke as a woman of reason, and Casanova cast her an admiring glance. He liked people who kept their composure.

Volnay found it harder to contain himself, so great was his aversion to this notorious womanizer. Chiara soothed him with a smile, and this time, as a subtle punishment to Casanova, she took only Volnay's arm, as far as the cafe to which, with signal determination, she had decided to take them.

A bright, friendly atmosphere reigned in the Petit Café des Tuileries. The place was a little noisy, but that suited their confidential talk. Mirrors dotted around the walls reflected paintings of restful Tuscan landscapes and scenes of the grape harvest, populated by country girls dressed quite inappropriately for the task. Despite the early hour, Chiara ordered a *rossolis*—an aperitif scented with rose petals, orange flower water, jasmine, aniseed and cinnamon, with a few cloves. The two men drank coffee, with an aroma of toasted bread.

'What a curious drink this coffee is,' pondered Casanova. 'The more one drinks, the less one sleeps, and the less one sleeps, the more one needs coffee.'

'I can understand why it should be your favourite drink,' taunted Volnay, 'you who go about your business by night.'

'Monsieur,' retorted the other sharply, 'I am no night owl; I live quite as much by day. Besides, I am known in every court in Europe.'

'Indeed,' Volnay persisted, 'the Chevalier de Seingalt has conquered the whole of Europe with his... *swordsmanship*. Did you know, Chiara, that he refers to that *sword* of his as "the principal agent for the preservation of the human race"?'

'Monsieur,' cried Casanova, squaring his broad shoulders, 'you forget yourself!'

Chiara was plainly amused.

'Please stop bickering, you two. Whoever saw such behaviour?'

She looked at them both for a moment, Casanova bubbling with vitality, enthusiastic and voluble, Volnay grave and self-contained, thoughtful, but driven by cold determination.

Which of the two might I choose, if ever I were forced to choose just one?

She dismissed the thoroughly improper thought and focused her attention on the conversation. She must play her cards carefully.

'So, Messieurs, let us speak frankly. A young wig-maker in the employ of the king has been killed, and you must do everything in your power to find the culprit.'

The two men said nothing. Both were on the defensive. Chiara placed a pretty hand on the inspector's wrist, and felt it tremble.

'Chevalier de Volnay,' she said, 'you first. Tell us everything.'

Volnay blinked rapidly. Ignoring Casanova, he gazed into the young Italian's eyes.

'I have sought no confidences from the Chevalier de Seingalt.'

The latter grunted scornfully, then swore in Italian, causing Chiara's cheeks to flush pink. Volnay continued, unperturbed:

'And so I am not about to confide in him now.'

The Venetian leant towards him, threateningly. His gaze was ice-cold. All trace of enthusiasm and good humour had disappeared.

'You are swift to judge me, and to condemn me out of hand, but beware! I may be a good-natured fellow in a lace collar, but I can soon take that off.'

The inspector paled.

'You would threaten an officer of the king's police! I can have you interrogated…'

Casanova threw himself back in his chair and laughed. People were starting to look in their direction. His laughter died suddenly in his throat, and he whispered quietly:

'And will you also interrogate the man who is concealing vital evidence?'

He glared at Volnay.

'Shall I elucidate?'

The inspector closed his eyes for a moment. No, the Venetian would not go so far as to say it out loud. Not here, not in front of Chiara. This was a cunning scheme to buy his silence, or worse.

'Mademoiselle…'

Casanova had turned to the young woman, who sat listening intently.

'Our friend Volnay removed a letter from the victim's body and has kept it hidden from everyone.'

'Did you really do such a thing, Monsieur de Volnay?' Chiara's voice sounded oddly choked.

She had not noticed the inspector's fingers closing around the hilt of his sword, nor that he was beginning to draw it from its sheath. But Casanova had caught the hiss of metal. He watched as the blade emerged. Chiara followed the Chevalier de Seingalt's gaze. She saw the inspector's clenched fingers.

'Volnay! Return your sword to its sheath this instant!'

Her voice was commanding, authoritative and utterly unexpected, thought Volnay, in such a charming creature. Almost in spite of himself, he obeyed. She leant towards him, and for a moment he thought she would slap his face, but she did nothing of the kind, and the closer she came, the faster his heart beat, for he suffered a new discomfort now. Casanova stared hard at them both.

'Volnay…'

For the first time since they had met, Chiara covered Volnay's hand with her own. A wave of tenderness broke over him.

'Do not allow yourself to be ruled by anger,' she said gently. 'Anger kills the intellect, and the spirit.'

She gazed deep into his eyes. Her own were dark as the blackest pearls, but softened by the same iridescent light.

'Do not act alone now, Volnay. No man can fight alone against the whole world.'

A heavy silence ensued, but the inspector felt strangely soothed by the contact of her hand on his.

'The letter exists,' he hold Chiara, ignoring Casanova. 'I can say nothing more, but it concerns—'

'The Comte de Saint-Germain, am I right?' she asked. Casanova accompanied her question with an approving nod of the head.

So they had guessed that, too.

'Indeed, the comte. But the letter is unconnected to the murder,' he added, sharply.

The magical moment had passed. Chiara's hand deserted his own, and he felt again that familiar, aching void. He remembered his discussion with the monk, on the subject of clothing. If the patina of a fabric could capture the accelerated passage of time, his own clothes would fall to shreds and rags when Chiara took her distance once more.

'Mademoiselle Hervé was meant to deliver the letter to the comte, is that it?' asked Chiara, in an odd tone of voice.

Instinctively, she sensed his distress. And placed her hand on his once more, as if she had guessed this was the sole precondition for his answer. Her touch was light and tremulous. He sensed her vivacious, ardent nature.

'Yes.'

'Then why didn't you ask the comte if he knew of it?' she asked in surprise.

This time, Casanova intervened.

'To ask such a thing would be to reveal the existence of the letter, in the hands of an officer of the police. It would serve to warn the comte, too, and perhaps others besides... Is he not a friend of the king and La Pompadour? Besides, we know now, though neither of you seems inclined to mention it, that the victim was a creature of the marquise.'

The Venetian stared deep into Chiara's eyes, causing her to blush and look away, at Volnay.

'And the servant you questioned acknowledges that a girl accompanied La Pompadour to the comte's residence,' ventured Chiara. 'You might ask the comte whether he received the girl together with her mistress? And why?'

'And the comte would tell me that she came to adjust his wig, or to proffer any other kind attention you please! I should be no further advanced…'

Volnay turned to Casanova.

'And on the subject of *kind attentions*, might this Mademoiselle Hervé have been a visitor to the Parc-aux-Cerfs?'

The Venetian made a show of pondering the question, his fingers tapping delicately on the rim of the porcelain saucer under his coffee cup.

'She was doubtless a little too old for the king's fancy, but certainly, nothing in her private morals would have prevented it.'

He shot Volnay a piercing look.

'Is there something in the letter you found that gives you reason to suppose she might have gone there?'

The inspector struggled to retain his composure, cursing himself for asking the question, whose answer he had already guessed. Mademoiselle Hervé was carrying the king's child. Clearly, she had enjoyed his favours, no matter where. And here was Casanova reading him like an open book, matching one piece of information with another, honing his intuitions.

'Tell us, then, Volnay,' the Chevalier de Seingalt continued. He seemed to be following a thread, from one thought to the next. 'Was the second victim a prostitute?'

If only I knew for certain! thought Volnay. He almost spoke the words out loud.

'The victim was unable to be identified,' he said drily, 'for reasons you may imagine. And we have no other clues.'

'Such a shame! But she may have been, surely?'

'What are you trying to say?' asked Chiara impatiently, leaning in more closely to her two companions.

Casanova settled himself squarely in his chair, focused all his attention on Volnay and pronounced eight words as distinctly as if he had counted them off on a rosary.

'She was found at the Parc-aux-Cerfs.'

Adding modestly:

'Otherwise, why would our friend Volnay have mentioned the latter?'

Volnay blinked rapidly. Nothing escaped the cunning Venetian. Chiara, for her part, was staring at them with unfeigned astonishment, struggling to grasp what lay beyond the words uttered by both men.

'One moment!'

The Chevalier de Seingalt leapt up from his seat. A familiar figure had just passed in front of the cafe window.

'The comte's assistant!' exclaimed Chiara, and her eyes followed Casanova as he rushed outside and urged the man to join them, with his usual infectious enthusiasm.

The comte's assistant was fulsome in his polite protestations while the others pressed him to take some coffee. But Chiara's charm and quiet authority broke his resistance, and she withdrew her hand from Volnay's once again, to focus all her attention on the new arrival. He had an open face, and the broad brow of a man accustomed to deep thought. He spoke readily on the subject of his master, heaping him with praise.

'Believe me, Monsieur le Comte de Saint-Germain is motivated solely by the good of all mankind. I have never seen anyone so attentive to others. He is a friend to man and beast alike—his heart beats for the happiness of his fellow creatures.'

His tone was perfectly sincere.

'He knows everything and foresees everything. I have never known such a clairvoyant mind as his.'

'Does his clairvoyance extend to making predictions?' asked Casanova innocently.

Volnay shot him an acerbic look. Even a scoundrel like Casanova could not suppress an interest in the esoteric sciences. The rumours regarding the comte's discovery of the philosopher's stone, and the secret of longevity, clearly excited him, despite his natural scepticism.

'Well, as you know, the past is more the comte's terrain,' said his servant adroitly.

Chiara moved forward as if transfixed.

'But people say he wrote the alchemical treatise *The Most Holy Trinosophia!*'

'The comte is well versed in chemistry, that is true,' acknowledged his assistant, cautiously.

'In chemistry and alchemy alike?' Chiara insisted.

The other gave no immediate reply, but applied himself to stirring his coffee with great thoroughness. Just when his silence was beginning to seem impolite, he answered:

'A great deal is said and thought about the comte. For my part, I have witnessed only scientific experiments, with convincing results.'

'Such as restoring purity to a flawed diamond,' suggested Chiara, who was leading the conversation now, while her two companions watched with interest.

'Mademoiselle, I can say nothing about the comte's experiments without betraying the trust he has placed in me.'

Volnay listened intently. For reasons unknown, the man's declarations sounded false. He decided to play along.

'They say that people visit the comte to obtain certain potions from him.'

The assistant paled very slightly. Volnay fixed him with a firm stare and delivered his well-aimed strike.

'Has the comte been visited recently by Mademoiselle Hervé, the king's wig-maker?'

The inspector thought the other man might faint. The assistant's complexion had turned deathly white, and his mouth opened and closed as though he lacked for air. Fat beads of sweat dotted his forehead, along the line of his wig.

'I have no idea. Excuse me,' he gasped, 'it's so very hot in here, I think I need to step outside.'

He rose clumsily, overturning his coffee cup and apologizing profusely until Volnay stopped him with a raised hand.

'You haven't answered my questions.'

The assistant avoided his gaze.

'I do not know the lady, and I know nothing about her visit. I wish you good day.'

He hurried away. Casanova eyed Volnay with a look of cold derision.

'So, what are you waiting for, to clamp him in irons? The man's as forthcoming as an ass digging in its hooves. If anyone deserves to be taken in for questioning, it's him!'

Both men sensed Chiara's disquiet. The assistant's reaction had done nothing to satisfy their curiosity. Casanova attempted to smooth her ruffled composure, without success. Soon, they took their leave, with many a sidelong glance, and a host of unformulated questions on every side. Volnay watched sadly as Chiara's carriage drove away, then bade Casanova a frosty goodbye. Suddenly, Chiara's carriage shuddered to a halt, and her slender, bare wrist was thrust through the window.

'Monsieur de Volnay?'

He ran after her and reached the carriage, panting for breath. The young woman's face peered anxiously out. Hastily, she opened her lips to speak.

'I must see you tomorrow, on the subject of the letter in your possession. Do nothing until then! Do you promise?'

He nodded mechanically. The coachman whipped his horses and Volnay stood watching with a strange pang as the carriage moved off. A new question posed itself: could Chiara be trying to get her hands on the letter, too?

Volnay smiled as he returned home and stepped through the door. The monk was giving the magpie a lesson in Latin rhetoric. He sighed, pointing to the bird:

'"Science without conscience is but the ruin of the soul." Alas, your very fine bird is capable only of repeating things, but not understanding them. Like much of the human race, indeed!'

He walked over to the table, on which he had placed a glass of wine.

'Forgive me for helping myself, but my excitement at the sight of a fine bottle is hard to contain! The Devil knows, it's barely three years since I was in prison, me! And making do with tepid water.'

He took a mouthful and smacked his tongue against his palate.

'A Suresnes. A distinctive flavour, but one gets accustomed to it. You should mix it with a little cognac—that would improve it.'

'I'm so glad it meets with your approval,' said Volnay, still smiling.

'Few things on this earth delight the heart of man so much as this sweet beverage.'

The monk's expression turned melancholy.

'There was a time in my life when I thought I would die. Since then, I consider every day a marvellous stay of execution which I am eager to enjoy.'

Volnay almost shrugged, but stopped himself. He knew that except for the occasional, very good wine, which he drank sparingly indeed, and one or two roast meats, the monk's pleasures were wholly of the intellect. He gave a brief account of his visit to the Comte de Saint-Germain, and his walk in the Tuileries afterwards, with Chiara and Casanova.

'Splendid,' said the monk, and he quite literally jumped for joy. 'You have just confirmed one of my more brilliant hypotheses!'

Volnay showed no reaction. He was secretly annoyed at the monk's visit, though his colleague kept a key to his house and could enter whenever he pleased. His mind remained focused on Chiara's hand, whose slightest touch brought devastation in its wake. He remembered the almost physical pain he had suffered when she removed it from his, leaving it orphaned. He was lost for words to describe the happiness that accompanied this suffering. The monk had no such thoughts. He consulted his scant notes and frowned.

'No news from the Brotherhood of the Serpent?' he asked amiably.

'You know we must never speak its full name,' Volnay reprimanded him, white-faced. 'Only "the Brotherhood".'

'Absolutely. And so?'

'Nothing!'

The monk seemed to have recovered his serene calm.

'Good! First, then, I shall tell you what I have discovered about the Comte de Saint-Germain before his arrival in France. In England, the comte is greatly appreciated in musical circles. His talents as a violinist are in great demand, and the composer Gluck has dedicated a work to him: *Reasonable, Well-ordered Music, for English Ladies Who Appreciate True Taste in Art*. He has his work cut out!'

The monk paused and moistened his lips.

'And so our comte left England in 1746. He reached France last year—April 1758. I regret to inform you that no one seems to have any idea what he did in the intervening twelve years. The comte's path through life is like the flight of a bird: it has left no trace. It is rumoured that he was in the Indies, and Tibet, or at the court of the shah of Persia. Which is quite possible, because he seems to have deep knowledge of the Orient. That said, when asked, the comte explains that he retired to his own estates, in Germany, in order to pursue his researches in chemistry, and even alchemy.'

'Is that all?' Volnay was disappointed.

The monk's eyes glittered.

'The comte's conduct is exemplary. He is rich but benevolent. There was never a more charitable man, nor one possessed of such perfect manners. The mystery of his own origins, and the origin of his fortune, remains.'

He paused to check his notes.

'He receives no income, but pays everything in cash and never asks for credit. You have seen his lifestyle at first hand, and there is no trace of money changing hands! As if he slept on a hoard of treasure.'

'Are you going to tell me about the philosopher's stone?' Volnay was sceptical.

The monk burnt with enthusiasm now. 'I have another theory about that. One connected to his birth. My research has led to the elaboration of a number of hypotheses: the first is that the man is of unknown parentage. *Ex incognitis parentibus*! The other is that he is the illegitimate child of a great figure in Europe.'

He broke off and stroked his beard.

'I'll spare you the avenues I explored and abandoned: his Rákóczi ancestors in Transylvania, the San Germanos in Savoy, even the one who calls himself Comes Cabalicus in Bohemia…'

He narrowed his eyes and frowned as if trying to put his thoughts in order. Volnay watched him, smiling. He knew the mime was purely for show, and that the monk's prodigious memory demanded no effort of retrieval.

'Let us consider the confirmed facts, like proper investigators,' the monk continued. 'When the comte was in England, a Jacobite rising broke out in Scotland and marched south. Foreigners were hastily rounded up, as enemies of the state. Among them, the Comte de Saint-Germain, who refused to reveal his true identity to anyone but the king of England. Do you hear me? His true identity! He acknowledged that he was not the Comte de Saint-Germain, and would only reveal his identity to a person of royal blood! Ergo, he was questioned by the king's foreign minister himself, the Duke of Newcastle, and released immediately.'

Certain of his audience's undivided attention, the monk continued, with evident zeal:

'And so, here in France, our own notoriously starchy monarch Louis XV receives the man as a close friend and speaks of him as if he were the scion of some noble family. And once, in public, the comte let it be known that he "is from a place that has never been ruled by foreign hands".'

To give greater emphasis to what he was about to say, the monk rose and paced about the room. His right hand slashed the air around him, as if wielding a sword.

'One family alone answers that description: the Wittelsbach male line, which reigned over Bavaria, Zweibrücken and the Palatinate. Ask me now where the comte's vast estates lie? In the Palatinate! One of its princesses was married off to a king of Spain. The Comte de Saint-Germain does have the look of a Spaniard, wouldn't you say?'

Volnay agreed, cautiously.

'You told me,' the monk continued emphatically, 'that the comte described how, at the age of seven, he lived the life of a fugitive, in the forest, with his governor. That there was a price on his head, and that his mother had fled. We know that the Palatine princess Maria Anna of Neuburg married the king of Spain, and had a secret liaison with a nobleman of the kingdom, the Amirante of Castile, a man of immense wealth, exemplary learning and a fine intellect.'

The monk stood on the spot and raised a finger in triumph.

'The man was a skilled painter and sculptor, too, and spoke several languages. On the death of her husband, a war of succession broke out, and Maria Anna of Neuburg suffered the pain of losing her lover: he died of apoplexy on the wrong side, the losing camp. She was forced into exile in France and lived for thirty-six years in Bayonne, under the surveillance of the royal authorities, having sent all her jewellery and gold abroad for safe keeping. The amirante's bastard was forced to flee with his governor, to escape being killed by his father's many enemies.'

The monk held both hands out in front of him, palms turned outward, in a gesture of further triumph.

'Which explains the Italian connection, subsequently, because it is said the Grand Duke of Tuscany, Maria Anna of Neuburg's uncle, sheltered the Comte de Saint-Germain as a child, in the Pitti Palace in Florence. The grand duke, the last of the Medici, was an excellent musician, spoke several languages, and was well versed in the sciences, in particular chemistry. Hence, the comte's impeccable education and gifts, inherited from his parents and honed by his guardian.

Later, Saint-Germain passed himself off as a Sicilian gentleman. And the Grand Duke of Tuscany possessed vast estates in Sicily. The comte's wealth is easily explained: gold and jewellery—the famous gems he shows to everyone—from his mother; paintings from his father, who owned the finest art collection in Europe, and the amirante's bottomless deposits in banks in Venice, Amsterdam and Genoa. From which I am able to calculate, with equal logic, that the comte is sixty years old, though he looks at least ten years younger thanks to his impeccable diet!'

Volnay clapped his hands. He was genuinely impressed. The monk bowed modestly.

'It is nothing. Am I not the most brilliant mind in Europe after Monsieur de Voltaire?'

The inspector stifled a grin. The monk was an admirable fellow, if somewhat proud of his own intellect, a failing that had brought his near-downfall in the past. But he had learnt no lesson from that.

'Interesting, but inconclusive for our inquiry,' said Volnay, pragmatically.

The monk sighed.

'Well it gives me food for thought! What news with you?'

'I am now persuaded that Mademoiselle Hervé visited the comte's mansion on the day of her death, and that she was seen there by one valet at least, and doubtless also by the comte's assistant, though not by the comte himself.'

'She was not invited into his presence, and could not have the letter delivered to the comte by a third party.'

'Which would explain the acute discomfort shown by the comte's assistant when we questioned him at the coffee house,' agreed Volnay. 'Perhaps he was the person she saw. He was clearly hiding something from us, whatever, but I cannot prove what that might be, as things stand.'

'I'll see to that,' said the monk serenely.

'Understood. I must report again to Sartine, and tomorrow I am summoned to Versailles, to see the king!'

The monk nodded.

'Watch yourself!' he said, pointedly. He thought for a moment. 'As to the second dead woman, I went walking in my habit in Versailles, in the Parc-aux-Cerfs. I described her to a number of shopkeepers, without showing the death mask, so as not to arouse suspicion. I said I had found the ring you removed from her finger, the one you entrusted to me.'

He opened his hand, revealing the ring, as if by magic, shimmering in the light.

'A woman shopkeeper recognized the ring, and my approximate description of the victim, in particular her clothing. She was indeed an occasional resident at the Parc-aux-Cerfs, known by her first name—Marcoline. She was one of a band of prostitutes who are accustomed to liven things up when the king tires of his little girls and hungers after some professional entertainment.'

Volnay nodded darkly. His investigation was becoming more convoluted by the minute.

'If only I could gain entry to the king's residence at the Parc-aux-Cerfs,' he sighed.

'A privilege granted solely to juvenile prostitutes and their matronly madams,' said the monk. 'And the occasional amorous adventurer…'

VIII

*Venice is not down there, Madame
la Marquise, it is up here!*

CASANOVA

Dusk fell over the city in a riot of blood and gold. Casanova inspected the street with a cold eye, then signalled to his coachman. The carriage left Paris and set out for the ill-lit streets of the Parc-aux-Cerfs. The quarter was no longer, as its name suggested, a game park. Though it was still a hunting ground, of sorts. The land had been set aside as a deer enclosure by Louis XIII, but was abandoned by his successor, who took little interest in hunting. Subsequently developed as a residential district, it extended between the Rues de Satory, des Rosiers, Saint-Martin and Saint-Médéric. A great many functionaries and employees of the Court of Louis XV lived there now. A handful of powerful aristocrats kept houses of pleasure there, too. The king's property was reached at the end of Rue des Tournelles, the site of the royal kitchen garden.

The notorious royal pimp Le Bel had found a modest but pleasant house for his master at number 4, Rue Saint-Médéric, near the barracks of the Gardes Françaises. To reach it, the king travelled barely a quarter of a league from the palace of Versailles. But the house was a decoy: it was far too small, and unbefitting. Public attention remained focused there, nonetheless, allowing the king to repair unnoticed to number 20, Rue Saint-Louis, in the most outlying section of the Parc-aux-Cerfs. A steward in the service of La Pompadour had taken care of everything. He had received a gift of land from the king for his pains, thereby extending his existing, inherited estate, upon which he built a fine lodge designed by Lespée, the inspector of the king's buildings. The rooms were decorated by the painter Boucher. All this was known to a man such as Casanova.

It was just as the carriage turned onto Rue Saint-Louis that it lost a wheel. The racket attracted the attention of the two men guarding the entrance to the royal house of assignation. Casanova climbed down from the coach and winked at his accomplice, the coachman. He explained the misadventure to the two guardians and slipped them a gold coin each before striding confidently up the driveway towards the house. He climbed the flight of steps leading to the front door and knocked. It was opened by a liveried valet decked in gold braid and the royal arms, but Casanova was immediately accosted by a woman of a certain age, far too painted and elaborately attired for his taste, who stepped out from behind the servant.

'A wheel on my carriage has shattered,' said Casanova, in his most suave voice. 'My coachman has gone for help. I wonder, would you allow me to take shelter inside for a few moments? The nights are still so cold!'

'Monsieur—'

'The Chevalier de Seingalt, at your service. Madame?...'

'Madame Bertrand.'

Casanova bowed low, taking the madam's rather dry hand down with him. The woman hesitated a moment, then glanced at the valet, signalling for him to leave them. She led Casanova to an elegant salon, casting frequent glances in his direction as they walked. Clearly, the figure and reputation of the Chevalier de Seingalt were a source of some excitement, as Casanova had dared to hope.

'Let us sit here, Chevalier. Will you take something to drink?'

She chose a seat beside him, and Casanova knew that if he stretched out a leg, his foot would touch hers. They were sitting in a round room with lilac-coloured panelling inset with mirrors that reflected their image into infinity. The door lintels were all decorated with amorous scenes: a nymph sitting on the joined hands of a pair of satyrs, another astride a satyr's back, naked women bathers laughing with delight, captured by the painter's brushwork in a shimmering bouquet of greenery, water and flesh. A painting hanging on the wall caught his attention. It showed a mischievous young lady high on a swing, revealing well-turned legs encased in white stockings, and a dizzying glimpse of her undergarments. One of her shoes had slipped off and flew through the air, uncovering an exquisitely arched foot.

Casanova fixed the woman with his ardent gaze. 'Thank you,' he said at length. 'I need nothing but your charming company.'

Madame Bertrand gave a small, embarrassed but satisfied laugh.

'You are too gallant, Chevalier.'

She blushed, adding:

'Too gallant indeed, it seems. Much is said about you and your exploits…'

Casanova affected a conceited tone.

'Ah, Madame! Believe me, whatever ill you hear of me falls far short of the truth!'

They both laughed, and their shared laughter drew them closer. The conversation turned to more intimate matters. The lady ventured a question: was it true that on a certain occasion in Venice, the chevalier had satisfied fifteen women, one after the other? Casanova gave her to understand that the number was exaggerated. Two or three might be subtracted from the total. Mademoiselle Hervé's name was slipped into their talk, but the madam showed no reaction. They chatted pleasantly in this vein until Madame Bertrand excused herself. She had orders to give to the staff and would be back in twenty minutes.

Left alone, Casanova set about exploring the house. He had planned nothing in advance, but followed the inspiration of the moment, as so often, taking advantage of favourable opportunities, and rebounding when things took a turn for the worse, for there was no fall from which he could not spring back onto his two feet. He knew it would be difficult to talk further to the madam, who studiously avoided any questions about the girls and their visitors in this place. He might learn something from a glance into the bedrooms. If he were to encounter one of the royal prostitutes, he could make them talk—and more besides.

Silently, he climbed the wooden staircase, noting a few rather crude copies of canvases by Boucher and Fragonard on the walls. He heard a burst of laughter, and hurriedly sought refuge on the floor above. Peering through the balustrade he saw two young girls holding hands, entering a bedroom. One was small, apparently of Spanish origin; the other was taller, blonde and very much to Casanova's taste. He supposed the girls were treating themselves to a moment's mutual pleasure. He listened intently, but was disturbed by the sound of an ill-tuned harpsichord. The music was coming from a bedroom that seemed bigger than the others. To his right, a door led to a small closet. Casanova smiled. Could this be what he had known in Venice?

He turned the handle. The door hinges were well oiled and made no sound. The space was a closet, but of a rather particular kind: a large painting hung on the wall that divided it from the next-door bedroom. Casanova examined it carefully, then unhooked it from the wall and placed it delicately on the floor. A hole had been bored in the wall. Casanova understood. Just as in Venice, where the French cardinal de Bernis had delighted in spying on him as he made love to his mistress, a young nun, the hole doubtless corresponded to the eyes of a figure in a painting on the other side of the wall. He pressed his eye to the hole and saw the king!

Louis XV was tall and well built, with a high forehead and thick eyebrows. He was past fifty, but he cut an imposing figure nonetheless. For now, from what Casanova could see, he had seated a young girl of about fourteen on his knees and had set about exploring every curve and hollow of her nascent breasts while she played the harpsichord. The melody was becoming increasingly discordant, as the king progressed in his explorations. His Majesty was implacable, and his expression was hard as flint.

The Chevalier de Seingalt shifted his position. When he looked again, the pair had undressed prior to slipping beneath the eiderdown. The room was cold, however, and Louis XV was still in his undergarments. The chase was on, and the king seemed to delight in pursuing his prey around the bed, scurrying to catch the child, who appeared afraid, though she may have been play-acting—it was difficult to tell.

Casanova was startled by the sudden touch of a hand on his arm. It was Madame Bertrand. Gently but firmly, she pulled him away from the wall.

'You should not be here, Chevalier,' she whispered icily. 'I was mad to have admitted you.'

Casanova feigned the depths of despair as she pulled him along a corridor.

'Alas, I am so inquisitive, it will be my downfall!'

'Did you recognize the gentleman?' she asked, with barely disguised anxiety.

'He put me in mind of a Polish count I once knew,' said Casanova, innocently. 'But I may be mistaken?'

Madame Bertrand fixed him with a cold, fish-like eye, then pushed him ahead of her into a bedroom that lay apart from the rest. She closed the door behind her and drew the bolt, before sizing him up with a calculating stare.

'You're as cunning as a Chinaman, Chevalier, but now you must pay.'

Casanova stiffened, but Madame Bertrand's eyes betrayed the punishment she had in store for him.

'Ah, Madame! I am at your mercy!' he declared, throwing himself to his knees.

Looking up, he suppressed a sigh at the sight of the hard-faced madam preparing to unlace her dress.

'Twelve or fifteen women?' she said in a hoarse whisper. 'What, then, might you be capable of with just one?'

The Marquise de Pompadour peered out into the night through the barely parted curtains of her carriage. In the darkness, the gateway with its pilasters decorated with gilt bronze stags seemed to taunt her.

Her mind filled with memories of the first years of her relations with the king. She had tried to conquer his incurable ennui by never offering him the same woman twice. One day, she had received her royal lover dressed as a simple village girl, for a rustic picnic on a cloth spread directly on the ground. On other occasions she had been a lady of Imperial Rome, reclining on her bed, or a Spaniard, or an androgynous page. She had made herself up as a Pierrot, with flour whitening her cheeks, and red paint on her lips. Each evening, she had organized intimate suppers with guests from a carefully selected circle of close friends, for his relaxation and entertainment. She had ridden out hunting with him, and built the king his own theatre. Nothing worked. When the excitement was over, the king's mood would darken, and he would sink once more into his never-ending lassitude.

Violent exercise and dissipation were essential to dispel the king's black moods. When he lacked either, his anxiety became unbearable. His unquenchable urge for new adventures and fresh, juvenile meat had to be satisfied. She had introduced—without success—a new diet calculated to warm her own somewhat cool temperament: chocolate with three types of vanilla and ambergris, truffles, celery soup and elixirs provided by a string of charlatans. Weary of her efforts, she had made arrangements for the house in the Parc-aux-Cerfs. She had been the favourite for thirteen years; she had done everything for the king, including taking on the mantle of the Royal Madam.

Just then, she spotted a silhouette slipping away from the building with an agility that spoke of long experience in such matters. She lifted the curtain and signalled for the figure to climb aboard. Casanova hesitated a moment, upon recognizing her, then greeted her respectfully and joined her inside the carriage.

'Madame, I am deeply honoured—'

She dismissed his words with a wave of the hand, and issued a brief command. The coachman cracked his whip. Casanova waited in deference, for the marquise to signal her permission to speak. She was the king's favourite, after all. He watched her closely, though he was careful to disguise the fact. His instinct told him that everything he had heard was true. Frigid: that was exactly what she was. For a moment, the arch-seducer reflected on the feat he knew he could accomplish—revealing her true sensuality to the second lady of France, after the queen. And immediately he decided against it. He was prepared to take risks with a woman for whom he felt a measure of desire, but this woman prompted no such feelings. She was unappetizing, he decided, despite her regal air.

She was past thirty, but still beautiful. Casanova had never seen her in the flesh before, only in paint. Nattier had painted her as Diana the Huntress, Carle van Loo as a Sultana, and then as a shepherdess, and Drouais as an embroideress. As a result, the original before him now was somewhat different from the woman of his imagination.

She was taller than average, and her dark blonde hair framed a near-perfect oval face with large, prominent eyes of indeterminate colour. Her features were soft and regular, and her lips parted in the most charming of smiles, to reveal fine white teeth. In spite of the many cares on her shoulders, her face remained open and amiable. Her health was fragile, and from morning till night, she was forced to present a smiling face to her friends and enemies alike and attend to the king's pleasure. Louis XV's maniacal egotism brooked not the slightest murmur of complaint from his entourage. The royal pleasure took priority over all else. One evening, overcome with fatigue, she had begged to be excused. The king had asked if she was suffering from a fever. When she told him she was not, he had ordered her down on her knees!

Now, her exhaustion was plain to see. Her blonde hair had faded, and patches of eczema had appeared on her face. Wrinkles clawed at the corners of her eyes, which were ringed with blueish circles. The king had walled up the secret staircase that once connected their two apartments. He felt nothing for her now but the deepest friendship. It was said the marquise kept a register in which she recorded all the king's adventures and infatuations, suffering in silence until she was able to score through the name of the person, when she fell from favour. She lived her life constantly on the alert, an existence that might drive any woman to despair, but not her, Jeanne Poisson, Marquise de Pompadour.

'Chevalier de Seingalt—'

She had broken the silence, conscious that Casanova, skilled courtier and man of the world, would not risk being the first to speak.

And so here he is, before me, she thought. *The famous Casanova. Here like all the others, with his obsequious air, ready to serve me, or betray my trust. Watch him—he has that light in his eye, that calm assurance. He is no novice, from what they say. He knows all the uses and abuses of this world. But I can handle him.*

'I have been waiting for you,' she said.

Casanova was unable to conceal his surprise. The marquise gave an ironic smile.

'Do you honestly think you can enter the Parc-aux-Cerfs as easily as all that? The footmen came to warn me the moment you set foot inside the house.'

'And you rushed here in an instant?' asked Casanova, sceptically. He had lost none of his lucidity.

The marquise was unperturbed. Truly, these people had ice in their veins, as Casanova knew only too well.

'They tell me you're a Venetian,' she said. 'Are you really from down there?'

'Venice is not *down there*, Madame la Marquise, it is *up here!*' Casanova tapped his temple.

For a moment, La Pompadour's lip trembled very slightly, and Casanova feared he had been too impertinent by far. He had expected anything but the sudden confidence that followed, the fruit of the marquise's profoundly disheartened state.

'The king is indifferent to everything; nothing truly interests him.'

Casanova froze. He devoured choice morsels of gossip,

but he would happily have gone without this. The marquise stared at him coldly.

'You're wondering why I have told you this? Some men, like you, have an understanding of human nature. The king suffers from acute ennui. It is his affliction.'

A severe coughing fit interrupted her words. Casanova's discomfort increased at the sound.

'Ennui,' she continued, catching her breath. 'Ennui, and a crippling fear of death.'

She sighed. Her features betrayed her immense weariness.

'Louis yawns after making love,' she said. 'Does that ever happen to you, Chevalier?'

The Venetian shook his head.

'You are a most fortunate man,' she sighed. 'But perhaps my temperament is not suited to his.'

Casanova translated: *I am frigid, and past pretending!*

'I betray no secret,' La Pompadour continued, 'if I tell you that the king has constant need of the pleasures of the flesh. And that has allowed some ladies to set traps for him…'

There was a heavy silence. Then she sighed:

'I do not want to lose the king.'

Casanova sat in silence, reflecting that this woman had captured Louis XV with all the artifices and wiles known to woman. She was frigid, but had simulated transports of ecstasy in their love-making. Neglected, she had transformed herself into the royal madam. She had pretended to share the king's passion for hunting, and cards, when she hated both. No indeed: this woman was determined not to lose the thing she had fought so hard to obtain.

'What do you ask of me, Madame la Marquise?' he asked in deferential tones.

For the first time, she looked into his face, and the Venetian fell under the spell of her large eyes.

'Be at my service, Chevalier. You will not regret it.'

Casanova hid his discomfort and affected a knowing look. He was capable of weighing up a person's self-esteem to the last ounce. The marquise's was boundless, he could see that. There could be no question of vexing her with a show of hesitation, or excessive reflection on the matter, before giving his answer.

'What must I do?'

'Your friend Volnay, the Inspector of Strange and Unexplained Deaths, is in charge of an investigation that is very close to my heart. Keep me informed as to its progress, at every stage. I will see to it that you are admitted to me, day and night.'

Casanova's mind raced. 'Day and night,' La Pompadour had said. But the marquise's icy expression dispelled any confusion.

'Your loyalty and discretion will be total,' she commanded. 'If you disappoint me, I'll have you sent to the Bastille, and you will see the light of day only through the bars of a cell.'

Casanova acquiesced, submissively.

'Be assured, Madame la Marquise, you will find in me your most loyal servant. I will spare no zeal in your service. I offer nothing but my arms and my blood, and they are yours, with joy in my heart.'

A little theatrical, but uttered with conviction. The marquise was no fool, but she received his speech with a smile of such warm encouragement that Casanova took her hand, and kissed it. For a second, he thought she might slap him, but her outrage and exasperation were quickly transformed into a most charming look.

'I am sure you will serve me well, Chevalier.'

She knocked firmly, once, on the side of the coach. The carriage drew to a halt. The Chevalier de Seingalt understood that he must climb down. He found himself in a dark, unfamiliar street. The coachman cracked his whip and the vehicle lurched heavily before going on its way.

'A plague on the great and powerful of this world! We are mere animals in their eyes: they pick us up and set us down at will!' Casanova muttered to himself angrily. 'This place is blacker than the Devil's own arse—I might be in hell itself for all she cares! And me, like some pathetic lackey, "Yes Madame, no Madame!" I can deploy my talents till I'm fit to burst, but there will always be something between me and such as them: the lack of a title, and the blood of a few ancestors in some godforsaken wooden stockade, centuries ago! One day, the people will see them all hang!'

He walked through the deserted streets, trusting to instinct and his innate sense of direction. The Rue du Hasard and the Rue des Mauvais-Garçons forced an ironic grin—chance and bad boys, indeed. After half an hour, he found himself on the Rue Saint-Louis. His carriage was still waiting, and he breathed a sigh of relief. The wheel was fixed. He would ride home to some well-deserved rest, and above all a decent meal, for his adventure had sharpened his appetite.

At the sound of iron-clad carriage wheels clattering over the cobbles, Casanova threw himself into the shadows. He saw a coach draw up in front of the gates to the royal house of pleasure. A distinguished-looking figure leant down for an instant, to speak a few words to the porter. He recognized the man's face. The Comte de Saint-Germain!

IX

La Pompadour, the Belle Marquise,
Brings many a courtier to his knees...

ANONYMOUS

Dawn. Rising with the first cockcrow, thousands made their way to Versailles, their place of work. To the right of the palace, a vast, green and pleasant plain reached to the horizon and beyond, dotted with windmills. In front, the road was crammed with riders and vehicles. The air was vibrant with the loud cries of the carters and the cracking of whips. When Volnay arrived, the palace courtyards were already filled with carriages and teams of horses delivering the courtiers and petitioners. The exasperated outriders yelled and swore at one another. Impassive, the inspector pushed his way through, walking as if in a dream, but making straight for the palace grounds.

All at once, the gardens of Versailles lay before him, the palace's terraces bright with flowerbeds, gilt bronze balustrades and the play of the fountains, rising and falling in a milk-white mist. He gazed for a moment at the enamel-bright blooms, then at the cleverly arranged jets in the water basins. Nymphs and Tritons cavorted, spouting sheaves of white spray into the sky. Gods and mortals revelled in illicit pleasures, disporting themselves in the stone-rimmed pools. His eyes followed the perspective of the rows of box hedges, and the avenues of fine sand, more neatly combed than a lady's hair. A world of order and beauty. And suddenly, everything seemed too straight, too perfect, to Volnay's eye. Nothing of all this was real, or true. It was all a carefully maintained illusion.

The harsh experience of life had shown him that Nature was curved and sinuous. The right angle was a product of the hand of man. Volnay turned his back on the naked nymphs, without regret.

The inspector wore his hair tied with a ribbon at the nape of his neck, unlike the royal courtiers, who wore short wigs, powdered white to conceal the difference in their ages. His doublet was of dark velvet, and he wore a hat decorated with a white plume. His flannel cape was fastened with a luxurious, diamond-headed pin. The ensemble was new, and well made, and yet it seemed to Volnay that he could scarcely have looked more laughably out of place if he had strolled around stark naked. The men were resplendent in their elegance, and the ladies' dresses were elaborate, architectural constructions, sophisticated and lightweight. Their gigantic coiffures were decorated with golden chariots, baskets of fruit carved from precious gems, or entire landscapes—great, towering artworks beneath which their faces quite disappeared. The Court was a temple of fine manners and sophistication, too, as Volnay discovered when his clumsy greetings drew a cool response from the beautiful, diamond-bedecked ladies.

He walked the length of the great mirrored gallery, splashed with the reflected light of its chandeliers. Above him, the lavishly painted vault extended over thousands of square feet. Allegories and heroic exploits were depicted against azure skies. The inspector narrowed his eyes, dazzled by the sunlight blazing on the gallery's gilded decorations.

His grave, austere appearance nonetheless impressed the king's officer, to whom Volnay handed his letter. Whether they had been summoned to the royal presence or not, all visitors met with the same fate—a long wait under the indifferent gaze of the Greek gods and goddesses overhead, while the sun embraced the marbled hall with its warm rays. Stoically,

Volnay waited until two o'clock in the afternoon, keeping boredom at bay by enumerating the colours in the paintings lining the walls: cream, beige, rose, sand, ivory, Veronese green, crimson…

At last, he was admitted to one of the king's offices. The royal desk was of Chinese lacquer. Mirrors lined the walls, their joints masked by magnificently worked, gilded flowers. The panelling was painted with small, picturesque subjects, picked out in gold and silver. The monarch dispensed orders to one of his servants. His coat and jerkin were richly embroidered with silver and gold thread, sequins and gems. Despite his magnificent appearance, Louis XV seemed dry and aloof, thought Volnay. The king glanced quickly at his visitor, and his eye was grey, dull and glassy. His demeanour communicated a total lack of interest or compassion for the human race.

At length, Louis XV dismissed his servant and turned his icy face to Volnay. He had just returned from one of the interminable hunting expeditions with which he sought to quell his burning sensuality. He treated his women as simple objects of desire, and abandoned them without regret, but the sins of the flesh terrified him, too, for he lived in fear of the Devil. The eternal contradiction between the king's vices and his near-obsessive fear of death was a source of unending torment.

One foot in hell, already, thought Volnay, beneath the mask of his impassive expression.

'Come closer, Chevalier, over here,' said the king impatiently. 'Monsieur de Sartine has given me a report of your business of the corpse without a face.'

'One of your wig-makers, sire, Mademoiselle Hervé.'

'Yes, yes.' The king's dismissive tone betrayed his complete indifference.

At closer quarters, Volnay observed the king's leaden complexion, and the sardonic, almost dissolute smile playing at the corners of his lips. The result of his assiduous cultivation of women of low life? It was said the king delighted in their foul-mouthed talk, and that he liked to give his whores nicknames—'Rag' or 'Scrap'—a measure of the esteem he felt for them.

'Chevalier,' said Louis XV, 'you saved my life once, and I trust you implicitly. But you're playing a dangerous game.'

Volnay stood beneath the royal gaze, unsure what to think. The king's character was secretive and impenetrable. Who could truly exercise a hold over him? Only La Pompadour.

'Will you tell me the truth, Volnay?'

The inspector blinked nervously.

'Yes, sire.'

'There are unpleasant rumours circulating about me in Paris, are there not?'

There could be no mistake—this was a test, and Volnay's answer was frank:

'They say that you snatch children, to satisfy your desires.'

The monarch's stare hardened alarmingly.

'And what do you think?'

'That these rumours are in part due to the many cases of children and vagabonds who are taken and sent to Your Majesty's colonies,' replied Volnay evenly, without looking up.

The king gave a start of surprise. He frowned as he tried to discern a possible hint of insolence in Volnay's words, then shrugged and turned his back. Volnay remained where he stood, unsure quite how to proceed.

The monarch walked to the window and gazed out, with a bored air. Suddenly, he stiffened. His attention focused on a group walking outside in the gardens. Volnay stepped silently to one side, to get a better view of the object of the royal interest. The king was watching a group that included a very young girl, barely more than a child. He understood. The king was a wild beast, forever on the lookout for fresh prey.

'Sire…'

The king turned, and his expression was hard as ice. His heavily lidded eyes were utterly without life.

'Find the murderer of these little white chicks but report your discoveries to no one but me.'

Little white chicks. Dear God, in the eyes of our king, we are mere livestock.

Louis XV returned to his desk, took a sheet of paper and began to write.

'This letter places you solely in my service for the duration of your investigation. You will report to no one but me. My steward will bring you sufficient funds for your requirements.'

Volnay's heart beat fast. Under the direct orders of the king! Sartine would not like that.

'Sire, permit me to ask if I might question your first valet of the bedchamber, Le Bel? He may have valuable information concerning Mademoiselle Hervé.'

The king span around.

'Question Le Bel? The very idea!'

He shook his head and said again:

'The very idea!'

'Sire, this is of great importance for the investigation. I need to know more about the victim.'

'The victim? Ah, yes…'

His tone hardened.

'Wait outside in the antechamber. I'll send him to you, but you are not to bother him excessively.'

Volnay felt suddenly as if he had ceased to exist in the king's eyes. Louis's dark melancholy, his irrepressible ennui, had swept over him once more. He stared vacantly into space.

He held out the letter with no sign of irritation or anger, merely indifference. Respectfully, Volnay took his leave.

When the police officer had left the room, Louis XV pulled a bell rope. Le Bel slipped into the office like a faun. He had been waiting for the summons behind a door.

'Le Bel,' said the king, 'I have seen a ravishingly beautiful child in the Marble Courtyard, thirteen years of age, blonde as wheat, wearing a blue dress. She was walking between two women. Try to discover who she is, and bring her to me.'

'At once, sire.'

The king pressed his forehead to the windowpane.

'I am like the ogre of folklore,' he sighed. 'I hunger after fresh meat, but I am cursed never to be sated. Never! Do the pangs of hunger plague you still, Le Bel, when you have eaten your fill?'

The first valet fidgeted uncomfortably. He had no idea how to respond.

'Go, Le Bel. Go and bring her to me here, for a drink of chocolate!' said the king, at length. 'Ah, I was forgetting… and when that's done, you will see the Chevalier de Volnay, that police inspector. For strange and unexplained deaths. He's investigating the murder of a young woman with no face.'

He turned and added, in an offhand tone:

'Mademoiselle Hervé, were you aware?'

Le Bel swallowed hard.

'Sire, permit me to ask what I am to tell him?'

The king raised an eyebrow in surprise.

'Why, nothing, Le Bel. Nothing!'

The Inspector of Strange and Unexplained Deaths sat on a bench seat waiting for someone to fetch Monsieur Le Bel, first valet of the king's bedchamber, a person of considerable power and influence, for no one lived at closer quarters to the monarch than he. Time seemed to stretch out for ever, like the marshmallow sweets of his childhood. Here at Versailles, no one cared how long you were made to wait.

One day, sooner or later, he thought, *someone must put a match to all of this, and hang the king from the nearest lamp post. But patience. The people's suffering cannot continue much longer, and enlightened minds aplenty are working to awaken them.*

Inevitably, affectionately, his thoughts turned to the monk. Throughout his youth, Volnay had chosen the path of violent action, fighting the vagaries of power and the accident of birth by joining the Brotherhood, in secret, while the monk had taken the path of wisdom and learning, to open the minds of others. That said, even the monk was capable of drawing his sword, on occasion, and dispatching his fellow man in the time it took to say two paternosters and an Ave Maria.

Volnay smiled sadly. He knew he was born to a solitary existence, shunning life in society. His intelligence, and his powers of deduction, had found the perfect outlet in the solving of complicated cases, and his values found expression in the service of justice and truth. Besides his habit-wearing colleague, his only friend was the magpie, to whom the monk had diligently taught the very direst oaths and heretical propositions.

After an hour's wait, Volnay was shown into a small salon, where a glass of cordial stood waiting. He did not touch it.

I want nothing from these people.

A door opened, and Le Bel entered the room. There was nothing remarkable in the man's looks, but his attitude oozed smug complacency, and an exaggerated self-confidence.

Rumours about the man were rife. It was said that once, when the royal park was filled with dense crowds for an evening of festivities, the king had spotted a fourteen-year-old girl being crushed and jostled in the throng. Enflamed by her adorable little face, he had ordered his valets to extricate her and bring her to him. Next day, Le Bel, first valet of the king's bedchamber and royal pimp-in-chief, was sent to purchase the girl from her aunt, a candle-maker. The aunt struck a hard bargain, and eventually sold her niece for fifty louis d'or and a contract to supply candles to the royal chapel. The girl was a virgin, and so, naturally, Le Bel saw to her deflowering personally. For eight days, this vile individual trained her in the service of a gentleman's pleasure, to His Majesty's subsequent delight.

This, then, was the slime-coated, slug-like creature before him now.

'Monsieur Le Bel,' he said, icily. 'I have a few questions for you.'

'Here?' said the other man in astonishment.

'Why ever not? We are alone.'

The valet smiled fleetingly.

'Clearly you do not know Versailles! Follow me.'

Once again, Volnay found himself walking down a series of corridors to a smaller, less richly decorated room. The window enjoyed the same view over the gardens, with their neatly trimmed avenues of box.

'I want to talk to you about Mademoiselle Hervé.'

Le Bel lowered his gaze in a faked show of deference.

'But I know nothing about her.'

'It was you who introduced her to the king!'

Le Bel's expression turned to outrage.

'You should know, Chevalier, that the king's private affairs are no concern of yours.'

For a moment, Volnay toyed with the idea of questioning him about the second victim, Marcoline, the occasional boarder at the Parc-aux-Cerfs, but he knew he was facing a wall. There was no sense in revealing one's hand more than necessary.

'Do you know of anybody who knew Mademoiselle Hervé?'

'I have told you, I know nothing about her at all,' repeated Le Bel, obstinately.

Volnay saw he would get nothing more.

Deep in thought, Volnay descended the great marble staircase, running his hand along the balustrade. At first, he failed to notice the gentleman waiting for him at the bottom of the steps, holding a plumed hat in his hands.

'Chevalier de Volnay?'

The man flung back the grey silk cape he wore around his shoulders and bowed. He was young, and his face wore a frank, open smile. His manners were polished, his smile courteous. He addressed Volnay with a measure of deference.

'Chevalier, the Marquise de Pompadour would be delighted to make your acquaintance.'

Volnay followed him without a word to the marquise's private apartments. All was delicacy and refinement. The rosewood furniture was inlaid with precious marquetry, and the armchairs were upholstered in blue silk, with a pattern of intertwined foliage. Perfume burners dispensed an agreeable aroma of incense and roses. On a side table, he noticed a copy of *Il pastor fido*, a tragicomedy by Guarini, hinting at La Pompadour's taste for the theatre and acting. The marquise wore a pink dress with a ruched and flounced overskirt of white satin, decorated with appliquéd threadwork and fringed flowers. She rose as he entered and presented her hand to be kissed. A tiny hand, burning hot. It was said that La Pompadour was in fragile health, constantly on the alert, at the beck and call of an egotistical monarch, and ever watchful of her innumerable enemies at Court.

'Chevalier de Volnay, I have been so impatient to meet you!'

Her practised eye quickly gauged the inspector's plain but elegant clothes, but she lingered on his face, as impassive and inexpressive as stone. She was unsurprised. Her spies had forewarned her:

He takes no sides, has no friends. An indefinable creature. Nothing seems to move him.

Volnay was laying eyes on the marquise for the first time. She had been beautiful, he decided, but what remained of her considerable charm was cruelly diminished by her extreme pallor. Volnay had heard it said that she had suffered the torments of Calvary on the deaths of her daughter and father, a few years before. To his great surprise, she produced a large sheet of paper and addressed him vehemently:

'Perhaps you have something to say about the effectiveness of His Majesty's police! Yet again, the servants found this pinned to the door of my mansion in Paris, this morning.'

The poster read: *Residence of the King's Whore.*

Volnay nodded in sympathy.

'This is truly scandalous, Madame, but it is not within my remit. I am in charge of—'

'Strange and unexplained deaths in Paris, and nothing more.' La Pompadour cut him short. 'I know. Must I kill someone to merit your attention?'

Volnay froze, but she seemed to recover herself just as quickly. Was she trying to throw him off his guard? All of a sudden, her attitude changed. She enveloped him in her warm gaze, and gave an exquisite smile.

'People have praised your exceptional talent at solving tangled mysteries. And with the use of new scientific methods known only to yourself.'

She seemed to be deploying all her charm to force him into submission and lure him into her camp. Volnay knew she could be dangerous, but she was not cruel, and was often compassionate, provided one did not stand in her way.

> La Pompadour, the Belle Marquise,
> Brings many a courtier to his knees.

'And so you are in charge of this extremely delicate inquiry into the death of a poor young girl with no face,' she observed.

'Alas, I have no clues to follow. Nothing at all, for the moment, I am sorry to say.'

'Really nothing?'

'Nothing.'

She was getting nowhere with this stern-faced policeman.

There it is, she thought. *One upright, honest man in all Paris and here he stands, before me, when what I need is a sinuous type with a spine like a snake. But integrity may go hand-in-hand with loyalty. He may not be such a bad choice after all. My adversaries stand little chance with him, and if he tips in my favour, there will be nothing more to say.*

With that in mind, her tone shifted to a more direct threat.

'Your role in the police force is quite unprecedented, and it hangs by a single thread: the goodwill of His Majesty the king. Monsieur de Sartine is unhappy at having a new inspector thrust upon him, for strange and unexplained deaths. He holds it against you, as you are no doubt aware?'

She leant closer, and Volnay was overwhelmed by her perfume, as if she had chosen to share the sumptuous bouquet of white flowers, with soft, velvety base notes, with him alone. Her tone was confidential now. That of a person of power, sparing a moment of her precious time to enlighten a subordinate whom she has judged trustworthy.

'Monsieur de Sartine is plotting to be appointed lieutenant general of police for the whole of France.'

Her gaze lingered over his face, and she added, with a hint of regret:

'Alas, if he succeeds, it will mark the end of your very particular status.'

She fixed him with a kindly expression, and Volnay knew what she was about to say.

'That said, everything in this kingdom depends on His Majesty's goodwill. A word at the right moment is all that's required... but do any of your friends have the king's ear?'

Volnay understood very well what she was after. He shook his head regretfully. The marquise's expression was radiant.

'What an idiot you are! Why would you not befriend me?'

She spoke now like a powerful minister to a valued but somewhat obstinate servant. Volnay struggled to contain himself as he replied:

'That would indeed be my dearest wish, Madame!'

Something in her attitude suggested that she had relaxed, very slightly.

'Well then, Chevalier, enough of this hide-and-seek. Who is the young woman whose face was torn off?'

The victim's identity remained a relative secret, but Volnay judged that it was known to too many already for the name not to have reached the ear of the most powerful person in France after the king himself. This, then, was a test of his loyalty.

'She was Mademoiselle Hervé, one of the king's wigmakers.'

The marquise did not so much as blink, but she rewarded Volnay with the smile of a schoolmaster at the sight of an unruly pupil stepping back into line, at last.

'What did you find on her body?'

He will lie to me, she thought, *but I know now that he has it in his possession!*

Volnay was not expecting so direct an opening. Rapidly, his analytical mind furnished the reply. Too many people knew now about the letter Mademoiselle Hervé had been carrying.

'I found a sealed letter on her person, Madame.'

She gazed at him, unblinking.

'Have you read it?'

'No, Madame,' he replied evenly. 'Because I knew the time would come when it would be reclaimed.'

The marquise considered him in silence.

Intelligent answer… He thinks carefully, and treads cautiously. Does he speak the truth? I must try to find out more. Really, this is a most remarkable man!

'You have just seen the king. What did he say to you?' she asked.

'He wishes me to report directly to him, in my investigation.'

'Do you know why?'

'Doubtless in order to wrest me from under Sartine's control.'

'Why?' the marquise insisted, coldly.

A second's hesitation was a second too long with La Pompadour.

'Because you asked him?'

The man's a devil!

'And why would I do that?' she asked.

'The letter may concern you closely, and your trust in Sartine is limited…'

She leant towards him, her eyes gleaming.

'Do I take it that you have scant esteem for Paris's chief of police?'

'Indeed, Madame, I have none.'

Her pale eyes assessed him in silence.

Why such frankness, at times?

'And whom do you trust?' she asked, archly.

'No one, Madame, other than my colleague the monk, and

194

my magpie. A very fine bird—she speaks Latin quite as well as she speaks French. She would delight you, I'm sure.'

The marquise looked at him in surprise, then gave a light shrug of the shoulders.

Books, an intelligent bird, a heretical monk who was almost burnt at the stake, and the corpses in his morgue. Is this truly the extent of this man's society?

'Have you mentioned the letter to anyone?'

'No one, Madame.'

His tone lacked conviction, but it would pass, Volnay thought. Again, the marquise took her time before asking:

'Can you bring it to me, here?'

He will tell me he's burnt it, but he has not, I'm certain.

'Yes, Madame.'

Such a disconcerting creature! Or else very clever… Well, let's be done with it.

'Why go to see Monsieur the Comte de Saint-Germain?'

Another test of his loyalty, but Volnay knew the ties of friendship between the comte and La Pompadour. He knew how to react, and his reply was cunning.

'I discovered that Mademoiselle Hervé had gone with you to visit the comte, on the night she died. I tried to find out more from him, while not confronting him directly on the subject. The visit brought me no further information.'

The marquise rose quickly. Volnay did the same.

'Bring me the letter this evening, after eleven o'clock, to my mansion. You will be handsomely rewarded.'

Volnay bowed.

'I ask no reward, Madame; I am merely doing my duty.'

And he withdrew, under La Pompadour's thoughtful gaze.

Volnay emerged into a courtyard crowded with carriages and horses, and looked about for his own vehicle and team, which he had entrusted to a groom that morning. He sensed a presence close behind him, followed immediately by the press of a dagger against his back.

'Chevalier,' said a soft but firm voice, 'make no sudden movement. You will turn to your right, then climb into this carriage. I will prick you and push you in myself if I must!'

Volnay cast a brief glance over his shoulder. He saw a man dressed in black, with an upturned collar. The features were familiar, and with them the milk-white, almost translucent pallor of the skin, affording glimpses, here and there, of the blood pulsing just beneath. The lifeless eyes confirmed his identity: Wallace, the man who had attacked him at his home. And there could be no Wallace without his master, Father Ofag, and the Devout Party.

'Oh, but after you, I pray, Monsieur Wallace!' he cried loudly, in mock indignation. 'We shall go together to see dear Father Ofag!'

To his satisfaction, the surprised faces of a number of courtiers and valets turned in their direction. He felt Wallace stiffen with anger, then contain himself. He climbed into the carriage. Wallace installed himself beside him, keeping the point of the dagger firmly against his ribs. The carriage windows were veiled, and Volnay felt quite disorientated when he climbed down from the vehicle once more. He found himself in a courtyard reached through a pointed, Gothic archway. He observed a central doorway with a round opening covered by an iron grille. The details might help him to locate the place if he escaped this encounter alive. He was taken to an austere building, its facade punctuated by isolated sash windows. A dark, deserted passageway led to a massive door guarded by a man with a sharply pointed chin. Wallace pushed him roughly inside.

Volnay looked around him. The room was austere and cold, such that its decor seemed to have been devised with precisely that end in mind. The only visible note of luxury was a richly illuminated psalter lying open on the worktable at an image of the naked body of Mary Magdalene, thinly veiled by her own, long golden hair, being transported to heaven by a flight of angels. The repentant sinner's finely modelled flesh, languid pose and rapt expression suggested divine ecstasy and extreme sensuality, in equal measure.

Hunched in a tall armchair, a man with grey hair and a smooth, infantile face stared at him through half-closed eyes. His hands were buried in his sleeves, as if to keep them out of sight. His demeanour was honeyed and thoroughly unwholesome, thought Volnay. Wallace left his side and whispered something in the man's ear. He seemed annoyed, then impressed as he pursed his lips and looked in Volnay's direction. Plainly, the henchman had described how the inspector had shouted out loud in the courtyard in Versailles that they were paying a visit to Father Ofag, for this was he. Volnay took advantage of his release to step forward, holding his chin high.

'You are holding an inspector of the king's police against his will!' he thundered.

The man gave an elegant, rounded gesture of reply. His features struggled to affect an expression of welcome.

'Greetings Chevalier. I am Father Ofag. Who is holding you, may I ask?' His tone was sickly sweet. 'You are my guest, and free to leave whenever you please. Though you might do better to listen, first, to what I have to say.'

He shot a troubled glance at the psalter and clapped it shut before turning to Wallace.

'You may leave us, my friend. Do go on, Monsieur the Inspector of Strange and Unexplained Deaths.'

Volnay proceeded with caution. He knew he must tread very carefully indeed.

'What do you want to talk to me about?' he asked.

'About a letter, taken from a corpse.'

Father Ofag lifted his eyelids to reveal a pair of near-translucent, pearl-grey eyes pierced by large, dark pupils. Volnay lowered his gaze and saw a chaplet hidden in his capacious sleeves. Ofag seemed to be counting off its beads as they spoke.

'I gave it to the Marquise de Pompadour with my own hand, this very afternoon,' replied Volnay icily.

He had answered almost without thinking. If Wallace and his accomplices, doubtless lurking behind the door, believed him to be still in possession of the letter, his days were very probably numbered. He might have claimed to have handed the letter to the king, but the Devout Party's spies kept a close eye on the latter, as he well knew. To answer that the letter was now in the hands of La Pompadour, their sworn enemy, was enough to prevent them from verifying the truth of his statement.

'Have you read it?' asked the priest.

'It was sealed,' said Volnay, unflinchingly. 'It was safer for me to hand it over intact.'

'Safer, indeed,' Ofag nodded, with a thin smile. 'Safer for an honest man, but not for anyone else…'

The priest observed him attentively, with a mixed expression of innocence and cunning.

'You are an honest man, are you not? That's what they say about you, at any rate. You may be telling the truth, but how shall I know? I could have you tortured, just to be sure…'

He intoned the words with the calm serenity of a man reciting his paters and his Ave Marias.

'Tortured?' retorted Volnay. 'You, a man of God? He would never pardon you, and neither would I! You would be left with no solution but to dispose of my body, but my disappearance would not go unnoticed. I have just emerged from an audience with the king, and after that, his favourite. Questions would be asked. And as you know, I made certain not to accompany your henchman without a word or two to the assembled company.'

Father Ofag nodded approvingly.

'Indeed. Your instincts served you well, at Versailles.'

The priest swept the air with his hand, as if to dismiss unpleasant thoughts.

'Killing, torturing... I prefer to chase such vile things from my mind. I would far rather count myself your friend!'

He smiled and added, thoughtfully:

'Perhaps you have been handsomely rewarded by La Pompadour for handing over the letter intact. Honest and clever, too...'

Volnay gave no answer: apparently, none was expected.

'You left the letter intact,' Ofag persisted, 'and so you must have seen the seal.'

Volnay knew that a show of cooperation was essential in such circumstances. He replied without hesitation.

'It bore the royal seal.'

Father Ofag struggled to conceal his astonishment. He thought for a moment, peering at Volnay all the while through narrowed lids.

'To summarize the facts,' he said, joining his hands in front of him on the table, inside his sleeves, as if in prayer. 'A wig-maker in the service of the king and the entourage of La Pompadour is killed and disfigured. Ha! You see? I know a great deal. Has it not occurred to you that the crime might have been ordered by the marquise? She lives in constant fear of a younger, more attractive woman taking her place in the king's affections. Imagine what the king's letter might contain: a noble title for the girl in question, her appointment to a position of power at Court, the acknowledgement of a bastard, if ever she was with child, and who knows what besides?'

Volnay pretended to play along, shaking his head.

'Given the king's notorious appetite for young girls, La Pompadour might as well try to hold back the ocean with her bare hands.'

'But perhaps this time the king was passionately in love? Women have driven men to lose their reason since Adam and Eve! Our flesh is not for martyrdom alone.'

Volnay stared at Ofag in surprise. The man was in a state of high excitement.

'And the second murder?'

Father Ofag frowned.

'A warning from La Pompadour to any aspiring mistresses of the king?' he ventured. 'Such an appalling death would suffice to cool the ardour of many. It would likely affect the king very badly, too.'

He fell silent. Volnay knew he was thinking of the king and his obsessive terror of death—the one thing that ensured the Devout Party remained in the royal favour, despite La Pompadour's profound aversion to their cause.

'Do you seek to harm the marquise, by means of this letter?' asked Volnay.

Ofag's eyes narrowed to fine slits, filtering a gleam of pure hatred.

'La Pompadour, first whore of France! Of course we seek to bring her down!'

He hissed the words like a serpent. The king's favourite was a source of vexation to the nobility and the clergy, thought Volnay. But not by virtue of her position at Court. What irked them most were her bourgeois origins. The first whore of France, as the Devout Party liked to call her, had established herself as a patron of artists and freethinkers, nonetheless, and Volnay was grateful to her for that, though he abhorred the official role of the favourite itself.

'Jeanne Poisson!' Ofag hissed the Marquise de Pompadour's name. 'Remember, Inspector, who she truly is: the daughter of a fishmonger! A cold fish indeed! With dead eyes and a scaly hide…'

Volnay blinked briefly. Ofag was wrong, Jeanne Poisson was the daughter of a financier's clerk—her family name left her open to any number of facile, callous puns in the mouths of her enemies.

'What do you want of me?' he asked calmly.

Ofag shot him a calculating stare. He had the eyes of a fanatic, but an intelligent fanatic, capable of considering everything in its proper perspective. He was weighing up Volnay in his mind.

'Truth be told, I do not know what to make of you, Chevalier de Volnay. Who is it you serve?'

'I serve the king, of course.'

Ofag shrugged.

'We all serve the king, each of us in his own way. Either you are on the side of La Pompadour, with her coterie of heretic philosophers, bound for the eternal bonfire, or you are on the side of the Faith.'

'I'm nothing but a simple police officer. Who cares what I think?'

Ofag jumped to his feet.

'We care, Volnay! Us! You've heard the verse doing the rounds all over Paris!'

He closed his eyes as if to call the words, and recited them all at once:

> 'Versailles, of old the height of taste
> Now seethes with vermin,
> Lay it waste!'

Ofag looked up, and beheld Volnay's manifest lack of interest. Clearly, the lines had left the inspector unmoved. He frowned.

'You may be indifferent to the ills of France, but less so, I hope, to my arguments. You know the king's temperament…'

It was Volnay's turn to frown. He had not expected to hear this.

'The king demands ever-younger girls. Some are barely formed, mere children… God in heaven! Where will it end? And the Marquise de Pompadour supplies them, together with Dominique Le Bel, that pimp in a valet's coat! We must lock her up! She has corrupted the king, Versailles, France itself… She and her enlightened friends have dared to trample the sacred boundaries established by the Faith. They will lead us all to damnation!'

And so Volnay understood the extent of Ofag's intelligence. He hoped to win Volnay to their side by appealing not to his sense of duty, but to his sense of virtue. Clearly, they knew him well enough to see how little he cared for the king, and all his government. But protecting the lives of children was quite another matter.

'Very good.' The inspector had made up his mind. 'Help me, and I'll help you.'

'Ah! You'll agree to an exchange of information? Very good! Very good!'

Ofag's mood brightened visibly.

'Wallace!' he called.

The door opened almost instantly, and Volnay turned to face Ofag's henchman, rather than show his back.

'You heard everything, I take it?' asked Ofag, with a knowing look at the inspector.

'Yes, everything,' said Wallace, evenly.

'In that case, we can explain to the chevalier the concatenation of events that led you to become a front-row witness to murder!'

Wallace gave a swift bow of the head.

'I was following La Pompadour's carriage; she was returning from a visit to the Comte de Saint-Germain.'

He pronounced the name with a shudder of disgust, then continued in the same, toneless voice:

'The carriage stopped for a moment, and a young woman climbed down. It was Mademoiselle Hervé, the king's wig-maker. La Pompadour had just secured her services, doubtless to distance her from the king, because she was a brazen little thing, and liable to pervert him still further.'

'One moment!' Volnay interjected. 'Why were you following the royal favourite's carriage?'

Father Ofag unlaced his fingers and shook his head disapprovingly.

'Don't answer, Wallace!'

He turned to the inspector and glared at him like a furious schoolmaster.

'Your question is quite irrelevant, Inspector! And utterly unconnected to the matter that interests you. Pray continue, my dear Wallace.'

'Mademoiselle Hervé climbed down from the coach. She exchanged a few words with the Marquise de Pompadour, and then the vehicle went on its way,' said Wallace. 'I chose to follow the young woman.'

The small smile playing at the corners of his lips sent shivers down Volnay's spine.

'Sometimes,' he explained, 'in my trade, one needs to follow one's instinct…'

Volnay didn't dare to ask what his trade might be.

'Something in her behaviour intrigued me,' Ofag's servant continued. 'She seemed to be carrying something in her hands, and looking all around her. She seemed impatient and, how can I put this?…'

He struggled to find the right words, and turned to his master.

'Excited?' suggested Ofag, quite unruffled.

'Indeed! That's it!'

Wallace's satisfaction showed in his face. A thin smile lit his cruel lips as he continued his account:

'She hesitated, then, as if she could wait no longer, she hurried into the small courtyard. My first instinct was to follow her, but then I held back, so as not to betray my presence. After a few moments, I heard a terrible scream. It was my turn to hesitate. What if she was not alone? With a lover, perhaps?'

He blushed violently, and Father Ofag cleared his throat.

'I heard a hideous, gargling groan. I froze where I stood,' he went on, with his head lowered. 'I was about to rush forward, when I saw her emerge, staggering and clutching at her face with her hands. She gave a last cry before sinking to the ground. Clouds covered the moon. I heard footsteps, and snatches of conversation. I hid myself, quickly. The man they call Casanova was approaching, with one of his conquests.'

He stood and waited, arms pressed close to his sides, staring straight ahead like a soldier awaiting orders. Father Ofag laced his fingers and turned to the inspector.

'You see, now you know everything. Your turn next…'

Volnay was perplexed.

'What can I tell you that you don't already know?'

He would have to find something, to satisfy the terms of his contract with the Devout Party, concluded just a moment before.

'You could always tell me about your reasons for visiting the Comte de Saint-Germain,' suggested Father Ofag with a treacherous smile.

Truly, thought Volnay, *Paris is a breeding ground for informers and spies. How many are at my heels?*

He decided on a mixture of truth and lies.

'The letter bearing the king's seal was addressed to the Comte de Saint-Germain. And so I decided to pay him a visit to try to discover more, but alas, it was not possible. I bribed one of his servants, and discovered that the Marquise de Pompadour had visited the comte on the evening of Mademoiselle Hervé's death, and that she had probably taken the girl along with her, though she was very probably not introduced to the comte.'

'A letter addressed to the Comte de Saint-Germain!'

Father Ofag's eyes shone with joy.

'This is most... What did we say, Wallace? Exciting! An intimate of La Pompadour's mixed up in all this! I am a passionate follower of Our Lord, and I abhor their kind. Anyone who claims to speak for the dead, or with the dead, is guilty of sacrilege! I'll have Saint-Germain's head, too! The Church denounces his claim to eternal life. Man was driven out of the Garden of Eden, and there is no escape from our mortal condition. Dig there, Chevalier, on that very spot! And come back and tell me what you find. Is that all? Heaven knows, I'm hungry for more—come back quickly with your news. I pray to God that he will ensure your success. Wallace will escort you out.'

'No need. I will find my own way.'

'I'm afraid I must insist.'

They bade one another goodbye, one with unctuous charm, the other somewhat stiffly. The inspector was about to pass through the open door when Ofag called out to him.

'Ah, Chevalier, one last thing. Your friend Chiara D'Ancilla works for the Marquise de Pompadour—were you aware? She is what your people call an informer, is she not? She has been trying to get hold of the letter for the marquise. She must be quite satisfied now. Surely you knew?'

Volnay stood rooted to the spot. His face had turned deathly pale, and the lines of a poem—an ode to treachery—sprang to his mind. He bowed his head coldly and followed Wallace from the room.

Father Ofag smiled and rubbed his hands, adding, as if to himself:

'So it seems you did not know, indeed.'

X

*The prettiest women are always ready to lend their
hand to machinations designed to betray us men!*

CASANOVA

The beggar had acquired nothing but a singular pain in the
backside, after sitting for hours on the irregular cobbles opposite a building with tall windows protected by wrought-iron
grilles. From time to time, he shifted his gaze to the church of
St Martin, some sixty feet away. Once, it had been a church of
the Knights Templar, people said. He was intrigued by a small
statue perched at the top of the central doorway. The figure
represented a demon with a woman's torso, but covered with
hair, bearing a set of horns and leathery wings, like a bat's.

When, at last, the assistant to the Comte de Saint-Germain
passed in front of him, the beggar scratched himself with a
leer of disgust, as if he were covered with vermin, then held
out his hand awkwardly. The assistant paid him no attention
whatsoever. The beggar spat on the ground and gazed after
him. When the man disappeared around a corner, he jumped
to his feet and hurried after him, eager to keep him in sight.

He had kept watch for two days and understood his target's habits now. The streets were thronged with miserable
wretches like him. He passed mostly unnoticed in the crowd,
but once or twice he had been pulled aside, as an unfamiliar
face in the neighbourhood. At those times, the dagger he
kept well hidden, and handled with dexterity, had dissuaded
his opponent from bothering him further.

The habit maketh not the monk, as the old saying went,
and never was a truer word spoken in his case. The monk,

for it was he, followed the comte's assistant at a careful distance. On Rue de Montmorency, they passed in front of number 3, a house of medieval appearance, with a dark, austere facade. The pillars bore the initials, now partly worn away, of the legendary alchemist Nicolas Flamel. The words *Ora et labora* could be seen, carved in relief: 'Prayer and work'. The monk glanced at them with interest, then continued tracking his prey to a rented apartment on Rue des Quatres-Fils. He waited patiently for the assistant to emerge, then hurried down a blind alley to a tiny court-yard, where he threw off his habit and, decently dressed underneath, slipped inside the building. Equipped with a set of keys supplied by Volnay, he opened to door to the assistant's lodgings.

Contrary to the impression of the building's exterior, the rooms were pleasant enough. The door opened straight into a sizeable, well-lit room with large windows and a fine chim-neypiece carved in wood. It was furnished with a long oak table and four chairs, a rosewood cupboard and a chest. Fine tapestries warmed the walls, and the floor was laid with Venetian carpets. They looked new—a recent addition to the decor, it seemed. The monk lifted one corner and examined the condition of the floor tiles underneath. He checked the tapestries, too. They were newly hung: the panelling behind them was the same hue as the rest.

Someone has earned themselves some money quickly, and lately, he thought.

Two doors led to a bedroom and a small laboratory. The bedroom contained a large bed and chest of drawers. A three-branched candlestick stood on a chest of exotic hardwood. The monk glanced into the final room and nodded approv-ingly. Here, too, everything looked clean and well maintained. Test tubes were arranged in order behind a set of scales. The room was lit by a single, tiny dormer window, and a scrubbed furnace glowed faintly in the half-light. He was about to examine it more closely when he was startled by noises at the main door.

How could the comte's assistant be back so soon?

He heard voices and understood that the fellow had gone to fetch someone. In the space of a heartbeat, the monk took stock of his situation. A key was turning in the door. The only solution was to hide under the bed. He hurried to the bedroom and wriggled out of sight, with some difficulty, just as the assistant and his guest entered the main room.

He heard a muffled conversation, then someone pushed open the bedroom door. The monk saw a delectable pair of ankles encased in the most adorable boots, right in front of his nose. The young girl sat down upon the mattress. The comte's assistant seated himself quite properly in the armchair. Hidden from view, the monk listened as he spoke.

'Mademoiselle, the years go by, wrinkles appear and beauty fades like the flowers of the field. The furrows that remain are the work of the Great Gardener above…'

The monk could not see the comte's assistant, but supposed he would be pointing up at the sky.

'But what if the bloom on the rose never faded? What if your beauty, that wondrous gift from heaven, were to survive the passage of time unblemished? A face such as yours, Mademoiselle, deserves to remain just as it is now, a timeless frame for those pretty eyes.'

Under the bed, the monk winced at the pompous, not to say 'flowery', language. He heard the assistant rise from his chair, saw his feet approach and felt the mattress sag under his weight. He was sitting beside the young girl now, and the monk sensed her discomfort. Her boots moved a few inches, as if their owner had shifted her position, to preserve a certain distance between her host and herself, as he continued his bombastic address:

'For beauty is truly a gift from God, is it not? Why then, should God see fit to take it back, after so short a time?'

The young girl heaved an unhappy sigh.

'But,' she objected, 'perhaps it is better this way? If God has so ordered the world…'

The assistant gave an amused chuckle.

'God has also given Mother Nature the power to remedy the problem. The Comte de Saint-Germain, with my help, has found ways to extract and capture Nature's powers, in phials of inestimable value. Oh, of course, he cannot part with them, and offers them only to a few people of the very highest rank. But since I assist him in the preparation of the elixirs, it so happens that I have one here.'

The monk heard the assistant get to his feet and guessed he was fetching the little phial from the top of his desk.

'Here is something truly priceless!' he declared. 'As rare and precious as gold, diamonds, emeralds or opals. A commodity such as many would kill to possess. And this commodity, Mademoiselle, can be yours.'

He boomed the words like a fairground peddler. The monk heard the young girl fidget in embarrassment on the bed.

'My parents have some property and possessions to their name, but I myself have nothing.'

'Nothing? Mademoiselle, you offend against your own charms.'

There was a silence, and the monk felt the girl's awkward embarrassment. The comte's assistant returned to the bed and sat very close to her.

'The sands of time are pouring away fast, like your life, Mademoiselle. The season of roses is so soon past. Permit this humble gardener to give you the benefit of his science.'

'I don't know if I should…'

The monk felt the mattress move. The comte's assistant was doubtless slipping his hand around the girl's waist, leaning still more closely towards her.

'Your face is so sweet, so beautiful… Oh, your skin is so smooth. I do not want you to change. No! Not ever!'

The monk heard a muffled sigh and supposed the two were kissing. He felt their bodies fall across the bed. He shook his head and suffered the rest with a resigned air.

Casanova observed Joinville with circumspection. The wine merchant's broad shoulders had sunk, and he kept his elbows planted firmly on the table, as if fearing to lose his balance. The man had been drinking, and the Venetian judged him incapable of tackling more than one matter at a time.

The pair were in a charming house on Rue du Petit-Bourbon, which Casanova had had the pleasure of visiting before. The walls were covered with rose-pink hangings, and the tables were dimly lit with candles.

The residence was populated by delightful creatures, whose caresses came at a price but were none the less passionate for that. Casanova had come here once with a painter of his acquaintance, who liked to say that the canvas was a flat bed and that a painter's brush stood permanently erect and yearning in the direction of his model. From that evening, Casanova cherished the charming memory of an amorous encounter with two exceptionally lusty young women.

A young girl with rosy cheeks and plump, hungry lips came to pour their drinks—wine for Casanova and beer for his companion. She swayed her hips as she walked, turning every head. Joinville observed her with a sidelong glance, and Casanova made a note to return one day and make her acquaintance more fully.

'She has a fiery temperament, that one,' said Joinville, who had caught his friend's eye. 'She comes twice.'

'Indeed?'

The wine merchant leant closer, his eyes shining.

'There's even a woman here who has a wine stain on her face, yet she commands a very high price!'

'Outward beauty is not all,' said Casanova, simply.

He was becoming impatient. He needed no advice whatsoever when it came to women.

'Well,' he said, 'I found your message, and here I am. Do you have the means to settle your debt?'

The other man gave an arch smile and pulled a sheet of poor-quality paper from his pocket, seemingly fresh from the printer's.

'There,' he said, 'a torrent of libels that will be all over Paris tomorrow morning. Read it, and you'll see that La Pompadour is accused of nothing less than having the king's young mistresses killed in the most hideous way, to dissuade whoever dares think to take her place.'

'The work of the Devout Party.'

The other man's smile broadened.

'So one might think, but it is not so—I know the printer well. He's a member of a secret society—'

'The Freemasons!' declared Casanova.

'No,' Joinville corrected him. 'They obey neither the Masonic law nor London. They are a Brotherhood. A very ancient and secret society. First known as the Fraternity of the Serpent, and now as the Brotherhood of the Serpent.'

'*Novus ordo seclorum*,' recited Casanova, who had turned quite pale. '"The new order of the ages".'

'What's that?'

'Their motto.'

'Is there nothing you don't know?' grumbled Joinville.

'Very little. And secret information is my speciality!' Casanova brightened, and took a sip of his wine. 'I have read a great deal—'

'Yes!' laughed Joinville. 'Few people know that Casanova is a translator of books from Latin and Italian, knows his classics back to front and can recite almost any snatch of Antique poetry.'

'Few people indeed,' said the Venetian pensively.

The Chevalier de Seingalt reflected on the new information. He had not foreseen this and pondered the matter darkly. The case was becoming highly complicated, even for someone like him. If it were not for Chiara, he would happily have withdrawn from the whole thing.

'The Brotherhood are mightily sure of themselves,' Joinville continued, lowering his voice. 'They distrust the Freemasons and detest the monarchy. People say they are dangerous, unpredictable. They are utterly without scruples, and will not hesitate to kill if it suits their ends. "Anyone, anywhere, anyhow", they say. Their Grand Master is a very old man now, and he has a hard time keeping them in check. Some are contesting his power.'

'Power is always contested,' said Casanova wearily, 'and young men must kill their elders if they are to live!'

'Well, if you're satisfied, I'm leaving,' grumbled Joinville, pulling himself clumsily out of his chair.

Casanova placed a hand on his wrist, holding him back gently but firmly.

'One last question. Do you know Chiara D'Ancilla, and who it is she serves?'

'A young Italian aristocrat, of excellent family. She lives in Paris with her father and dabbles in science. Her apparent naivety masks a greater love of plotting and intrigue than one might think. They say she is one of La Pompadour's creatures.'

*

The carriage set Volnay down on the muddy banks of the Seine, just before the Pont Notre-Dame. At once, the inspector was engulfed by the tumult of the street, the cries of the vegetable-sellers and water-carriers. He walked the length of a block of houses along Quai Mal-Acquis, jostled by the throng of chair-carriers, pickpockets and street peddlers. The tumbledown assortment of buildings looked like a house of cards ready to collapse at the first breath of wind. A bowl of peelings crashed without warning at the inspector's feet. Not wishing to dirty himself any more than was necessary, Volnay made his way past a row of small, well-known, very ancient hotels—Le Mortier d'Or, La Corne de Cerf and L'Arche de Noé—before turning onto a narrow street, the Rue de la Chouette-Clouée. The only apparent danger here was a troupe of about ten prostitutes, baring their breasts under the noses of the few passers-by, in hopes of luring them to a filthy nest of straw infested with fleas and bugs, there to engage in various age-old erotic entertainments.

He had lost valuable time at Versailles, and later with Father Ofag. The setting sun extended its last, bloodied rays over the rooftops, like sharp fingers gouging livid red scars. Inexorably, it sank. The horizon flushed purple, and cinnamon.

Volnay pressed close to the wall, to avoid the foul gutter running down the middle of the street, and the buckets of slops that were emptied into it at regular intervals. He brushed past a young woman with long legs, her stockings hitched up with suspenders. Her beautiful face was framed by bronze-coloured hair, which she wore thrown back in a long mane, over her shoulders. Her pale eyes gazed deep into his, and she gripped his arm as he passed. The young woman smelt bad, but she exuded an animal sensuality—her only perfume—and her skin was a soft shade of honey. She smiled insistently, but said nothing. She leant more and more heavily on Volnay's arm, trying to force him off the street and drag him upstairs. In the half-light, her mouth glistened like an open wound. Volnay pulled himself free with some difficulty. The touch of her hand as it drew him to her was a fresh challenge to be overcome. He got past the woman, and turned back to look at her. She was staring after him, saying nothing.

The inspector quickened his pace, away from the young prostitute's imperious gaze. Overhead, the swiftly gathering clouds announced rain. Overhanging facades were a common feature in this quarter. Volnay was heedless of the danger they posed. Suddenly, he felt a tight grip on his arm. He found himself backed against a cold wall, with a dagger at his throat.

'If you were not our brother you would be dead already,' growled a voice. 'Consorting with the Devout Party!'

Volnay froze. He knew what these people could do—he had been one of them. For a fleeting moment, his life passed before his eyes: an endless string of regrets, a funereal march of missed opportunities, the flames of a bonfire, a weeping child and—heaven knows why—Chiara's mouth. Chiara's eyes. He felt droplets of blood beading his neck, and heard another voice, calm and cold. The voice told him to wait, not to move—a carriage would be coming. The inspector sighed heavily. After Father Ofag's henchmen, it was the turn of the Brotherhood to take him off to some secret place, to be killed, or to meet one of their number. Was there any man in Paris more threatened than he?

He heard a muffled sound followed by an exasperated cry.

'Another spy! Dear God, that's two he had on his heels.'

He saw a twisted body pass by, carried between two men with broad, strong shoulders. A man with a sharp, weasel face seemed to be in charge. His eyes shone with a disconcerting, yellow light. He patted the lifeless body with a grin that made the inspector shiver.

'Don't fret,' said the man holding the knife to his neck. 'He's worth more to us alive than dead! You should be more worried about yourself…'

But Volnay felt no anxiety. The spectacle of his past had reminded him that he felt no particular attachment to this life. He made no effort to discern the heavy features of the man holding him now between life and death. Instead, with calm detachment, his methodical mind tried to match the two spies who had been tailing him to their paymasters.

One is with the Devout Party, that's for sure, but the second man? Why not with Sartine, who cannot bear to be kept out of things? Or even the Marquise de Pompadour?

He was dragged into a tiny courtyard, still held in a tight grip all the while. Again he saw the weasel-like man pass by, and he committed the man's features to memory. He looked dangerous, and utterly without scruples. Half an hour passed, and the muffled sounds of a horse and carriage were heard making their way along the unpaved street. He was pushed into a highway coach, its windows masked by leather curtains. The door closed behind him. Volnay was not especially surprised to find himself opposite the big man with piercing grey eyes whom he had met at the inn, with other members of the Brotherhood. He took a moment to study the man's face. His strongly lined features were severe but impassioned, and his gaze was of such intensity that he seemed to want to force his way into your mind. He was unquestionably a leader of men, capable of sending you to your death before you had even understood why.

'Good evening, brother.'

The German-accented voice was as gentle as Volnay remembered from their last meeting. The voice of a man so certain of obedience that he had no need to speak with any greater force.

'You've had me followed since the beginning of the investigation,' said Volnay.

The other man waved his hand in irritation.

'Who is not following you, my friend? You have three spies on your tail, as well as our own, and perhaps others too, for all I know! Your every visit is known within hours, by Sartine, the Devout Party and the Marquise Pompadour. Arranging a tête-à-tête with you without their knowing is something of a challenge, believe me! My men are blocking the street for the moment, but we have very little time.'

'What do you want?'

'First, a warning, Chevalier. There are people around me who cannot understand how it is that you have dealings with the king, La Pompadour and the Devout Party. Some of those people hate the last of these: the religionists are the opposite of what we are, and what we want to be. But those who hate them are mistaken. The Devout Party is not our primary target, and nor does Father Ofag consider us his enemies, at present.'

'Then Father Ofag knows of you?' Volnay was worried. He squinted in the dark interior of the coach.

The fat man gave a condescending smile.

'He is as well informed as Monsieur de Sartine's police force. Indeed, he may even be their source, for a fee. There is nothing that cannot be bought and sold here in Paris, as you well know. There is no trust, no loyalty anywhere outside the Brotherhood. Except…'

He considered Volnay with a mixture of curiosity and respect.

'Except for you. The one person who says nothing, sells nothing, an islet of loyalty in an ocean of betrayal. But loyalty to what? To chimeras! The stuff of dreams!'

His stroked his beard complacently with his heavily ringed fingers.

'I don't understand you,' he continued, thoughtfully. 'And yet we resemble one another: we desire equality for all, and respect for the rights of every man, freedom of thought, an end to torture and the sale of public offices, society's release from governance by the Church, and the representation of the people in the government of France!'

His tone had become increasingly strident. He knew it, and lowered his voice once more, like a man with long experience of such precautions.

'I cannot understand why you do not return to our midst. Is it the influence of that heretic monk, with his fantastical ideas, or the exclusive society of your talkative magpie that has turned your head once and for all?'

Volnay blinked rapidly. The reference to the monk and the bird filled him with secret dread.

'Leave the monk out of this,' he said.

The other man gave a short, unpleasant laugh.

'Your monk has secret dealings with Sartine. We followed him to an inn. Surely you knew that?'

Volnay sat motionless. He could not think, only feel. Had the monk reviewed his options and decided to change sides rather than become trapped in a situation with no way out? Impossible!

'But we are here to talk about us,' insisted the large man. He sensed that Volnay's determination was wavering. 'You cannot continue alone against all the rest. We want the same thing, you and I.'

Volnay nodded slowly, with an empty stare.

'When I was younger,' he said bravely, 'I wanted to over-throw degenerate kings and tyrants who are accountable to no one. Then, one day, I asked myself who would take their place.'

'Us! We can take their place!' hissed Volnay.

'And therein lies the problem.'

A heavy silence fell between them. The inspector was the first to speak.

'What do you want from me? What are you trying to do now?'

'To stir up public opinion, Volnay. Public opinion! We are gaining ground. The people's outrage is growing against the most flagrant injustices, the most shameful scandals. Tell me more about the murders of these two young women. I order you, brother!'

Volnay was breathing heavily. His heart knocked against his ribs. He knew that he was bound for ever by his old oath of allegiance to the Brotherhood. He knew, too, that if he refused to speak, he would die. A thin cord around his neck, and it would all be over. Even Wallace inspired less fear in him than the servants of the Brotherhood of the Serpent. He told the man everything, choosing his words carefully and sparing nothing except, as for Father Ofag, the fact that he had read the contents of the letter discovered on Mademoiselle Hervé's body. The other man nodded as if unsurprised by any part of what he heard. He sighed, then addressed Volnay in angry tones:

'A short while ago, a young virgin of fourteen was taken before the king. Le Bel had not had time to deflower her and provide the usual training, and finding herself suddenly confronted, with no explanation, by a sinister man undressing himself without a word, she scurried like a terrified hunted animal all around the bed. By dint of chasing around after her, naked, the king caught a cold and was confined to quarters. The story got out. The Court merely laughed, because morale—and morality—there have reached their lowest ebb. But the people were outraged. Now, the mothers of Paris hide their daughters when they go out, for fear of crossing his path. I have travelled in the countryside, and across Europe.

Everywhere, people tell me: "He'll be killed!" I have even heard people whisper that, one day, there will be a great bloodletting, to rid us of this ill.'

He scratched in his luxuriant beard again, but there was a hint of awkwardness now.

'We do not seek the king's death, but the death of his office. We have no desire to make a martyr of him. But to discredit him, to ensure that the monarchy is viewed with horror, yes! That is our aim.'

He fixed Volnay with a penetrating stare.

'Is it yours, too?'

Volnay felt the blood drain from his face. There was a time in his life when he would have stopped at nothing to achieve precisely that end, but sometimes men learn, and change.

'Yes,' he managed to say. 'My aim is to destroy the monarchy.'

'The Fraternity of the Serpent has existed down the ages,' said the Brotherhood's leader, still staring hard into Volnay's eyes. 'It has died and been reborn; it has adapted to political systems, and influenced them. And yet the massacre of the Templars almost destroyed us. It took centuries to rebuild what we had lost. Now, we must recover our rightful place, stolen from us by the Freemasons: we shall be first! And for that, we must strike hard at those who refuse to hear us. You say you have always wanted to destroy the monarchy. Are you prepared to pursue that end by any means, however vile?'

The coach was silent as the grave. Volnay felt the blood pulsing at his temples. He heard himself speak:

'By any means!'

The other man observed him for a few moments.

'Well then, good. We shall destroy them together: the king and all who serve him, Sartine and La Pompadour alike. Listen carefully, I am about to give you my instructions. Diverge from them by so much as a hair's breadth, and you are dead.'

The Chevalier de Seingalt glanced through the letter he had just finished, then scattered a little sand over it to dry the ink. The letter read as follows:

Madame,

My sincere and disinterested attachment to you, and to the good of your beloved country, force me to warn you that new elements requiring prompt action necessitate our meeting. I request an audience as soon as possible, at your mansion, so that I may reveal them to you. I am thankful for this happy opportunity to prove my eagerness to act in your service.

I remain, Madame, your most humble, respectful and obedient servant,

Chevalier de Seingalt

He rang, and a liveried valet in a braid-trimmed coat hurried to his side.

'Go immediately to the Marquise de Pompadour and give her this letter. Be sure to tell her that it is of the greatest urgency and importance. Wait for her reply and hurry back here. Do not stop at an inn along the way!'

There was much to tell. As usual, the monk refused to say anything until he had moistened his lips. An excellent bottle of Champagne wine served the purpose.

'You left very early this morning,' he told Volnay. 'The young Italian woman came and rang at your door. Naturally, I didn't open it to her, but dear God, how charming she is!'

Volnay gave a gesture of exasperation.

'I quite forgot! When we parted yesterday in the Tuileries, she told me to do nothing until I had seen her again. She must have had something important to tell me.'

He smiled dully.

'I should have done as she said!'

The monk shrugged. He had taken Volnay's best chair, and sat gazing at the gilded spines of the books opposite with an unfocused smile. He received the news of his partner's promotion to the direct service of the king with circumspection.

'One day you're at the summit, the next, right down at the bottom. The Tarpeian rock is very close to the Capitoline Hill… The king never shows any emotion. He can chat amiably with a minister in the morning and send him into exile that same evening. Your position is delicate.'

Volnay told him about the rest of his audience with Louis XV, and how he had felt himself to be in the presence of some cold-blooded animal, a creature brimful of nothing but a terrifying void.

'The king is not evil,' declared the monk. 'But he is implacable. He is cold, and inconstant. He has no feelings, no pity. None for other people, and none for you. We must distance ourselves from him as soon as possible, or he will suck us into his void.'

Volnay told him about his fruitless interview with Le Bel, followed by his visit to the Marquise de Pompadour, and to Father Ofag. The monk was astounded. He even forgot to pour himself another glass of wine.

'What an extraordinary day! But not altogether surprising, in the end, because everyone is at your back. Everyone is trying to secure some personal profit from this business. First the Brotherhood of the Serpent, and now the Devout Party, making good ground right behind!'

The monk's expression hardened.

'Father Ofag… Another one who wanted to burn me alive because I claimed that Christ possessed nothing on this earth but the poor clothes on his back. Cursed spawn, preaching in the morning and dogmatizing all day long!'

He broke off when he saw Volnay take hold of a glass and pour himself some wine, glancing sidelong at his colleague. Hastily, he held out his own glass for Volnay to fill.

'Now it's my turn to surprise you,' he said. His spirits revived. 'I chanced on a fine scene at the lodgings of the assistant to the Comte de Saint-Germain. The villain sells potions to women—potions he claims to have perfected with his master.'

Volnay froze.

'Potions? Precisely the sort of thing likely to interest Mademoiselle Hervé, according to her grandfather, and the neighbour at her lodgings.'

The tips of his fingers were touching, and he gazed into empty space. The monk leant closer. He knew this pose: it often preceded a moment of sudden revelation, an idea that would spring fully formed from Volnay's reasoning, and resolve the most complex questions.

'A potion contained in a phial. How stupid of me, how idiotic… The comte was right about one thing: complex problems arise from the simplest of causes.'

Volnay seemed to have entered a deep trance. His voice was barely more than a whisper.

'Could that be it? Wallace said she was holding something in her hands when she climbed down from the carriage. Could it be?…'

He turned to the silent monk.

'Tell me more!'

The other man gave a shudder of disgust.

'When a woman has no money, but is young, and pretty, the comte's assistant takes his payment… in kind, on the spot, even before she has time to remove her dress. Believe me, I heard everything!'

Volnay looked incredulous.

'Here and now, in our century of enlightenment, people are peddling elixirs of eternal youth. Even love potions…'

His tone shifted indefinably as he uttered these last words, but the monk said nothing.

'What do you expect?' retorted the monk. 'The encyclopedists and philosophers are brilliant indeed, but they are few in the face of the ignorant masses. Swindlers pass themselves off as men of science, for their own profit. They use mathematical formulae and Kabbalistic numerology, and they calculate the positions of the stars to tell your fortune.'

He gave a sad smile.

'Our scientists and our philosophers have forgotten that by sacrificing faith on the burning altar of reason, they deprive humanity of one vital thing: hope. And there will always be people ready to supply that vital need: soothsayers, healers, Kabbalists, sorcerers… They are the custodians of hope in the life beyond.'

Volnay shrugged, opened the door to the birdcage and placed the magpie on his shoulder. The bird cackled loudly:

'Damn the Pope! Damn the Pope!'

He glared at the monk.

'Did you teach her that?'

His colleague shifted uncomfortably in his seat and changed the subject.

'You must keep your promise. Go to the marquise's mansion and give her the letter you found. If you do not, the direst consequences will ensue. As for me, you see, I am dressed in my layman's clothes, and I shall accompany you.'

Volnay protested, but his colleague cut him short.

'I'll stay outside, at the entrance, but we'll take our swords and pistols. It's getting dark. To shake off the spies let us hurry first to the inn, the Leaky Barrel. If we're followed, we will leave there by the back door. Until we reach the marquise, our lives hang by a thread.'

Volnay caught his arm.

'First, I need to test a hypothesis. We must return to the spot where Mademoiselle Hervé's body was found.'

They made their way quickly through the motley throng, cutting through the bird-catchers' and grain merchants' quarter, where a bitter smell filled the air.

'I forgot to mention, I've been contacted by the Brotherhood,' said Volnay, casually.

The monk gave vent to a vehement, blasphemous curse involving the king and the Pope.

'What do they want?'

'Same as usual, an end to the monarchy.'

The monk glanced quickly around them. The darkness was thick now, and silent. He hurried on, pulling Volnay behind him, with a firm grasp on his arm.

'As far as the Brotherhood are concerned,' he growled, 'the people are naturally ignorant and stupid. They want to free the people from the chains of monarchy, but only so that they may substitute those of an enlightened elite that will confiscate all power, to its own advantage. Their morals are no better than the king's. You were one of them. The worst mistake of your life. Do not make it twice!'

'A young man readily chooses the most expedient way,' said Volnay in a hoarse whisper.

'You are still young, and every man follows a twisting path in this life!'

Volnay seemed not to have heard him.

'I wanted to avenge my father.'

The monk's expression hardened suddenly.

'Madness! Madness! Do you believe for one minute that we can go back? Must you remain a child your whole life?'

Distress pierced his voice. Cursing, he led Volnay firmly through the streets, as if the younger man had been struck blind. They paused only once, in front of the Saint-Jean cemetery, its tombstones shining faintly in the moonlight. The darkness distorted their sense of direction.

'It must be this way,' said the monk, 'but a man is easily lost in this half-light.'

Volnay shot him a piercing glance. He voiced the question that had tormented him since his talk with the leader of the Brotherhood.

'They told me you met Sartine at an inn.'

The monk froze with a wounded air. The moonlight cast tangled shadows at their feet. Time stood still.

'I was forced to strike a deal with Sartine,' he said wearily, at last. 'A plan of action with manifold advantages: I keep him informed, and he leaves us in peace for the duration of the inquiry. If I had not... Well, he is capable of things beyond imagination.'

Volnay's eyes burnt with anger. The monk knew that blazing, Arctic hue, the blue-grey of cold rage. No good would come of it.

'Calm yourself! Be calm...' he intoned. 'Proceed as you will but allow me to watch your back.'

He looked around, peering into the shadows lining the street. Then he glanced back at Volnay. His expression was serene, almost radiant.

'I am loyal,' he said simply.

He pronounced the word as if it were the loveliest ever spoken. All at once, the tension eased. Volnay nodded briefly, then planted himself in the middle of the crossroads, and quickly identified the entrance to the courtyard. On the far side, a bread oven glowed red in the darkness.

'There! There it is!'

The monk shrugged and followed him. The yard was filled with wooden packing cases and sacks of flour.

Volnay paced every inch of the space, examining the joints between the cobbles. 'Still,' he muttered, 'I cannot fathom why, as Wallace described, Mademoiselle Hervé hurried past her own staircase, which we know to be here beside the entrance, and further on into the courtyard?'

'Look up from time to time,' advised his colleague. 'It rests the eyes. Perhaps this little phial is what you're looking for?'

He held it aloft, with a sardonic look.

'Hunting the hat on your head? I almost trod it underfoot when we entered here, but I said nothing. It doesn't do to find the thing you seek too soon!'

The young woman was dressed in a grey satin cloak trimmed with fur. With not a flicker of movement in his face, the Chevalier de Seingalt watched as she emerged from the mansion of the Marquise de Pompadour. Nothing surprised him any more. He hurried to draw level with her, secretly delighted to see the blood drain from her face at his approach.

'You! Here?' he exclaimed, with forced jollity.

The young woman seemed to wilt on the spot.

'Chevalier! Whatever are you doing here at this hour?'

'Why, I've come to visit the Marquise de Pompadour. Just like you.'

'Are you quite out of your mind, Monsieur?'

The Venetian smiled, and gallantly held out his arm.

'Let us walk a moment together, if you will. The evening promises to be mild, and this gentle breeze is most pleasant.'

Pale as death, she slipped her hand through his arm.

'I am conscious,' said Casanova, 'that I have arrived an hour early for my appointment. We should never have met here, but there it is. I wanted to get a sense of the place before presenting myself. One never knows what one will find!'

He laughed.

'And fate has smiled! You, here. An intimate of the marquise, as it now seems.'

Chiara opened her mouth to protest.

'No, no, do not speak—a lie will quite spoil your pretty face,' said Casanova. 'I knew you felt a certain liking, an affinity for the Marquise de Pompadour, but to think that you would be one of her spies... Well, it is often thus. The prettiest women are always ready to lend their hand to machinations designed to betray us men!'

The young woman's eyes blazed with anger.

'You don't understand! The king is disgusted by the works of our philosophers—he speaks of them with horror. But the Marquise de Pompadour supports them. She has rallied to the new ideas, she advocates progress. Without her, France would have been thrown back a hundred years. For my part, I have chosen to follow the party of thinkers on the higher, more arduous path, not those who grovel and flatter in hopes of securing some small favour.'

'Should I feel targeted?' asked Casanova, in wounded tones. 'But why should the marquise meddle in our petty affairs? And what has all this to do with the murder of the faceless woman?'

Chiara's face was expressionless.

'I cannot say.'

'Do you not trust me?'

'No!'

The Venetian burst out laughing.

'I adore plain, honest speaking. It has always delighted me, and it is so rare nowadays. We all know, since yesterday, that Volnay removed a letter from the body of the first victim, but what I did not know, until lately, was that the marquise judges the letter sufficiently compromising for her to charge *you* with its recovery.'

A quick glance at Chiara's face told him he had hit home.

And, he thought, *the marquise's faith in your talents is such that she has asked me to follow this affair, too! But let us keep that to ourselves. In this life, the secret of success is secrecy itself!*

His sharp eye caught a movement on the other side of the street. He squinted to identify its source, and the smile withered slowly on his lips.

'Well, Chiara, we are clearly not in luck today…'

She followed his gaze and froze as she recognized Volnay.

'What of it?' sighed Casanova. 'Chance is a fickle mistress indeed, and it seems that we have all arranged to call on the marquise this evening…'

Chiara gave no reply. She watched anxiously as Volnay strode towards them, his face an expressionless mask. Behind him, an older man with a short, greying beard and a sharp, lively demeanour hurried to try to hold him back.

'Well, here you are, both,' fumed Volnay as he drew level with them. Accomplices by day and night! Mademoiselle, what of my faith in humanity now?'

'You are mistaken, Monsieur—'

'I know everything, Mademoiselle, and rest assured, I am fulfilling the damned mission entrusted to you by the marquise, this very evening. I am about to hand her the letter, and I trust you will keep out of my way from now on!'

He turned to the Chevalier de Seingalt, who stood bolt upright, with an impartial smile on his lips.

'And that remark goes for you too, Monsieur Giacomo Casanova!'

The Venetian adopted a pained expression, and drew closer to his compatriot.

'Chevalier de Volnay,' said Chiara, blushing deeply, 'I can explain—'

'Too late, Mademoiselle. I discovered the whole truth a few hours ago. I did not believe it at first, but Father Ofag has been kind enough to tell me whose side you are on.'

He saw her start in surprise at the mention of the name, but shrugged and went on:

'Rest assured, I quite stupidly put my life in danger by keeping the letter from him. I told myself that whoever wanted it would have to snatch it themselves from the point of my sword. But it is of no interest to me now. The Devil take you all—you, him, her! Here's an end of it: there's your damned letter, you can take it to the marquise yourself!'

Chiara's face had turned white as bone. She saw Volnay's older companion smile and address her a small signal, as if to say: 'All will be well.'

'This is all horribly embarrassing,' bemoaned Casanova, delicately wrinkling his nose. 'Such vulgarity!'

Volnay made as if to draw his sword and run the man through, but the monk gripped his colleague firmly by the arm.

'Let us go.'

He led Volnay away, leaving Chiara alone with Casanova. The young woman appeared quite lost. She signalled to her coachman. Her carriage stood waiting at the entrance to the mansion, unable to enter the courtyard, which was already filled with vehicles and their horses. The groom hurried to fold out the steps and open the coach door. As if in a trance, Chiara climbed inside, followed—after a moment's hesitation—by Casanova. The coachman cracked his whip, and the horses moved off.

'What's this?' frowned the monk. He spoke quietly, under his breath. 'What's this? She's climbing into her carriage and making off in the opposite direction with the letter. She hasn't taken it to the marquise! We are betrayed.'

The carriage was moving away, bouncing over the cobbles. The monk swore, and dashed across the street after it. A carriage almost ran him over, and Volnay was forced to pull him back sharply, before he was trampled under the horses' hooves. They both fell to the ground and watched as Chiara's carriage disappeared around a corner.

'God in hell!' swore the monk. 'Why give her the letter?'

Volnay looked lost. Conflicting emotions played over his features. It was some time before he managed to speak.

'I don't understand.'

'Me,' hissed the monk between his teeth, 'I understand only too well. Those two have played us for a pair of fools.'

Inside the coach, Casanova was the first to recover his spirits. His instinct dictated the safest course of action.

'Mademoiselle? Recover yourself, you are quite pale.'

He patted one of Chiara's hands, and his eye fell on the letter, clutched tightly in the other.

'Give that to me,' he commanded.

He took the letter and stowed it in his waistcoat pocket.

'Mademoiselle, doubtless you have your reasons for not taking the letter to Madame la Marquise. Rest assured, I am wholly at your service.'

His habitual reflexes returned. Never one to waste an opportunity, he set about unclenching her fingers and entwining them with his own.

'Chiara—'

All at once, she seemed to jump out of her skin.

'The letter! Why didn't I take it to Madame la Marquise?'

'I have no idea. I thought perhaps you had changed your mind.'

She cast him a scornful look.

'Who do you take me for? I serve the marquise, and I serve her with loyalty.'

She called to the coachman.

'Stop! Turn around and take us back to the Marquise de Pompadour!'

She turned to Casanova, her eyes sparkling.

'Give me back that letter!'

'Chiara, is this quite reasonable? The letter will be safe with me...'

Her dark gaze speared him to the seat.

'Give it to me or I'll see my lackeys have you whipped.'

He sighed, forced a smile, and gave her what she was asking for.

'This is all rather unnecessary, Chiara, is it not? I am your friend...'

Chiara threw herself back in her seat. She seemed on the verge of tears.

'I don't know.'

Turning the coach about was a difficult operation. The Rue Saint-François was narrow and dark. The coachman struggled to manoeuvre the two horses harnessed between the shafts. He swore and cracked his whip, heightening their nervous agitation.

A little way down the street, Wallace dismounted from his horse and called sharply to the two henchmen close by. The men hurried towards him, their swords knocking against their sides.

'They have the letter—we must seize our chance! Gentlemen, you know what you must do. May God bless the steel in your blades!'

The metal shafts hissed and rang as they were drawn. Chiara's horses reared in fright. Casanova risked a glance through the carriage window.

'Ah! An interesting turn of events!'

Quickly, he assessed the situation. The carriage was blocked sidelong across the street. Paralysed with fear, the coachman had dropped the reins. The Chevalier de Seingalt heaved a sigh and turned to his companion.

'A pair of filthy villains, daring to have their way with a ravishing young woman such as you!'

He opened the carriage door as he spoke, and jumped nimbly to the ground. The two henchmen approached, brandishing their long, threatening swords.

The Venetian drew his own weapon, muttering under his breath:

'*Ne Hercules quidem contra duos!* Not even Hercules fought alone against two!'

'Chevalier!'

Chiara had climbed down silently from the carriage, and clutched his arm. Gently, he pushed her behind him, without taking his eyes off the two men.

'Have no fear, Chiara, and above all, stay far behind me.'

It occurred to him, on a sudden, that he would never know a finer death than this: to fight and die for a young woman, before her very eyes. His heart beat fast. The knowledge of what he would do for Chiara terrified him.

The two henchmen moved closer all the while. Casanova greeted them with a smile and a smooth flourish of his sword, then plunged it straight at the heart of the more dangerous-looking of the two: the man with a three- or four-inch scar down his cheek.

'There!' he breathed, straightening up with a show of false bravado.

The thrust was ill-defended and slipped between his opponent's ribs. The man clutched one hand to his side, drenched in blood. Casanova dodged an attack from his partner, gripped his sword hard and fought the man off vigorously. The wounded man staggered back to take stock of his injury, while his partner launched a second attack. Again, Casanova parried the thrust, effected a feint, then attacked again. A skilled swordsman, he identified his opponent's weakness in seconds. When his attacker lunged, he knew what to do. Parry, riposte, and he scored a fine hit on the man's arm.

'There!' he breathed again, with satisfaction.

Clearly, the henchmen were unprepared for their opponent's skill. The two attackers seemed to be collecting themselves when a third figure emerged from the shadows, pale as death. Casanova was filled with foreboding: the man drew his sword as smoothly and easily as if it were an extension of his own arm.

'Now that's hardly fair,' muttered Casanova. 'I'm beginning to tire!'

Again, he felt the death wish seize his gut. He cast a final glance at Chiara over his shoulder. She stood watching him.

Casanova heard the pounding of feet. Cautiously, he glanced round to see Volnay running towards him, followed by his companion, older but still sharp and alert. He heard the ring of the new arrivals' swords being drawn in their turn. The wounded henchmen turned and fled, and Wallace quickly found himself surrounded.

'Three against one?' he exclaimed in surprise, hesitating as to his next move.

'Well I'll be damned!' said the monk brightly, presenting his sword. 'I doubt another chance to kill you quite so easily will come our way any time soon…'

Wallace parried his thrust and backed away to the wall. With a single gesture, Volnay halted his companions as they moved forward, swords pointed.

'Wallace, answer my questions and your life will be spared.'

The other man glared at him coldly. His milk-white face glowed faintly in the half-light. The fire in his pale, colourless eyes was such that Volnay could barely hold his gaze.

'Do I look like one who will tell his life story to the first man that asks?'

Volnay's mind was made up.

'Then I will take you man to man, and we can talk while we fight.'

He observed Wallace carefully as he spoke. His tall figure was planted firmly on the ground, yet he gave the impression of a curious lightness, too. Wallace gave a thin-lipped smile. His pale, ice-cold eyes stared at Volnay as if he were already dead.

'If you insist.'

He tore forwards. A timely reflex spared Volnay a good six inches of steel in his chest. He brandished his sword at arm's length, holding his adversary at a distance.

'Gently does it, Monsieur Wallace, the briefest exchanges are not always the best.'

Volnay concentrated on keeping up a solid defence, seeking out his opponent's sword so as to leave him minimal room for manoeuvre.

'I know that you are not Mademoiselle Hervé's killer.'

He parried another attack, caught his breath and continued, still on guard.

'But for the second victim, I cannot be so sure.'

'And why not?' demanded Wallace, circling him, ready to lunge.

Volnay kept his left flank covered, and parried with ease to his side.

'Did you kill her?'

'In God's name, no! To what end? I don't even know who she is.'

He concluded his phrase with a sudden, quick jab at Volnay. Volnay crossed his right arm and drove the blade aside, with a sharp clash of steel that resonated the length of the street. Windows began to open, and people leant out for a better view. Another parry and riposte from Volnay drew a ripple of polite applause.

'A fine defence!' said Casanova appreciatively, turning to his neighbour.

'Indeed!' A smile wrinkled the corners of the monk's eyes. 'Though a little less *piste* may be in order, and rather more of the street.'

'Quite so, quite so…' said Casanova, eyeing him with curiosity.

Volnay repulsed another attack. He took no risks, and tried to keep himself at a reasonable distance, to anticipate the next assault.

'Was it you who ordered the attack on the monk, while he examined the first victim's body?'

Wallace gave a sinister laugh.

'There is no lesser Christian on this earth than your monk, as you well know! His life is worthless!'

Again he jabbed his sword, and swiftly produced his dagger, swiping at the hilt of his opponent's blade, and finding Volnay's wrist. The inspector yelped in pain and dropped his weapon. A trickle of hot blood ran down his hand. At the same moment, Wallace gave a gasp of surprise, beat his arms as if to take flight, then fell on his face like a dead weight. The monk stepped forward to pull his damascened dagger from the man's back—a fine, six-inch blade, thin and razor-sharp.

'Forgive me,' he said, 'for interrupting, but I had made no

promise to spare his life, and I simply could not stand by and hear myself accused of being a bad Christian! For shame!'

The Chevalier de Seingalt stepped forward, holding a dagger in his left hand.

'I was preparing to do the same. You're a fine swordsman, Volnay, but rather too courtly for this day and age, I fear.'

He turned to Wallace's body, raised the point of his sword in a salute, and pronounced a brief eulogy:

> 'In death, as he in life had done,
> He turned his filthy rump to heav'n
> And showed his arse to everyone.'

Skilfully, the monk dressed his colleague's flesh wound with a handkerchief supplied by Chiara. The young woman's face was utterly white. With some effort, she smiled at Volnay, though her eyes were filled with sorrow. Ever discreet, the monk waited at the mansion gates, while the others went inside. The Marquise de Pompadour received all three in her music room. A superb harpsichord took pride of place. Sheets of music for guitar could be seen in one corner. A bouquet of roses contributed its fragrance to the prevailing aroma of beeswax.

La Pompadour was elegantly dressed, as ever, but Volnay noted her pale complexion and drawn features. The marquise looked ill. The king had broken his toy. She welcomed them in appropriate style, but her gaze turned frequently to Chiara, as if to seek an explanation for this intrusion *à trois*.

'Madame la Marquise,' said the young woman in clear, confident tones, 'Fate has seen fit to set all three of us in pursuit of the same letter. We judged it fitting that we should bring it to you together. Everyone gathered here has shown absolute discretion, as you know.'

La Pompadour gave no reply. She had tried to secure the service of each of the three individuals now present, but the only one in whom she truly trusted was Chiara. The girl watched her now, in silent adoration, as she rose and walked over to the musical instrument. For an instant, the polished wood of the harpsichord reflected the marquise's frail figure, as her fingers brushed the ivory keys.

'Who has read the letter? Tell me the truth.'

'I have, Madame la Marquise,' said Volnay.

Chiara shook her head. She was quite overcome. La Pompadour turned to her and waited.

'The letter was in my hands for a just few minutes,' said the young woman. Her expression was deeply troubled. 'I swear to God, I have not given it so much as a glance.'

Next, the marquise looked at Casanova, who bowed graciously.

'For my part, Madame, I have not so much as touched it,' he lied, with breathtaking aplomb.

The marquise considered him for a moment, but Casanova was an habitué of the stage, and did not bat an eyelid. After a while, La Pompadour nodded. She rewarded Chiara with a smile, and Casanova with a purse of gold. For Volnay, she seemed to hesitate before finally proffering her hand to be kissed. Dutifully, the inspector brushed her slender, burning fingers with his lips. He felt no particular emotion: if the marquise thought to secure his personal attachment through her gesture, she was quite mistaken, as she very quickly under-stood. Volnay took a step back, a little surprised at the strong smell of rice powder that hung about the marquise's person.

The same graceful hand was outstretched to him now. Still without a word, the marquise took the letter and read it.

'Is that all there is?' she asked evenly, when she had finished.

Volnay was caught off guard. He observed her more closely. She seemed perplexed, but quickly adopted the usual impassive mask.

'Yes, that is the letter, Madame,' said Volnay, staring her straight in the eye.

The favourite's expression was impenetrable. Volnay understood that something was wrong. A sidelong glance at Casanova confirmed that he, too, was watching her reaction with careful attention.

'Do you take me for a complete fool?' asked La Pompadour.

Volnay glanced at Chiara, dumbfounded, and received a look of equal astonishment in return. Casanova himself appeared thoroughly taken aback.

'I cannot think that the king sent Mademoiselle Hervé to the Comte de Saint-Germain for such a purpose,' said the marquise, and her voice trembled slightly. 'But if he did, I doubt whether the comte would have received her, even bearing a letter such as this.'

'He did not, Madame,' said Volnay, solemnly.

The marquise fixed her pale eyes on his, as if to draw his gaze and dissolve it in her own. When she released him, Volnay felt his violent heartbeat subside. Deathly silence reigned in the room. All eyes followed the marquise as she moved towards the fireplace, where, despite the mild spring weather, a pile of logs burnt with hellfire. She approached her hand to the flames, and suddenly the letter caught alight. She spread her fingers sharply, and the paper twisted and writhed as if convulsed in pain, on the hearth.

'Forget all of this,' she said calmly. 'All of it! One word, and you will end your days in the Bastille.'

She turned to face them, and for a single, eternal moment, all were struck by the last rays of her faded beauty.

'*Adieu*,' she said.

Volnay felt Chiara blanch at his side. They took their leave with suitable deference and reached the door. The sound of La Pompadour's voice called them back, as they were about to step outside.

'Ah, I was forgetting—Chevalier de Seingalt, I have heard that, together with the Duchesse de Chartres, you were practising a personal variation of the Kabbalah. Such tricks and practices are wholly incompatible with your present situation. Remember that in future, if you do not seek my displeasure.'

Casanova bowed, proffering his most dazzling smile.

'I have sworn my loyalty to you, Madame, as you know. Your wish is my command! Before I leave, I must warn you of certain damaging libels that will be published tomorrow if you do not take immediate action with Monsieur de Sartine.'

The marquise listened impassively, and rewarded the information with another purse of gold, under Volnay's disapproving eye. They emerged into the courtyard without another word. It was almost midnight, and they were alone—an uncomfortable trio standing in the pale moonlight, all in a state of some consternation. They stared at one another in silence. Had they given La Pompadour the wrong letter? Casanova observed Volnay with undisguised suspicion. The inspector knew that there had been only one letter on Mademoiselle Hervé's body, though it was not, it seemed, the letter the marquise had been expecting.

Chiara was the first to attempt a reconciliation.

'You must not think ill of me, Chevalier de Volnay, I never thought to harm you, I—'

'Mademoiselle,' he said in icy tones, cutting her short, 'you seem to have forgotten your game of deception, but I have not.'

He turned to Casanova.

'As for you, Chevalier, I have scant appreciation for your role in this affair, but I am grateful to you for protecting this lady with your sword.'

He gave a short, shallow bow, as if against his better judgement, then turned to walk away, leaving Chiara blushing deeply and Casanova with a nascent smile. Driving in the young woman's carriage, to her mansion, the Venetian observed her in silence. Her features were an astonishing blend of gentleness and firm conviction. He closed his eyes for a moment, lost in thought.

Love was the sole aim of his existence. Obviously, as a younger man, he had desired riches, before the highs and lows of life had fostered a more philosophical outlook, leading him to refuse lucrative positions, and the hands of wealthy young women, offered to him in marriage. His freedom was without price, but what price must he pay for Chiara? He was surprised to find himself wondering what was going through her mind, as she sat deep in thought.

Chiara was lost in a reverie. She had lived her life thus far without seeking the attentions of men, but not without lovers, either. A total of two, to date, because while she had learnt how to seduce a man, she had not perfected the art of entertaining others behind his back. She had abandoned her first lover for the second, and left the latter for his own sake, because she despaired of his stupidity. Neither had proved particularly disappointing, but they had failed to touch the depths of her heart, or to ignite her passion. Today, she knew that she had invaded the lives of two more men, and that her choice had not yet alighted on one or the other.

She liked Casanova's adventurous nature, his refusal to conform to life's rules and his determination to play them along, for his own advantage. By comparison, Volnay's upright integrity bored her, but she admired him nonetheless. Both were free because they had decided to remain true to their own selves. But the fact remained: Casanova made her feel like a woman, while Volnay made her feel like a child.

'Why has everything worked out this way?' she asked abruptly. 'And what's troubling him, anyhow, that he should speak to me so rudely?'

'You mean Volnay?' asked Casanova, nonchalantly.

'Who do you think I'm referring to? Is my reputation so low that you think men line up to insult me in turn?'

'He was indeed most discourteous,' agreed the Chevalier de Seingalt.

'On the other hand...'

'On the other hand, you betrayed him, just as you betrayed me.'

Chiara sulked in silence until they reached her residence. The Venetian climbed down from the carriage and followed her inside, as if invited, though she had said nothing on the subject. She received him in her bedroom. A bed of daffodil-yellow Peking silk stood on a rosewood floor. Casanova's eye wandered over the walls, stretched with filmy lengths of gauze. Chiara invited her guest to sit in an armchair.

'I am truly sorry for betraying you,' she said, 'but who can I trust?'

Casanova smiled.

'No one, believe me!'

'You are poking fun.'

'No, I am quite serious.'

Chiara shrugged.

'You spend your life seeking entertainment in others.'

'I poke fun at stupidity. Nothing else.'

There was a brief silence, broken first by the Chevalier de Seingalt.

'Why do you work for the Marquise de Pompadour? By which I mean, what drove you to choose her camp?'

She looked at him, scandalized.

'But I have told you: I believe that she represents the future of things.'

A sudden thought seemed to strike her, and she lowered her voice:

'Whereas you represent the past.'

Casanova sat in silence. Not as a result of what had just been said, for he had turned worse situations than this on their heads in the past, but for the unexpected pain her words had caused, piercing him like a dagger. The thought of a future without Chiara was intolerable. He determined to take his fate into his own hands.

'Your pleasure is my greatest passion, Mademoiselle, though I am nothing but a poor miscreant whose life consists of duping others, and enjoying the pleasures of love, gaming and the table.'

Chiara was fascinated in spite of herself. She shook her head.

'Why tell me such things? Why do you persist in showing yourself in your very worst light?'

'Because I want you to know me as I truly am.'

'But I know who you are,' she said, 'and what I like in you is that you never try to do otherwise.'

With her unerring woman's instinct, Chiara understood that there was nothing dark, nothing wicked in the schemes of this infectiously good-humoured rogue, this impish voluptuary, for whom womankind was both religion and sacrament. Still, she wanted to know more, for nothing had touched her so much as the child he had once been, and who lived in him still.

'Tell me more about the episode with Bettina. At the time, you were aged…'

'Almost twelve, but let us speak no more of her: she broke my heart with another, and Fate saw to it that I would never pluck the flower I so desired, with her.'

Again, he avoided Chiara's gaze, preferring to observe her from behind, in the play of mirrors.

'At that time,' he said, 'my mother, who had been summoned to perform in St Petersburg, desired to see me in Venice. I was taken there. I hadn't seen my mother for two years, and I had forgotten she was so beautiful, so wonderfully beautiful. Abbott Gozzi doubtless thought so, too, because for all the time he spent in conversation with her, he was unable to look her fully in the eye. When we arrived, he told me to go and kiss her, and I hurried into her arms, but she did not return my kiss.'

Chiara paled, but said nothing. Casanova went on, seemingly in spite of himself:

'That refusal,' he said, speaking slowly and with unusual emphasis, 'was the greatest betrayal I have ever known in my life. There is nothing worse than a mother who will not accept your love.'

Father Ofag laced his fingers. He pouted sorrowfully.

'You wake me in the dead of night to tell me that you have killed my faithful Wallace,' he moaned, 'and you stand before me here, with no shred of remorse or repentance, bad Christian that you are!'

'Your faithful Wallace,' retorted Volnay, 'attacked the carriage of the Marquis D'Ancilla's daughter with two vile assassins. I am indeed without remorse.'

'Dear God! What an outrage! How dare you?'

'There is no one to contradict me. I was there, and I have the word of the Chevalier de Seingalt and that of Chiara D'Ancilla. A patrol of the night watch has also visited the scene, to take away the bodies. And lastly, the incident was witnessed by the coachman, and a streetful of people watching from their windows!'

Father Ofag's normally boyish face was a mask of deathly white. 'Dear God! The scandal! The scandal!' he raged.

'Not necessarily, but only you can ensure that the news is contained. Everyone knows your connections to Wallace; you cannot erase them. But you may correct your servant's mistakes.'

'Whatever do you mean?'

Father Ofag was listening attentively now.

'The carriage of the young noblewoman Chiara D'Ancilla was attacked on a narrow lane by two robbers. Finding himself nearby, Wallace rushed bravely to her aid. He killed the two villains, but received a fatal blow, and died shortly after, where he fell. Perhaps this version will suit you better?'

Father Ofag's eyes shone. He straightened up, and his natural colour returned.

'That's my Wallace, a brave and noble soldier of God! But...'

He blinked rapidly and a look of cunning stole over his face.

'What do you want in exchange?'

'A letter in your own hand, acknowledging Wallace's misdeed. I will deposit it with a lawyer, and it will remain confidential until the moment of my death, which I hope will be neither accidental nor untimely... In case you get any wicked ideas!'

'Is that really necessary?' asked the cleric in honeyed tones. 'My word will suffice, and I shall withdraw from this whole business immediately.'

'Your word...'

The inspector guarded against speaking his true mind out loud. Father Ofag tried one last time to plead his case. He swung his rosary before his eyes with his left hand, as if to hypnotize him. Volnay followed its movement with his eyes, feeling suddenly ill at ease.

'The king has need of our party, to assist him in wise government, in accordance with Christian principles.'

'The role of a monarch,' Volnay interjected, 'is to give his subjects adequate sustenance here on earth, and not in Paradise.'

He moved closer and planted himself firmly in front of the cleric, with one hand on the hilt of his sword.

'You will withdraw from this business immediately,' he decreed, 'but you will also sign this letter for me. If you refuse, your enemies will use this occasion to their advantage, and the police will very soon be here at your door.'

Father Ofag sighed and took up his quill.

'A man such as you, Chevalier…' he said, looking at Volnay half fearfully, half in admiration. 'Truly, it is a great shame we cannot be friends.'

The monk paced nervously in the passageway, his hand in readiness on the hilt of his sword. He kept a wary eye on two evil-looking men, both heavily armed and wearing buffalo-leather jerkins and scuffed boots.

More of Wallace's henchmen, he thought.

With relief, he saw Volnay emerge, unruffled.

'Another two minutes,' he said, 'and I would have skinned these vermin alive to get inside!'

'Why?' asked Volnay in astonishment.

'I feared for your safety.'

'You're getting old!'

The monk's face reddened.

'Not at all. I'm growing younger by the day! Did he sign?'

'Without too much persuasion.'

'He has a pliant soul.'

The inspector nodded. Quickly, they left the building and found themselves on the dark street outside. A bell sounded in the distance.

'We need a carriage,' said Volnay.

They made for the more-frequented streets in search of a coachman, taking care to walk down the middle of the road, their hands ready on their swords. Shadows slipped silently from one alleyway to the next, but brigands and policeman weren't the only people abroad at this hour. It was one o'clock in the morning, and already thousands of country folk were pouring into Paris, making their way to the market halls laden with fruit and vegetables. They called out noisily to one another.

'Where are we going, anyway?' asked the monk.

'To Rue Saint-Louis, in the Parc-aux-Cerfs. The king granted me complete freedom to pursue my investigation this morning, and on his authority, I will have no difficulty gaining admittance to question the madam and her boarders about Marcoline, the second victim.'

'Now there's a place I have never seen and should very much like to visit!' said the monk, stroking his beard with an expression of rapt delight. 'But when are we to sleep?'

'When we have solved this case.'

XI

Follow God; fate will find its own way.

The nearby church tower was ringing ten o'clock when some-one came to knock on the monk's door, studded with great black nails. He uncovered the peephole, and the young woman smiled as she heard a muffled expletive. The bolts were drawn back and, cautiously, the door was opened a crack. The monk blinked like an owl in the white light of day. Chiara observed him for a moment. He was taller than most men, with smiling eyes but a thoughtful expression. A narrow, slightly hooked nose pointed firmly above a finely drawn mouth and a deter-mined chin. He would look very fine struck on a medal, she thought to herself.

'Here you are in your monk's habit,' Chiara noted. 'It all depends, then, on the hour of the day!'

The monk said nothing, but his expression darkened considerably.

'As you now know,' she went on, confidently, 'I am a loyal servant of the Marquise de Pompadour, and I am ashamed that the Chevalier de Volnay has not chosen the same camp, as a man of science. I know who you are, too, reverend sir. Indeed: the loyal colleague of the Inspector of Strange and Unexplained Deaths cannot hope to pass unnoticed for long.'

The monk had stood motionless until now. He stood aside for her to enter, with a smile playing at his lips.

'We had better continue this most interesting conversation inside, Mademoiselle.'

He showed her into a small study, its walls lined with an impressive quantity of books. Some were bound in dark brown or tan calfskin, others in red, green or yellow morocco leather embossed with delicate, lacework patterns and rolled borders. Older, rarer copies were decorated with graceful, scrolling motifs and fleurons, or inlaid with mosaics. One book lay open on the worktable.

Chiara inclined her head in curiosity.

'What are you reading, Monsieur?'

'*The Palace of Secrets, or Nocturnal Dreams and Visions Explained by the Doctrine of the Ancients.* The work is more than a century old, but I remain curious to pierce the mysteries of sleep and dreams.'

Chiara looked doubtful.

'It serves no purpose whatsoever!'

'Wrong! One day, you will see the birth of a new profession: the interpretation of dreams! As for me, I carefully set down all my dreams upon waking, and I ponder their significance over breakfast.'

She gave a small, tinkling laugh that seemed to echo around the walls.

'You are most surprising!'

'So you know who I am, Mademoiselle?' asked the monk casually, after inviting her to take a seat.

Chiara refused the offer, preferring to run her finger over a map showing the whole world, its lands and oceans.

'Soldier, duellist, monk, philosopher, doctor, anatomist… Do you really think you have been forgotten, Monsieur de—'

Swiftly, the monk placed a finger over her lips.

'Do not speak my name—even these walls have ears!'

'And what are you afraid of?'

'That they will hear!'

She considered him with curiosity.

'Is it true what they say about you?'

'That rather depends on who's talking,' observed the monk wickedly.

Chiara's face lit up with a smile.

'Those who love you say that you were a great scholar, ahead of your time. The others—'

'Yes?'

She shuddered.

'That you were the Devil himself.'

'The Devil in a monk's habit?'

'You wear it very little!'

He laughed.

'Why should I? I broke my vows long ago.'

'Why?'

'They say that a Christian is driven to action by grace, and a philosopher by reason.'

'Do you no longer have faith?'

'Well… not really, no.'

'So you do not believe in God?' she insisted.

'Not really, no.'

And he added in the blink of an eye:

'*Sequere deum, fata viam inveniunt*: follow God; fate will find its own way.'

Chiara looked at him with evident curiosity.

'Tell me about the Chevalier de Volnay.'

'And why should I tell you about him?'

She stared him in the eye, with that natural arrogance that is the preserve of the highest-born in this world.

'You will tell me about him for the very good reason that I desire it! Or do you wish me to reveal your identity at every dinner and salon in Paris?'

A faint, cold light showed in the monk's face.

'Your threats do not scare me. Sartine knows who I am.'

'Indeed. But your sentence, though it was never carried out, has not been cancelled. It is merely—what's the word?'

'Suspended,' said the monk.

Chiara nodded.

'That's it: suspended. Any rumours about you could force even untouchables like Sartine to act against you. Our chief of police can hardly boast in public that he employs an excommunicant.'

There was not a flicker of movement in the monk's face, but his eyes turned deepest black. It occurred to Chiara suddenly that he would make a formidable enemy.

'But come now,' she said anxiously, 'I am not your enemy. And don't look at me like that. I have acted on behalf of the Marquise de Pompadour, for sure, but it was for the good of all.'

'Many a private advantage is served for the good of all,' said the monk.

The young woman gestured nervously. Her fluttering hands betrayed her impatience, too.

'I merely wish you to reconcile me to the Chevalier de Volnay!' she exclaimed.

'Why?'

'But...'

She blushed faintly.

'I do not wish him to think ill of me.'

A smile played at the corners of the monk's mouth. His eyes shone more amiably now.

'Why do you wear a habit?' asked Chiara suddenly.

'Because I am forced to, young lady. When, a long time ago, I was excommunicated by the Church for publishing my works, I fled to the countryside.'

He looked at her for a moment. She was listening attentively, with an almost friendly expression.

'But that was not enough,' he said. 'The royal powers issued an arrest warrant, because I had dared to assert that a man should be free to come and go, both physically and in his thoughts.'

He raised one finger with a slight, thin smile, as always when he wished to stress a great truth or principle.

'Because, Mademoiselle, if thoughts are not allowed to circulate freely, there can be no other freedom. But those in power do not wish it, because the more people think, the more learning and intelligence they acquire, and that flies in the face of their leaders' plans for their subjugation.'

'You are just as I imagined,' she smiled.

'I beg your pardon?'

She leant towards him, her eyes shining. With disarming frankness, she reached out and took his hands.

'I have read your words, passionately. You have spoken so many truths, ahead of so many people! You are possessed of a great heart and mind.'

'I vouch merely for the good of all in a century where too many think only of their own interest. The tragedy of mankind is that we bring everything down to our own level and put ourselves at the centre of all things.'

Chiara watched him thoughtfully, noting his ardent gaze, his faint, ironic smile, tempered with obvious good nature.

'Tell me more about Volnay.'

'Alas, sighed the monk, 'he saw his father, the man he admired more than anyone, retract his words on the bonfire, and abjure what he had believed all his life. After that, the poor man fled in shame and died of sorrow when his son was not yet twelve years old. I had taken refuge in Geneva at the time. I have spent my time fleeing France, and then returning to her.'

He fell silent and seemed to think for a few moments.

'In short, I took the boy in, because he was the son of my best friend, and I loved him. When he reached adulthood, he took the curious decision to enter the police force. To repair some past injustice? Chance smiled on him, and he saved the king's life and was made Inspector of Strange and Unexplained Deaths, the post that has sparked so many rumours. Two years ago, the king authorized him to bring me back to France, but on two conditions: the first was that I serve the king as part of his police force—hence I am Volnay's partner and colleague. The second was that I wear this habit as penitence, and that I go out and about as little as possible. Which is why, as a rule, I live like some old owl, surrounded by my test tubes and my books, and the handful of corpses of interest that Volnay brings me here.'

Chiara was remarkably quiet throughout the monk's account. When he had finished, she heaved a long sigh.

'That explains everything,' she said.

The monk nodded. He saw that she was satisfied with his explanation. And so was he. Indeed, it was so convincing he almost believed it himself.

Chiara rose gracefully from her seat.

'Your laboratory must be of the first order. May I visit it?'

The monk gave a thin smile and led her to the room. The strangeness of the place seemed to seep from its very walls. Chiara walked for a moment among the round furnaces with their domed lids, the crucibles, the alembics and the test tubes. She admired the instruments carefully arranged along each table.

'What is this?' she asked suddenly, pausing in front of a glowing furnace in one corner.

'One of my experiments. I have kept that material alight for two years.'

Chiara knelt down with a loud rustling of silk.

'Projective powder, to enact the transformation of base metals into gold!' she declared excitedly.

'Ah!' said the monk. 'You are one of us!'

He closed his eyes briefly, opened them again and recited, in a solemn voice:

'Whatever is below is similar to that which is above. Through this the marvels of the work of one thing are procured and perfected.'

'Separate the earth from the fire,' Chiara intoned straightaway, *'the subtle and thin from the crude and coarse, prudently, with modesty and wisdom.'*

The monk seemed to reflect for a moment, on the revelation of her knowledge. Chiara appeared to him now in a new light: no longer a spy and a schemer in the service of the Marquise de Pompadour, but an open, enlightened mind, full of boundless curiosity.

'However scientific our cast of mind, it always comes down to this, does it not?' said the monk, in a fatalistic tone. 'The magnum opus and the philosopher's stone! How to get rich and remain forever young. The universal dream of mankind. But who led you down this path?'

Chiara hesitated, then shrugged.

'When I was twelve years old, I found a chest full of old books in one of my parents' country houses in Italy. One dusty manuscript told the story of Nicolas Flamel and his wife Pernelle—how they discovered the elixir of youth and the powder of sympathy. I was amazed. After that, I read Paracelsus—'

'Oh, Paracelsus! One of our greatest thinkers. So many alchemists sought one thing only: the secret of the transmutation of steel into gold, but he sought the power of healing. You know how?'

'Yes,' said Chiara, in a matter-of-fact tone. 'Using natural, edible substances like fennel, nutmeg and cloves. He was looking for the Active Principle, for the preparation of medicines—the quintessence, because the quintessence of a plant is so effective that half an ounce will accomplish more than one hundred specimens of the same plant in its natural state.'

'*Modus praeparandi rerum medicinalium*,' said the monk sagely. 'Paracelsus used alchemy as a medicinal art to pre-pare remedies, and not as a technique for the transmutation of base metal into gold. He replaced the heating up of metal by fermentation, or digestion.'

He broke off suddenly and scrutinized Chiara's face intently.

'Why are you so interested in Volnay?'

Chiara blinked for a moment in surprise. Then her eyes lit up.

'Who says I'm interested in him?'

'You asked me to tell you about him, and I sensed an inter-est—a tenderness—on your part.'

The monk's tone was cordial, and his intelligent gaze was filled with goodness and understanding. Chiara blushed del-icately nonetheless.

'You are mistaken, and my lack of feeling is requited, for the Chevalier de Volnay shows no interest at all in me.'

'That remains to be seen. I have found him noticeably pensive lately. As for the Chevalier de Seingalt, well, he's quite a different case altogether, is he not?' observed the monk wickedly.

'He is most… obliging,' agreed Chiara.

'Obliging? Casanova? More a creature of instinct and sensation, in my view. While Volnay is doubtless too much the master of his own impulses.'

He muttered the rest under his breath:

'At least, he aspires to be so.'

Chiara gazed around at the test tubes full of multicoloured liquids. The room was suffused with an intensely studious atmosphere, quite at odds, it seemed to her, with the monk's wayward nature.

'You never say anything about yourself,' she told him, in the reproachful tones of an infatuated daughter to her father.

'My memories are as ragged as I am! My parents followed convention. They had predestined their eldest son for a career at arms, and their second—me—for the clergy. But our tastes were precisely the reverse, and we longed to change places. I was a young hothead, and I loved nothing better than a good sword fight. My older brother was gentle and reserved. The education I received made a scholar of me nonetheless, but when my brother was killed in combat, I exchanged the cloth for a soldier's uniform, to seek my revenge. And that is how I came to take part in the Polish war of secession, and the invasion of Lombardy and the Duchy of Palma, with the French and Piedmontese troops. I fought against the Austrians in San Pietro and Guastalla. In the army, I learnt how to fight, but also—thanks to a military doctor—how to treat the sick. When I returned to France, I relinquished my uniform and joined the encyclopedists. You know the rest... tried, imprisoned, escaped, returned.'

'You are remarkably sage and scholarly now,' said Chiara.

'I was guilty of so many stupidities as a youth that it fairly hurts my brain to think of them now. And so I have tried to live at a distance from my passions, though a vague yearning for love tugs at me even now... But Volnay—he is still young, in the grip of folly and mad daydreams, just like you.'

They shared a companionable silence that grew until it set them apart once more.

'Volnay told me about the letter,' said the monk, at length. Chiara had been expecting this.

'Yes, the Marquise de Pompadour entrusted me to recover it, but I know nothing of its contents. All I discovered yesterday is that it was not the letter she had been expecting.'

'Yet it was indeed the letter that Volnay found on Mademoiselle Hervé's body. There was no other, I assure you.'

She covered his hand with her own and squeezed it affectionately.

'I believe you. In which case, the poor victim must have handed the original letter to someone else, unless someone stole it from her.'

'Wallace is dead,' said the monk. 'The truth cannot come from his lips. Clearly, the Devout Party do not have the letter, or they would never have expended so much effort on its recovery. Our best hope is to try to find out more from the marquise about its contents.'

Chiara frowned.

'She does not trust me enough for that. The Comte de Saint-Germain, on the other hand…'

The monk shuddered. Him again!

'Yes,' Chiara continued, staring thoughtfully into space, 'the comte is the only person who seems to have her complete confidence. One might almost think…'

She left her sentence unfinished, but the monk had heard too much already. Somewhere in his mind, a corner of the sky brightened. To set the seal on their new-found friendship, the monk presented Chiara with a phial of *aqua ardens*, distilled from old wine, an infusion of quicklime stones, sulphur and tartar of Montpellier.

'I ground the powder myself, and distilled it in a well-luted alembic,' he said. '*Aqua ardens* has infinite applications, as you know. It will be highly useful to you in your experiments!'

*

The comte received the marquise in silence but signalled that she was free to talk. They were in a closed room, with the shutters drawn. The walls were lined with panelling decorated with touches of rose-tinted gold. Sunlight filtered through the shutter slats, bathing the room in a soft glow, and contributing a touch of unexpected colour as they lit up a Chinese vase of painted enamel on copper.

'This room is sealed off from the world, with inner and outer windows. As you can see, I have had thick drapes hung all around; there is a double door, and a guard is standing now in the passage outside.'

The Marquise de Pompadour nodded.

'Do you still have some of the potion? I am so tired…'

'Madame,' said the Comte de Saint-Germain, 'I fear for your health. My potion will help you to feel better, but if you do not change your habits, you will not live beyond another four or five years.'

The marquise sighed.

'Four or five years is plenty. One can achieve a great deal in that time. And I am unafraid of death. I shall be together at last with my dear departed daughter.'

A tear formed in the corner of her eye, and she wiped it away delicately.

'Be of good courage, Madame,' said the comte. 'There is still hope.'

'It always pleases me to hear you say so, my dear comforter and guide…'

Her words trailed away. The comte covered her hand with his own—the hand of a friend, and she took no offence, though she had a horror of physical contact.

'Trust me!'

'But I do trust you. You are my friend!' she declared.

'A friend who is greatly concerned for you, Madame.'

He leant towards her.

'The letter, Madame la Marquise—the letter stolen from you by Mademoiselle Hervé is still in unknown hands. The king's mischief has distracted us. A request for me to kill the germ of life in a mistress who is with child! Truly, he is deranged! But we must find the other letter.'

La Pompadour's pursed lips betrayed a hint of vexation, but she said nothing.

'Try to remember, Madame,' urged the comte. 'I entrusted the letter to you myself, here in my own home, so that you might show it to certain individuals. You had it about your person when you climbed into your carriage. But papers may fall from a pocket, in a carriage. And so Mademoiselle Hervé picks it up discreetly and conceals it on her person. Or removes the papers while you are dozing. Then she asks the carriage to stop near her Paris residence, and not in Versailles. And the rest we know. Did you see nothing, notice nothing?'

Stricken, the marquise shook her head.

'Madame,' the comte continued, 'you must continue to play on your informer, Casanova, and on your young disciple, Chiara.'

'She detests that—'

La Pompadour broke off. The comte had lifted his hand, with his fingers spread wide, and brushed her face. Suddenly, she saw his eyes roll back in their sockets, and felt him stiffen. She held her breath. The comte stood frozen, and a bright aura seemed to surround him all at once, but whether from the rays of the sun or from some other, more mysterious source, she could not tell.

'Madame…'

The voice resonated as if from beyond the grave. The comte's hand dropped to his knee.

'You have had another vision!' exclaimed the marquise.

The comte stared fixedly at her for a moment, before his features softened.

'I have seen the letter in his hands...'

'Volnay's hands?'

'No, the monk.'

The monk contemplated the furnace glowing red in the darkness. The room was exceedingly warm, and a light sweat beaded his brow.

'So you do not wish to see her?'

Volnay hesitated. He thought of a few lines he had read:

> Let us tear ourselves from her gaze, her eyes.
> We love not, if we can say our goodbyes.

'Never, no.'

The monk sighed to himself. He knew how stubborn Volnay could be, that he was capable of losing the thing he most desired, for ever, out of sheer obstinacy. His colleague expected too much of others and could only be disappointed in return.

'You must reconcile yourself to her,' he insisted. 'We have learnt today that the letter you recovered from Mademoiselle Hervé's body and which you gave to the marquise was not the letter she was looking for. And so there is a second letter about which we know nothing, though its importance is such that we have both been attacked. I tremble at the very thought of the revelations it contains. Imagine! Sartine, La Pompadour, the Devout Party and the Brotherhood are all out to find it!'

'Chiara, like the marquise, knew nothing of the existence of two letters,' said Volnay. 'Her surprise was unfeigned. She truly believed she held the letter the marquise so desired in her hand.'

'She was sincere,' agreed the monk. 'I saw it with my own eyes. But the fact is, the contents of the second letter must be so dreadful that the marquise will never reveal them. Not to Chiara, not to anyone…'

He stretched his hands out in front of him, in a gesture of supplication.

'To the point: we have two unexplained murders and, still, one letter to recover. We learnt nothing last night at the Parc-aux-Cerfs. We shall never succeed alone. You must seek a reconciliation with Chiara!'

'No.'

'But I shall give you another reason,' declared the monk, in triumphant tones.

'And what is that?'

'You are in love with her!'

The grounds were planted with tall trees. Chiara touched their coarse, flaky bark as she passed, one after another. She seemed reassured by the contact.

'Thank you, Chevalier, for agreeing to see me again. I know that in your eyes I am an unworthy spy…'

Shrouded in exhaustion and despair, Volnay struggled to stare straight ahead, avoiding her gaze, as he replied.

'The whole system is perverted, Mademoiselle. Spies and informers everywhere. The whole world is watching itself, spying on itself, betraying itself. And this filthy cloaca is the fount of law and order in the kingdom.'

Chiara shivered, in spite of herself.

'I had no wish to be a part of it in this way.'

'And yet you were.'

Volnay looked up at the sky. He had sensed a change in the air. The fat, tow-coloured clouds overhead appeared consumed by slow fire.

'For my part,' he continued, 'I am devastated by the thought that my conduct might have put you in danger, and that without…'

He seemed to choke on his words, as if clots of blood were caught in his throat. Chiara took pity, and finished his sentence:

'Without the Chevalier de Seingalt's swordsmanship, our plight would have been dire indeed.'

Volnay nodded briefly. It cost him dearly to crown his rival with laurels.

'But you came to our rescue in your turn…'

She placed a hand on his arm, as if he had offered it. Once again, Volnay was stirred by conflicting emotions.

'Will you ever forgive me?' asked Chiara, quietly.

Seconds passed. They had stopped walking and stood looking at one another in silence, as if astonished by a sudden revelation.

'You will forgive me! You must!' she said impetuously, and leant closer. 'I do not want your scorn; I desire your friendship. You and I are one of a kind. The creed of natural selfishness acknowledges no moral rights or obligations, and we are united in its condemnation. Nor do we believe in God: humanity is all our religion.'

He stared at her in wonder.

'Have I given so much away that you can think such things of me?'

Chiara burst out laughing.

'The occasional hint, yes. Now, what will you say if I tell you: *our priests are not what we think them to be…*'

'*Their science is naught but our credulity!*'

'There! You read Voltaire. I knew it! You see, we were made to get along together!'

'To go forward together?' asked Volnay, unexpectedly. He regretted the question as soon as it was asked.

There was an embarrassed silence. The inspector was the first to speak.

'You are in a position to help me,' he said slowly. 'With your help, Mademoiselle, we can trap the comte's assistant.'

Chiara's eyes widened. Volnay hurried to explain himself, reassuring her as to the nature of the role he had planned for her.

'Be careful of the Comte de Saint-Germain,' she said. 'We do not know his true identity, and Casanova told me that, a few nights ago, he saw him entering a certain house in the Parc-aux-Cerfs.'

'The comte! In that den of debauchery?'

Volnay was astonished and made no secret of his surprise.

'I will do as you say, Chevalier,' said Chiara, 'for you.'

'For me?'

Chiara nodded sadly.

'Yes, because there is no other role left to me in this business, as you know.'

She stared into space.

'I have disappointed you. I know that. Believe me, I regret it. But you have not answered my question. Can we be friends?'

For a moment, Volnay feared she would take his hand, and that he would lose all control of his faculties. But she did not, and he regretted it even so. The slightest touch from Chiara filled him with happiness, and he knew now how badly he felt the need of such moments.

'Perhaps I am not the first woman to disappoint you, Chevalier?'

Volnay clenched his jaw.

'There was one…'

'One may sometimes be enough,' murmured Chiara, thoughtfully.

There was a long silence, as each pondered what they would say next.

Chiara spoke first. 'For my part, I have had no occasion to be disappointed in men, because I expect no more from them than they are able to give. Perhaps you expected too much of womankind?'

'Is a measure of constancy too much to expect? One day, you are everything to them, and the next, nothing. You meet them in the street and they go on their way as if you never existed.'

This time, Chiara reached for his hand and clasped it in hers. Volnay did not resist. The blood pulsed at his temples, and he prayed his disarray would pass unnoticed.

'What happened?' she asked.

He hesitated, until Chiara's hand pressed his still more firmly.

'There came a time when we told one another that our feelings could never change, that we could never be otherwise. Two weeks later, she had forgotten everything, in favour of a mere youth, a ladies' man with a smooth tongue in his head.'

'And did she marry him?'

There was a long silence. Even the birds seemed to have stopped singing.

'No, Mademoiselle,' said Volnay dully. 'She did not marry him, because I killed him.'

A shattering silence followed. Chiara's hand deserted Volnay's.

'How so?'

'A duel…'

'I see.'

They had reached a terrace planted with box trees. The sun disappeared behind the clouds.

'It looks like rain,' said Volnay, simply.

'I don't mind getting wet,' she said. 'I adore the rain, as I adore everything in nature. Do you like the rain, Chevalier?'

'No.'

'But you love science, at least?'

'I am more inclined to poetry, and letters.'

'With the exception of volumes of anatomy, to help solve unexplained murders,' she observed, in a gently mocking tone.

A winding avenue of trees led them to a copse, in the middle of which stood a hidden group of marble cupids, their arrows primed to prick the hearts of unwary souls who ventured their way.

'For my part, I take an interest in anything new,' said Chiara, with renewed enthusiasm. 'We have so much to accomplish, and only the Marquise de Pompadour can help us.'

There was a silence. Plainly, the inspector was dissatisfied with this latest turn in their conversation.

'You seem to have very little regard for the marquise,' said Chiara, regretfully. 'And no greater liking for the king, or the nobles at Court.'

'Your kind feel nothing but indifference for the misfortune of others.'

Volnay's tone indicated this would be his last word on the subject. Chiara hid her discomfort with another question.

'Have you always been a man of such rigid conviction, Chevalier? What were you like as a child?'

Volnay did not reply immediately. He remembered childhood games in gardens: swings, and playing at hide-and-seek or blind man's buff. A thousand things that woke in him a feeling of nostalgia and regret.

'The child in us dies in the world of men,' he sighed, between his teeth. 'I had a fine childhood, but it was shattered with one blow, and me with it. I should like to recover the innocence of that age...'

A cloud masked the sun. Around them, the flower beds shivered.

'It looks like rain,' said Volnay a second time.

Chiara's hands were clasped behind her back and she stood with her head cocked to one side, revealing a smooth, white neck.

'The people of this earth are not as bad as you think, and there is good in everyone. Take Casanova—'

'Bad example,' hissed Volnay. 'The man's a tremendous fraud, cold and manipulative.'

Chiara shook her head.

'He is far from cold, I can assure you.'

Volnay shot her a swift glance.

'You see,' he said, bitterly. 'You're defending him, and you like him, despite his reputation.'

Chiara's response was to the point.

'His reputation precedes him wherever he goes,' she said, 'because he makes no effort to hide his true nature. In our century of hypocrisy, he is a creature of sincerity.'

Silence.

'Like you,' she hastened to add.

Volnay made no reply but stared at her with an expression of renewed hope. Chiara gave a charming frown.

'But even you, Monsieur, you hide your true nature somewhat. You are not as cold as you would like us to believe. Am I right?'

There was no time for Volnay's answer: the first drops of rain were splashing on the ground. Chiara cried out as if hurt, then grasped his hand and pulled him along.

'Follow me, you who so dislike the rain!'

They sheltered in a dense, leafy grotto that gave protection from the sudden shower. Chiara shivered, and in a gesture more instinctive than calculated, Volnay put his arm around her shoulders. Surprised, she turned her enquiring face to his. The inspector closed his eyes for the briefest of seconds.

Chiara's mouth was a scarlet wound he must soothe. His lips brushed hers, ready to pull away at the slightest sign that she might recoil. But she did not. It was as if she had decided to confront the truth at that moment.

She closed her eyes and allowed herself to be kissed, timidly at first, then more and more passionately. Her tongue seemed to take on a life of its own, offering itself liberally to the chevalier's. For a moment, she held him so tightly in her arms that he stiffened. Little by little, as if by instinct, her ardour cooled, and she relinquished his mouth at last, recoiling slightly and adjusting her hair.

'You see,' she said, taking a deep breath, 'your true nature burns far hotter than may be imagined at first sight. Why did you flee from me?'

He was still holding her in his arms. He felt that if he let her go, he would lose her for ever. Great happiness, and muffled pain, mingled in his heart.

'I fled from you,' he said, 'because your presence woke such pain in me that I judged it wiser not to provoke it further by seeing you.'

'And so why aren't you fleeing me now?' breathed Chiara.

'Because there is nothing more terrible than my feelings for you, and nothing sweeter, either. Do not reproach me for this confession.'

Chiara gazed in silence at the scar that ran from the corner of Volnay's eye to his temple, then placed a hesitant finger against it, following its contours.

'I would reproach you more for keeping silent about your feelings,' she whispered, her lips barely two fingers' breadth from his.

And he kissed her again, and again.

'This garden is a place of marvels,' she said at length, breathlessly. 'And of traps…'

A soft, hesitant light filtered through a thin, bright haze of cloud when Volnay left Chiara's mansion. Even the foul, muddy street was powerless to overcome the happiness he had recovered after so many years.

Volnay's next scheduled visit was to the Comte de Saint-Germain. The comte was in the small paint workshop he maintained in Paris, and welcomed the inspector without affectation, but with his habitual show of extreme politesse. Urbane and charming as ever, he embarked delightedly on an explanation of the day's activities.

'What you see here is crushed, baked clay, mixed with coloured powders of my own composition, a little gum arabic as the binding agent, and fresh clay to thicken the preparation. Note how the clay ensures a cohesive mix of pigment. I stabilize the mixture with honey, because it's an excellent captor of atmospheric humidity.'

He took a step back and contemplated his work with a satisfied air.

'I love the powdery, velvety aspect of woad. Its granular consistency gives it an incomparable brilliance, as it refracts the light.'

He took a piece of cloth and enhanced the colour by rubbing and padding it skilfully over the coloured surfaces.

'And how goes your investigation?' he asked brightly.

Volnay told him everything about his assistant and confided his innermost thoughts on the matter. He knew that the comte—the creature of the great and powerful—would make no move if he believed the inspector was harbouring secrets. The Comte de Saint-Germain remained impassive, but he stared fixedly at Volnay, as if trying to read his thoughts.

'Well,' he said at length. 'So be it! I shall do what is expected of me.'

Volnay hesitated. The Comte de Saint-Germain gestured for him to approach an easel near the window, whose curtains were closed. He pulled them open, flooding the room with golden light. Volnay was dazzled for a moment and stood blinking while the comte hurried to turn the picture around, with a conjuror's flourish.

'I committed this little work to paper after your visit in the company of that charming young lady, who quite struck me with her beauty.'

The pastel was a portrait of Chiara. Bending closer, Volnay saw that the composition was organized in a pyramid structure, formed by the figures of the young woman, Casanova and himself. Chiara's eyes sparkled like uncut gems in the darkness. The train of her gown led the eye to a sheet of drawing paper held in one, trailing hand, to which she seemed to be pointing with the other. Volnay bent closer still and saw that the sheet was filled with an esoteric symbol: an equilateral triangle inside a pentagon, inside a heptagon, inside a nonagon. He committed the image to memory, before turning his attention to Chiara's portrait.

The artist had worked to guide the viewer's gaze progressively around the picture. In the foreground, a carpet exerted a *trompe-l'œil* effect, conferring depth and providing a solid base for the pyramid. Following the line of her dress, the eye rose to meet Chiara's face, wearing a thoughtful expression. She was looking at Volnay, though her body seemed to lean towards Casanova. Surely this was more than straightforward observation?

'I did the portrait from memory,' said the comte.

Volnay realized he was referring to the image of Chiara. She looked resplendent, and he felt a sudden urge to possess the picture at all costs.

'It's for you,' said the comte, as if reading Volnay's thoughts.

'It's not quite finished. But then, whatever we may think, this story is very far from over…'

He turned to face the inspector.

'Remember two things, my young friend. First there is rarely only one truth, but several. All the rest is mere opinion.'

He glanced at Chiara's portrait and continued:

'And second, if we are to define happiness, it is surely the joy of clasping in one's arms a person whom we love, and who loves us in return.'

Volnay returned home in the golden light of sunset. His thoughts returned to the young woman he had held in his arms. It seemed his lips were still moist from her kisses.

'Can I go on living without her?' he thought suddenly, in despair.

It had rained again in the night. In the morning, the wet cobblestones steamed. In his apartment, the comte's assistant brandished the phial with an inspired look, as Chiara pressed a hand to her forehead.

'Dear God, my head is burning.'

The assistant hurried to her side and offered her a seat.

'Would you like a glass of water, or a little eau de vie?'

'A glass of water, please,' said Chiara, in deathly, hushed tones.

Once he had left the room, she hurried to the main door and quickly drew the bolt. Volnay was the first to rush in, sword in hand.

'Charlatan!' he growled, when the assistant returned, and froze before them.

'But… but…' he stammered. 'Whatever does this mean?'

'It means enough is enough!' said a voice imbued with undeniable charm, but an equally undeniable accent of authority. The comte followed Volnay into the room. The assistant paled.

'So,' said the comte, 'this is how you repay my generosity—by stealing my potions and selling them!'

He stretched out his palm, and the assistant slipped the phial into his hand. The comte uncorked it and sniffed the contents quickly.

'You poor wretch,' he growled. 'You are a dwarf among giants—do you have even the slightest idea what you are doing?'

'Perhaps he was content to imitate his master,' said Volnay, without a shadow of a smile.

The comte span around to face him.

'Ha! Believe me, Monsieur,' he said, in horrified tones, 'I would go stark, staring mad before I would give a person a drug I knew nothing about!'

'What's in the phial?' asked the inspector, smoothly.

The comte gave no immediate reply.

'People ask a great deal of me,' he said darkly. 'One day, a woman of a certain age came to me for a liquor to preserve her hair and prevent it from turning white over the years! They say I possess powers of rejuvenation, even healing. I practise my skill as a chemist, but not to that end.'

Quickly, he slipped the phial into his pocket and turned to his assistant. His face was an expressionless mask.

'The Inspector of Strange and Unexplained Deaths entrusted me with the phial you gave to Mademoiselle Hervé, in exchange for your vile gropings. It contained a substance capable of purging impurities from the surface of diamonds. When the young woman rubbed it over her face, her skin dissolved instantly, and she died in atrocious pain.'

Volnay seized the assistant by the collar and pushed him roughly against the wall.

'You realized your mistake when you learnt of the young woman's death, and you paid the henchman to attack the monk while he was examining her body. You wanted to recover the phial, did you not? You were afraid the young woman had kept it with her, and that it would be traced back to you!'

The assistant opened and closed his mouth in a kind of stupor.

'Answer!' roared the inspector, throwing him to the floor.

The man gave a strangulated sob and rose to his knees.

'No! No, I swear! I betrayed my master to secure my fortune, and I abused the trust of pretty young women, I admit. My mistake caused Mademoiselle Hervé's death, but I did nothing more after that. Nothing!'

Volnay was surprised by the sincerity in the charlatan's tone. The man was trembling in every limb, and he doubted he would have been capable of bargaining with a hired hench-man of the very worst kind. The attack had been another of Wallace's plans after all, it seemed.

'You'll spend the rest of your days in a damp, dark dungeon,' he growled. 'At best.'

The Comte de Saint-Germain intervened.

'Chevalier, I beg you to consider this: my assistant is a rogue who deserves a measure of punishment. He has abused my trust and exploited my reputation to make money, and take advantage of women's credulity.'

He gave the man a hard stare. The assistant seemed to crumble on the spot.

'He deserves a moment's reflection within the walls of the Bastille,' said the comte firmly. 'But not to end his days there. A trial would deliver the harshest penalty and throw my name and my activities to the dogs of public opinion one more time. If you are in agreement, I will speak to the chief of police, even to the king himself, and ask for a letter of the royal signet. I believe that when an arrest is made for some minor misdemeanour, for which no further investigation is required, and when the inspector judges it appropriate to send the miscreant to prison, by way of correction, then it is up to the chief of police to determine the length of the sentence.'

'You're very well informed,' said Volnay quietly, narrowing his eyes.

'Invariably!'

'I don't know whether—'

It seemed to Volnay that the Comte de Saint-Germain had just tried to signal something to him, discreetly. But he gave no reaction, and the comte continued:

'Some things are best kept out of the public domain, wouldn't you agree?'

Chiara was the first to respond, nodding vigorously.

'The comte is quite right. We must proceed with care.'

Volnay shot her a look of hesitant surprise. The young woman seemed to have responded to the comte with a discreet signal of her own. He thought quickly. He knew he was in danger. He was being pressured, and spied on, from all sides. He needed support, and why not the support of the Comte de Saint-Germain, the intimate creature of the king and La Pompadour? He called to his men, outside on the landing, to take the assistant away in his carriage while he and Chiara remained in the room, with the comte.

'Are we alone?' asked the latter.

'Yes, Monseigneur.'

'I must thank you, Chevalier. Little did I know I was harbouring a viper in the bosom of my household. You have enabled me to scotch the creature. And I am grateful for your silence. You will understand the sensitivity of this whole business, for me. I have so many enemies… As for you, Mademoiselle…'

He turned to Chiara and bowed gallantly to kiss her hand.

'I cannot thank you enough for agreeing to play along with this farce and catch the villain. I am indebted to you both.'

Volnay stepped forward, ready to seize the moment.

'I still have a great many questions, Monseigneur, and I will be direct with you. What of the letter addressed to you by the king, asking you to take care of Mademoiselle Hervé's condition?'

The comte stared at him for a long moment.

'I cannot deny my knowledge of it—the Marquise de Pompadour told me the contents of the letter she had discovered, when you handed it to her in the company of your two friends. I give you my word that I had never read it beforehand. I believe the king lost his head when he wrote it. How could I end a new life? It was madness even to contemplate such a thing!'

There was a hint of cold fury in his voice, but the comte swiftly eased the tension with a sweet smile.

'A momentary lapse on His Majesty's part. This young woman didn't dare hand me the letter, and addressed my assistant instead, who is ever ready to ingratiate himself with the fairer sex, as I now understand. She came to elude the estate of motherhood, and he sold her eternal beauty. Who could resist?'

His words had the ring of truth, but a doubt remained in Volnay's mind. He had had enough, and determined to come straight to the point.

'Forgive me, Monseigneur, but you were seen entering the Parc-aux-Cerfs—a certain house on Rue Saint-Louis…'

The comte looked at him serenely.

'You are fearless, Inspector, and irreproachable. An honest man in a world where scarcely anyone dares speak his mind. Your courage will be rewarded, but I must ask you to be discreet.'

The inspector nodded briefly.

'I went to that place, indeed,' the comte continued. 'A young woman by the name of Hélène de Pal, taken there against her will by her father, had resolved to drink poison. With my support, she simulated the tragedy with a pill which I procured for her. The doctors were unable to revive her at the scene. At the appointed time, I arrived with an antidote to bring her back to life. Her repentant father agreed to give her in marriage to her lover, as the young woman desired, rather than prostitute her to the king. That is all the reason for my visit to that place.'

Volnay considered him for a moment in silence, sobered by what he had just heard, and by the sincerity in the comte's words. He believed him, though he had no proof, but the extraordinary tale opened up still further horizons, and hinted at quite a different Comte de Saint-Germain.

'Today's episode has allowed us to solve the mystery of the first murder,' said the inspector, pensively. 'But not the second. If the last victim had not been at the Parc-aux-Cerfs, I should have thought her death was the work of a madman aping the first killing, and clumsily at that. But the fact remains…'

'She *had* been at the Parc-aux Cerfs!' Chiara finished his sentence.

In the street, Volnay gently stayed Chiara with his hand.

'I must accompany this man. He is quite beside himself, and now is the best possible time to question him. Fear loosens tongues better than interrogation.'

Chiara stared at him, in a new light.

'You are quite pitiless, at times.'

'I have an investigation to lead, and nothing will stand in my way,' said Volnay with characteristic dread determination.

'And do I stand in your way?' she asked, in a pale voice. 'Or am I your goal?'

Volnay looked awkward.

'Well, you have certainly served my cause…'

Chiara drew back as suddenly as if she had been struck.

'And is that why you came to see me, and kissed me, Monsieur the Inspector of Strange and Unexplained Deaths?'

'I seek after truth, Chiara, only the truth.'

Chiara's hands grasped Volnay's.

'Do not sacrifice what truly matters to discover the secret cause of things.'

'I cannot relinquish the quest for understanding,' said Volnay obstinately.

A gulf yawned between them.

The iron-clad wheels of the inspector's carriage clattered over the cobbles. The comte's assistant stared at him in terror.

'Will I be tortured? Unlike you, I am a tremendous coward, and I have told you everything, outright.'

Volnay shot him an icy smile. The man had abused every possible trust, and a woman had died by his mistakes, for which he showed little enough remorse.

'You should have thought of that before,' he said simply.

Volnay thought for a moment. One detail still bothered him.

'When she climbed down from the carriage, in front of her home, Mademoiselle Hervé did not go straight up to her rooms but hurried further into the courtyard. I do not know why.'

His prisoner returned his gaze, utterly at a loss.

'I have no idea. What was there in the courtyard?'

'Nothing in particular. A baker's oven, on the far side.'

The assistant's face lit with a flash of understanding.

'Then, er… She was following my instructions, no doubt.'

'Explain yourself.'

'I advised her to warm up the phial before rubbing the contents over her face. With the heat from the oven, the results would be immediate.'

Volnay threw himself back in his seat, eyes half-closed.

'And so her impatience led her there. Now I understand.'

The assistant trembled like a plate of veal jelly.

'Monsieur,' he said, 'my fate is in your hands. Help me and I will give you information that will put the Comte de Saint-Germain firmly under your control.'

The inspector fought not to let it show, but a wave of curiosity flooded his consciousness.

'And why should I wish to exercise control over the Comte de Saint-Germain? I am no master blackmailer, nor am I at war with your former master.'

The assistant leant closer and addressed Volnay in confidential tones.

'Believe me, sir, the Comte de Saint-Germain is a redoubtable adversary. He is a true Kabbalist, and a follower of the magus Hermes Trismegistus. He is the author of *An Open Entrance to the Closed Palace of the King*. He possesses a globe of smoked quartz into which he conjures spirits. He violates ancient taboos, dating back to the time of Moses, to do it! You cannot imagine the things he is capable of!'

'Well, tell me about them,' said Volnay evenly. 'I'll make up my own mind when you've finished.'

To his great surprise, the assistant seated himself next to the inspector. He smelt the man's sweat, and a distinctive odour that he knew well, from having sniffed it on so many suspects under interrogation: the smell of fear.

The inspector listened, in growing astonishment, to what the assistant had to say.

'And so,' he summed up, when the assistant had finished, 'you're telling me that—'

'The Comte de Saint-Germain has truly discovered the secret of the transmutation of lead into gold!'

XII

I fear marriage more than death!

CASANOVA

The monk pursued his inquiries among the friends of the second victim, Marcoline. In so doing, he visited Casanova at his residence, La Petite Pologne. The chevalier received him warmly, but as soon as his guest was seated, he addressed him with a knowing wink.

'You don't often emerge from your lair by the light of day, monk. Our man of God favours the night!'

The monk's eyes glittered fleetingly with a cold, harsh light. Then it was his turn to smile.

'Moonlight stimulates the circulation, as you well know, Chevalier de Seingalt. A tonic for mind and body alike!'

Casanova moved closer and stood before him, with his hands on his hips.

'And so, do you think I failed to recognize you when we drew swords together against that whey-faced devil? Do you think that while I never forget a woman, I forget the faces of men? In a word, do you honestly believe I could forget the accomplice of my escape from the Piombi, in Venice?'

The monk's face was expressionless.

'The fact is, I have barely had occasion to present myself to you,' he said calmly. 'I am pleased you recognized me: the man who scraped a hole in the ceiling, to reach the roof of the doge's palace, after all!'

Casanova laughed heartily.

'Heaven knows, I was never one for manual labour!'

'Nor I,' retorted the monk, politely, 'and yet I scraped a hole in the floor, too.'

'By the Devil, so you did! But we must celebrate our reunion!'

The monk bowed, smiling.

'I have nothing against reunions, if there's a decent wine.'

Casanova ordered Cyprus wine and a piece of smoked tongue. The bottle was brought, and duly dispatched, and the tension eased.

'Contrary to popular opinion,' said Casanova, 'I am a lover of the religious life. My last relations with a nun continued for twelve hours straight, hard as a rock throughout and all under the watchful gaze of a future cardinal of France.'

'He moves in mysterious ways, His wonders to perform…' observed his visitor solemnly.

'You're a devil of a monk!' declared Casanova, laughing. 'You speak Latin, handle your sword like a hired assassin, and you're a greater heretic even than I! How sad to have gone our separate ways the moment we got out of prison. I like you.'

'And I you, my dear philanderer.'

They clinked glasses.

'Yes,' said Casanova, 'our kind recognize a kindred spirit at first glance.'

The monk blinked knowingly. He knew what Casanova was thinking. Adventurers are eternal rebels. They know how to recognize another soul for whom any constraint is provocation. Casanova returned the acknowledgement, with a barely perceptible nod of the head. The monk leant closer.

'One piece of information, and you shall have my blessing, my son. After we parted in Venice, how did you get away? I was forced to disguise myself as a washerwoman!'

Casanova shrugged his shoulders lightly.

'A capacious robe suits you very well! As for me, I took shelter with the wife of the police chief of a nearby town, while her husband was out, hunting me down in the woods.'

The monk nodded.

'Clever!'

Casanova observed him attentively.

'My turn to ask you a question. I never knew how you came to be locked up in the Piombi.'

'Oh,' said the monk, 'the merest trifle. I compared the Most Serene Republic's Council of Ten to a pack of red-arsed baboons.'

Casanova gave a short burst of laughter.

'Any criticism of the Ten is strictly forbidden!'

'But there it is—I am drawn to forbidden things.'

Casanova looked at him thoughtfully, with the air of a man reunited with a former brother-in-arms. He raised a questioning eyebrow.

'You're not here to rake over old memories. You have something to ask of me.'

The monk nodded.

'Circumstances have embroiled you in a criminal investigation. Your zest for first-hand information, and your hopes for the hand of our young friend Chiara have drawn you in further. And so I am going to give you an opportunity to help us. Discreet inquiries have revealed the name of the second victim: Marcoline. She had two friends, Léonilde and Maria. Occasional bedfellows at the Parc-aux-Cerfs.'

He stroked a finger along the edge of his glass, watching for Casanova's reaction.

'You know what will happen if we question them. They will snap shut like a pair of oysters, and we will find ourselves pressured by Sartine to keep our distance. On the other hand...'

The monk's smile etched a thousand tiny wrinkles at the corners of his eyes.

'On the other hand,' he continued, 'pillow talk passes unnoticed and will doubtless deliver more satisfactory results.'

Casanova thrust his glass into the air.

'To the Devil's own monk! And delightful entertainment in prospect…'

The sun was a tarnished copper disc when the Chevalier de Seingalt climbed down from his carriage. He took a few cautious steps, knowing that his prey would turn the corner of the street at any moment, then hurried forward, jostling the two young women as he passed.

'Oh, dear Lord!' said one.

Casanova swept the ground with the brim of his hat, and delivered a flurry of apologies. The women stared at him in curiosity, noting his elegant clothes, his autocratic bearing and his pleasant, open face. The Venetian returned their scrutiny. He remembered the pair from his incursion into the Parc-aux-Cerfs, on Rue Saint-Louis. One was quite tall, with a narrow waist. She wore a red velvet dress with slashed sleeves, decorated with ribbons and tassels. Her pale face was framed by twin cascades of dark blonde hair. Her cheekbones were high and well defined, and beneath her slightly hooked nose her generous, scarlet-painted lips offered a glimpse of fine white teeth. The other girl was smaller and thinner, with a more highly coloured, exotic complexion and lank, black hair. Her watchful brown eyes were flecked with gold. She held her hands clasped behind her back and affected a frown of annoyance.

The Chevalier de Seingalt bowed graciously.

'Ladies, again, I beg you to excuse me! I am quite in a whirl. My clumsiness has its reasons, and I can but hope you will suffer to hear them, by way of explanation and apology. I have come straight from a gaming table where I have won a small fortune, and I can think of nothing but the best way to spend it as quickly as possible.'

The darker, thinner girl said nothing, but the tall blonde smiled indulgently.

'Consider yourself excused, Monseigneur. And if you are in need of advice on how to spend your winnings, I am sure we can offer some ideas.'

Casanova burst out laughing, and the young women warmed immediately to this cheerful, unaffected, vigorous and thoroughly likeable man.

'Truly, I need your help!' he declared, shaking a purse full of gold. 'Allow me to escort you to the theatre in my carriage, and after that we shall take supper at my mansion.'

The smaller girl, who was seemingly of Spanish descent, spoke first:

'But we do not know you, Monsieur.'

Casanova gave a signal, and a magnificent carriage pulled up beside them.

'Is that your carriage, Monsieur?' asked the taller girl.

'Mine, indeed. But allow me to introduce myself: the Chevalier de Seingalt, at your service.'

The taller girl dropped a slight curtsey.

'I am Léonilde, and this is Maria.'

The coachman folded down the steps. Casanova helped the first girl to climb aboard, then held out his hand to Maria. She hesitated a moment, then smiled in turn and leant her weight on his arm rather more than was necessary to step up into the coach. Certain of splendid entertainment later that day, Casanova was bright and spirited, sparkling for the benefit of the two demoiselles, who were flattered to have attracted the attentions of such a well-known gentleman.

Léonilde couldn't help but ask: 'Why has a fine man such as yourself never married, Chevalier?'

'Why, because I fear marriage more than death!' replied Casanova, laughing.

'And yet they say you will stop at nothing to seduce a woman,' said Maria.

'More than you could possibly know!' declared the Chevalier de Seingalt. 'Once, in Germany, my determination to find a way into a certain lady's bed led me to be locked up inside a church day after day, hidden in a confessional. Then I took a staircase leading from the sacristy to her apartments, where I would wait for up to five hours for the door to be opened. I took my delicious reward for the long hours spent waiting, but was careful not to wake her husband, sleeping soundly nearby! But the interminable waiting in the cold took its toll on my health, and I left her for another, more accessible lady.'

The girls laughed, and Casanova joined the chorus. He dispensed a constant stream of witticisms and tall tales. The trio sipped bitter orange punch in a delightful cafe in the Palais-Royal, then attended the theatre before retiring to the chevalier's mansion for supper. Casanova ordered a magnificent table laid with oysters and lobster, truffled red partridge baked in pastry, and a ragout of escalopes of foie gras in Madeira wine.

The party uttered cries of amazement and delight while, under the table, surreptitious touches ignited their mutual desires. Feet searched and found one another; hands slipped beneath the cloth while they drank from the same glass. Oysters were passed from mouth to mouth, because, as Casanova said, an oyster should always be drunk with the saliva of one's beloved. Naturally, the trio moved on to the bedroom, but not before Casanova had swallowed down his habitual aphrodisiac of raw egg whites.

The room was decorated with panelling painted with a shower of birds and blossoms, interspersed with small medallions depicting amorous scenes. The bed was dressed in cream muslin embroidered with small garlands of golden acorns, and scattered with far more silk pillows than was necessary. In the adjoining room, the young women gasped in admiration at the water closet, with its marble toilet bowl and flush valve, and its seat inlaid with fragrant, hardwood marquetry.

'You may try it out later,' agreed Casanova. 'But for now, we have better things to do…'

The magpie cackled brightly as the first rays of sunshine touched her cage. The monk and the Inspector of Strange and Unexplained Deaths shared a breakfast of soup, cold meats, bread rolls and jam.

'You're not eating much,' said Volnay.

'Blame it on Casanova's Cyprus wine,' grumbled the monk. 'It's left me with an almighty headache.'

There was a confident knock at the door. The monk cast Volnay a wicked glance.

'Talk of the Devil… What a hearty constitution! A sleepless night, and you rise with the sun to tell us all about it.'

Volnay invited Casanova to sit with them. With a notable lack of ceremony, the chevalier pulled up a chair and helped himself to a chicken breast, devouring it in two mouthfuls.

'You will be proud of me, my friends! The job was done in a matter of hours, thanks to a fat purse, natural curiosity, the promise of pleasure, a well-stocked table, fine wine and the delights of conversation.'

'And?' Volnay was impatient.

'And then conversation ceased, I went into action, and triumphed!'

'So you had a pleasant evening?' asked the monk, wryly.

Casanova responded with a rhyming couplet:

> 'Ye gods, such delight, as I pressed my suit,
> And with it the juice of forbidden fruit!'

'And what did you find out over the course of this restless night?' asked the inspector, irritated by the monk's complicity.

'More than you would ever uncover in the course of your inquiries! A woman's bed is the best place to discover the secrets of the entire world. Can you imagine—the two minxes began proceedings by undertaking together what they are in the habit of doing with their men! But we exhausted every possible combination thereafter, I do believe.'

Volnay clicked his tongue in irritation.

'Spare us a recital of your exploits. You sniffed the sweat of their armpits. Where's the glory in that?'

Casanova affected an air of profound astonishment.

'For my part, I have always adored the smell of every woman I love, and the more abundant her sweat, the more I am seduced.'

Volnay rolled his eyes and said nothing. The monk smiled, with a rapt expression that spoke of old but vivid memories springing to mind. Seeing that his audience had stopped listening, Casanova sighed.

'I admit that it was hard work bringing the conversation around to Marcoline, but I succeeded, at length.'

He pulled the last leg of chicken towards him.

'It was the smaller of the two, the wild girl Maria, who knew her a little. Marcoline visited the house in the Parc-aux-Cerfs only occasionally. She had scarcely known the royal bed, being called upon only when the usual courtesans were unable to satisfy our beloved king. May God save him!'

He crunched the bones between his teeth and discarded what was left, with a troubled air.

'That was all I discovered…'

The monk heaved a sigh of disappointment, and Volnay shot him a glance, as if to say *I told you so!*

'On the other hand,' Casanova went on, 'my good lady Léonilde, whom I should be delighted to see again, delivered up some precious information. Shortly before her death, Marcoline had bagged herself a fine pigeon: a mature gentleman, not especially handsome, but with a decent fortune that more than made up for his shortcomings. She had loosened his purse strings all right, and intended to continue, though the man had shown greater reluctance of late.'

'Blackmail?' asked the inspector.

Casanova's expression was non-committal.

'She did not pronounce the word, but it was in her eyes!'

'And that's all?'

'Dear God!' exclaimed Casanova. 'I'm no policeman!'

He held out a glass and the monk hurried to fill it, satisfying his own thirst for information as he did so.

'Was this Léonilde able to give you a description of the man?' asked Volnay insistently.

'A vague portrait: fifty to sixty years of age, no distinctive characteristics, but a remarkably maladroit lover, it seems.'

The monk rose quickly to his feet.

'I take it from all this that our victim was leading her lover a fine dance! I'll take care of young Léonilde, though, alas, I'll not follow your interrogation techniques. Where can I find her?'

Casanova gave a sly smile.

'She left my residence less than an hour ago, and is probably now enjoying a well-earned rest. Otherwise, she plies her charms in a house on the Rue de Savoie, near the Palais-Royal.'

'Noted. I won't hurry there now, though. I have an experiment to finish first.'

He turned to Volnay.

'I suggest you call on Marcoline's landlady and question her neighbours. Perhaps one of them can tell you more.'

The inspector nodded. Left alone, he and Casanova stared at one another in silence.

'I'm going home to bed,' said the Venetian. 'I'm quite exhausted.'

But he made no move and peered at Volnay with sudden interest.

'You said you were tired,' said the inspector, irritably.

'Yes, those ladies were an inexhaustible fount of sensual delight.'

'Like any whore.'

'No, Volnay,' said Casanova, insistently. 'Like every woman. Their bodies are charged with a living energy all their own. A life source. If God exists, she is a woman!'

'I cannot follow you into such terrain.'

Casanova gave him an understanding look.

'I understand your difficulty, Volnay. You do not love women, you fear them.'

'I don't fear them,' retorted Volnay. 'I merely protect myself from any source of pain.'

Casanova shook his head disapprovingly. Volnay's words ran counter to his entire philosophy of life, and he felt a sudden urge to share it with this young man.

'Pleasure is never a source of pain.'

'But true feelings are! And that, you cannot possibly understand.'

'Do not believe it,' said Casanova, vehemently. 'I have feelings for every woman I bed, and the pleasure she takes is four-fifths my own.'

'Truly, Casanova, you make me laugh! You seduce women in order to advance your own position in society.'

Casanova's expression darkened.

'My conquests are rarely of such quality. Let me tell you a story: one evening in London, I encountered a young lady with whom I made love on the spur of the moment, in a carriage. When we parted, I asked her to introduce me to her friends. She answered coldly that such a thing was impossible, as she did not know me. "I have told you my name," I said. "Surely you know who I am?" "I know very well who you are," she replied, still more coldly, "but escapades such as these are not a letter of introduction."'

He looked up and stared the inspector hard in the eye.

'Believe me, the touch of naked skin on skin changes nothing. To the aristocracy, we are less than flies!'

The inspector said nothing. Casanova's face clouded like a sky turning to rain.

'I know you despise me, Volnay. That's unimportant. True, I adore parties and whoring. I have sacrificed everything for my one delight, the pursuit of desire, rich one day, poor the next, but losing none of my good cheer along the way. I have known the best and the worst of times, but I have always been my own master, and no one has ever held me in their power. Can you say as much?'

'Yes. No one has power over me,' said Volnay, adding sourly: 'And I flatter no one.'

Casanova was unperturbed. There was a hint of defiance in his reply:

'I have achieved my wealth by my own talents and merits. The nobleman takes the trouble to be born, and nothing more. And still he takes pride in the fact, the imbecile. He shines by the accident of birth, not the brilliance of his intellect. He pressures his subjects, shearing the wool from their backs, and you find me more dishonest than such as he? Ha! You have no idea what it is to come from nowhere, and to arrive somewhere.'

'I am a self-made man,' said Volnay coldly. 'I'll take no lessons from anyone on that score.'

The two men locked eyes for a moment, challenging one another. Casanova was indifferent to the inspector's hostility, as he was to the hostility of any of his own sex. He felt no hostility in return, either. Rather a sense of respect, and a measure of indulgence, as for a wayward student who stubbornly refuses any advice he may be offered. For his part, Volnay grudgingly admitted that Casanova was possessed of some talents. He was brave and daring, despite his faults. He even secretly admired the essential components of Casanova's life: his high spirits, good humour and wit, his love of intrigue, his courage, his travels, his light-heartedness, and his passion for women.

'Have you never wished to stop and settle somewhere?' asked the inspector.

Casanova made no attempt to disguise his surprise at Volnay's sudden curiosity.

'At a woman's side, often. But the feeling soon passes. And never in a city, except Venice…'

He seemed overwhelmed by a sudden feeling of nostalgia.

'Ah, Venice! Her palaces cast their shadow over my mind. The water she bathes in courses through my veins. Venice lives within me, wherever I go. Venice is a woman: she is mine; she is chastity itself, and a thorough wench. Venice gave herself to me like a whore, then cast me aside. And now I am her client, he who wakes alone, with his purse stolen.'

It was the lament of a soul in exile. Volnay knew Casanova was speaking from the heart, and considered him in a new light.

'Why don't you return home?' he asked.

'Home! Where is home?' exclaimed the Chevalier de Seingalt. 'I was born in Venice, and if I were to return there, I would be left to starve. I was raised in Venice and thrown into prison in Venice! And to think…'

His expression darkened.

'And to think that I do not even know the whereabouts of my own mother.'

There was a long silence. Volnay was discovering Casanova's true nature, more profoundly human than he could have imagined, and the prospect frightened him. Chiara would never succumb to an unscrupulous adventurer, but to a vulnerable wounded man…

'Leave Paris,' said the inspector, suddenly.

'What?'

'You'll never have Chiara!'

Volnay had shouted the words, and Casanova gazed at him with compassion.

'Woman is the undisputed centre of our world,' he said gently. 'No one could feel more desire, more concern for womankind than I do. I love each one as if she were the first, and the last. That's my secret. But it seems that Chiara may indeed be the last.'

Volnay swore vehemently under his breath. There was a fluttering of feathers in the magpie's cage.

'Casa's a cretin! Cretin Casa!' cackled the bird suddenly.

Casanova peered inquisitively at Volnay.

'What did your magpie just say, Monsieur?'

The monk donned a coat, gilet and breeches in striped blue taffeta, and made his way to the Rue de Savoie, in search of Léonilde. She was nowhere to be found. He visited a number of houses frequented by girls of her kind, to no avail, and set out instead for those other notorious dens of pleasure and solicitation: the cafes of the Palais-Royal, where young women of the world were very much at home. The city buzzed like a hive in the early afternoon sunshine. The monk was delighted to walk out in his finery, proud of his new-found elegance and the admiring looks he drew from the females of the species. He found her walking in the gardens of the Palais-Royal, and greeted her. She seemed to fit Casanova's description.

'A piece of gold, young lady, if you will tell me the nicknames our esteemed monarch applies to his girls!'

Taken by surprise, the young woman eyed his fine clothes and flowing, needle-lace cuffs.

'I have no idea, Monsieur. Grace, Belle, Beloved?'

The monk laughed aloud.

'Our beloved king calls them Ride, Rag, Grub and Sop!'

The girl was speechless.

'But you couldn't know that, of course,' he continued. 'Take this coin—it suits your complexion better than mine!'

She took it without a word.

'May I know the name of the charming person here before me?'

'Léonilde.'

The monk hid his satisfaction.

'Do you read, Mademoiselle?'

Léonilde stared at him. What a curious question!

'No, sir. I have no use for books.'

'That's a shame—a pretty girl like you would have much to gain by expanding her knowledge.'

'I received a religious education, sir.'

The monk nodded approvingly.

'Tell me more. I am interested in matters of religion.'

'Not I, Monsieur. Whenever I misbehaved, my punishment was to be shut in a cellar where they buried the nuns. I wept in terror for hours at a time.'

A ray of pity lit the monk's face.

'We each have our cross to bear. Indeed, that's why I never rush to judge my fellow man.'

She considered him with curiosity and liking. It was her lucky day. After a fine, wealthy nobleman, she was being accosted by a man of quality, to all appearances good-hearted and intelligent. She wasn't always so fortunate. Two days ago, she had spent three hours attending to the needs of a vegetable-seller from Suresnes, with rotten teeth and an inability to ejaculate. She had suffered his foul breath and his ineffectual thrusts until he had decided to hit her, at which she had cried out, until the madam intervened, remonstrating gently with the sheepish offender. When her client had left, the wicked woman had scolded her, and even slapped her for rousing the entire household over so little.

'Are you fond of ice cream?' asked the monk, abruptly.

He took her to the Procope. The parlour served ices flavoured with rose petals, toasted orange flowers, brown bread and fresh butter.

'Did you know, Léonilde, that the Chinese and Arabs had the secret of iced sweetmeats? The caliphs of Baghdad drank syrups mixed with snow—*chorbet*. At the court of Alexander the Great, mixtures of finely chopped fruit—*macédoines*—were served with honey, in dishes topped with snow. Nero would dispatch horses to gallop back from the far mountains with iced mixtures of rose water, honey, fruits and pine resin. And by the grace of God, Marco Polo brought us the *sorbetière*!'

'I've heard that story. Yet I doubt Marco Polo ever got as far as China—in fact I even doubt he set foot in Asia,' said Léonilde, raising a sceptical eyebrow. 'The adventures of Marco Polo are certainly the fruit of his own imagination, and yet people still speak of him, centuries later.'

The monk nodded and steered the conversation to the subject of Marcoline. The young woman was no fool.

'The Chevalier de Seingalt has told you about me, hasn't he?'

'Why should he have done that?'

She frowned delicately.

'I spend the night with him. He asks me about Marcoline. And next day, here you are asking me the same thing.'

'You're right,' the monk admitted. 'The chevalier did indeed talk to me about you.'

'That's rather dishonest of him, especially after he gave proof of his tender feelings towards me, seven times over, in the course of the night.'

'Proofs of that nature are fleeting indeed.'

'And you,' she stated, plainly disappointed. 'You are a dishonest man, too.'

'My natural disposition is to be frank, but experience has taught me to exercise caution,' said the monk.

She stared him in the eye.

'What do you want to know?'

'I'm looking for the man Marcoline was blackmailing, and her probable killer.'

The blood drained from Léonilde's face.

'She's dead? Dear God!'

She moved closer.

'I never saw him, but what she told me about him seemed very strange to me.'

And she told him everything she knew.

'Ah,' said the monk. 'That is indeed most peculiar.'

XIII

*The most delightful place on earth loses its charm the
moment one is condemned to live there in perpetuity.*

CASANOVA

'Rise, oh most desired sun!' said Casanova on waking.

And the sun had risen at his command, so that he stepped
out of bed in a thoroughly good mood, and set out to pay
Chiara a visit.

The young noblewoman kept the Venetian waiting. She was
washing her face with sweet almond oil, in a room decorated
with crystals and seashells. A ceramic stove purred gently
beside a bath filled with still-steaming water. The traces of
her bare, wet feet dried fast on the marble floor. Her dressing
table was covered with pots of ointment, small soaps perfumed
with the rarest essential oils, and phials of rose and orange
flower water.

Chiara was in a sorrowful mood, and the rituals of her
toilet helped her to forget her troubles. She had offered
her lips to Volnay, and now she had heard nothing from
him for almost three days! It seemed clear to her now that
the indifference he had shown her when he left with the
comte's assistant, proved that the inspector had accepted
their reconciliation solely in order to set the trap that had
delivered the charlatan into their hands. She bore a grudge
against Volnay now, and against the male species in general,
hence the coolness of her greeting to Casanova once she
had dressed—in a long, white muslin gown tied at the waist
with a pink ribbon.

'How are you, Chevalier de Seingalt?'

'Exceedingly well! Beset with thoughts of you, my nightly dreams are delightful indeed, and put me in the best of spirits.'

'I'm pleased to hear it.'

Somewhat taken aback, Casanova tried in vain to cheer her, and was on the point of leaving when Chiara spoke:

'Give me your arm, we shall take a walk.'

They went down to the cool shade of the gardens.

'Do you believe we can go back in time?' she asked when they were under the trees.

'No, Chiara, I do not,' said Casanova firmly.

It had just occurred to him that the thought of Volnay was the only thing standing between them.

'Truly?'

She seemed to think for a moment. Like the springtime all around them, her thoughts returned to the beginnings of life.

'We are children for so short a time, after all,' she said.

Casanova had no idea what to say.

'And so, do we become what we are destined to be, as children?' she asked.

'Indeed, perhaps we do. The world is there all around us, and the people around us affect the way we see it, from the start. Do you know who my parents were? Actors! They trod the boards, and now my stage is the royal courts of Europe. I spend my life playing my own part, and I admit that here, today, I am beginning to tire of it...'

As so often when he spoke about his life, and his boundless freedom, Chiara looked enchanted.

'And yet your life is one great adventure book, filled with women, and gaming, and travels. You've even added a few touches of magic!'

Their hands joined for the briefest of moments, then parted.

'Will you leave here, Chevalier?' she asked suddenly.

'Yes, one day,' said Casanova, evasively.

'And why? Do you not like Paris?'

'The most delightful place on earth loses its charm the moment one is condemned to live there in perpetuity.'

She walked on a few paces, joining her hands behind her back like a little girl preparing to misbehave, or speak out of turn.

'Would nothing keep you here?'

'You keep me here, Chiara. You. Not this ridiculous investigation, about which I understand not the slightest thing.'

She enveloped him in a warm, appreciative gaze, then gave a doubtful frown.

'My dear old liar. How delightful it would be to listen to your talk, and abandon myself to you, in your arms!'

She leant forward to kiss him tenderly on the lips, then stepped back. Casanova stood as if turned to stone.

'But,' she added indulgently, 'I do not trust your feelings for one second—only your desire. And for me, that is not enough.'

They walked on, along a path of fine sand lined with firs and beech trees.

'No one believes that I am capable of feelings, like anyone else,' sighed Casanova. 'And yet I loved my mother more than anything in the world, and she refused to acknowledge me.'

There was a long silence. A bird began to sing.

'And so what is love, for you?' asked Chiara.

Casanova thought for a moment, then said slowly:

'A sacred monster that we may define only in paradoxes. A bitterness sweeter than anything imaginable; a sweetness more bitter than anything on earth.'

Chiara fidgeted uncomfortably.

'You're becoming melancholy and disenchanted. That's not like you at all!'

They had reached the edge of a copse. Ahead lay a glimpse of a leafy arbour, the very spot where Volnay had kissed her. Chiara shivered and turned on her heels.

'Let us go back inside. You can tell me the source of this melancholy.'

Suddenly, Casanova was close beside her, smiling and joking.

'Be my princess! I'll build you a palace of precious gems. I'm *sure* the Comte de Saint-Germain will be able to help!'

As if by magic, his hand closed around hers. Laughing, he led her after him, and she held him back, because she knew where he was taking her. The box hedges raced past, and the ground seemed to slip from under her feet. She pretended not to understand; she feigned reluctance, but her heart was beating fit to burst and the blood pounded in her ears. They ran up the steps, under the astonished gaze of the footmen, and crossed a painted, gilded passageway. Breathless, she stopped him in the doorway to her bedroom, but he laughingly slipped past her and seated himself with authority on the fringed silk covers of her bed, inviting her to join him.

Casanova breathed her scent, impatient to know where her perfume ended and the smell of her skin began. The hem of her dress was split to reveal an underskirt, explored now by Casanova's hand, like a mariner discovering a new world. She ventured to protest, but he stopped her mouth with a long, deep kiss.

Chiara never knew how it happened. She resisted for a time, then weakened as he kissed her, before surrendering herself, trembling. The soft mattress cleaved to her body; she lay her head against the white eiderdown, and realized that she was listening to him, answering him, allowing him to touch and caress her. Casanova's hand reached under the blue, boiled satin underskirt that flattered her waist, crushing the lace beneath. Her body surrendered, surprised and delighted at his expert touch. His weight did not oppress her, and his warmth communicated itself to her. Above them, on the canopy over her bed, plump cupids embraced solemnly. She felt suddenly transported into their midst, among the fleecy clouds that decorated her ceiling.

Dazzled, Casanova covered her smooth, radiant body with a thousand kisses. He made love to her passionately, but when he pulled away to spare her, she held him to her and whispered:

'Draw blood!'

'I want to melt into your body,' Volnay had written, thinking of Chiara.

The setting sun cast a strange glow over the streets as he stepped outside. After the storm, the bright puddles looked like sky holes in the street. He thought of the rain that had brought them together in the leafy arbour. The rain was his ally. He set out for the mansion of the Marquis D'Ancilla.

Her body breathed once more. She had experienced the climax of passion. Overhead, the cupids gazed sadly down. Chiara lay across her bed like a discarded flower. She turned her head slightly to one side and saw that it had rained during their love-making. The windowpanes were dotted with constellations of teardrops. She thought of another shower of rain, from which she had sought refuge in another man's arms, and her eyes brimmed with tears.

'There are caresses that wound, like repeated blows,' she whispered.

'Cheer up,' said Casanova. 'Gloominess is the death of me.'

*

Volnay watched as Casanova's carriage drove out from the forecourt. He saw the Venetian's profile framed in the coach window. Driven by a sudden sense of impending disaster, he hurried forward. The gates had not closed. He saw Chiara, who had accompanied Casanova to his carriage, pacing the courtyard. Her soft, dream-like expression told him straight-away what had happened. He froze, struggling to master the pain that spread through him now, like poison. Then, silently, he turned and walked away.

XIV

Is there a living soul on this earth who
has seen me eat or drink?

COMTE DE SAINT-GERMAIN

The comte's trio of visitors bowed. One was a man in his seventies, of dignified bearing, with a white beard covering a determined chin. The other two men, both of mature years, were utterly dissimilar from one another. The face of one was adorned with a nose shaped like a potato, and eyes that sparkled with intelligence. The last, but far from least, of the three was painfully thin and starved-looking. The skin of his face lay close over the skull beneath; his cheeks were hollow, and dark, yellow-brown rings circled his eyes.

The Comte de Saint-Germain greeted them with his habitual show of politesse, addressing each in turn: 'Monsieur le Duc,' 'Master' and, finally, 'Captain.'

'Monsieur le Comte,' said the oldest of the three, the man whom his host had addressed with the title of duke, 'we have come at your invitation. We represent the Masonic lodges of Saint-Pierre and Saint-Paul, the Arts Sainte-Marguerite, the Parfaite Union, the Louis d'Argent, the Loge de Buci and many others besides. All stand ready to unite and take action, but not as a federation under a single leader.'

'Do you know who I am?' asked the comte.

'I know who you claim to be!' said the other man delicately. 'But I am none the wiser for that. The Marquise de Pompadour speaks very highly of you. But that will not suffice, though we hold her in the very highest esteem.'

The comte said nothing, but walked over to his desk and opened a locked drawer, from which he removed a sheet of parchment.

'Here is the document you have come for.'

The three men studied it closely; then the oldest man muttered:

'The man who must come will show three signs: the parchment, the talisman and the gold. You have shown us the parchment, which is in order. Do you have the talisman?'

The comte presented it to them, folded in a piece of purple silk. It was a polished, round plaque, encased in metal and imprinted with curious designs. The obverse showed the mysterious number 'two hundred and sixty', arranged over eight lines; the reverse showed the planet Mercury as an angelic youth with wings on his back and heels, brandishing a caduceus like a sceptre in his right hand, and with a star on his head bearing the Latin name 'Mercurius'.

The two younger men were unstinting in their compliments, but the oldest man smiled into his beard.

'They say this talisman has the gift of eloquence, and the power to incline its owner to learning in every branch of the sciences. It suits you perfectly, Monsieur le Comte, no doubt about that!'

His companions glanced at him in surprise, then nodded silently.

'The parchment, the jewel—both are here, although you might have stolen them both,' said the gaunt-faced man. 'But if you are truly who you claim to be, then you must be in possession of the *lapis philosophicae*, the philosopher's stone!'

'O ye of little faith!' exclaimed the comte. 'And your faith in God depends on the proof of miracles, no doubt?'

Still, he led them smiling into his laboratory, picked up a phial and held it before their eyes.

'Behold, and honour the *aqua Tofana*,' said the comte.

The three men clustered around him, feverish with excitement. The Comte de Saint-Germain prepared the mixture using the *aqua Tofana* and a little mercury ore, then left it to heat in a crucible over a hot flame.

'This, mixed with *aqua Tofana*, is the philosophers' mercury, whose secrets I cannot reveal. But know that I have used a mercury ore known as *terre d'Espagne*, filtered through a fine linen cloth to remove any remnants of slag. This mercury is essential to the Work, for it combines both sun and moon. The mineral alloy obtained is sufficiently subtle that it can withstand the tyranny of fire. I reduce it to ashes, to cleanse it of its impurities, then I make it react, to gold or silver. At this stage in the process some call it the Virgin's milk, or the dragon's tail.'

The group watched in fascination as the mixture putrefied and turned black.

'This phase is termed the Raven, or the Dark Work,' said the comte.

The heat was tremendous, but the comte showed no sign of sweating. He took another phial filled with a greenish liquid and mixed its contents with the black amalgam.

'The green lion's blood, one of the Work's most secret materials.'

He poured the resulting mixture into an athanor, and continued heating it.

'The Work is wholly natural, but we control its circumstances, and an even distribution of heat is primordial. The virtue of a well-directed fire operates upon our Work.'

After an hour, the mixture turned sparkling white.

'The White Work...' breathed the oldest of the three onlookers in admiration.

The group held its breath. They knew that, at this stage, the stone was capable of turning lead into silver, but that if it was heated further, the white would turn red, the colour of the perfect philosopher's stone—the Red Work, through which the dead entity of gold would be wholly transformed, and brought to life.

'This all seems quick enough to you,' observed the comte, 'but make no mistake, I have laboured for months and months to produce the *aqua Tofana*, and the green lion's blood.'

The comte poured the White Work into a long-necked glass bottle and sealed it, then placed it to heat in the athanor.

'The longer the mixture is cooked, the more subtle it becomes, and the more subtle the mix, the better it is able to penetrate and transform the material.'

He continued heating the mixture, and added a little mercury.

'Mercury alone perfects the Work,' he said solemnly.

When the mercury began to give off black smoke, the comte hurried to another furnace, from which he removed a glowing piece of charcoal, using tongs to transfer it to the bottom of the crucible, where he gave it a sudden blast of fire. Melted in the flame, the mixture turned saffron yellow. The comte added a few pinches of powdered gold. The composition turned orange, then took on the appearance of coagulated blood, then turned a glossy red.

'The Red Work!' chorused the trio ecstatically.

Deftly, the comte poured the mixture into an ingot mould, and the group watched in amazement as it cooled, turning gradually to a beautiful golden hue.

'You hold a boundless fortune in your hands!' declared the oldest of the three men.

'Gold is never an end in itself, gentlemen,' replied the Comte de Saint-Germain sagely, 'but we shall use it to finance a revolution one day!'

*

The Master's estate was thoroughly well maintained, with a judicious mix of woodland, vineyards, orchards and fields. Blossoming apricot and peach trees greeted Volnay with a first wave of colour as he entered the property. Further along, roses, narcissi, amaranth and daffodils spread carpets of colour at his feet, and in the heady bouquet of fragrance, Volnay recognized the scent of jasmine, tuberose and roses, mixed with the subtler perfume of lilac, almond blossom and gardenias. The gentle murmur of streams rose to his ears, accompanied by birdsong. Fountains burst skywards, filling the air with the glitter of silver and gold.

Volnay stopped his horse and surveyed the property. Truly, this was Paradise on earth. A place of fragrance, colour and light to bewitch the senses.

He narrowed his eyes for a moment and followed the silvery-blue ribbon of a sunlit stream. He drew closer, and surprised a chaffinch drinking the water. The bird flew off, its damp wings leaving their imprint on the air. Volnay imagined this enchanting place filled with people to his taste. But the figures quickly vanished when he saw Chiara at the centre of them all. He felt a fresh surge of anger and spurred his horse forward.

An elderly man appeared at the top of the steps. He watched Volnay's approach with benevolent curiosity.

'Behold my young disciple, galloping out to meet me at this late hour, in search of some good advice. Come down from your horse, my friend, and follow me—you must be quite exhausted.'

They passed under the portico, and a servant led them to a colonnaded terrace, where they were served a sumptuous drink of fragrant mocha beneath a pergola overgrown with wisteria.

'The Brotherhood wants me dead,' said Volnay quickly, as soon as they were alone. 'They wanted to use me in an affair that touches on the king, and La Pompadour.'

The Master folded his hands and frowned. He was tall and thin, and stooped slightly under the burden of the years. His angular features were tanned and leathery, from over-exposure to the sun.

'What sort of affair?'

Volnay sighed. It was true—the Master was indeed living cut off from the world nowadays.

'The death of two young women, discovered with the skin of their faces torn away. The first death was an accident. The motive for the second murder remains to be discovered. She was very probably killed by a man she had been blackmailing. She was disfigured so as not to attract suspicion.'

The Master shuddered. His cordial good humour had vanished.

'What possible interest is that to the Brotherhood?'

'The two young women were among the king's mistresses, and the Brotherhood seeks to discredit him. You know the state of the country, and the rumours circulating about the king. Discrediting the monarchy paves the way for its eventual overthrow.'

'A most undesirable outcome,' said the Master, with renewed firmness in his voice. 'We came close to committing an irreparable act once before, when we primed Damiens to kill the king. I for one am glad we thought better of it in time, and that you were able to stop him.'

'Damiens died in atrocious suffering,' Volnay reminded him.

The Master stared deep into his eyes.

'I was wrong, I admit it. Which is why, after that inglorious episode, I retired gradually from the world, leaving Baron Streicher in charge of the Brotherhood.'

'Baron Streicher—the large man with the luxuriant beard, and the piercing gaze?'

'The same.'

Volnay bowed his head and contemplated his empty cup. The Master's sharp eyes were on him still, silently exerting their authority.

'Is there anything else you wish to ask me?' he asked after a few moments.

Nervously, Volnay moistened his lips.

'The Comte de Saint-Germain is mixed up in this business, too, though I cannot say how, exactly.'

The Master frowned.

'*Sanctus Germanus!*' he hissed softly, before quickly pulling himself together.

'Volnay, listen carefully to what I am about to say. Trust me and ask no questions: keep as far away as possible from the Comte de Saint-Germain!'

The inspector stared at him in astonishment.

'To return to the Brotherhood,' the Master continued firmly, 'we are no longer alone in our stand against absolutism and ignorance. The Freemasons have emerged. Their many lodges are highly active, and the Brotherhood's ancient lineage gives us no prerogative over them. We would be wise to join their cause.'

'I doubt Baron Streicher will agree.'

'Who is working with him?'

'No one I know, but he uses the services of a disreputable crew of henchmen, ready to kill on his command…'

The Master fidgeted uncomfortably.

'It must not come to that. I still exert a good deal of authority over them. We will talk to the Freemasons. I'll send you word of the place and time, and the means of entry. Take care and speak of this to no one, not even your friend the monk. Do I have your word?'

'Why not the monk?'

The Master was plainly embarrassed. He cleared his throat.

'Your somewhat erratic friend may be the soul of discretion, but his antics are not to my taste. He is far too unpredictable.'

'You are wrong to think of him that way,' Volnay reproached him. 'I trust the monk as I trust my own self.'

The Master broke into a condescending smile.

'You are wrong,' he said. 'You may be surprised to find you do not know him quite as well as you think.'

'What do you mean?' asked Volnay impatiently.

'Only that.'

Volnay frowned, unhappy with this turn in the conversation.

'There is one thing I don't understand,' he said. 'The Brotherhood decided, on your authority, to form closer ties with the Freemasons, and their leadership in London. Why has it not done so?'

The Master sighed.

'The Brotherhood is the oldest secret society in the world. It dates back to the civilization of ancient Sumer, five thousand years ago, the source of every structure in our modern society: the state, the army, the administration, commerce, justice—'

'Slavery, the subjugation of the people,' added Volnay without a pause.

The Master raised his eyebrows. He was visibly irritated.

'Well,' he said drily, 'we seek to alter radically the face of this world, as you know. But we are prevented from closer union with the Freemasons by our choice of the means to that end.'

'The monarchy prevents the progress of society, and ideas, but must it be brought down by violence?' asked Volnay. 'And inevitably we must ask: to be replaced by what? The Brotherhood of the Serpent is seen as the custodian of higher wisdom and knowledge handed down from the first Masters, at the dawn of time…'

'And that is the crux of the problem for Baron Streicher and his friends. Their sense of superiority prevents them from rallying to the Freemasons' cause, where all the lodges are equal, though London exerts a moral authority of a kind. Truth be told, Baron Streicher sees himself as the legitimate ruler of all mankind!'

A heavy silence ensued.

The racket of carriage wheels woke Volnay in the dead of night. Driven by curiosity, he rose and peered out of the window, in time to see a figure in a black cloak and hat. Footmen hurried to open the doors and escort him inside.

'You, here, *Sanctus Germanus*!' declared the Master. 'The storm is gathering! But come inside, refresh yourself and take something to eat.'

An impenetrable smile lit the visitor's face and the Comte de Saint-Germain's stentorious voice rang out mockingly:

'Is there a living soul on this earth that has seen me eat or drink?'

A door creaked, and the two men disappeared. The footmen busied themselves in the entrance; then silence fell once more. Volnay stole out into the passageway. His bedroom was on the upper floor; no one would see him. He stood motionless in the darkness, at the top of the stairs. Voices rose to him from time to time, like the rumour of a distant storm. A moment later, a door opened and footsteps rang out across the tiled hallway. A shadow passed. He recognized the elegant silhouette of the Comte de Saint-Germain.

'Take care!' he said firmly. 'If you persist in your mistaken course, you will be in grave danger.'

'Your words do not scare me,' said the Master, his features set in stone. 'You think you can frighten me, but I have been careless of my own safety for a long time now.'

The comte nodded. He stood in the doorway, and turned one last time. His face radiated the serene wisdom of a thousand past lives.

'Take care!' he repeated. 'Your willing charm is not enough.'

The doors opened, and Volnay shivered in the rush of cold air. For a moment, he determined to hurry downstairs and ask his host the meaning of all this noise, and the meaning of the comte's attitude and threats. But he had witnessed something he would never have seen had he not behaved like a vulgar spy. It was difficult, in such circumstances, to go downstairs and join his host.

Regretfully, he returned to his room, but was unable to sleep. He felt a sense of dark foreboding. He tossed and turned in his bed, fell asleep shortly before sunrise, and woke to the sound of silence.

Volnay sat straight up in bed. The pale, early-morning light filtered through the shutters, but the house was utterly still. He tried to quell his anxiety and go back to sleep, but to no avail. A furtive rustling alerted him. He listened out but was unable to locate its source. He got out of bed and began to dress. Was it a stifled noise from downstairs? Softly, he lifted the door latch. The staircase lay in semi-darkness. Volnay took the back stairs, used by the servants, and found himself outside the door leading to the kitchens. Still there was no sound. He held his breath, and pushed open the door. He saw the cook, seated at the table, and his spirits rose. Then the blood froze in his veins. Her pose was grotesque, her limbs twisted and seemingly disconnected. A scarf of blood circled her neck. Nearby, on the floor, lay the body of her husband, his throat also cut. And over there, the body of a servant...

Volnay's hand reached for his belt. He stifled a gasp. Icy sweat seeped through his skin. He had left all his weaponry upstairs in the bedroom. His gaze swept the room, searching for a knife. He found a good-sized cleaver, used for chopping game, grasped it and felt its satisfying weight. Handled effectively, it would do some damage. The door to the servant's hall stood wide open. He heard footsteps and returned to his hiding place on the back stairs.

'Down there, they all went that way,' said a guttural voice. 'Only the Master and his guest to deal with now.'

'Do it straightaway, before they're awake, and post the men on the two staircases, to block any chance of escape.'

'Leave it to me.'

The assassin left. Volnay thought quickly, struggling to calm the wild beating of his heart. He must save the Master at all costs. He bounded up the stairs; he had very little time, but it would be suicide to take on a band of armed men without his weapons. He lost precious seconds fetching his sword and pistol from his room. He heard the attackers gathering below. He raced to the Master's bedroom. Awakened by the noise, he was sitting straight up in bed, his nightcap tied firmly under his chin, as Volnay entered.

'You?'

He stared at Volnay, aghast.

'Whatever's happening?'

'There's a group of armed men downstairs,' said Volnay hurriedly. 'They have killed the rest of the household. They're coming up here to slit our throats.'

He tried to barricade the door with a small chest of drawers as he spoke.

'There are men blocking both stairs,' he panted. 'We must use the window.'

Volnay saw in alarm that the Master had made no effort to get out of bed.

'The comte…' he breathed wearily. 'I should have listened to him.'

His features hardened. He stared at Volnay with a look of fierce determination.

'Jump out of the window, take a horse from the stables and fly! Quickly!'

Volnay froze in despair. The men were beating on the door. Shouts rang out along the passage.

'I won't leave you.'

'Too late, my friend.'

The Master's voice was calm. He tore off his nightcap and added:

'I have been ready for this for a long time!'

The door crashed inwards and two men fell into the room, tumbling over the chest of drawers. Volnay went into action straightaway, driving his sword through one ragged doublet, then another. A swarthy face, criss-crossed with fine scars and partly hidden beneath a broad hat, appeared in the door frame. The man wore a foot soldier's buffalo-skin doublet to protect against sword thrusts. He brandished a long rapier, and used it to good effect, repelling Volnay speedily across the room while three more of his kind poured in behind.

The last to enter was plainly the executioner-in-chief, the man who had received the order to post his troops on the stairs before the final assault. He had a pointed, ferret-like face and wore a gold ring in one ear. Above taut, leathery cheeks, his yellow eyes flickered like candle flames guttering in a draught. Volnay recognized him: he was a member of the Brotherhood. The assailant's sinister face broke into a bestial grin. He pointed a finger at the inspector and hissed:

'He who betrays the Brotherhood dies by the Brotherhood!'

And before he had even finished speaking the words, he threw his dagger straight at Volnay, who deflected it in mid-air with his sword, in a desperate reflex. Another attacker seized the moment to deliver a fatal blow, but Volnay's sword sprang to block the blade, as if of its own accord, and drove it aside. He felt a trickle of hot blood run down his neck. As if through a fog, he saw the Master offer this throat to the sacrifice.

'No!'

Volnay howled, and his cry accompanied the Master to his death. A hideous gurgling followed. The inspector was seized with a wild rage. He raced forward, delivered two or three blows, scored a couple of hits, and felt the tip of a blade slice his scalp. He fought on for a moment, in a blood-soaked mist, making the most of the narrow space between the bed and the wall to avoid a mass assault. Fleetingly, he caught the eye of the weasel-faced thug. The man was smiling. He had drawn his pistol, and pointed it straight at Volnay. The inspector uttered a loud cry, turned, and threw himself against the window.

The wooden frame shattered under his weight with a deafening crash, and he plunged into the void in a hail of glass. It was not far to fall. He crashed to the ground, but rolled nimbly to one side. He had lost his sword as he fell, but recovered it and turned around. One of his attackers had jumped too, but landed badly. Volnay ran him through where he lay without a second thought. A metallic wasp buzzed close to his ear. The weasel-faced man swore, and yelled out in exasperation:

'The prey will not hold still, dammit!'

He was being hunted like an animal. A delicate mist floated over the fields as he ran. Beyond the dappled meadows and hills, the dark, dense mass of the forest rose in the distance. The landscape was more rugged now. An expanse of fallow fields stretched before him, hatched with shadow.

The forest loomed on the horizon, and Volnay heard the sound of galloping hooves at his back. His lungs were on fire, but he redoubled his pace in desperation, never once turning to look back. The thunder of hooves sounded in his ears as he reached the cover of the first trees. He had not used his pistol, until now. He planted one foot firmly on the ground and turned. His first assailant was upon him. Calmly, he took aim, and fired. Desperately, the two riders approaching fast reined in their horses. Volnay raced through the clumps of trees. He reached the undergrowth and ran deep into the forest, over a carpet of moss.

The further he ran, the darker it became. The foliage became thicker and thicker. The atmosphere was close, and stifling. The silence was broken only by the moan of the wind. He leapt over a small stream in one bound, running further and further from civilization. The smell of damp wood and mould filled the air. There was an unreal quality to the silence.

Volnay had no idea how long he spent roaming the forest, pushing ever deeper into its heart. He lost all sense of direction, even of time. Above him, squirrels leapt from branch to branch. The sun beat down on the thick canopy of leaves, but did not pierce the darkness beneath. He sank down and leant his back against the trunk of a tree, to rest and tend to his wounds.

His mind floated like pollen on the wind. Chiara was there, smooth and white-skinned in the darkness. Volnay closed his eyes and pictured the young Italian's dazzling, unrivalled beauty, her dark eyes gazing deep into his, and the thought filled him with happiness. He felt his arms around her waist, and his heart beating against her bosom. A first, sweet surrender. The first of many…

Night fell, and the ivory gates of his dreams shut tight. A gentle breeze blew in his ears. The undergrowth rustled, and night creatures emerged from the thickets. The whole forest seemed alive with whispers. He heard the ripple of water, and found a spring at the bottom of a small hollow. Cautiously, he climbed down to slake his aching thirst. Kneeling beside the trickle of water to wash his wounds, he heard a rustling among the leaves and strained his ear to listen.

At first, he had been terrified by the silence. Everything lay still, as if a great predator stalked the forest depths, so that the very trees held their breath. Then he heard more rustling, and a shadow loomed beside him. Slowly, he turned his head. He saw a branch pushed to one side, across the clearing, and the swift gleam of a pair of eyes. A lithe form stepped from the undergrowth and stood motionless, watching him.

Volnay's eyes widened in terror. A wolf. The creature stared at him with its golden eyes. Slowly, his heart beating wildly, he rose to his feet. Branches cracked, he heard the dull sound of paws pounding the forest floor, and silence fell once again. The creature had vanished.

Volnay waited for the furious pulse at his temples to subside, then plunged his hand into the spring and rubbed the cool water over his face. Cautiously, he continued on his way, but night was falling, awakening ancient fears that drove him to seek the light and emerge from the shelter of the trees. Just then, he thought he heard the sound of muffled, regular blows. Volnay nodded to himself; he knew what they signified. He walked in their direction, with hope in his heart. Drawing nearer to the sound, he found traces of human existence. The woodcutters had scarred the forest, leaving trails of sap, oozing like blood. All at once, he came upon their camp. Small fires glowed, and a cluster of finely sharpened axes stood planted in the ground. He hurried towards them and asked his way. The men eyed him suspiciously, but a handsome coin dampened their curiosity.

He followed the path pointed out to him by the men, and reached the forest edge. The road passed close by, lined with stunted bushes. A short distance away, he saw the silhouette of a ramshackle inn. Windows rattled in the evening wind, shutters slammed, and the signboard creaked back and forth. Volnay approach cautiously and glanced inside. No sign of the assassins on his tail.

The inn reeked of burnt fat and woodsmoke. The floor of the ill-lit room was strewn with filthy straw. Volnay took a seat and scanned the drinkers' congested faces. Nothing to fear. No comely serving girl either, but a tall, surly woman distributing pitchers of sour wine that grated on the tongue, with an air of fierce devotion to duty. The blood coating the inspector's scalp had dried to a dull brown crust, and his clothes were in a pitiful state. The woman eyed him suspiciously. As luck would have it, the jacket Volnay had thrown on hastily contained his fat purse.

He ordered slices of roast bacon, devoured them and asked to see the innkeeper, bargaining with him for the price of a horse. The deal was soon struck—the price was clearly of little concern, and a worn-out creature stood patiently waiting for death in the stables. Volnay rode slowly back to Paris, taking care to avoid the busier highways. At every crossroads along the way, tall crosses and saintly shrines offered their illusory protection against the forces of destiny. But in his heart of hearts, Volnay knew that danger and death would overtake him soon enough.

At sunrise, a key turned in the lock on Volnay's front door. A furtive shadow slipped inside. The man drew back his hood.

'*Damn the law! Damn the law!*' cackled the magpie suddenly.

The monk approached her cage, smiling.

'I see my lessons have not gone unheeded!' he said quietly. 'You're a fine pupil, sweet bird, but don't let Monsieur de Sartine hear you say such things!'

Then he called out:

'Are you there?'

He went to the bedroom. There was no one there, and the bed was cold.

'He didn't sleep here,' he muttered, running his hand over the mattress. 'That's unlike him. He's not one for staying out all night in bad company, as some of us did in our youth.'

The monk returned to the magpie's cage.

'Where's your master? He was supposed to see me yesterday afternoon, but I waited in vain. He sent no word. Strange…'

He peered at the bird's feeding dish, narrowing his eyes.

'Well, it seems he wasn't planning a lengthy absence— you've almost nothing left to eat. That's not like him either. An unexpected occurrence, then.'

He thought for a moment, and made his decision.

'You'll come with me, my lovely. Your master loves you dearly, and I will not leave you here all alone.'

He took hold of the cage and placed it on Volnay's desk.

'I'll leave a note. And pray there's no trouble with the king.'

'*Damn the king!*' cried the magpie.

'Enough of your insolence,' said the monk amiably, 'though it is music to my ears!'

The monk returned to his own lodgings and donned his gentleman's clothes. He cut a fine figure, and stood admiring himself in the glass, when the magpie became suddenly agitated.

'What is it, my lovely?' The monk turned in surprise.

The magpie was flapping around her cage, scattering seed as she fluttered her wings. The monk stood for a moment, then hurried to the window.

'The Royal Watch! Clever bird!'

He slipped a purse into his pocket.

'Essential munitions. Things are clearly taking a turn for the worse…'

He climbed onto a table and opened a small window high in one wall.

'I'll be back for you, have no fear!' he told the magpie. 'But for now, I had best keep out of their way.'

He eased himself out through the narrow window with agile grace, and pulled himself up onto the roof.

'Fine work for a man of my age!' he muttered happily.

XV

Be of good cheer and earn your beauty!

CASANOVA

Volnay entered Paris at dawn. He must warn the monk immediately. His friend and the magpie were the only creatures he cherished now, in this miserable world. He wound his way through the narrow, dirty streets of the Faubourg Saint-Antoine to avoid being seen. He held a handkerchief to his nose, against the stench of urine. The destitute, filthy, ragged crowd parted to let him through. He left his horse at an inn, and mingled with the throng, anxious to discover whether his house was being watched. He saw two riders posted outside, their hats pulled low over their faces, capes around their shoulders, swords at their sides. They were waiting for his return. The monk must be either dead or in hiding. Slowly, he turned around, careful to resist the urge to run. A firm hand was placed on his shoulder. He turned, and found himself face-to-face with three archers of the Royal Watch, in their grey jerkins and red coats.

'Chevalier de Volnay? You are under arrest. Kindly come along with us.'

They led the inspector to a carriage drawn by four horses, and ordered him to climb inside. Seated in the coach, Sartine eyed him coldly.

'Better late than never, Monsieur the Inspector of Strange and Unexplained Deaths!'

One of the watchmen saw Volnay into his seat, then climbed down from the coach.

'The riders are mine,' Sartine continued. 'As soon as I heard what had happened at the Master's house, I had your house searched, and the monk's. We found nothing in either, only your strange collaborator's cursed alembics and furnaces, for his heretical experiments!'

A cold smile lit his face, but stopped short of his eyes.

'The monk has had the good sense to make a run for it, at least. He's a skilled dissembler, always able to disappear in plain sight on the streets of Paris, as you and I well know. But I've got you! Murderer! The Master's entire household!'

'It wasn't me!'

Sartine trained his lifeless eyes on Volnay.

'The question is not whether you are the murderer, but whether you can prove that you are not.'

He rapped the coach window, ordering the coachman to move off.

'Where are you taking me?'

'To the Châtelet. We're delivering you in comfort, at least!'

Volnay ventured a glance through the carriage window. The two riders had placed themselves either side of the vehicle.

'Don't even think of it,' said Sartine, reading his thoughts. 'They would strike you dead on the spot, and I have another armed man seated next to the coachman, under the same instructions.'

All was lost! Volnay felt the tears well in his eyes.

'The killings were ordered by the Comte de Saint-Germain!' he yelled.

'Oh, indeed?'

Sartine shot him an ironic look, then continued:

'The king greatly enjoys the company of the Comte de Saint-Germain. He delights in the tales of his travels through Africa and Asia, his anecdotes from the courts of Russia and Austria, even the sultans! There is little prospect of my calling on the king, to tell him—on the word of a police inspector arrested for murder—that his friend the comte has connections to a dangerous brotherhood.'

'A brotherhood?'

Sartine tore off his wig in a sudden access of rage.

'Do you think me an utter fool? Did you truly believe that because you had been placed at the head of this investigation, I would charge no one else to shadow your inquiries on my behalf?'

Volnay sighed, thinking of the many spies that he knew had swarmed around him from the beginning.

'I knew you would,' he whispered, at length, as much to himself as to Sartine.

The chief of police stared at him scornfully.

'As for the people killed at the estate, are they not members of some secret brotherhood, to which you yourself belonged in the past? You joined the police, and by a remarkable stroke of luck—or careful planning—you brought yourself to the attention of the king and secured the post you hold today. I've been making inquiries about you. Dear God, the things I discovered! I could have withdrawn your commission, or had you clapped in prison, but I did neither. It pleased me to think that my Inspector of Strange and Unexplained Deaths was a man with a past even stranger than the crimes he was investigating. It gave me a hold on you, should the need arise. But that's of no use to me now. You are a man without a future.'

Volnay shook his head, bitterly.

'You knew I had been a member of the Brotherhood of the Serpent? You're like the Cyclops in the legend of Ulysses. You do me the favour of eating me last…'

'You have a talent for stirring things up,' said Sartine.

He fell silent. Volnay glanced out of the window. They were crossing the Pont-Neuf. Crowds thronged the bridge. In the distance, the grim silhouette of the Châtelet rose like a bird of prey. They heard the coachman cursing and calling out as he pulled the horses' reins to the right or left.

'What do you know about the Brotherhood?' asked Volnay, quietly.

He was trying to distract Sartine's thoughts, so that he might drop his guard. The chief gave a short laugh. He liked to display his vast knowledge, especially of things that were supposedly secret.

'The Brotherhood of the Serpent! A conspiracy acting in the shadow of royal power, which aims to bring down the latter and replace it with government by and for the people. Its current motto is *Lillias pedibus destrue*—"Crush the fleur-de-lys underfoot!" A pyramid structure: novices observe a five-year probationary period before being initiated into the first of twelve levels of knowledge. There are secret signs and sacred words that allow members to communicate under cover. They say the Brotherhood of the Serpent survived the fall of ancient Sumer by joining with the Egyptian mysteries, and establishing itself in Europe with the rise of Christianity.'

He paused, and lovingly stroked his wig.

'Its ancient motto is *Novus ordo seclorum*: "The new order of the ages". And it has recently adopted another: *Annuit coeptis*: "Our endeavours find success".'

Sartine recited the information like a diligent schoolboy. He continued in the same, neutral tone:

'Recruitment to the Brotherhood is chiefly limited to France, Italy and parts of Germany. The Brotherhood of the Serpent has not agreed to join the wider Freemasonry movement, because the two hold somewhat different beliefs. Your own, murdered Master was the architect of the attempted rapprochement. Which suggests the existence of a violent

321

faction, of which you are very probably part, that has secured the upper hand and seeks to uphold the Brotherhood's independence, by force if necessary.'

'You're remarkably well informed,' said Volnay, with studied indifference.

Barely had he spoken the words, when he dived towards the carriage door, slipped through Sartine's hands, startled the escort's horse and raced to the parapet of the bridge. The crowd stared as Volnay jumped down into the Seine, while the first shots rang out above him.

Volnay stayed huddled in a warehouse until dark, shivering in his wet clothes. When he emerged, they were almost dry, but his sorry appearance left much to be desired. Worse, he was coughing, and had lost his purse in the river. Staggering with exhaustion, he wandered the loud, busy streets thronged with hurried passers-by and beggars, peering enviously into the windows of shops selling hot pastries and meat pies baked in wood ash. Standing back to let a carriage pass, he glimpsed a familiar profile silhouetted in the window and threw himself at the coach door.

'Hands off my master's carriage, peasant!'

The coachman's whip cracked across his face and Volnay yelled in pain. Casanova put his head out of the coach window.

'Whatever's the matter?'

'This villain was blocking our path, Monseigneur!'

Volnay tried to move closer. The whip cracked overhead.

'Chevalier de Seingalt!'

He fell to his knees.

'Chiara!' he cried, without knowing why.

'One moment!' Casanova called out. 'I'll have no one whipped like a cur. And who is this queer fellow, who knows my title, and the name of my love?'

Cautiously, he climbed down from the coach and approached the inspector.

'Chevalier de Volnay? Is that you? What a state you are in! Whatever has happened?'

Volnay staggered to his feet. His cheek burnt.

'I cannot go on—I beg your sanctuary.'

Gently, the Venetian took him by the arm, glanced briefly around the street, then helped him into the carriage.

'You have got yourself into a fine tangle, my young friend,' he said, feelingly. 'You're wanted for the murder of an entire household to the south of Paris!'

Volnay nodded. He was dazed.

Casanova continued:

'Knowing your exceedingly upright character as I do, I should be surprised if there were any truth in the rumour. But a rumour it is…'

He gave Volnay an ironic smile.

'Rumour, Inspector! Perhaps now you understand how its victims suffer!'

Volnay said nothing. To have fallen into the hands of the man who had stolen Chiara from him was unbearable. But he was too weak to leave.

Casanova shot him a swift glance.

'My friend, I cannot take you to my mansion. My coachman is a trustworthy fellow until his tongue is loosened by a well-stocked purse, and Paris swarms with spies, as you know. The higher orders may be unaware of a connection between you and me, but I am a well-known figure, and as such I am under constant surveillance from the king's police.'

He narrowed his eyes and considered Volnay with a mixture of gravity and human sympathy.

'Here's what we shall do: we'll get down from the carriage in a moment or two. I'll order the coachman to wait, and take you to a house where you will be well treated, and where you may even find a measure of enjoyment. With discretion, mark you. A young woman, Sylvia, lives there with her mother. They rarely entertain at home; they both work in a very respectable house. The women are in my debt—I have done them one or two small services. I should add that when I call on them, I honour mother and daughter together in the same bed. Neither is jealous of the other. There, you have it all!'

The street was crowded with an endless stream of vehicles, riders, fruit-sellers, water-sellers and passers-by. Casanova and Volnay strode into the throng and were soon lost to sight. They reached a street lined with improvised stalls selling an array of spices. Tooth-pullers plied their trade, too. Casanova led Volnay to a tall, two-storey house. Grey columns decorated its facade, supporting a flower-decked balcony. He gave a series of loud knocks on the door, followed by another series of quieter knocks. Shortly, footsteps were heard inside, and the door opened.

'Chevalier!'

A tall woman stood in the open doorway. She was not yet forty, but her appearance suggested a faded flower. Despite her regular, pleasant features, she exuded a dry, authoritative air, likely to appeal to admirers of severe, self-assured women.

'Madame, may we come in? My companion is dead with fatigue, and needs to rest.'

At that moment, Volnay suffered a violent coughing fit and shook from head to foot.

'Is he ill?' asked the woman anxiously, frowning.

'As ill as any man who has spent the day in wet clothes after suffering two or three blows in a sword fight,' said Casanova hurriedly. 'The poor fellow was forced to leap into a tub of water to escape a jealous husband who came home too early, after which he spent all day shivering in a leafy arbour before slipping discreetly away. I found him in this sorry state. Obviously, I could have taken him back to my residence, but the jealous husband is aware of our friendship, and may well have come calling. If you were able to lodge him here, discreetly, for a few days, I should be forever in your debt.'

The Chevalier de Seingalt spoke with such conviction that the inconsistencies in his story were quite forgotten. As if by magic, he also produced a pretty purse, bulging with coins. The door closed behind them. Safe at last, Volnay felt his legs give way beneath him. The shock of the previous night, the murder of the Master and his household, his flight through the forest, the encounter with the wolf, his ride through the night to Paris, and his spectacular escape from Sartine's carriage swam before his eyes, and he was close to collapse.

'Quick! He is about to faint!' cried the woman.

Casanova supported Volnay. With the help of the robust woman, he took the inspector to a neat, clean bedroom, where a decent mattress awaited. Volnay opened his eyes one last time, and saw the woman's dress stretch under the weight of her bosom as she bent over him.

'You need to rest,' she said in a husky voice. He felt her remove his boots. A freshly laundered sheet covered him like a shroud. Immediately, he sank into a deep sleep, like an exhausted child.

The mistress of the house treated Volnay with almost maternal care, and was at equal pains to keep Sylvia, her undeniably charming daughter, at a safe distance. The girl had her mother's regular features, and chestnut curls framed her pretty oval face. She had a slightly aquiline nose, and hazel eyes with long, dark lashes. Only her somewhat calculating eye hinted that here was a woman of pleasure, with no small experience of the world.

The mother closed the door firmly behind her. She had brought the inspector a bowl of chicken broth, wine, cheese and a thick slice of white bread. Volnay devoured his meal and fell asleep again immediately. A small noise woke him, several hours later. He opened his eyes. With the shutters closed, and the slats pulled down, the room was almost completely dark. He saw the gleam of a pair of eyes in the shadows.

'Dear God! What has brought you to such a place as this?'

'Chiara!'

He felt a wave of happiness and suffering that was quite detached now from the simple pleasure of the kisses they had exchanged just a few days before.

She seized his hands.

'The Chevalier de Seingalt told me you were here. He can help you. He is accustomed to… complicated situations.'

Volnay stared at her delicate, blue-veined hand, and covered it with his own. She shivered, then gazed deep into his eyes. She stayed that way for some minutes, and much was shared, though unspoken. Then their tongues loosened and they began to talk. Volnay told her about his visit to the Master, and everything that had happened since. Chiara listened with the careful attention accorded when visiting the sick, then cleared her throat, and spoke in turn:

'I am going to see the Marquise de Pompadour. At this stage, she alone can help you and save you from that wicked man Sartine, and the Brotherhood.'

She rose to leave.

'Chiara, I…'

A tear shone in the corner of the young woman's eye.

'I know, yes.'

Volnay was unsure they were referring to the same thing, but he sensed the strength of her feelings, and said nothing. He felt a fleeting urge to go to her, collect the teardrop on his fingertip and put it to his lips, to savour its taste. The taste of happiness, perhaps?

'The Chevalier de Seingalt is waiting for me,' she said, in more confident tones.

'Casanova…'

'He saved you, and has treated you as a friend, remember that! I must go now, but I shall be back, with good news.'

She opened the door, and turned to him one last time. But Volnay lay stretched out on his bed, as if in a faint. To associate Chiara and Casanova in his mind demanded an effort of will quite beyond his powers. He heard her light footsteps on the stairs. Just as on that terrible night at the Master's house, his curiosity, and his despair, got the better of him. He emerged from his room and stood motionless at the top of the winding stair. He bent forward to listen.

Casanova was waiting for Chiara downstairs.

'Well?' he asked.

'He needs help. I will go to the marquise.'

'The wisest course, indeed…'

Casanova's finger followed the trace of Chiara's tear.

'Gaiety, Mademoiselle, is shared by a happy few, but sorrow mirrors the ghastly sufferings of souls condemned to eternal punishment. Be of good cheer and earn your beauty!'

He wanted to embrace her, but she pushed him away.

'Not here.'

'One kiss…'

'I'm not sure. Perhaps later. Volnay is here…'

'Upstairs, in his room.'

There was a rustle of silk, and a woman's stifled sigh, then: 'No, I say, not here!'

Volnay was destroyed. He returned to his bed; he did not hear the rest of their conversation on the doorstep.

'Chiara…'

'No, I tell you! You will never have me again if you carry on so. I never want to feel your hands on me again!'

'Then what about my mouth?'

He pulled her roughly to him and forced his lips on hers. She yielded briefly to the pleasure of his kiss, then pulled away, trembling.

'You are exceeding the bounds of decency, Monsieur! If you dare take me one more time, I'll have you roundly thrashed by my lackeys!'

'But Chiara…'

'There is nothing more to say, Chevalier. Neither my heart nor my body are yours. Oh, and one more thing—you are old, sir, and your kisses are marred by the unpleasant smell of an older man's mouth.'

They both turned to see the young woman who had answered the door to them standing in the kitchen doorway, watching them attentively. She wore a pale-coloured dress that showed her slender hips to fine effect. Her breasts were prominently displayed atop a tight corset, barely covered by a delicate lace handkerchief tucked into the low neck of her dress.

'Let us go,' muttered Casanova, uncomfortably.

Sylvia watched them leave, with the beginnings of a smile at her lips. She went up to Volnay's room and asked innocently:

'Who was the gentleman who accompanied that young lady here? He seems much taken with her…'

She stole a sidelong glance at Volnay. He was staring into space, and said nothing.

'The young lady, too, indeed,' she added quickly. 'She was kissing him most passionately on the doorstep.'

Sylvia watched the blood drain from Volnay's face, with satisfaction. She came to his bedside, hesitated for a moment, then ran her hands though his mane of black hair.

'It's all a mess!' she whispered.

Only afterwards did she see the tears in his eyes.

The beggar narrowed his eyes and peered at the front door of the house.

'Is this the place?' he asked the coachman who accompanied him.

'Yes. I got down from the carriage out of curiosity, and watched them as they walked along the street. I saw them go in through that door. Now give me that second coin.'

The monk's face shone with a cold smile, in his beggar's rags.

'Take it. And may God forgive you for betraying your master, the Chevalier de Seingalt, poor Christian as you are!'

'I should not have betrayed, him, as you say,' said the other man bitterly, 'if you had not also promised to reveal to me the secret of heightened vigour, when I honour my wife in the performance of my conjugal duties.'

'She or any other of her sex,' joked the monk.

'Hold to your promise!'

The monk sighed.

'Very well. All you have to do is urinate three times into the wedding ring while reciting *In nomine Patris*. And if you've lost the ring, the keyhole of any church door will do.'

'Is that all?' asked the man, doubtfully.

'Indeed,' said the monk solemnly. 'Alternatively, eat a roasted woodpecker seasoned with holy salt before the conjugal act. For identical results.'

'Very well…'

The monk sighed as he watched the man walk away.

'People will believe anything in this day and age.'

XVI

I feel the thunder anew but am powerless to strike the bolt.

CASANOVA

Father Ofag narrowed his eyes. His fingers drummed absently on the table as he waited for the person who would deliver him the letter at last. The letter that had caused the death of his beloved Wallace, a pure heart in a rugged setting. The letter had alarmed the Marquise de Pompadour and the proud, sinister Brotherhood of the Serpent. Perhaps even Sartine knew of its existence. All Paris was looking for it and now, at last, it was to be brought to him on a silver platter. Naturally, the seller was asking a great deal of money, but what was gold compared to the downfall of the Marquise de Pompadour and her henchmen?

A few minutes more… Ofag was modest in triumph. He was a man of the shadows, a soldier of God. He cared little for monuments or statues, so long as his life's work was complete.

The sound of boots echoed on the stairway. At last, the bearer was announced—the bearer of the letter that even the most capable police officer in Paris had failed to find. The man stepped into the room, and Father Ofag exclaimed:

'Chevalier de Seingalt! What a pleasure!'

He disliked the new arrival thoroughly, but hid his aversion beneath a forced smile. Casanova strode towards him. For once, he was plainly attired in a generous black cloak. A long sword hung at his side, and a dagger was tucked into his belt.

'So! Has my favourite thief brought me the letter?' asked Ofag, in an access of uncharacteristic cheer.

Casanova looked offended.

'I am not in the habit of thieving, and I am disappointed that you should hold me in such low esteem. Here is the truth of the matter: I come to the aid of a woman who has been struck to the ground, I kneel beside her, and discover that she is dead, and her face torn away. My companion falls into a faint. And as I prepare to come to her aid, too, my hands discover a letter on the body of the dead woman. Alas, it finds its way into my pocket!'

'And so it occurred to you to offer it for sale.'

'I soon saw that the letter was of interest to a great many people! Be thankful I have chosen to sell it into the hands of good, Christian folk.'

'May God forgive you, for you have sinned indeed,' said Father Ofag indulgently.

'Honestly, I don't think there's much to forgive,' said Casanova smoothly. 'An honest ruse is the sign of a cautious mind. And he who is incapable of exercising that, is a fool.'

'Have you got the letter?' asked Ofag impatiently.

Casanova gave a cold smile that stopped short of his eyes.

'The bidding has been intense,' he said solemnly. 'You'll have to double your price if you wish to remain in the running.'

A heavy silence ensued. The clergyman was the first to speak:

'Heathen! For the salvation of your soul, and your duty to the preachings of Our Lord Jesus Christ, you should seek lasting treasure in heaven, over temporal riches here below!'

'I beg your pardon?' said Casanova. 'I bring you your enemies' heads on a plate, and here you are haggling over the price and telling me to take my payment in heaven?'

'*Tum podex carmen extulit horridulum!*' growled Father Ofag, green with rage.

Casanova stiffened. He understood perfectly well what he had just heard. He was accused of farting out of his own mouth!

'We shall strike a bargain right now, or not at all!' declared Ofag. 'I'll agree to your price, but I must have the letter!'

Casanova tensed at his threatening tone. He had arranged a motley escort of hired thugs, who stood waiting outside, on the stairs. Ofag knew they were there, but doubtless had other tricks up his sleeve. The Venetian's fingers closed tight around the hilt of his sword.

'Gently, my friend, gently…'

Father Ofag had spotted the gesture, and it unsettled him.

'There will be no attempt made against you. I gave you my word at the outset of our dealings. I am acting for the greater good of Christendom, you know that.'

'I'm sure Christendom will be most grateful,' said Casanova, without a trace of a smile.

'Do you have the letter with you?'

The Venetian sighed. It pained him that anyone should still think him as naive as all that.

'Of course not! Send a man to me with the money, and I will hand him the letter.'

He paused for a moment, then added:

'Please.'

The monk was escorted into the Comte de Saint-Germain's workroom with all due ceremony. Left alone, the two men eyed one another at some length.

'I'm delighted to see you again, Monsieur de—'

'No names, please!' interjected the monk. And he softened his brusque tone with a polite bow of the head.

'As you wish,' said the comte. 'But I know who you are, by any name.'

The monk frowned slightly.

'In truth, it matters little who either of us is.'

'There's truth in that,' breathed the comte, with a brief gesture of the hand, to which the monk responded in kind.

'I honour and respect the *aqua Tofana*,' intoned the monk serenely. 'I am the sword of fire that chases out the impurities of this earth. I am the invisible and unavoidable blade that will reach you wherever you may be.'

The comte nodded. He showed no sign of surprise.

'I am the diamond scales,' he responded. 'I weigh the fate of mankind.'

A long silence ensued.

'I believe I know whence you come,' said the monk. He held his breath. 'Am I right? Are you who I think you are?'

'You will have no firm answer, my friend. I am of no place, and no time,' replied the comte, and his voice was like the faint murmur of a stream. 'Beyond time and space, my spiritual being lives its eternal existence. By diving deep into my thoughts, journeying back down the ages, I may become whomsoever I desire.'

'In that case, I believe we can do business,' concluded the monk, with an impish gleam all his own.

There was a knock at the door of Volnay's new lodgings. Sylvia went to open it. Outside, there was no sign of the Chevalier de Seingalt, no elegantly dressed noblewoman, but an old man with a basket of eggs, who addressed her straightaway, before she had a chance to speak:

'I've come with the eggs you ordered for your patient. Give me a coin—we may be watched. There is a letter for him under the straw.'

'A letter for who?' asked Sylvia, pale-faced.

'For your patient. Quickly, the coin! I may be watched!'

The young woman did as she was asked. No sooner had she done so than the strange peddler turned on his heels and hurried away. He disappeared around the corner of the street, limping as he went. Thoughtfully, Sylvia closed the door and slipped her hand beneath the eggs. She found a sealed letter at the bottom of the basket. She held it up in front of her in hopes of reading something, but to no avail. Slowly, she climbed the stairs. When the handsome young man had read the letter and fallen asleep once more, she would discover its contents for herself.

Volnay was sitting in the room's only armchair, lost in thought. He received the letter with surprise, but read it attentively. Sylvia busied herself about the room, dusting the shelves unnecessarily, straightening the sheets, passing back and forth behind Volnay in the hope of catching a line or two of the letter's fluent hand.

'*I am here,*' wrote the monk simply. '*Do not venture out. Tell the mistress of the house that I will visit you at nightfall.*'

Tired of waiting, Sylvia wrapped her arms around Volnay's neck and read the letter outright.

'So you're to have a visitor. I am forewarned!' she said. 'Another lady?'

'Not at all,' said Volnay, unsure whether to unfasten the arms from around his neck, or to stay caught in their delightful embrace.

So the monk had escaped from Sartine and picked up his trace! Perhaps he was there right now, below the window, doubtless heavily disguised. Life had taught him the hard way to exercise caution when required.

'Good!' said Sylvia, in satisfied tones. 'I must go out now. Promise me you'll be good while I'm gone? I shan't be long.'

She sat herself on his lap. Volnay showed no reaction, so she placed a kiss on his lips, then rose and left the room, laughing. Volnay sat alone in the darkened room, lost in thought. He barely seemed to have noticed Sylvia's departure.

The oracles had spoken. The Marquise d'Urfé must be inoculated by Casanova that very day, in order to be reborn later in the body of a male infant. Casanova had prepared the credulous, superstitious noblewoman for the procedure, over a period of months—and Chiara and Volnay had denounced the proceedings from the moment they had all first met. To support his actions with the ageing marquise, whose fading charms did little to spur him on, Casanova was accompanied by a young assistant, charged with restoring his vigour, if such were to prove necessary. She was presented to the marquise as a water sprite, freshly risen from the waters of the Seine, and readily accepted as such. The water sprite had presented the marquise with a slip of paper, upon which was written: *'I am mute, but not deaf. I rise from the Seine to bathe you. The hour is upon us. We must do the bidding of Oromasis, king of the Salamanders.'*

Assisted by two servants, they had first made an offering of gold to the Seven Planets. The Marquise d'Urfé had provided the requisite coin, but little suspected that the coffers which were subsequently tossed into the waters of the Seine contained nothing but lead. After that, they had repaired to La Petite Pologne, the residence of the Chevalier de Seingalt, for a purifying bath, before taking their places in a spacious bedroom. The windows stood open, for it was a hot day, and Casanova was to perform the act of inoculation three times, for enhanced credibility. And so, as the monk approached along the central avenue leading through the grounds, he was greeted by the mingled cries and moans of two women.

'The monk!' growled Casanova, emerging from the bedroom when his servant came to announce the caller. 'He can come back another time, or wait!'

The chevalier was in a bad temper. The second assault had continued at some length, and his hair was plastered in sweat, mixed with powder and ointment. The elderly marquise had encouraged him by wiping his brow as he worked, and the young water sprite delivered caresses calculated to help him retain his habitual vigour. He could have cheated and faked the climax of their coupling, of course, but he disliked such stratagems and wanted to give the marquise proper value for her money.

And so the monk was asked to wait in a small room set aside for coffee. Encouraged by the water sprite, Casanova was able to prepare for the third act of coitus, dedicated to the god Mercury. The chevalier was accustomed to fresh, youthful bodies. The marquise's withered breasts, wrinkled skin, black-painted eyebrows and furrowed complexion caked in white make-up robbed him of his powers. Conscious of the situation, the water sprite demonstrated considerable feats of imaginative intervention, but alas, the instrument of the marquise's pleasure remained dormant. Confronted with the chevalier's impotence, the water sprite saved the situation by drawing on her extensive learning in the Venetian arts, and initiated the marquise in the delights of Lesbos. The spectacle stirred Casanova to renewed action, grunting and sweating under the younger girl's encouraging eye, congratulating him on his ability to satisfy the god Mercury. But he whispered in her ear:

'I feel the thunder anew, but am powerless to strike the bolt.'

The water sprite assisted the Marquise d'Urfé in her attainment of *la petite mort*, but gave Casanova an unequivocal sign: he would have to fake his climax, though he disliked cheating.

Casanova sighed, stiffened and simulated an impressive series of convulsions that left the marquise quite speechless.

After a few moments, he got to his feet and told her:

'The word of the Sun is in your soul, and you shall bring forth your own self, changed to the opposite sex, early next February!'

Then he sent the marquise home, with instructions to remain in bed for one hundred and seven hours.

A window overlooked the garden, and the room was attractively arranged with furniture upholstered in moiré silk embroidered with a delicate chain motif. Casanova joined the monk after almost an hour, his face still red with effort.

'Forgive me for making you wait, my dear friend,' he said. 'I was seeing to a matter, the resolution of which was rather more complicated than expected.'

'It's a pleasure to wait in such charming surroundings,' said the monk politely.

He was dressed liked a cleric, in black, so as to pass unnoticed in the crowd. As often before, he found himself a fugitive in this life, though he seemed unmoved by the latest turn of events. He looked around the room. A painting on the wall caught his eye. It showed a young girl sitting on the grass with her lover beside her, attempting to slip a hand around her waist. Taken by surprise, the girl was half-turned towards the viewer, and had lost one of her shoes, revealing a seductively arched foot.

'A fine work, is it not?' said Casanova, walking over to the picture.

Suddenly, he froze. The monk was holding the narrow blade of a dagger to his throat.

'Chevalier de Seingalt, you're going to have to speak the truth for once,' he said in a tone of quiet determination.

With six inches of steel against his windpipe, Casanova nonetheless kept his calm.

'Gently, monk, whatever's the matter?'

The other man grinned.

'I have been thinking a great deal recently, and realized at length that I had been scuttling crabwise, sidelong to the truth, while staring it in the face! The Marquise de Pompadour, the Devout Party and heaven knows who else are looking for a letter. Volnay took only one from the dead woman's body, and I trust him as I would trust my own self. What, then, happened between the moment when the young woman stepped down from the marquise's carriage, carrying the letter, and the moment when Volnay arrived at the scene of the crime?'

He eased the pressure on the blade, for a moment, but continued talking.

'Wallace followed the young woman as soon as she emerged from the carriage. He lost sight of her when she ventured into the small courtyard. Later, when she had collapsed in the street, Wallace approached the body but was forced to hide when others arrived on the scene. And who was out walking that night? You! I questioned the men of the Royal Watch, who were first on the scene after that. They found your lady companion unconscious, and you told them that she had fainted at the sight of the corpse. You were entirely at liberty to remove the letter. The truth shines bright: it was you, because it could be no one else! My logic never fails to dazzle me.'

'You're mistaken. The letter must have been stolen by the man Wallace,' said Casanova calmly.

'Wrong! He said he took nothing from the dead woman's body.'

'He was lying!'

'Why would he? Everything about him announced that he is telling the truth. If he had taken it, he would have hurried

338

away from the scene with it. But he did not. On the contrary, he remained on the spot, then set out to hunt for the letter.'

'Perhaps he was looking for the second letter.'

'Which was of no importance, given that he had the first? And if he had taken one, why not both? No, Wallace took nothing from the dead girl. It was you!'

'Your logical mind is playing tricks,' said Casanova, breathing more harshly now. 'It has landed you in prison more than once, remember that!'

'My logic is irrefutable, and we are all quite stupid not to have seen it from the very first. If you do not hand over the letter I'll slash your face so that no woman will ever desire you again. I can do it! I'll make you the most repugnant creature on earth!'

'You would do no such thing—I, your saviour from the Piombi!'

The monk grinned.

'My poor friend. I remember our escape all too well. You had me scrape so hard my arms are still stiff!'

'You would never have succeeded without me. It was I who procured the tool you used.'

'And once we were out, it was I who dragged you away by force when, at the sight of the Grand Canal in the sunshine, you burst out sobbing like a child that has been forced to go to school!'

'I was thanking God with all my soul, for His mercy,' protested Casanova, 'and my tears expressed the gratitude I felt in my heart.'

'God is dead,' hissed the monk, 'and before long, you won't be in the best of health either.'

Swiftly, he pressed the blade of his knife to Casanova's face.

'No woman will ever look at you again, I swear!'

A bead of blood shone on the Venetian's cheek.

'No! No!' yelled Casanova. 'A world without women is death itself. I would give you the letter, if it were still in my possession.'

'Cunning,' said the monk, 'but you're a fool. You've kept it, to orchestrate the bidding to the very last second. That's enough talk. Say goodbye to your boyish good looks! Chiara will gaze in horror upon such a face as yours!'

The monk felt Casanova's body stiffen against his.

'Behind the painting! It's behind the painting!'

The monk stared around the room. His eye came to rest on the young girl with her silk-stockinged foot. He pushed Casanova in front of him, then struck him hard in the nape of the neck with the handle of his dagger. He held Casanova's body against him, then let him fall to the floor. He approached the painting and examined it once again, reflecting that truly there was nothing more enchanting than a young girl's tender abandon, in the grip of love's first pangs, nor anything more sensual than a pretty foot without a shoe. Alas, all that was behind him now! Carefully, he took down the picture. Behind it, a letter was fixed with two nails. He prised them away, took the letter and read it.

Anyone watching would have seen a look of utter stupefaction paint itself over the monk's features.

'Would you care to hand it to me now?' said a cold, calm voice behind him.

The Chevalier de Seingalt had recovered and got to his feet. He stood massaging his skull and pointing a pistol. The monk froze.

'I'm too kind... I should have struck harder. Now Volnay is done for!'

Volnay walked across to the window and opened it wide. The air was mild and sweet. He breathed deeply. Gathering his strength, he pushed open the shutter slats and glanced down into the crowded street. One had left his cart, laden with cabbages, carrots and leeks, immediately underneath the window. He saw the door open and close below, and sighed at the thought of the flirtatious young woman now climbing the stairs. He opened the shutters wide, then turned. Three men walked into the room, dressed like gentlemen and each wearing a sword at his side. Volnay's blood froze in his veins. Sartine had found him!

One of the men stepped forward. He had a swarthy complexion, and his face was sharpened by a soft moustache twisted into long, slender points. He rolled one end carefully between his fingers before he spoke.

'Monsieur, no harm has come to the two women sheltering you here. You have my word. Come with us, we're here to help you. We must act swiftly. I fear this may not be a safe house much longer.'

Volnay nodded.

'Lead the way, gentlemen.'

He gestured for them to walk ahead of him down the stairs, then turned suddenly and leapt from the window, hoping the vegetable cart was still standing just below. He landed on a bed of watercress and leeks, then jumped down to the ground in a flurry of greens and began to run. He collided with a water-carrier, who cursed him roundly, and overturned a basket-seller's stall.

'Quick, this way!'

An old man with a faintly familiar face was gesticulating for Volnay to follow him. Cries rang out behind him. The inspector hesitated for a second, then hurried after the man through a door and down two covered passageways leading to a small courtyard. They crossed it and found themselves in another, narrower street. The old man hurried to a door studded with thick black nails, pushed it open, then clutched Volnay by the wrist, pulled him inside and slammed it shut behind them. He pressed his hands against Volnay's mouth, urging silence. They heard the sound of running feet outside, then nothing. A candlestick on a table shone a faint light around a sparsely furnished room with a beaten earth floor. The stranger's lips stretched in a thin smile as he moved to the centre of the room. With one hand he tore off his knitted hat and wig, and his false moustaches. As if by magic, he seemed to straighten up. When he turned, the candlelight cast a discreet glow on a high forehead furrowed with discreet thought lines.

'You!' cried Volnay. 'God in heaven! Whatever are you doing here?'

'Once I had found out where you were, I rented this house by the week,' said the monk. 'Your place was under close surveillance.'

'Surveillance? By who?'

'Who knows who the spies are working for? That was why I sent you a message. I planned to get you out of there by night, dressed in women's clothes. You would have made a most charming hostess! But instead, here you are in broad daylight, with a posse on your heels.'

'I scarcely had any choice in the matter,' grumbled Volnay. 'A group of men came for me.'

'What did they look like?'

Volnay described them briefly. The monk nodded thoughtfully.

'I see. Ham-fisted lot!'

'Whatever do you mean?'

'I'll explain later. For now, you're going to throw on these vegetable-seller's rags and come with me, and hope there's no one on our tail. Hold fast! Things can only get better.'

'Where are we going?' asked Volnay, though he was resigned to understanding nothing of the monk's schemes.

'To see the only person who can protect you now: the Comte de Saint-Germain!'

XVII

By the particular grace of God, I have borne
everything calmly, and with fortitude.

COMTE DE SAINT-GERMAIN

The Comte de Saint-Germain was impeccably attired, as
ever. He held a phial sealed with wax at arm's length, as if to
verify the perfect whiteness of its contents. Quietly, the monk
cleared his throat to announce their arrival.

'Come hither, Chevalier de Volnay,' said the comte, turning
to greet them. 'And my thanks to you, my friend, the mysterious monk, for bringing him to me. You are aware of what
remains to be done now?'

The monk nodded silently, clasped Volnay tightly in his
arms, then left the room. The inspector was beyond surprise
now. The comte pointed to a tray on a table covered with a
red velvet cloth.

'This carafe contains a maraschino liqueur, with black
cherries. You're quite pale. Take a glass. You'll find it's softer
and sweeter than a kiss.'

The inspector stood motionless.

'And this,' said the comte in a soft voice, 'is the universal
spirit of nature.' He shook the phial gently. '*Atoétér.*'

He spoke as if to himself:

'Stir all things, that the truth may surface, nothing but
the truth…'

'The truth!' said Volnay, bitterly. 'Where can the truth hide
now? Everything exists in appearance only, and behind your
fine painted panels, appearance itself is an illusion. The truth
is nowhere!'

'Or rather, the truth lies elsewhere,' said the comte.

'You have used me!'

'And what would you have me do otherwise?' exclaimed the comte. For the first time, there was a note of irritation in his voice. 'You were charged with a criminal investigation by the king himself, and everyone was watching you! When I learnt of the theft of the letter, from the Marquise de Pompadour, our suspicion fell straightaway on Mademoiselle Hervé, because it could only have taken place in the carriage. And we already suspected her of spying for Monsieur de Sartine. Which is why the young woman's death caused us such torment. We thought that you had kept the letter. The marquise sent Chiara to your house, and we had it searched, unbeknown to you, unlike Wallace, who turned the place upside down. After that, we tried the monk's lodgings—'

'You didn't dare!'

The comte signalled for Volnay to calm himself.

'Again, the Devout Party were ahead of us. We would never have made an attempt on the life of our illustrious monk, for whose science and humanity we have the utmost respect. But to them, he is a worthless heretic whose very existence is an aberration in the sight of God. Which explains the murderous attack on him. But they were no more likely to find the letter with him, than with you—were they not? The mystery thickened. Mademoiselle Hervé's murder, and its appalling consequences, tormented us still. Who could have committed such horror? And why? Fortunately, you gave us the key to the mystery when you brought my assistant's trafficking to light. A misappropriated concoction, not the letter, was the cause of Mademoiselle Hervé's death. Sadly, as fate would have it, the missing letter was in her possession.'

'And the second victim?' asked the inspector.

'With a second murder, the mystery thickened, as you are aware!' said the comte. 'We feared some ill-judged action on the part of the Brotherhood of the Serpent, to discredit the royal house. The Brotherhood had joined the dance. They were impatient, eager to outstrip the Freemasons in the Western world, and the Orient. But remember that all the while, Sartine—though careful to keep a low profile—was keeping watch. He set his spies to follow your every move.'

The comte interrupted his own account.

'You supplied the letter, and we could all breathe once again, but only for the briefest of moments: the letter was not the one we had all been expecting. Who could have imagined our king would supply Mademoiselle Hervé with such a message, for me!'

His eyes blazed with a brief flash of anger, but he continued in the same measured tone:

'Everything was suddenly more complicated. But I had plenty to occupy me: the new leader of the Brotherhood, Baron Streicher, feared the Grand Master's return. I went by night to warn the Master and bring him back with me to Paris, but he would not hear of it. I did not know you were a guest in his household, or I should have guessed what would happen next, and brought you both back by force! Your visit to the Grand Master must have precipitated things. They understood you had come to warn him, and in so doing you signed the death warrant for the entire household. "He who betrays the Brotherhood, dies by the Brotherhood."'

'But after that…'

'I tried to protect you as best I could, once I had picked up your trail in Paris. I had the house, and your enemies, watched. I feared for your safety, and I decided to have you captured and brought here. Alas, you preferred to escape by

346

jumping out of the window. But here you are nonetheless, happily enough!'

'How did the monk know he could trust you?' asked Volnay, thinking aloud.

'Because I gave him a sign.'

'A sign?'

The comte made no reply, but smiled mysteriously. Volnay was exasperated.

'Where is the monk? I demand his return!'

The comte took him gently by the arm.

'We shall go and join your friend. He has gone ahead, and is following my instructions. A man can hope for no better lieutenant than him!'

'How can you send him your orders?' asked Volnay.

'You'll see soon enough.'

Volnay followed the comte. He was dumbfounded. They left the mansion by a hidden door and climbed into a carriage stationed a few streets away. A swarthy man stood beside the door, twirling his moustaches between his fingers and watching them as they approached with a meditative air.

'Here is a man we can trust,' said the Comte de Saint-Germain, pointing to him. 'I gave him the task of bringing you to me.'

Volnay was beginning to understand. He addressed the man:

'Forgive me, Monsieur, for not following you earlier.'

'No matter, sir,' said the other politely.

His hand touched the hilt of his sword as he added evenly:

'I failed to exert my full powers of persuasion!'

The carriage seats were upholstered in beribboned grey velvet and set with silken cushions. A leather blind protected the passengers from the gaze of the street. The carriage moved forward slowly, and little by little, the din of the city ceased. The road was bumpier; the vehicle shook and lurched. The first, scattered trees gave way to woodland of oak, wild cherry and larch, dotted with yellow shoots. A dense pine forest swallowed them whole, and spat them out. Lifting the curtain over the door, Volnay saw the proud ruins of a castle on a distant crag.

'One thing bothers me,' he said. 'Why, in your position, would you bother to circulate such rumours about yourself?'

'I am not their source!' declared the Comte de Saint-Germain. 'But I have made use of them, indeed, because what police force would suspect me, a man whose name is on everyone's lips, of being a man of the shadows, operating in secret?'

Night was falling when they stopped. It seemed to Volnay that they were in the midst of the ruins he had seen earlier. A round, half-collapsed tower stood beside a ditch filled with rubble and a few, scattered pools of dark, stagnant rainwater. A tall, round keep was still standing, peppered with holes. For the rest, all that remained were crumbling expanses of wall, foundation stones and pillars strewn over the ground and overgrown with ivy and weeds. They followed a barely distinguishable path covered with moss and ferns.

A silhouette wearing a white veil materialized from behind a column. Volnay felt an icy sweat drench his back. The spectral apparition seemed to float towards them. His heart pounded, but he soon recovered his reason: beside him, the comte showed no surprise or fear.

'A useful phantom, for keeping unwelcome strangers at bay,' observed Volnay.

The comte gave a small laugh.

'You're beginning to understand,' he said.

'Yes, you're bringing me to a secret gathering—the sign you addressed to the monk indicates that you are one of them. Which is why the monk knows he can trust you. He's a Freemason himself.'

The comte considered him gravely.

'Yes. And you, Volnay, you once committed the folly of joining the Brotherhood of the Serpent.'

The inspector lowered his gaze and said nothing. The Comte de Saint-Germain watched him pensively for a moment, then shrugged indulgently.

'It is time. Follow me.'

He led Volnay to the ruins of one of the castle buildings, doubtless the guards' quarters. They entered through a narrow opening and slipped between walls of rubble and crumbling brick. Volnay spotted a door, intact in one wall, beneath an oval archway topped by a keystone bearing a Greek cross carved with the words *semper dilige, semper ama*. The comte pushed hard against it. The hinges were clogged with rust. They found themselves in a room open to the sky. Stone flags covered the floor, surrounded by weeds. The far end was completely overgrown by weeds. The Comte de Saint-Germain strode into the room. Clearly, others had trodden this space before him. He knelt and, with Volnay's help, began to clear the dirt from an iron trapdoor, opening it to reveal a damp, mossy staircase, down which they carefully made their way.

Volnay was startled by a clang of metal overhead. The trapdoor has been closed behind them! His companion was unperturbed.

'Stay close to me,' said the comte. 'And say nothing unless asked.'

He seemed to think for a moment, then added:

'In fact, it would be wiser for you to say nothing at all.'

They had reached a long passageway with decaying, yellow-stained walls. They followed it to a cave with a dry well, at the heart of a veritable web of openings. Four galleries opened into the space. Without a moment's hesitation, the comte took the left-hand passage, leading to another room with a partially collapsed, vaulted roof. Volnay felt a fresh sense of dread. The place was vast, and the darkness seemed alive. The comte took a step forward and the inspector did the same. The darkness seemed to tremble. A torch was lit, and another, and a third, until the shadows were partly consumed by a string of flames, projecting a livid red light around the walls.

The inspector shivered. Before him stood a hundred motionless shadows, all dressed in white, their faces concealed like spectres beneath their hoods. The Comte de Saint-Germain stepped forward fearlessly into their midst. They formed a circle around him and Volnay, who held his breath. They were surrounded by faceless, eyeless spectres clad all in white. He could see the outline of their swords, pistols and daggers beneath the folds of their immaculate robes.

'Who are you?' said a voice.

The Comte de Saint-Germain raised one hand and made a sign in the air.

'*Ego sum qui sum.* I am he who is. I am the most senior of the Freemasons!'

Three men stepped forward and removed their hoods: the three mysterious visitors who had witnessed the accomplishment of the Red Work in the comte's workshop.

'He is who he says he is,' they said, speaking with one voice. 'Welcome, Comes Cabalicus, companion of the Kabbalah. Welcome to you, Sanctus Germanus, holy brother!'

A rumour ran through the rows of figures. The comte silenced it with a gesture.

'Masters of the Grand Orient and Occident Lodges,' he said, 'I have come because it is time. By the particular grace of God, I have borne everything calmly, and with fortitude. But I cannot tolerate murder in the name of freedom!'

A deathly silence followed. No one moved. Every muscle was tensed to the extreme.

'The revolution is afoot!' declared the comte in a loud voice.

A cry of joy rose from the ranks of the white ghosts, but he stopped it with another gesture.

'But it will not come tomorrow.'

Again, no one moved.

'Some sought to hasten its coming and thereby destroy it altogether. One Grand Master has been killed, and all his household. An attempt was made to cut the throat of the man standing beside me here. I suspect the murderers have introduced themselves into our midst tonight! Let us all remove our hoods, and see who is who!'

No one moved, and the Comte de Saint-Germain strode towards one of the spectres, placing a firm hand on his shoulder.

'Wise and learned friend, uncover yourself!'

Without a moment's hesitation, the monk threw back his hood.

The comte turned to a slender silhouette standing beside him.

'And you, sweet friend of Italy, uncover yourself!'

The slender silhouette hesitated for a moment, then lifted a delicate hand to its forehead. Volnay stifled a cry of astonishment. The hood fell back to reveal Chiara's beautiful, luminous features. Spontaneously, the monk reached out to grasp her hand. The wall of figures all around them seemed suddenly to collapse. Hoods were thrown back one after the other, and friends turned to one another in astonished recognition. Quickly, the Comte de Saint-Germain paced around, taking Volnay with him. Not a single face from the Brotherhood of the

Serpent! The monk and the comte exchanged disappointed looks.

'Friends,' said the comte, 'ensure that in each of your homes, there is a spacious, hidden chamber served by underground passageways, so that the brothers may attend meetings in safety. You must tread praise and blame, fear and hope underfoot, for your mission is none other than to do all in your power for the greater good of humanity, and never to dishonour mankind with base actions. Men have been motivated by a misplaced love of their country, to wage wars against one another, when all are brothers, differing only in the tongue we speak, and the clothes we wear. Our lodges are spread throughout the world. Today, we bring together the lights of all the nations to form a single movement, from France to the Americas! One single republic across all the world!'

Everyone left before sunrise. The comte, Volnay, Chiara and the monk were the last to leave the vaulted chamber. Carefully, they replaced the trapdoor. The ruins of the castle were bathed in moonlight. Slowly, they stepped forward, crunching the sand and stones underfoot. Volnay glanced at Chiara as she walked, her head lowered, saying nothing. The comte was pensive and silent. Only the monk showed his habitual good humour, whistling quietly between his teeth. Suddenly, he stiffened, every inch the old soldier.

'There are people here!'

Everyone froze. It seemed to Volnay that he sensed stifled breathing in the darkness, the fever of expectation, and a flash of steel in the light of the moon.

'Gentlemen,' said the comte calmly, 'it is time to draw your swords.'

Everyone did as they were instructed, and Volnay placed Chiara behind him. There was a rush of drawn steel. Ghostly figures floated towards them through the ruins, clad in long capes. They were twenty in number, their faces hidden beneath large, broad-brimmed hats. Slowly, they advanced to surround the group, swords in hand.

'Mademoiselle… Gentlemen,' said the monk, in tones heavy with irony, 'it's a fine day to die!'

The comte raised one aristocratic eyebrow. His smile flashed in the darkness.

'My dear monk, I fear you may have spoken too soon. Remember, I am he who knows!'

As he spoke, a troop of men in black, armed with swords and pistols at the ready, jumped out behind the oncoming assailants. At their head was the Comte de Saint-Germain's trusted guardian, the man who liked to twiddle his moustaches between his fingers. The cloaked attackers span around in panic—nothing is worse than to be ambushed from behind, just as you believe victory is assured. Pistol shots, the clatter of swords, cries and groans were heard, but a harsh, powerful voice rang out, exhorting them to group together and hold their position. Baron Streicher had no intention of surrendering.

One of the attackers, who had approached the Comte de Saint-Germain's little group, seemed not to have heard. He raced forward, eyes staring. The monk skewered him carefully on the point of his sword then pushed the body away with his foot, to extract the blade with greater ease. The comte had not moved a muscle. Already, another attacker was racing towards them.

'The youth of today,' sighed the monk, parrying a sword thrust, and attacking in turn. 'Determined to keep us all hard at work!'

Disorderly, hand-to-hand fighting broke out in the midst of the ruins now. The blades scattered sparks in the moonlight, and the clash of metal echoed all around. From time to time, a shot lit the darkness.

Suddenly, a man threw himself forward, whirling his sword and clearing a path through the dark silhouettes. He was followed by another swordsman. He caught Volnay's eye for an instant. There was a howl of rage, and the man chased after him, followed by his accomplice. Volnay recognized his pale, weasel face. With extraordinary presence of mind, he blocked the fatal blow the man was preparing to bring down upon him, and delivered a sharp stab with his dagger, then parried another thrust, crossing blades with such force that his fingers ached. From the corner of his eye, he saw the comte fighting with a new arrival, equally determined to try his luck. The monk was also locked in combat, his forehead pouring sweat.

'Forgive me for not asking first,' he told his adversary, 'but I'm afraid I'm going to have to kill you.'

Volnay fought with clenched teeth, but found it hard to face the crazed onslaught of the heavily armed man. He retreated in despair, anxious to ensure he remained between his attacker and Chiara. Suddenly, the weasel-faced man gave a howl of pain. Chiara had hurled a sharp rock directly at his head. Volnay struck his sword from his hand, and swiped the tip of his blade along the man's throat without a second thought.

The fighting was coming to an end. The comte and the monk had each dispatched their adversaries, and were congratulating one another. Some of the attackers lay groaning on the ground. The men in black were running them through, one after the other. Their leader delivered his report to the comte, with his usual sangfroid.

'All dead—'

He broke off at the sound of a scream of agony in the night, followed by a hideous gurgle.

'All dead now,' he corrected himself, with not a shadow of a smile. 'Baron Streicher was with them. He fell in the midst of our assault, but the others carried on fighting without him.'

'After what they did to the Grand Master and his house-hold, they could expect little clemency on our part,' said the monk. 'Which is just as well.'

Slowly, they returned to the comte's carriage. White-faced to the point of translucency, Chiara held back. The monk offered her his arm. Volnay fought not to turn around and clasp her to him. Seated facing her in the coach, he tried to catch her eye but failed. At length, he turned to the comte.

'Monseigneur, there are two mysteries that remain to be resolved. Where is the letter you were looking for, and who took it? And who killed and disfigured the second victim, Marcoline?'

The comte nodded gravely.

'I shall solve the first before your eyes, at my mansion, but to my great consternation, I have no answer to the second!'

Volnay smiled, and his face seemed to flood with renewed happiness.

'As to the latter, Monseigneur, I have an idea, but I need you to make it a reality!'

XVIII

My memories are a constant source of happiness.
I'd be a fool to make regrets that serve no purpose.

CASANOVA

They stood in the comte's laboratory, a splendid room that was its owner's pride and joy, and which Chiara and the monk seemed greatly to appreciate, commenting in detail on the many different experiments a person might carry out with such fine equipment. A furnace glowed red in each corner. The monk scurried from one copper crucible to the next like an excited child, inspecting the spatulas and the residues at the bottom of the dishes, admiring the acids, and the phials sealed with wax, discovering gold and silver dust here, mercury or copper vitriol there.

In particular, the comte was experimenting with coloured pigments, and explained how he hoped to discover a new blue dye that would earn fortunes for French traders.

'But the Great Work?' Chiara pressed him, breathlessly. 'The Great Work?'

The comte smiled indulgently.

'My experiments have resulted in three types of product: a volatile fluid, an oily substance and lastly a solid residue. Too often, alchemists use the four elements: earth, air, fire, water. But I mix them with three substances: sulphur, mercury and salt, because the three together form a solid body. When alchemy decomposes something into its constituent parts, the sulphurous principle separates like a combustible oil or resin. The mercurial principle flies into the air like smoke, or manifests itself as a volatile liquid, and the saline principle remains, as a crystalline material, or an indestructible amorphous substance. Take a piece of wood and set it on fire—the sulphur burns, the mercury is exhaled as smoke, and the salt remains in the ashes.'

Unlike his two companions, Volnay was thoroughly bored by the Comte de Saint-Germain's explanations. He was far from displeased when a servant appeared to interrupt them.

'Forgive me, Monseigneur,' announced the newcomer with all due ceremony. 'Madame la Marquise is here.'

'Hurry, man! Show her in,' said the comte briskly.

They all left the laboratory for an adjoining salon, its floor covered by a vast carpet or Persian silk.

'Your Lordship…' said the servant.

The comte bowed low and the marquise entered. She urged the comte to stand up straight, pressing his hand.

'Do not bow, my friend,' she said. 'You are my equal, if not my master.'

She turned to Volnay, who stood watching, dumbfounded.

'Such is the case, Chevalier. Things are not always as they seem, and he who trusts to appearances is but a fool.'

Volnay watched as the marquise's shadow obliterated the silk carpet's elaborate arabesques.

'Do you have the second letter, Madame?' asked the comte.

The marquise gave a solemn smile.

'Thanks to the monk, to yourself and to our friend here.'

On cue, Casanova entered the room, drawing a gasp of surprise from Volnay and Chiara together. He was magnificently dressed and wore an expression that was bold and contrite in equal measure. Solemnly, he held out the letter, to the Marquise de Pompadour.

'Madame, I was wrong to conceal the letter, but now I can make amends. For you, Madame…'

And he bowed, adding, for Chiara's benefit:

'And for the young lady's beautiful eyes!'

Chiara flushed with indignation. She seemed to be discovering the man's extraordinary duplicity and audacity, all at once. Volnay, for his part, would happily have ripped out the Venetian's guts there and then. So many days, so much effort wasted in search of a letter that had been in the hands of their accomplice all along! The monk simply rolled his eyes to heaven, in which he had little enough faith as things stood. He could not believe Casanova had been touched by the grace of God. But the fact remained that the Venetian stood smiling sweetly at Chiara like a love-struck boy, as if he had just proved his undying passion, and his natural good faith.

'You have done a great wrong,' said the marquise, with great severity.

Then her features softened.

'But you have done the right thing, at last. All is well that ends well.'

The Chevalier de Seingalt bowed once more.

'And besides,' added La Pompadour, 'I am not so very surprised by your good deed. Did you not write in one of your letters: "Wretched the nation that dies of hunger and poverty or is massacred by all Europe to fill the coffers of he who has betrayed it"? Because that is indeed what you wrote to one of your friends—is it not, Chevalier?'

Casanova paled very slightly, then nodded.

'Ah yes, Monsieur,' said the marquise, 'we intercept letters, and open them here in France, just as they do everywhere else. The postal inquisition is a thing to be feared. You should take greater care in future, brother…'

Everyone in the room started at the word, except the comte.

'Yes,' said the Marquise de Pompadour, 'the Chevalier de Seingalt, like everyone here, is a Freemason, though he has taken a very different path from ours!'

'As for you…'

She turned to the monk.

'Monsieur, or dear brother—since the term has a second meaning in your particular case—you were the first to solve the riddle. You called the Chevalier de Seingalt to order, and reminded him of his duties. I cannot express my gratitude too highly. You are the bearer of a fine name, a great name, and I hope to recover it for you one day. No one deserves it more than you.'

The monk acquiesced with a gesture of exquisite humility though his eyes sparkled with his characteristic intellectual pride.

Carefully, the Marquise de Pompadour opened the letter and read it slowly, with an air of intense concentration. Finally, she gave an indecipherable nod and held the letter out for the comte to take.

'Kindly burn this.'

The comte took it carefully, as if he dreaded to touch it, then read it through. He looked up.

'Have you read it?' he asked Casanova.

The Venetian gave a wry smile.

'Of course! I needed to know its true value.'

The comte smiled briefly.

'Thank you for your honesty.'

He turned to the others.

'Each of you played a part in this adventure, and each of you was initiated into certain truths, this past night. You may read the letter, then, like the Chevalier de Seingalt. You will see that it designates me as the leader of the Freemasons in France and throughout Europe. I gave it to the Marquise the

Pompadour so that she might make me known to certain of her friends, but I kept a copy as a precaution.'

The marquise touched him gently on the arm.

'And I should never have taken the letter. Too dangerous…'

Her pale eyes surveyed the company.

'Now you understand why so many people were searching for the letter so actively. To compromise the comte is one thing, but to compromise me is to thrust France into the hands of the Devout Party, or the first adventuress with an ounce of brain between her ears to slip between the king's sheets.'

The Comte de Saint-Germain held out the letter to Volnay, who refused it politely.

'I do not need to read it, Monseigneur; your word is enough.'

The comte gave a slight nod of the head, before offering the letter to Chiara, and the monk. Each refused it with the same courtesy. And so the Comte de Saint-Germain held it over a candle flame, before carrying the burning paper to the chimneypiece, where it was consumed. Only when the flames licked at his fingers did he let it go.

At that moment, a liveried servant knocked and entered.

'Monseigneur, they are here,' he said simply.

The comte sighed and turned to Volnay.

'Monsieur the Inspector of Strange and Unexplained Deaths—I trust you know what you are doing! There can be no turning back now.'

At that moment, Sartine entered the room, and the temperature seemed to drop by a good ten degrees. A heavy silence engulfed everyone present. Only the monk's eyes sparkled, as always at the beginning of a fine experiment, or a thorny problem. The comte stepped forward, frowning.

'Thank you for coming, sir.'

Sartine bowed gallantly before the Marquise de Pompadour, then greeted the comte.

'It is my duty,' he said in grandiloquent tones, 'to present myself wherever Madame la Marquise commands.'

He glanced around the room and fixed his gaze on Volnay.

'Though it brings me into strange company indeed,' he said gruffly.

'Monsieur de Sartine,' said the marquise hurriedly, 'listen to me, I beg you. Have you followed my instructions?'

Sartine bowed once more, with extreme deference, but his eyes were as cold as ever.

'Madame, as you suggested in your letter, I have been to the ruins of the castle you named, and found the bodies of a number of fanatics, identified as members of the Brotherhood of the Serpent. One corresponded exactly to the description given by the peasants who saw them hurry away from the home of the former Grand Master of the aforementioned Brotherhood. Next, I summoned the person you indicated. My obedience is blind, as you see, but I hope that it will not provoke any trouble…'

'Have no fear,' said the marquise. 'The king will be most grateful to you.'

Another knock at the door. The same servant opened it a fraction and whispered a few words to the comte, who nodded.

'Here is our man,' he said solemnly.

'And so it is time for me to go,' said La Pompadour.

The comte prepared to leave the room with her, but she stopped him with a gentle, weary gesture.

'Stay there, my friend—Chiara and the Chevalier de Seingalt will accompany me.'

She left, accompanied by Casanova and Chiara, who refused the offer of his arm. Volnay stared after them, darkly. In the doorway, Chiara turned and addressed him:

'Chevalier, please come to my residence as soon as you are able.'

Volnay's heart skipped a beat. He turned white as a sheet, then deep red. The monk suppressed a smile and the comte pretended not to have noticed. He sat down heavily in an armchair. The burden of worry had caught up with him, and for the mere shadow of a second, Volnay thought he saw the weight of the years on his shoulders. More years than any of them could imagine.

The door opened once again. Father Ofag entered the room and stood stock-still when he saw the inspector and the monk.

'What does this mean, Sartine?' he asked hurriedly. 'Why am I called with no explanation to Monsieur le Comte's residence?'

He broke off to greet the comte with a brief nod of the head. Lowering his eyes, he was dazzled by his host's sparkling shoe buckles and diamond-encrusted garters.

'You will excuse my humble appearance,' muttered Ofag sarcastically. 'Our Lord Jesus Christ owned nothing more than the clothes on his back.'

The comte ignored the slight and bowed graciously. Ofag stared around the room and caught sight of the monk.

'What do I see here?' he hissed, sounding for all the world like a human snake. 'A heretic in the dwelling place of an immortal!'

The monk shrugged lightly.

'If I must be dismissed as a reprehensible thing, I should prefer to describe myself as a philosopher.'

'Sinner!'

'I was indeed a sinner in my younger days,' admitted the monk. 'And I have aspirations to return to that noble estate in the very near future.'

Sartine stepped forward. His expression remained neutral. He was venturing into unknown territory.

'The Inspector of Strange and Unexplained Deaths in the city of Paris thought it best to gather us all to hear what he has discovered…'

Volnay interrupted him. 'It would be proper, first, to give thanks to God for permitting me to solve this case,' he said, firmly.

The monk's eyes narrowed, but he said nothing and did as Volnay said. The others followed suit. As if on a reflex, Father Ofag pulled out his rosary. The inspector looked up suddenly.

'That's a fine boxwood rosary you have there, Father Ofag.'

Everyone stared at him as if he had gone quite mad.

'May I see it?'

The inspector held out his hand. Ofag hesitated for a moment, then handed him the string of beads. Volnay walked over to the window, to examine it in the daylight. The room held its breath.

'There's a bead missing, Father Ofag,' said Volnay coldly.

'Indeed, Inspector, I lost one, and have had no time to time to take it to be repaired. It is a family heirloom.'

Slowly, the inspector put his hand into his pocket. He pulled out a handkerchief and unfolded it with extreme care, before removing a boxwood bead.

'Would this be the one?'

Father Ofag's assurance deserted him.

'It may be.'

Volnay walked slowly across to where he stood. His eyes were twin points of steel.

'Do you know where I found this?'

The other man's breathing was faint. He avoided Volnay's gaze. He shook his head, but made no attempt to speak. The inspector continued, in icy tones:

'I found this wooden bead beside the corpse of a young prostitute who officiated from time to time at the Parc-aux-Cerfs. The young woman was a venal creature, as it appears, and she had found herself a plump game bird to pluck. A man whom she was blackmailing.'

'You are building a case on the head of a pin!' cried Ofag.

The inspector drew closer to him, seized his wrist and pushed up his sleeve, revealing a forearm marked by three long red scars. He glared at Ofag, who cowered in shame at the thought of what was coming next.

'Three long scratches, all drawing blood. The blood beneath the fingernails of your victim! You preach virtue all day long, but the beast is there within you, as it is inside us all. You needed a woman. You happened upon a certain Marcoline. You became infatuated with her. But women like Marcoline are obsessed with their personal gain, and nothing else. She decided to blackmail you, under threat of selling your secret to the highest bidder—which she might very well have done at some point.'

Volnay stepped back, blinking, under the force of the implacable hatred he read in Father Ofag's eyes.

'You committed a sin of the flesh with a prostitute of the king,' he continued. 'We may turn a blind eye in the case of a prelate like the abbé de Bernis, but when the perpetrator is the moral conscience of the Devout Party, it's a different matter altogether.'

'She was a whore! The Great Whore—the Whore of Babylon!' spat Ofag suddenly.

His terrifying expression startled everyone in the room. He recovered himself and added, unctuously:

'Until now, the dignity of my office has preserved me from temptation, but the flesh is indeed weak, and the Devil has the art of erasing all trace of grace from our souls. I was seized with the full horror of my sin—it disgusted me...'

'*Omne animal triste post coïtum,*' sighed the monk.

Ofag gave no reaction, but continued his solemn confession.

'I wanted to terminate our arrangement, but she refused—she relished her hold over me!'

His lips parted in an unpleasant grin.

'I could not allow that woman of low virtue to bring down the good name of the party of God! May the archangel Michael protect me, I accept my due punishment. And may God and the Blessed Virgin herself support me and come to my aid! I shall answer for my sins to them, and never to you.'

Volnay nodded. He looked sickened.

'Not an ounce of remorse!'

'She was a whore, and deserved nothing more,' said Ofag.

The inspector blinked briefly.

'A fine demonstration of the esteem in which you hold your fellow man.'

He continued speaking, rapidly now, as if eager to finish.

'You killed Marcoline with your own hands, to be certain no ruffian would try to blackmail you in turn. But you were unsure whether she had spoken about you to someone, and whether the crime could be traced back to you. And so you had an idea. The death of the young, faceless woman had horrified the whole of Paris. By reproducing the act, you would deflect suspicion. But the act revolted you. You butchered Marcoline's face, and in so doing you signalled the distinct nature of your own murder. But you couldn't have known that.'

Father Ofag showed not the slightest reaction, but fixed his icy gaze on Volnay. Volnay walked across to the window. A carriage lurched forward in the courtyard outside, taking a beloved creature with it.

The monk crossed the room first, and placed a hand on Volnay's shoulder.

'When did you discover this?'

'When I returned to Paris, I saw the crosses standing at every crossroads, and experienced a kind of revelation. The clue I had recovered at the scene of the first murder, the boxwood bead, was from a rosary! I remembered Father Ofag's rosary, and his fascination for Mary Magdalene. An irrational suspicion was born, and it was confirmed when we were all reunited just now. You told me that Léonilde had confided that Marcoline's lover often made the sign of the cross, and that he liked to keep his hands out of sight, in his sleeves. All that remained was to find three bloodied scars on Ofag's arm, matching the blood under three of Marcoline's fingernails. There we have it.'

'We do indeed. But you might equally have found nothing,' said Sartine.

'Intuition, sir. Intuition.'

For the first time, the police chief's face showed the hint of a smile.

'Well played, Volnay! Failure would have sent you straight to the Bastille, for good, but your success absolves you of all blame.'

He turned very slowly to Father Ofag.

'You will come with me.'

The cleric took a step forward. He stared into Sartine's eyes.

'We need to talk, sir. Now!'

Sartine nodded vaguely.

'Let us go and join the Marquise de Pompadour in another room.'

'What?' exclaimed Ofag and Volnay, together.

'She is waiting for us in a side room, right here.'

The monk and Volnay exchanged glances.

Sartine and Ofag left the room without a word.

'Whatever's happening?' Volnay asked the comte, who responded with an embarrassed gesture.

'We have discussed it with the marquise; it's better this way,' he said.

The two men soon returned. Father Ofag appeared in sombre mood, but relieved. Sartine was unruffled. He spoke in icy tones:

'We have struck a deal, endorsed by the marquise. My heart and mind are saddened to think of it, but some interests must be held above all others, and the interest of France is one such. The murder of the girl Marcoline will never come to light, and I have promised to ensure that what has passed here is dismissed from their memories by all present.'

He turned sharply towards the inspector and the monk.

'And that goes for both of you!'

The monk placed a hand on Volnay's arm, refraining him from giving an ill-considered answer, in the heat of the moment.

'So be it,' he said, simply.

The chief of police showed a gleam of satisfaction. He took his leave of his host and led Father Ofag from the room. The comte accompanied them.

'So there it is, my son,' said the monk philosophically, when they were alone.

And he accompanied his exclamation with the comforting smile of a parent to a child who has just discovered all the misery and wickedness of the world.

'I shall never become accustomed to it, father!' said Volnay.

'What of it? The marquise has muzzled her worst enemy and Sartine will become chief of police for all France.'

'And justice?'

'Justice will wait, my son, she will wait a while longer…'

There was a long silence.

'Father?'

'Yes, son…'

Their story had taken a decisive turn, thought Volnay. He had lost his father as a boy and found him again too late. He had forged his own character, for the most part, and kept his distance from the world now. He had kept his doubts, his questions, and his feelings to himself.

'One question has always tormented me. Perhaps now is the time to ask it.'

'I'm listening, my son.'

'On the pyre, when did you decide to recant?'

The monk gazed at him, feelingly.

'When you began to weep, my child.'

Volnay lowered his head. A tear welled in the corner of his eye.

He knew me too late, thought his father, fleetingly. *How to recover so much lost time, and tell him my love?*

'Let us meet at home tonight,' said the monk, clasping him in his arms. 'We have so much to say to one another.'

'Tomorrow, father. This evening, I must meet someone else.'

The monk's face lit up with a smile.

'Of course, my boy. And a most delightful person at that!'

Before leaving, Volnay brushed his father's beard with his lips, in an extraordinarily gentle embrace.

Through the window of her music room, Chiara spotted Volnay in the forecourt. She watched him, and saw an impossibly upright and sincere heart, and islet of loyal devotion in an ocean of turpitude. And the young woman knew, at the same time, that he would never be hers because it was too late, for him and for her. Suddenly, unexpectedly, Volnay's eyes gazed into hers. Calmly, she faced her fate, like the Spanish regiments at the Battle of Rocroi when, deserted by their every ally, they had made a final stand, forming squares to resist the French cavalry charge on a devastated battlefield.

They gazed at one another for a long time. There was no anger in Volnay's face. She understood then that he had loved her more than any other man before him, more even than Casanova, whose heart he knew she had touched.

A passing adventure, she wanted to tell him. *And you see, it has not lasted. You and I are not like that. There is little I can give you. I could probably never make you laugh, but I place my heart in your hands, if you will have it.*

She gazed into his eyes and saw that he was deeply troubled.

Does he still want me? she asked herself. *All he need do is give me a sign, take one step towards me. He hesitates. He's coming towards me. No, he stops. Surely he will not turn away? There, he has turned his back on me. He is leaving. Wait! Turn, and you will see my tears. No, it is over. He's gone. He cares nothing for my love.*

Casanova had clasped her lightly around the waist, but Chiara resisted vigorously, and pulled herself away.

'Your boldness knows no limits,' she growled. 'You betrayed us in the most appalling manner, by hiding the letter in the hope of selling it, and still you dare to call on me! To think you reproached me for spying on behalf of the marquise!'

Casanova frowned.

'I am not a wicked man, Chiara, but a man of instinct. I behaved badly when I followed that instinct, I admit.'

'You betrayed us all!'

'That was before I knew you. I would never have sold the letter!'

'After the monk unmasked you.'

'Oh, that… He was my good conscience—proof that I am possessed of one!'

Chiara opened her eyes wide.

'To hear such a thing coming from your mouth, I might faint away!'

'It is a mouth that longs to place itself upon yours!'

Casanova was pressing his suit once more, and Chiara pushed him away unceremoniously.

'You seduced me, you took me, and you were going to abandon me like all the others. I know you handle these things very capably, and no one ever holds anything against you. Your visits become less and less frequent, you become less and less insistent, and then one day you leave for another country, and that's that.'

Casanova frowned in annoyance.

'No, Chiara! That's not how I want things to be between us. There is nothing I will not do for a glance, or a smile, from you.'

He added, huskily:

'I would even stoop to kiss the ground beneath your feet…'

Chiara was standing at some distance now.

'Yes, you still desire my body, very much, and my heart, too, because you have a great need to be loved, and perhaps you even love me a little.'

She continued, staring into space:

'But that love is light, and fleeting: it passes like a cloud in the sky. You are sincere in the heat of the moment, but what remains over time? You'll be sorry to have lost me, tomorrow, but the day after, you won't give it a second thought. Next week, your gaze will alight on a seductive figure with a slender waist and fine, white skin. The death of one love fills you with sorrow, but the promise of new love fills the void in your heart.'

'You are mistaken. I want to stay with you for the rest of my life. If it weren't for the difference in our situations, I would ask you to marry me.'

'If I found myself alone with you in all the world, I would be no more reassured as to your constancy,' replied Chiara, bitterly.

Casanova paled very slightly.

'Why do you doubt me, and the constancy of my love?'

Chiara's expression was grave.

'Quite simply, Giacomo, because constancy is not in your nature.'

It was the first time she had called him by his first name. He felt an upsurge of joy in his heart at the sound, as from a lover's caress.

'I love you, I adore you.'

He had taken her hand and covered it with kisses, lingering over the blue veins of her wrist. She pulled it away.

'You do not love one woman, but all womankind. And in order to love womankind, you feel the need to love us all.'

For the first time in a long while, Casanova lost his self-control. His mouth was dry, as if crammed with dust. He swallowed hard.

'There have been many women in my life,' he stammered, 'and I remember them all. They have loved me as my mother never did...'

Chiara cast him a sorrowful look and answered in the tone of an adult addressing a child.

'It is not you that I love, Giacomo, and you will never find your mother's love through me.'

Casanova froze. So that was it! His mother Zanetta's face came to him in a flash—so beautiful, so wondrously beautiful. Chiara's face!

He rose heavily to his feet. All at once, Chiara found him old, weary and desperately sad. She called him back.

'Giacomo?'

'Yes?'

'You will end your days alone, without wife or children, friends or mistresses, because no one will be drawn to you in old age. You will cherish no memory of good deeds done, other than to have taken, and given, pleasure: great pleasure, indeed, as I now know. But what suffering follows.'

She held back her tears.

'I do not know whether you will ever find your mother,' she continued, in a broken voice, 'but take my advice: stop along the way, and take the time to be happy.'

Casanova's face was deathly white. He bowed before her.

'Chiara,' he said, 'my memories are a constant source of happiness. I'd be a fool to make regrets that serve no purpose.'

Casanova emerged into the courtyard once more, his heart frozen in eternal darkness. His mind was beset with contradictory thoughts. Habitually, in such circumstances, he would hasten to forget his woes in a gaming parlour, or a brothel. But nothing appealed to him now. His latest love left nothing but the scalding pain of nameless sorrow. He found Volnay waiting for him at the bottom of the steps.

'Good to see you, dear friend,' he declared, with forced bonhomie.

Volnay raised his head, fixing his rival with his steely gaze. His veins were torrents of fire, yet he felt cold as death. He gripped the hilt of his sword and took a step forward. For a second, he glanced away from Casanova, to the windows of Chiara's apartment. He thought of her, of their encounter, and the looks they had exchanged. A sense of a missed rendezvous floated on the air, exacerbated by the Venetian's impertinent presence.

'I have two things to say to you, Chevalier de Seingalt,' he said.

XIX

He cannot love, who can say farewell.

CRÉBILLON FILS

Daybreak.

Volnay sat stroking his magpie for a long while, before writing a letter—his first—to his father, asking him for his forgiveness, and to take care of the bird if anything should befall him.

> *My dear Papa,*
>
> *I have decided to fight a duel with the Chevalier de Seingalt, this morning. I know that you will not approve of my decision, but I can no longer live with the knowledge that that adventurer has seduced and dishonoured my Chiara. There must be blood, or I shall be driven mad. I know that I am making the wrong choice, yet again, but this is the only path I can take.*
>
> *I hope that I shall return to you very soon, and clasp you in my arms. If it is not to be, forgive me, and hold me in your heart, and your memory. I entrust my magpie to your care.*
>
> *Your most loving son.*

He hesitated, then wrote a second letter for Chiara, before walking to meet his fate. It contained only a few words:

> *Later, when I am dead, you will love me more and more…*

*

A delicate veil of mist seemed to float over the field. Slowly, with a long hiss of steel and wounded nerves, Volnay drew his sword. Casanova smiled and drew his own weapon. He had recovered his spirits since his visit to Chiara, but the pain endured.

'One mystery remains to be solved, Inspector—your purpose throughout all this.'

'I don't understand,' said Volnay, simply.

Casanova gave a frivolous wave of the hand.

'Come, come—you are the final mystery! Solving these murders was not your chief purpose, am I right?'

'Indeed.'

'Your primary objective was to kill the king, was it not?' asked Casanova amiably, while putting himself on guard.

Volnay gave no answer. Coldly, he slashed the air with his sword. As a confirmed dueller, the Chevalier de Seingalt made no show of bravado, but maintained a conventional stance, at a reasonable distance from his adversary, ready to strike if necessary.

'May I ask, then, why you saved the monarch's life from Damiens's attack?' he insisted.

'The people were not ready,' said Volnay. 'To kill a tyrant is one thing, but to replace him is quite another.'

'But you were in the king's presence just lately. You could have—'

'It was not the place for it!'

He raised his sword, to warn his adversary, then struck out. Casanova parried the thrust.

'I fear, Volnay, that you may not be as thoroughly trained as I am,' he said calmly. 'If you only knew the number of jealous husbands I have confronted, sword in hand! And I am still here to tell the tale!'

He launched a well-judged attack that almost hit Volnay,

who pulled back quickly. Both men took a few steps back, eyeing one another firmly.

'The wrong moment, the wrong place! You're a mightily cautious assassin, Volnay. Unless…'

Casanova's blade whistled through the air.

'But yes! The right place and time—you wanted to kill the king in the Parc-aux-Cerfs! A king assassinated in the midst of his harem of children could never aspire to martyrdom!'

Volnay launched a furious attack.

'I can answer you, since one of us will soon be dead. That king wanted to burn my father at the stake! That's why I joined the Brotherhood of the Serpent.'

'And you wished to act alone?'

'The history of kings is the history of the martyrdom of their peoples!' hissed Volnay between his teeth. 'I ran out of patience!'

Casanova allowed himself to be fully engaged in quarte, parried in a half-circle, then thrust in tierce on the arm. His blade tore out a square inch of Volnay's white shirt. The move had a sudden, calming effect. With a cold gleam in his eye, the inspector engaged in quarte, parried, then with his weight firmly on both feet, launched a false attack. Casanova did not allow himself to fall into the trap, but parried calmly, and stepped back. He seemed barely out of breath.

'As I was saying, my dear fellow, I've fought many a duel, and have often been forced to run a cuckold through or bite my tongue. Though I am no killer, believe me.'

'You are full of nothing but our own self!' fumed Volnay. 'A puppet without a soul, spouting nonsense!'

Casanova sighed.

'I fear you have no idea how crude and callous are the words you have just spoken. That was uncalled for! If we had not been rivals, we should have become friends.'

Their swords clashed again.

'I care nothing for your friendship,' growled Volnay. He attacked in quarte on the arm and met with a parry and riposte for his pains.

Casanova thrust immediately and touched Volnay's arm.

'You are wounded,' he said chivalrously. 'I suggest we stop there.'

Volnay gave no answer, but hurled himself at Casanova. Their swords scraped briefly, and Casanova dodged to one side. His sword shone in the first rays of sunshine. It was stained with blood.

'You are quite mad, Volnay!'

With one hand pressed to his bloodied side, Volnay threw himself into the fight, yelling:

'Buffoon! You had to have her, too!'

'We are cast in our roles by womankind, not the reverse,' panted Casanova, parrying with all haste.

'And Chiara cast you as the romantic lead,' growled Volnay, stepping back.

'Fool that you are!' cried Casanova. 'I had her, indeed, but it's you she loves.'

The declaration seemed to goad Volnay to still greater heights of fury. He lost all self-control, swiping the air with his sword, and slashing his adversary's jacket left and right. Casanova thought himself hit, and stepped back, still on guard.

'Volnay!' he yelled. 'Life is a gaming table. I accept my gains, and my losses. I have banished jealousy from my life—it complicates relations and makes those it torments ugly. Banish it as I have, I implore you!'

Contrary to all expectation, the inspector lowered his sword and began pacing around Casanova.

'What did she say when you left her bed?' he yelled. 'That you were a magnificent lover? That she had never known such pleasure?'

Casanova was breathing heavily. He was no longer a young man of twenty.

'She told me that there are caresses that wound, like repeated blows.'

He shivered suddenly. Volnay was roaring like a man possessed. The point of his blade split the air, aiming straight at Volnay's heart.

'Get back or I'll kill you!' Casanova cried, as Volnay impaled himself on his sword. Slowly, the Venetian pulled the blade free of his adversary's body. Volnay was released and sank slowly towards the ground.

Volnay watched as his life passed before his eyes, like a host of bright butterflies. He noticed one shining brighter than all the rest, before the darkness fell. Speedily, Casanova clutched the nape of his neck, to save his head from striking the ground. He held him suspended for a second, then placed him gently down. Volnay lay motionless in the grass. And so, the Chevalier de Seingalt bent over him. In an astonishing act of gentle contrition, he kissed him on the lips.

EPILOGUE

My dear Volnay,

I was delighted to have news of you from our beloved mutual friend, and I am comforted to learn that you are in good health. We are fortunate indeed that after impaling yourself so unfortunately on my sword, the comte and your monk came so speedily to your aid and administered such exceptional care. They are both remarkable men, in very many ways, as you well know.

As for me, as you have doubtless learnt, I was forced to leave France in some haste. Twenty girls, each prettier than the last, were employed in my workshop making painted fabrics. A modest, and most charming seraglio. I became curious to know my worthy workforce better, but they—and my curiosity—exacted a high price. Indeed, I 'knew' them all, wonderfully well, and when I tired of one, I was obliged to assuage another's jealousy (I cannot bear jealousy, as you know), while at the same time sparing her predecessor's pains, by continuing to pay her a wage!

My fortune was lost—indeed, I was ruined by my own workforce! And so, I was forced to sell shares in my workshop to a swindler who took me to court and ordered the seizure of my business. People will attack a man when he's down! The wrath of a great many bad people was unleashed against me, all of them determined to see me brought low, and accusing me of every misdemeanour: forged signatures, abduction… I was even accused of fornication with a number of holy sisters. I, a respecter of religion, and its practitioners, to the very highest degree!

In short, I decided to liquidate my remaining assets and repair to Holland. My health is good, never better. When I have a little time, I shall write the Story of My Life. *A tale worth the telling!*

What of our delightful Italian friend? She loves you, you may be sure of that, though she has returned to the country of her birth. But beware, when the pearl of great price is located, the guardian dragon is never far away.

Take good care of yourself and be attentive when destiny calls. Sometimes, the gods intervene in the affairs of men in strange, even indecipherable ways. They bring many, seemingly irresolvable matters to their proper conclusion. And things often turn out not at all as expected…

Your devoted friend,

Giacomo Casanova
Chevalier de Seingalt

AVAILABLE AND COMING SOON
FROM PUSHKIN VERTIGO

Jonathan Ames
You Were Never Really Here

Yukito Ayatsuji
The Decagon House Murders

Olivier Barde-Cabuçon
*The Inspector of Strange
    and Unexplained Deaths*

Boileau-Narcejac
Vertigo
She Who Was No More

María Angélica Bosco
Death Going Down

Joyce Carol Oates (ed.)
Cutting Edge

Frédéric Dard
Bird in a Cage
The Wicked Go to Hell
Crush
The Executioner Weeps
The King of Fools
The Gravediggers' Bread

Friedrich Dürrenmatt
The Pledge
The Execution of Justice
Suspicion
The Judge and His Hangman

Martin Holmén
Clinch
Down for the Count
Slugger

Margaret Millar
Vanish in an Instant
A Stranger in My Grave
The Listening Walls

Baroness Orczy
The Old Man in the Corner
The Case of Miss Elliott
Unravelled Knots

Edgar Allan Poe
The Paris Mysteries

Soji Shimada
The Tokyo Zodiac Murders
Murder in the Crooked House

Masako Togawa
The Master Key
The Lady Killer

Tiffany Tsao
The Majesties

John Vercher
Three-Fifths

Emma Viskic
Resurrection Bay
And Fire Came Down
Darkness for Light

Seishi Yokomizo
The Honjin Murders
The Inugami Curse